"Strube is one of Canada's more expressive and creative prose stylists. It is, at heart, a uniquely intimate exploration of the perilous fragility of the human body, and the indomitable strength of the human soul."
— *Toronto Star* on *On the Shores of Darkness, There Is Light*

"Quietly elegiac and despairing, the novel keeps true to Strube's singular vision." — *Maclean's* on *On the Shores of Darkness, There Is Light*

"Strube's true talent, which was as readily on display in her last novel, 2012's Milosz, is for layering characters and situations and subplots on top of each other, one by one, until the entire Shangrila apartment building buzzes like a beehive." — *Globe and Mail* on *On the Shores of Darkness, There Is Light*

"Canada's best bet to succeed Alice Munro." — *Toronto Star*

"[Strube] describes Milton's absurd predicament in smart, eccentric prose . . . And yet, while we wince at Milton's blunders, we applaud his limping progress toward a true connection with others and a hard-won faith in his own capabilities." — *The New York Times* on *Milton's Elements*

"Strube deftly navigates around the human heart in a way sometimes reminiscent of Carol Shields. The writing is so effortlessly accomplished that it makes me wonder where Cordelia Strube sprang from."
— *Books in Canada* on *Alex & Zee*

"Often witty and pointedly observant in the face of pain and absurdity."
— *Newsday* on *Alex & Zee*

"Filled with wry and shrewd observations about the agony of growing up."
— *Chatelaine* on *Lemon*

"A remarkable literary feat." — *Maclean's* on *Blind Night*

"Strube's sure way with words, her mordant punchlines and equally sharp assessments of urban life on the edge of normal make this familiar story a compulsive read." — *Globe and Mail* on *Alex & Zee*

"[Strube] tells a loopy story in clear, unadorned prose and with gentle irony." — *Montreal Gazette* on *Milton's Elements*

"*The Barking Dog* is a rare achievement, an unstintingly honest, hilarious and dreadful delight." — *Globe and Mail*

"Her portraits of characters caught in urban angst are riddled with laugh-out-loud humour. . . . Strube's rueful insistence on contemplating human darkness is tempered by a certain wistfulness, a yearning for something finer, a flicker of hope that is never quite extinguished. . . . A book that crackles with anger, righteousness and a strange kind of passion for living."
— *Edmonton Journal* on *The Barking Dog*

"The bare-knuckled prose, reminiscent of early Margaret Atwood novels, is entirely free of metaphor or lyricism."
— *Toronto Star* on *Teaching Pigs to Sing*

"A heart-wrenching and daring subplot that leaves the reader shuddering . . . Strube knows very well those on the edge often have superior insight into what makes people tick." — *National Post* on *Blind Night*

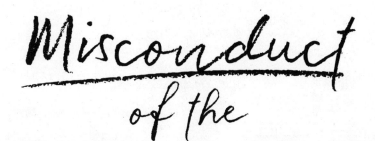

Misconduct
of the
HEART

Misconduct of the HEART

of the

Cordelia Strube

a novel

ECW

Published by ECW Press
665 Gerrard Street East
Toronto, Ontario, Canada M4M 1Y2
416-694-3348 / info@ecwpress.com

Editor for the Press: Susan Renouf
Cover design: Michel Vrana
Author photo: Mark Raynes Roberts

This is a work of fiction. Names, characters, places, and
incidents either are the product of the author's imagina-
tion or are used fictitiously, and any resemblance to actual
persons, living or dead, business establishments, events,
or locales is entirely coincidental.

LIBRARY AND ARCHIVES CANADA CATALOGUING IN
PUBLICATION

Title: Misconduct of the heart : a novel / Cordelia Strube.

Names: Strube, Cordelia, author.

Identifiers: Canadiana (print) 20190206284
Canadiana (ebook) 20190206292

ISBN 978-1-77041-494-5 (softcover)
ISBN 978-1-77305-489-6 (PDF)
ISBN 978-1-77305-488-9 (ePUB)

Classification: LCC PS8587.T72975 M57 2020
DDC C813/.54—DC233

The publication of *Misconduct of the Heart* has been generously supported by the Canada Council for the Arts which last
year invested $153 million to bring the arts to Canadians throughout the country and is funded in part by the Government of
Canada. *Nous remercions le Conseil des arts du Canada de son soutien. L'an dernier, le Conseil a investi 153 millions de dollars pour
mettre de l'art dans la vie des Canadiennes et des Canadiens de tout le pays. Ce livre est financé en partie par le gouvernement du
Canada.* We acknowledge the support of the Ontario Arts Council (OAC), an agency of the Government of Ontario, which
last year funded 1,737 individual artists and 1,095 organizations in 223 communities across Ontario for a total of $52.1 million.
We also acknowledge the contribution of the Government of Ontario through the Ontario Book Publishing Tax Credit and
through Ontario Creates for the marketing of this book.

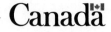

PRINTED AND BOUND IN CANADA   PRINTING: SOLISCO   5   4   3   2   1

MIX
Paper from
responsible sources
FSC
www.fsc.org   FSC® C103304

For Carson

"Give sorrow words. The grief that does not speak
Whispers the o'erfraught heart, and bids it break."

—WILLIAM SHAKESPEARE, *Macbeth*

ONE

Bob is up my ass about the kitchen staff not completing their e-learning, a Corporate time-waster.

"Bob, my cooks don't speak English. How are they supposed to e-learn?"

"If they don't complete it, cut their shifts," Bob says with the Latino/ Pakistani accent he thinks is funny. Last week he used it on a Sri Lankan cook who'd just escaped an arranged marriage. "What are you doing?" Bob demanded, jabbing his hairy finger at her salad prep. "Stop it! Stop it! Stupid! Stupid! Thin slices only!"

I'd like to lock Bob in with the frozen meats, but we're in my office, actually a closet with barely enough room to stand. Bob, his phone clamped between his ear and shoulder, holds up a finger to shush me when Desmond, the district manager, takes him off hold. "Des," Bob bleats, "it's not *my* fault a cook fell in the fryer."

I visited Jesús in the burn unit this morning. He couldn't lift his gauze-wrapped arm, had to wipe his tears with his left hand.

"Jesús," I say loudly so Des the DM can hear, "will be off for at least a month. I want him back. He's a good worker and has a family to feed." I don't mention the nurse's warning—severely burned kitchen workers rarely return to their jobs, the scar tissue is too heat sensitive.

"Des wants to know how it happened." Bob holds out the phone, which I don't take because talking to Desmond makes me feel like bugs are trapped in my skull. A self-proclaimed outstanding leader and a body builder in love with his own image, Desmond wears muscle-hugging attire while babbling Corporatespeak.

"Jesús was trying to clean the hood," I say loudly at the phone, "removed the grill and baskets, slipped and plunged his arm to the bottom of the fryer where the gas jets are. Presto, third-degree burns." I don't add that Jesús, dehydrated from the dinner shift, was hungover and had passed out. Or that our general manager—Bob—cuts labour costs by ordering the night crew to pull high-risk stunts like cleaning the fryers while the kitchen is still open.

Bob hangs up and wags the phone at me. "Stevie, you need to be keeping a closer eye on your staff. I don't want to have to write you up to Corporate."

I push past him, knowing he won't write me up because I'm cheap and can cover every station. He adjusts his Chappy's ballcap—rumour has it there's a bald spot in that patch of shoe-polished hair—and points at me. "Corporate's not happy a customer survey says we're the stingiest Chappy's in the chain. You need to be thinking about that." He frequently tells me to think about things it's not my job to think about.

"Corporate's told us to weigh portions, Bob. Weighed means smaller. Praveen *was* being generous with the sour cream on baked until you threatened to write him up. And we've had numerous complaints about the new roll policy." The latest proclamation from HQ stipulates only *one* roll per customer with a single pat of butter, exclusively with an entree, not a salad.

If I actually ran this kitchen instead of troubleshooting 24/7 because Corporate's too cheap to cough up for a plumber to snake the drains, the fryer debacle would never have happened. I told Jesús to prep for Fish Friday. If he'd followed my instructions, he wouldn't have been hanging over the fryer. But I'm only a kitchen manager with a vagina so why take orders from me? Particularly when you want to catch World Wrestling Entertainment on your phone. Jesús has the entire kitchen crew watching Hell in a Cell. I get why my mostly male staff enjoy viewing women in spandex thrashing each other, but it slows the line. The Divas Championship has the entire crew arguing in various languages about who's number one. Jesús insists the Bella sisters "own" the Divas locker room.

I can't shake Bob. He trails me while I make sure the line is ready and stocked, and the cooks at their stations. "Another reason," he says, "we failed the office report is the break room. It's *disgusting*. Staff toss things in there willy-nilly. We're not required to provide a break room. If staff don't keep it clean and tidy, Corporate will take it away."

We need the break room because Corporate forbids kitchen staff from eating in the dining room. Even off-duty employees are banned from the dining delights at crappy Chappy's. HQ believes staff socializing stirs up "gossip"—Corporate code for union talk. A couple of months ago, a Nicaraguan disher thought working conditions at Chappy's ought to be better than in some cantina back home and talked union. His hours were cut in a hurry.

When I look up from the logbook, Conquer, my head cook, throws a frozen steak at the wall. "Jesús forgot to take the steaks out," he growls. "I'm going to have to fart on these fuckers before I grill them." Conquer is a Viking, piercingly blue-eyed, square-jawed and too mountain man for Bob, who scuttles back to his office while Conquer makes a show of blowing on the steak. A papered chef, he considers himself above the riff-raff like yours truly who've worked their way up the ranks. He insists on being called Chef but doesn't wear the hat, just a bandana—biker style—that's soaked in sweat halfway through a shift. "I need pans!" he roars.

Our Eritrean disher got hauled off by the feds so I head for the dishpit, roll up my sleeves and grab the hose. Conquer follows in hot pursuit, noticing my bruises—not for the first time. "You going to tell me who does that to you?" he demands with Chef authority. I ignore him. He thinks all women want his Nordic ass. Grabbing my wrists, he scowls at the purple splotches on my arms. "One of these days soldier boy is going to kill you."

My son, Pierce, has what he calls night visions that get violent, like he's handing a water bottle to a little Afghan girl just as her head gets shot off by an AK. The hit hollows out her skull leaving her staring at him with the back of her head missing. Or he gets captured, hooded and tied to a chair. The insurgents drill holes in his ankles with a power tool, loop a wire around his neck, throw him to the ground and step on his back, pulling up fast and sawing away until his spine snaps.

Conquer slams pans around. "That kid is going to fuck you up. Seriously."

"Seriously, it's none of your business."

"What was he doing over there anyway?"

"Who?"

"Your kid."

I never think of him as my kid. *I* was the kid. My parents raised Pierce while I grew up playing musical fuckchairs and chain-drinking to steady the turbulence in my head. Never the hard stuff, just wine, preferably Chardonnay.

"Seriously, what was he doing over there?" Conquer snatches knives from the draining board.

"HR," I say. "And Logistics." This usually shuts up the military masturbators horny for war porn. They assume Pierce had an admin job and never saw combat. In warspeak, HR stands for human remains. Somebody has to pack the body parts into caskets. Pierce told me when newbie soldiers flew in they'd watch movies, toss a Nerf ball around and share spliffs. Weeks or maybe months later, he'd recognize one of them in a body bag, the outlines of the soldier's shredded limbs visible through the plastic. If it was winter, corpses looked like frozen meat. Sometimes tampons—a quick blood stauncher in the field—stuck out of bullet wounds. If soldiers burned, their charred remains were put in body bags. When all that was left were pieces of flesh, bone and ash, they'd be scooped into what Pierce referred to as Tupperware. In HR he sprouted grey hairs and grew whippet thin. Back home he sat on my couch mainlining Bud, muttering he didn't know what he was doing "over there." By then an Afghan mafia, led by the puppet president's brother, had a vise grip on Kandahar and was getting rich off NATO-led efforts. "The Afghans have to figure out their own shit," Pierce told me. "We can't fix it for them." He shook his head as though I were arguing with him, which I wasn't. Fourteen years of "just wars" and the Middle East isn't safe anywhere.

I finish up in the dishpit and deliver pans to the mighty Conquer.

"You mean logistics as in transporting supplies?" he asks.

"Convoys."

"Great. So tell him to get a driving gig. Delivering pizza or whatever. It'll get him off your couch."

"He's not fit for the road just yet." Pierce drives fast and erratically to avoid buried IEDs. If he wasn't behind the wheel on convoys he'd hang off the truck, throwing candy far from the vehicle so the kids chasing them wouldn't get hurt. With five- and six-year-olds running around with AKs, convoys didn't stop for children. Kids whose families were murdered for co-operating with NATO forces were strapped with explosives and pushed into the road. Pierce learned fast that IEDs can be hidden on bodies of any age or gender, in bicycle seats, corpses human or animal, piles of trash, rocks, even hung from trees. Soldiers lost faces and genitals, not just arms and legs.

In the walk-in fridge I discover that Daniel, the bar manager, is storing extra beer behind the bags of carrots. I shove the cases aside to sort through the veggies, rotating stock, throwing out the mouldy stuff. Produce is a constant problem; quality costs more and Corporate won't pay.

"Who's going to cover for Jesús?" Praveen asks, looking worried. He has vitiligo, the Michael Jackson skin disease that lightens pigment in patches. The skin around his eyes is white.

"Tareq can do grill," I say. Tareq drives Conquer the racist nuts because he's got attitude; a good worker though, and the inventor of the Butter Chicken Burrito—a big seller.

Sometimes remembering Afghanistan seemed physically painful for Pierce. He'd squirm and say, "There's no moral or immoral. All that shit goes out the window. It's like a car crash. You make a split-second decision then it's over."

The first time his convoy was under attack, Pierce panicked and pissed himself. Back at the base, ears aching from mortar explosions, he crawled in Kandahar dust to hide the urine stain. He and his sergeant sat down to write up a transport plan in a spare corner near the intelligence office and overheard a call on the radio coming in from a squad on patrol. The gunner's femoral artery had been hit. He was going into shock and bleeding out. Frantic, they requested a helicopter to pick him up. The command told the squad to stay in place. This went on for an hour, the squad's communications guy—with mortar fire in the background—begging them to send a medevac, and command saying a chopper was on its way. It wasn't. The gunner died. "Why do you think they lied?" I asked. Pierce shrugged, staring at nothing like it was something threatening. He still wanted to go back though, to his "people." He didn't belong in our world, where knobs lose their shit over phones dying.

His cough drives me nuts. He hacks up Afghan dust laced with fecal particulate from porta-johns and Kabul's open sewage system. Shit dries up in 40-degree heat and becomes airborne. Most days the sky is brown.

When he signed up he told me he was "doing the right thing for once." I told him it was George Junior's cash-grab poppy war. Naturally Pierce didn't want to hear this. That first Christmas he called my parents, not me. They were already losing bolts. "Why isn't he home?" they asked with the stunned look of the demented.

"He's fighting a politically contrived and unjust war," I said.

"Why?"

"To satiate corporate greed. War's good for business. Ike said that. Remember Ike?"

They chewed toast. They live on toast. I shut their stove down because they frequently forgot it was on and used it as a countertop. Peggy melted an electric kettle on it. Reggie decided the oven was a car part that needed oiling.

It bothered Pierce he wasn't a frontline trigger-puller shooting "bad guys." I told him the insurgents thought *he* was a bad guy, and that good guy/bad guy thinking fuels profitable wars on terror. A mentally unbalanced loner finds acceptance online with radical Islamists and runs down two uniformed soldiers in a Quebec parking lot. Bam, he's a bad guy. A homeless crackhead, pining for Saudi Arabia and the Quran, given the runaround by the passport office, goes postal and shoots a soldier on Parliament Hill. Bam, he's a bad guy. The politicians, after cowering in the Parliament Buildings, act like heroes when interviewed. Most of the gunfire, says a bureaucrat, was "the good guys getting control of the situation." Thirty shots to control one homeless, mentally unbalanced crackhead radical. "Our lives are changed forever," a civil servant whimpers. Oh, really? Try raising a family in the Middle East while the good guys bomb the shit out of it.

"War breeds war," I told Pierce. "Every time you bomb civilians, terrorists are born."

It's the Parliament Hill shooting that has pitched Pierce into a deepening gloom. Last night he thwacked his head, called himself a shitwad and said he wanted to die. He hasn't been to a barber in months and his greying hair and beard make him look closer to forty than twenty. Pacing and jabbing the air, he yanked at his *Jesus loves you but everybody else thinks you're a jerk* T-shirt like it was skin he wanted to rip off. I stayed crouched on the floor, hoping he'd quiet down. The Bosnian cat lady upstairs complains about the noise even though she stays up all hours playing pop radio. Pierce flung open the fridge and, after a couple of beers, started blaming me for what a fuckup he is. Which is fine by me if it stops him beating up on himself, but it just draws attention to the fact that there is no one else—just us rejects hating on each other in the dugout. "Whenever I look at people," he muttered, "I know what they're going to look like dead with their legs or arms shredded, their jaws blown off, their eyes ripped out."

I update the specials board and check with the prep cooks about deliveries, then spot-check the Fish Friday supplies. Daniel, the obese bar manager, sashays in from the dining room and hugs me. "Oh my god, oh my god, oh my god," he says, "you smell so good, what's up with that?" I tell him he shouldn't be storing beer in my fridge. He tells me about his night clubbing. "So I'm listening to the drag queens," he says, "like, leaning on the stage, and this guy comes up behind me and starts grinding on me."

I taste the Thai soup to make sure it won't burn customers' mouths off and inspect the floor drain to determine if my frantic plunging has had any lasting effect.

"I'm okay with it," Daniel assures me about the grinding. "Then the guy starts massaging my back and I'm like, 'Oooh, nice.' He was old but, like, *hot* old."

The drain is still slow. I start plunging again and tell Praveen to pour boiling water down it.

"Then he shoots his hand down my pants," Daniel says, "and starts fingering me and I'm like, 'Eww, no way, get off me.' Next the old perv shoves me up against the stage. Security had to pull him off me."

When the cat lady stamped on the floor, Pierce stopped still, combat ready.

"It's just the Bosnian," I said. "If you don't keep it down, she'll get us evicted."

He hacked and spit Afghan dust into the kitchen sink for about twenty minutes then said, "Who made them the enemy anyway?" Gripping his head like it might explode, he slid down the cabinets and sat on the cracked linoleum. "They're goat herders. They pray five times a day. Who the fuck made them the enemy?"

I suggested the CIA, George W. and Mr. Cheney, but Pierce's face was a slammed door. I could feel it reverberating.

He was never diagnosed with PTSD. To avoid paying him disability, Veteran Affairs decided he had a pre-existing mental disorder. There have been too many payouts to traumatized vets who can't go to crowded malls where explosives could be strapped to bodies, strollers, backpacks, who can't drive under overpasses where snipers might have them in the cross-hairs, who pick fights because that's what they're trained to do—confront conflict with violence—not look after the kiddies while Mommy works at McDonald's to make the rent. To get full disability these days (roughly

$1,150 a month—an MP's lunch money), a vet has to have a broken body, not just a broken mind.

Before being sent home, soldiers are expected to "decompress." They fill out psych evaluation forms, answer questions on a scale of one to ten—subtle questions like "Do you feel suicidal?" They all say they're fine because that's what soldiers who aren't wussies do, plus they want to get home. Sitting on commercial flights in their dirty cammies, they try to blend in.

Suicides come later. Pierce's friend Jake seemed confident, fearless, a dutiful soldier following orders, thinking "I've got a future with the military. They'll look out for me as long as I'm willing to get blown up." But he didn't get blown up. He sat around camp in the blood-boiling heat, fondling his rifle, thinking maybe he'd get through another tour without having to fire it and that maybe that was good because he wasn't sure he could *actually* kill somebody. He developed a dependency on nicotine and watched porn and war vids, trying to keep sand out of his crack and his balls unstuck. Finally his superiors pointed his unit in one direction and said go get 'em, boys.

The Canadians lugged their gear and guns around with sweat and dust stinging their eyeballs, but the insurgents weren't stupid and didn't make themselves targets. They hid in irrigation ditches, trees, cratered mountains, garbage, burkas, dead bodies. After a long, searing, choking silence somebody started firing at the Canadians and they fired back. It was noisy and exhilarating for a few minutes until they figured out they were being shot at by Americans. A guy who'd shared his Twizzlers with Jake got hit in the gut and clawed at Jake's feet pleading, "Don't let me die." Jake held the soldier's head in his arms as he bled out waiting for the medevac.

Jake returned home, developed a gaming addiction and decided never to form an attachment to a *real* person again because they might bleed out. He left butts and beer cans lying around and yelled at his mother when she asked him to pick up after himself. She started wishing he'd be called back because worrying about him over there was easier than living with him here. Jake was re-deployed despite his mental setback. Veteran Affairs docs doped him with pharmaceuticals to make him less jumpy and depressed. Drugged, back with Afghan dust plugging his nostrils, he discovered he liked firing his rifle, shouting and pushing people around and generally not giving a fuck. When he became too psycho—despite fourteen pills a day—the CF disqualified him from remaining in the military and started the prolonged release process for soldiers diagnosed with PTSD. Scared he was losing his mind, Jake tried to get help. But cuts to Veteran Affairs meant VA centres were being shut down and case managers laid off. Told to call Service Canada, Jake got voicemail, was directed to choose an option then put on hold again. Like most vets with PTSD, he lost patience with the phone maze, became more agitated and withdrawn and started self-medicating with whiskey, taking little sips 24/7—no binges, just a steady drip feed. He drove his mother's Malibu all night long with the doors and windows locked even though the air con was busted. When she complained about the cost of gas he yelled that the car was the only place he felt safe; he liked the confined space. He drove until he was ready to pass out. The only sleep he got was in that car. When the transmission broke down Jake stopped going out or sleeping and holed up in his room adorned with Harry Potter posters, gaming or watching TV. One night he swilled Canadian Club and all the meds the VA docs prescribed to get him "stable." His mother found him dead with shit and piss leaking out of him.

When Pierce called to offer condolences, she told him Jake had applied to be a firefighter but was rejected because of his PTSD. A month after his death, she emptied his closet and gave his clothes to the Goodwill. Now she looks for them on strangers.

Since Jake's suicide, my son hasn't left the dugout. Every night when I get home, I'm scared I'll find him dead in shit and piss.

TWO

Noah, my neo-hippie creative writing teacher, insists we write "fragments" in our "diarios" daily. He majored in Latin American Studies and diario means diary in Spanish. All the yoga moms bought pretty bound notebooks in which to pen their fragments. I'm using a spare logbook from Chappy's. Noah is in his twenties but stooped like an old man from bending over his laptop, pumping out poetry. He calls what we scribble in our diarios "automatic writing." He doesn't want us "overthinking it," cautions us to not let our left brains override what comes spontaneously from our right. The yoga moms write spontaneously about their dud husbands or genius children. Not one yoga mom has a stupid kid, apparently.

Fish Friday without Jesús was arduous. Praveen didn't stir the beer batter properly and plated a piece of fish that got sent back by the almighty customer. "Fired!" Bob squawked, alarming the South Asians and Africans. The truth is the old goat doesn't have the balls to actually fire anybody. He leaves it to me or Siobhan, the house manager.

Reeking of fish grease, I arrived home to find soldier boy at his usual post on the couch, staring at the TV, where a brawny detective was visiting his angel-faced, cancer-riddled daughter in hospital. When the little girl asked if she was going to die, the detective said, "No, baby, we're going to make you all better." This made Pierce boohoo, although he tried to hide it, leaning his elbow on the armrest and covering his eyes. TV schmaltz totally wrecks him now—the boy who never cried. The fragment I wrote was *Life's a joke. Wish I was in on it.*

Noah wants me to "riff" on this in my in-class writing. The in-class writing is based on prompts poetry man pulls from his beaten-up leather man purse: seashells, pebbles, photos, Tarot cards. I riff: *I used to try to figure shit out, like why in a dream my apartment is full of seals. Or why I was gang-banged in a Ford Fiesta and tossed behind a dumpster with blood streaming down my legs.*

I stop writing and stare at Noah hunched over a Thomas Hardy novel. He's wild about the guy and asked us to read *Far from the Madding Crowd.* Monique, the blue-haired old lady, and I were the only ones who did. The yoga moms didn't have time—too much social media to attend to, I guess. Monique expounded in her French accent about "Ar-dee's exquiseet prose," how she could feel the English rain caress her face in the meadow. I said the book made me horny for a sheep farmer. We had a busser who claimed his cousins in Manitoba fucked pigs. A man who fucks pigs is capable of getting lost in the sensation of the moment, I said. That's a plus in my book. Noah stared at me, shoved his pen in his mouth and wiggled it around.

To distract myself from the yoga moms and their online shopping grievances, I try to picture Noah in a coital position. He ties his hair back in a man bun and has a scruff of facial hair he fondles compulsively, but his personal hygiene seems adequate. He looks at me in that needy way lost boys do. I attract strays. Probably because I appear to know where I'm going—a trick I learned post-rape. If you faked purpose, the psychos left you alone. Meanwhile, the "nice guys" got turned on by the rape and wanted to see what I'd let them do to me. Initially I avoided all sexual encounters, but after a couple of months I let the nice guys do all kinds of pervy shit. I was punishing myself, trapped in a body I despised that didn't belong to me. Drinking my shame away wasn't an option because I felt sick 24/7. No surprise then that by the time the baby bump became undeniable, it was too late to abort. Denial kicked in and sex became a power trip, something I could control. Nobody could hurt me because there was nothing left to destroy, which is why I relate to my traumatized son. In bed at night stuff comes back, just like it comes back to Pierce in his night visions—atrocities he can't forget. He doesn't know how to use his body anymore. He walks with slightly bent knees as if walking down a hill, fearful of falling. The world has expectations he can't meet. Nobody understands him. This is how I've been feeling for years, but I can't tell him this without revealing he is a product of rape.

Putting out for hubby isn't something the yoga moms do for free. I hear them discussing negotiations. Mostly they spread their legs to keep him from sniffing around secretaries and waitresses. Until recently Siobhan, our house manager, screwed married men because she said she could boss them around. But then she met Edvar, the Brazilian bombshell bachelor, who bossed *her* around, and she decided she was "literally in love for the first time." A couple of days ago she checked Edvar's phone and discovered sexts to some other hottie. Pretty revolting stuff—enough to make any well-adjusted woman ditch the perv—but Siobhan said she's going to use it, "literally hold the sexts over him" to force him to buy her nice things and take her nice places. When she confronted him about the sexts, Edvar told her he suffers from depression and was abused as a child, which is why he needs approval from hotties.

My ass vibrates and I consider ignoring it, but it could be a crisis like my parents burning their house down or my son killing himself. It's Chappy's. I shove the phone back in my jeans and study my illegible chicken scratch. Hmm, maybe riff on something less depressing. *I was walking behind an old lady the other day when a little blonde girl ran up to her with outstretched arms, saying, "I missed you. I love you sooo much!" How wonderful, thought I, for the old lady that her granddaughter loves her sooo much. Then I noticed that the old lady was carrying a miniature dog and that the girl was talking to that. She took the miniature dog from the old lady and said again how much she had missed it and that she loved it sooo much.*

Monique stops clicking her ballpoint, pries the lid off a yoghurt and spoons it. Halfway through the yoghurt she unwraps a granola bar and crumbles it into the container. This makes a considerable amount of crackling and slurping noise when you're trying to concentrate on your diario. The yoga moms clench their veneered whites, but Monique keeps spooning and crunching.

On rainy days the city stinks of dog and cat shit. Forget climate change, we're going to be asphyxiated by domesticated animal feces and urine, poisoned by pet waste seeping into our water supply. Each time a condo owner buys a miniature dog, we are nudged closer to the apocalypse. When the world ends, the pets will devour the flesh of their owners. I told this to the Bosnian cat lady who creeps around outside in mini-nighties talking what sounds like dirty Bosnian to her cats. When she strokes their tails, the cats shove their butts in the air like they're hoping the Bosnian will shove her finger up their sphincters. It's disturbing, but not as disturbing as her globby, saggy legs under the mini-nightie. When I asked her to cover up in communal areas, she said she was European and they always walk around naked.

My ass vibrates again. It's Chappy's. They'll hound me until I surrender. "What is it?"

"The drain," Praveen gasps. "It's backing up."

"Where's Bob?"

"In his office watching *Eat Pray Love* again. He won't come out." Bob morphs into a Netflix junkie when he's "off sugar and stressed to the max."

"Bob says he's not calling a plumber," Praveen says. "He says plumbers cost too much on weekends."

"Keep mopping and plunging." Annoyed by the disturbance, the yoga moms glance up at me, snarling silently. Monique, unperturbed, keeps munching and scribbling. I want to be like her when I grow up, blue-haired and giving zero fucks.

I knock on Bob's door. "We have to call a plumber."

He does his wounded billy-goat yelp but doesn't open the door. "This is ridiculous," he says. "I can't get a moment's peace here. I haven't been able to get *any* paperwork done with all this higgledy-piggeldy and constant interruptions."

"The kitchen floor drain is backing up."

"It was working fine when I got here. You need to be paying attention to what your staff put down the drains. Maybe, if they completed their e-learning, they would learn that *our* drain policies are a little different from where they come from."

"Bob, I can't keep talking to you through the door."

"Then stop talking. And don't think I haven't noticed they aren't using the hand sanitizer. They need to use the sanitizer *at all times*. Stop it! Stupid! Stupid! Stupid!" He's talking to his computer.

I find a wire hanger and stretch it to snake the drain, extracting gobs of greasy, slimy muck. Fishing with the hanger, combined with energetic plunging, partially opens the drain. Praveen and Tareq watch dumbfounded. Must ask Bob if there's a section on plunging technique in the e-learning.

"It's working a little better," I tell them. "Keep an eye on it and when it starts backing up, start plunging right away."

"What if it's busy?" Praveen asks.

"Who's dishing?"

"Jamshed. He's slow." Praveen pulls on his forearm hairs—a weird nervous habit. Tareq shrugs. He doesn't like taking orders from a woman and grumbles in Bengali, no doubt saying something nasty about me. These boys talk behind my back right in front of me.

"One of the line cooks will help," I tell Praveen, knowing this is unlikely. Pitching in isn't something the motley crew does. The world's conflicts percolate right here at Chappy's: ethnic, religious, tribal. A clusterfuck of international relations.

"I shouldn't be here this early," I whisper to Praveen. "Pretend I'm not here."

"Sorry, miss?"

"Pretend I'm not here. I'm not on shift yet."

Praveen blinks at me, cocking his head, the skin discolouration around his eyes making him look birdy.

Time to suit up, grab a java and hide in my office/closet. Daniel's in there messing with his hair, pulling styling products from his GoodLife Fitness bag. He uses the camera on his phone as a mirror.

"What are you doing in my office, Daniel?"

"Oh, hey bae." He hugs me. "Bob and I went clubbing last night, and the Bobster is miffed because he did *not* get lucky. I slept at his place and borrowed his fedora. Result: catastrophic hat head. I need to reset." He squeezes goop from a tube and works it into the hair on top of his head. The sides are shaved, which doesn't flatter a fat man.

"Can't you fix your hair in the locker room?"

"No privacy. Oh, btw, the espresso machine is being finicky again."

"Not my department."

"Like I don't know that, but Siobhan's busy being flirty with the tour bus guides."

"I don't need to hear this, Daniel. I'm only the kitchen manager."

"Who else can I talk to around here, seriously. I mean, I'm a minority."

"What, because you're gay?" Or super-sized. His girth has been known to squash cakes while he's slicing them.

"Sometimes I just get this vibe from Olaf. Like he thinks I'm too gay."

"Olaf is gay," I say. Olaf is the hot blond wannabe rapper every gal and guy in the dining room wants to fondle.

"He says he's bi-curious."

"He's gay, Daniel. And so are Bob and Desmond. As far as management is concerned, you are in the majority."

"Do you really think Desie is gay? How delicious. He's so Dwayne Johnson." He hugs me again. "You always make me feel better. What's up with that? You are just so lovable."

Wrong. Nobody loves me and I don't love anybody. My counsellor, wearing cherry red cat-eye specs and matching lipstick, told me I have a discomfort with closeness, and a fear of intimacy and abandonment. This discomfort and fear explains why the little girl telling the grandmother/miniature dog she loved it sooo much snagged my attention. Guess it's easy to love a small, hairy creature with a walnut-sized brain—even though it will devour your flesh when you're dead.

My counsellor urged me to differentiate the rapists, as though the colour of their skin or hair mattered.

My son's hair is all over the apartment, and I'm tired of picking up the wiry strands. He looks more like a Black man with this overgrowth, despite his pale skin. We never talk about this, of course, or his Black penis. When he was little and noticed other white boys' penises were white, I told him not everybody is white or Black, that we're all a mix of colours. "My hair's brown," I said, "and Grandma's is yellow. My skin's darker than hers and lighter than Grandpa's." I showed him the seahorse-shaped birthmark on my thigh to prove that I too had some brown skin. He bought this for a while. When my dad took him to swimming lessons, Pierce scanned the change room for Black penises on white boys and vice versa. Reggie told him he was white and to forget about his privates. Reggie had wanted a son but was stuck with me, who'd caused an emergency C-section that left Peggy sterile. Pierce was a godsend, Reggie said.

I never told my parents about the rape. Like everyone else, they assumed I was a slut who'd got what she deserved. My father, the male slut—funny how we don't have a *slut* word for men—figured it was in the genes. This was a good cover and meant Pierce could dream up his father any way he liked and blame me for his disappearance. Being the product of rape isn't something anyone should have to live with. It wasn't—and isn't—Pierce's fault the rapists shadow his every move. I can't see their faces clearly but can smell and feel their bodies and hands on and inside me. No matter how many glasses of anaesthetizing fluids I guzzled, I could not numb the violations of rapist number one, two, three or four. For this reason I avoid touching my son. When he was little and forgiving of his absentee mom, he'd climb on my lap and wait expectantly for me to put my arms around him. I never did. He smelled of boy—slightly animal. Now he smells of man. And his hands look uncomfortably familiar.

THREE

A kitchen with good cooks runs itself; they'll step in and help without being asked. Where you have misogyny, racism, language problems, a mix of tribes and experience plus a lopsided rush where customers are slamming the same station—and WWE—you have mayhem. And then, of course, there's Daniel hugging me. "Oh my god, oh my god, oh my god, you are so Ali MacGraw. Bob and me watched *Love Story* last night. Best movie ever. Ryan O'Neal was such a snack. Have you seen it? It's Bob's mom's favourite movie. He grew up watching it and cries every time Ali dies. I said to him, 'Who does Ali remind you of?' And Bob said, 'A dying person,' and I said, 'She looks just like Stevie must've looked when she was younger—same hair, big brown eyes and cute nose.'"

"The younger me only looks like Ali when she's dying?"

"She's sad when she's dying, and you're always sad, aren't you, bae?" He hugs me again. We're low on Ranch dressing. I call another Chappy's to see if they can spare any. Daniel remains a sweating heap obstructing my path. He slides a cherry ChapStick over his lips. "Be honest with me, do I have B.O.? Siobhan says I smell."

"You is rank, cuz," says Olaf, the blond wannabe rapper, swinging by the hutch for his order.

"Oh my god, oh my god, oh my god, really? I'm going to have to kill myself." Daniel wipes sweat from his forehead. "I even used Old Spice Swagger High Endurance."

Helga returns a steak. "The customer says he had to wait eighteen minutes for it and it's tough as leather."

I display the plate to the Viking behind the chargrill.

"Tell him to fuck right off!" Conquer roars. "Eighteen minutes my ass." He jabs a knife into the steak. "Nothing wrong with that. Tell him to eat it raw, the assfucker." He throws his tongs across the kitchen.

"Conquer," I say, "grill him another one, medium rare."

I take the offending steak out the back door, where I know I'll find Gyorgi, the Slovakian busboy, smoking. Gyorgi's previous dream job was at the Darlington nuclear plant, where he carried bags of nitroglycerine and boxes of blasting caps from the safe storage site to where they're blasting. Sharing an apartment with a crowd of other Slovakian labourers, Gyorgi can't sleep until one of them goes off for a shift, leaving a vacant bed. He's six-foot-something, in chronic need of calories and known to eat food off dirty plates. "Save it for later," I say, looking up at him because I'm only 5'7".

Gyorgi takes the steak. "Thank you." The boy is big on eye contact. So refreshing when you're surrounded by thumb-bots glued to their phones. "How are you today, Stevie?"

"I'm fine, Gyorgi. How are you today?"

"Fine also. Thank you for asking." Except for his one tiny earring signalling an allegiance to some vaguely alternative point of view, my sense is Gyorgi is a straight arrow, hardworking. I've got my eye on him for the kitchen. Siobhan won't let him go easy; he's a great busser.

In my two-minute absence, Tareq manages to stick a knife through his palm while trying to separate frozen burgers. Prior to the takeover, a knife service swapped the dull knives for sharp ones weekly. Corporate reduced this to bi-monthly. Combine long shifts, dull knives, hangovers and wrestling featuring Junkyard Dog beating the crap out of One Man Gang, someone's going to need stitches. With the first aid kit out, Praveen is disinfecting and wrapping Tareq's hand. Covering both their stations while calling the board and grabbing the chits spitting from the printer, I start an order for a table of six, telling Jamshed to get more club sandwich toothpicks out of the dry storage room. Meanwhile, King Bob has stepped out of his office holding a chair. He sets it in front of the hutch and climbs onto it—with difficulty due to his size-too-small skinny jeans. He claps his hands several times in quick succession to get our attention. "I am announcing a zero tolerance policy for earbuds. Anyone caught wearing earbuds will be fired on the spot." He makes a throat-slashing gesture for emphasis.

The earbudded staff don't hear him. He claps again and stamps his feet on the chair, making it wobble. "No more cyber-loafing!" he shouts. "Do not for *one* second," he points the infamous hairy digit, "forget that I am ever-present and *always* watching!" The ESL crew gawp at him. "No more earbuds." Bob points to his ears then at the door and shouts, "Fired!" Only then does he notice the wound care going on in the corner. "*What* is going on here?"

Tareq, wearing earbuds, missed Bob's performance because he was trying to avoid bleeding to death.

Bob points to the bandages. "How did that happen?"

"Blunt knives," I say. "They should be sharpened weekly."

"It has nothing to do with blunt," Bob says. "It has to do with *earbuds*." He yanks the buds out of Tareq's ears and jabs the digit at him. "Consider this your last warning." Tareq, incapable of registering fear of goaty white men—possibly because he committed violent crimes back in Bangladesh—shows no sign of human frailty. His pitted face remains in a sneer.

"Are you still able to work?" I ask him, suspecting he's been knifed before and continued on his merry way. He nods, scowling. I miss Jesús. Faced with havoc Jesús says, "Chill, dude," or "Take it easy, bro," or, when confronted by Viking wrath, "Booyah, Big Bark." I must remember to download some Mexican wrestling for him. American wrestling, apparently, is for pussies.

Noah asked us to write a fragment about what we want out of life. I wrote: *World peace so I can grab some shut-eye.*

Every night, before Pierce goes to sleep—if you can call his sweaty jerking around on the couch sleeping—he secures the perimeter by setting up empty beer bottles to foil invaders. "Who's going to invade *us*?" I ask. We live in a crappy Scarborough triplex with paint peeling off the cracked stucco. Pierce, on autopilot, arranges the bottles in the windows, barricades the door with the easy chair and, all night long, does perimeter checks. Little noises like the fridge gurgling flick his soldier switch. Once I popped a tab on a can of juice and he dropped to the floor. Night or day he peers through the windows with binos because you never know when a parked car could be rigged with an IED, or a passing phone user could be coding a bomb. Even a kid on a skateboard might be strapped with explosives. Hypervigilance kept the soldier alive in Afghanistan. Back home he's just nuts.

What was different about his assault last night was I didn't resist. This is it, I decided, The End. No more Wing Nights at crappy Chappy's.

No more blanching cases of slimy, dismembered chicken. No more office reports and billy-goat Bob in my face. Even with Tareq holding the line, we're still short-staffed. I suppose I could hire Pierce to dish part-time; he needs employment, not only to get off my couch but to cover his beer tab. Then I could move Jamshed to prep and Praveen up the line. No one has to know we're related. Post-rape, in search of a new and improved me, I changed my last name to Tree. Only a nice, positive person could be called Stevie Tree.

With the rush over, I help reset the kitchen, clean the line and restock stations. The house staff expect to be fed after lunch but never order off the menu, riling the cooks, particularly Conquer. Siobhan, on a low-fat diet, wants everything sautéed in some chemical substance sprayed from a can. She gets away with finicky ordering when Tareq is on the line. Ogling her in her pleather mini, his boner becomes visible through his whites.

Next I investigate the break room where belongings are tossed "willy-nilly." Wade, the binge-drinking waiter with boy-next-door good looks, stands behind the door sipping chicken noodle soup.

"Are you having a moment?" I ask.

"I'm so hungover," he mutters. Like most of our university grads, Wade can't get a job in his area of expertise: evolutionary biology. He shares his evolutionary knowledge by revealing important facts like male sage grouse mate with cow manure because they can't tell the difference between a female sage grouse and a pile of shit. "Like most males," Wade explained, "they're eager to mate with any female, even if she's substandard, to spread their DNA."

"Is the booze worth it?" I ask him.

He holds his hand over his eyes as though I'm shining a light on him. "Don't preach."

"Whose crap is this?" I point to plastic bags stuffed with clothes, water bottles, coffee thermoses and other random accessories. Wade shrugs. He's starting to look like a spreading forty-year-old, not a man in his twenties. I remember this about drinking, the creeping fat. Suddenly you look in the mirror and go, "Fuck me. I'm a fat person. How did that happen?" Pierce is getting paunchy. In Afghanistan he lost thirty-six pounds. Three years later, with the grey hairs and couch potato fat, he looks like a middle-aged barhop.

Siobhan trots in, reeking of designer perfume she buys cheap in Chinatown. "There you are, hot stuff," she says to Wade. "Your order's up. Move it. You literally have two more tables out there."

"Can't *you* take their orders?" He slouches against the notice board peppered with Bob's coloured memos punctuated with frowny faces. Because of Bob's dyslexia, his missives are challenging to decipher (e.g., *Propre hygien must be miantianed at all timse!!!!!*)

"I just barfed a little in my mouth," Wade whimpers. "Can't I go home?"

"Barf in the toilet," Siobhan says, fluffing her pixie cut. "We literally have a tour bus coming in."

"Time to die," Wade groans.

"Whose crap is this?" I ask Siobhan, pointing to the bags.

She stares at the pile like she's never seen it before. "I have no idea."

"Maybe," I suggest, "a homeless person *literally* sleeps here and uses it as his storage locker." They both stare at me, computing if this is a feasible explanation.

"The new reality is," I say, "Corporate is going to take away the break room if staff don't keep it clean and tidy."

"Classic Corporate behaviour." Wade massages his temples. "So where are we supposed to nap?"

Siobhan pushes him out the door. "Go charm customers, Mr. Personality." She sits on a busted chair ejected from the dining room and examines a run in her nylons. "I'm so upset about Edvar."

This is my cue to ask what happened. Instead I tidy the break room while she sighs woefully and checks her phone. Within seconds she will scar me with her life experience.

"He's into, like, literally no hair down there," she says. "He wants me to get lasered, like, my entire snatch."

"Really? So he wants to fuck a child. How charming."

"Seriously, do you know anything about laser hair removal? Like, does it hurt?"

"Hmm let me think. Laser beam destroying hair follicles on delicate skin. Sounds like an ouch."

"All guys want girls hairless. It's from watching porn. Like even butt cracks are supposed to be hairless now."

"Well," I say, "tell Edvar to get *his* crotch and butt crack lasered." Siobhan may not be the sharpest tool in the shed, but she deserves better than Edvar.

I head out to the maintenance cabinet, grab a garbage bag, a red Sharpie and a label. Conquer's playing solitaire on his phone, which means it's slow on the floor—good news for me, bad news for Corporate. At the end of the day, Bob, rubbing his hands together, will demand, "Did we make good money today?"

Back in the break room, Daniel crowds the table, eating Pink Lemonade Cake. He points at it with his fork. "Whoever invented this should win the Nobel."

I shove the miscellaneous items into the garbage bag and stash it in the corner.

"So, bae," Daniel says, "I hope you noticed I'm wearing my dyke uniform to keep you company." He's wearing a grey and black striped cardigan, a black tie and a grey knitted infinity scarf. "Jokes! I love you," he squeals. "I know you're het. Just once in a while you could vamp it up a bit, girl. What do those legs look like under those whites? Ali looked super cute in little plaid skirts and tights. And little hats, like berets and toques with pompoms. You'd look adorbs in hats."

I print in red Sharpie on a label: *THE CONTENTS OF THIS BAG WILL BE DISPOSED OF IN 48 HOURS UNLESS OTHERWISE REMOVED.*

"Shots fired," Daniel says. "What are you coming as on Halloween? I always dress up as a hooker. Best costume ever. Helga's going to be a flower."

Halloween, another consumer compulsion. When I was a kid you carved a pumpkin. Now you decorate your porch with plastic skulls, skeletons and bats made by third-world undernourished children to entertain overnourished first-world children who need sugar like a cancer patient needs cigarettes.

"I love it that Corporate wants us to dress up," Daniel says. "I wonder what Desie'll come as. Maybe as the Rock in *G.I. Joe*. Oh my god Dwayne looked uber sexy in his armour vest. Amazon sells them. Desie could totally come as the Rock."

The newspaper on the table shouts headlines about the murdered soldiers and "the terrorists." Even on home turf, it's becoming obvious somebody's got it in for the Canadian Forces. This won't help get Pierce off my couch. When he was first discharged, he stayed in my parents' bungalow but his skittishness got on their nerves. "What's wrong with him?" they asked. "Why doesn't he sleep at night? Why's he always locking the windows and doors?" Reggie and Peggy—the party people—never locked their windows and doors, spent their mentally competent lives entertaining anybody willing to play board games with them. In the heyday of Trivial Pursuit the bungalow was packed with drinkers and smokers. I was a little tike, shoving tea towels under my door to block the stench of booze and cigarettes, trying to hold my pee all night but occasionally scurrying to the bathroom where I'd find Reggie feeling up a neighbour's wife.

After checking the fridges and freezers, ensuring stock is rotated, I notice Jamshed sweeping dirt under the beer kegs again. "Jamshed, use the dustpan and pick up the dirt." The man is hairnet-challenged, can't keep it centred on his head.

"For real?"

Jamshed uses "for real" to cover most English exchanges.

"For real, use a dustpan. You can't sweep dirt under things. You have to pick it up and put it in the garbage."

"No problem." He stands waiting for me to walk away, offering no indication that he plans to locate a dustpan for real.

Bob appears, gripping two binders. "One for kitchen," he says, thrusting the red one at me. "And one for front of house. Des came up with the task binder idea. You need to be getting your staff to check for duties in the task binder instead of standing around wearing earbuds."

"They can't read English, Bob."

Bob reminds me of my ex. Wolf, like Bob, told me what I *needed to be doing* and I figured he had to be right because self-improvement continued to elude me. Wolf forbade me gluten, refined sugar, alcohol, caffeine. Cleansed, I waited to feel better, to glow. Wolf took me to the gym and showed me how to work my traps, delts, abs and glutes. He took me running and demonstrated how to improve my stride and heel strike. After a few months of intense purification, he pointed out the cut in my biceps and delts. Wolf was very pleased with me and I hoped this would make me very pleased with me. For two years I tried to please Wolf and myself. We had Pierce over on occasional weekends and Wolf told me what I needed to be doing with him. I needed to be a role model and teach by example. Wolf tried to get the three of us cross-training but Pierce just wanted to use the Wi-Fi. That sums up the hold I had on my teenage son: internet usage. Wolf told me I needed to be monitoring what Pierce was up to online. This was beyond my capabilities. All I wanted was to eat brie and baguette and drink Chardonnay.

"You," Bob says, pointing the hairy digit at me, "need to be paying attention to how your staff handles equipment." He's back on sugar and hyper. Earlier he was smoothing his Chappy's polo shirt over his abdomen to show Daniel what staying off sugar for two weeks did for his figure.

"Look at me!" Bob said. "Look at this *skinniness!*" Then he piled a plate with two slices of Creme Caramel Apple Loaf and smothered it with whipped cream.

"Bob," I say, "we need scrubbies."

"I'm not buying you scrubbies."

"Why not?"

"Because your staff broke the ice machine."

"How do you know it was my staff?"

"Daniel says they drink Coke with ice non-stop. Maybe they don't have ice machines where they come from."

"You can't not buy scrubbies because the ice machine is broken. You said yourself another reason we failed the office report is we are the dirtiest Chappy's. How are we supposed to become the cleanest Chappy's without scrubbies?"

"If your staff can't respect the ice machine, why should I buy them scrubbies?"

"It's a shit machine, Bob. Siobhan's always complaining about it."

"Well, all the other Chappy's have the exact same ice machine and theirs aren't broken. What am I supposed to tell Corporate? All they see is more money being spent on *our* Chappy's, the stingiest and dirtiest, and the only one that *failed* the office report."

"We have way more customers than the other Chappy's. We deal with busloads of tourists wanting iced drinks. It's an old ice machine. It can't handle the demand."

"The other Chappy's have no problems with the exact same ice machine. I'll be in my office and I *do not* want to be disturbed. You have no idea what it's like. I hardly slept last night." He pokes Praveen, who stopped slicing Spanish onions on the slicer for three seconds to wipe his eyes. "If there's time for leaning," Bob scolds, "there's time for cleaning."

"We can't clean without scrubbies," I say. The fact that I have to beg for every dime spent *miantianing propre hygeine* in this dive is another reason I hate my job.

"You need to be making sure your staff uses the hand sanitizer *at all times.*"

If I'd stayed with Wolf, I would not be here. All I remember about that muggy morning was I couldn't face twig tea and going for a run, couldn't do stretches and swallow psyllium husks and probiotics. Wolf, already colon-cleansed and in Lycra, stretched his calves and said he was disappointed in me. I said I was disappointed in me.

He sat on the bed and put his hand on my knee. "You've come so far, Steve. Don't quit now."

He always called me Steve, which made me suspect the dieting and body sculpting was supposed to transform me into a man. Except that Wolf wanted to procreate. He could only ejaculate entering my vagina from behind—another cause for suspicion.

I rolled onto my side. His hand fell off my knee. "I've come so far where, Wolf?"

"You've made lasting lifestyle changes. Not many people have the willpower to turn their lives around."

My life just felt backwards, not that it had ever felt frontwards, but at least it had felt like mine. I shoved my pre-Wolf belongings into a saggy duffel bag. He looked stricken when I left, like an investor who's found out his stock is worthless.

After shopping for brie, baguette and Chardonnay, I showed up at my parents' and caved to my addictions. Reggie and Peggy, watching *Oprah*, barely acknowledged me so accustomed were they to me screwing up and seeking shelter. Pierce resented my presence until I bought some weed and shared it with him on the back porch. Those months before he signed up were the closest we have ever been—not like mother and son but like two misfits finding peace on the back porch while the prickly, scorched days softened to black.

Daniel hugs me again. "We'll make it all better, bae." He frequently says this and I have no idea what he's talking about. "See my background." He holds out his phone displaying a shot of a shirtless, ripped young man in provocatively low-riding jeans. "That's one of the Jonas brothers. Ten years ago he had hair. I like this look. Bald is hot. Like not cancer bald, buzz cut bald. Did you party last night?"

"Move your beer cases out of my produce fridge, Daniel."

"You are so single it's not funny."

In my office/closet, with the tension from the daily grind crawling up my shoulders, I prepare orders for the main supplier. Daniel's right. It's not funny.

FOUR

Walking home I stop at Dollarama for scrubbies. A wisp of a girl with bald patches stands ahead of me in line. Tenderly she lays plastic Halloween decorations on the checkout counter and I regret what I said about them. My mother always told me I see the bad in everything. Even now—when Peggy can't remember how to use a fork—she remembers to say, "You always see the bad in everything."

Before the rape I didn't think everything was bad. Life would get better. There were things to get through first, like school, living with your parents, but life would get better. Now I know life gets worse until one day you can't remember how to use a fork.

In Warden Woods, leaves crunch under my runners, and branches spread crimson, tangerine and ochre across a Windex blue sky. Sitting on my favourite mossy stump, breathing in earthy decay/renewal, I tell myself to endure with grace like a tree. When you want to rip people's faces off, think tree. What would a tree do?

A portly man in a hoodie that says TIS BETTER TO BE THE COMMANDER THAN THE COMMON MAN scrambles towards me. "Have you seen a little dog?" he asks, panicked.

"I've seen many little dogs."

"I mean *now*, like, in the last twenty minutes."

"No. Sorry."

"Oh my lord. If you see a little brown and white dog, *please* give a

26

holler." He charges into the woods, and every few minutes while I'm trying to endure with grace like a tree, I hear him calling, "Esther!"

One of the things I try to avoid pondering while enduring like a tree is my parents, which means I can't stop thinking about them; their decline and the impact it's having on me financially. With home care eating up most of their social security benefits, there's not much left for taxes, utilities and groceries. Each month I contribute more to keep the gig going. A decent nursing home would cost twice what it costs to keep them in the bungalow, not that they'd go willingly. Best case scenario, they drop dead simultaneously. They've always done everything together, that's if Reggie wasn't groping neighbours' wives or at Reggie's Auto fixing cars. Reggie's Auto was constantly on Reggie's mind, and Reggie was constantly on Peggy's mind, which worked out until they had a daughter who should have been on somebody's mind. All that accidental freedom made me long for rules: be home by ten, do your homework, clean your room. One Christmas Reggie bought me a TV. The message was clear: stay in your room and watch *your* TV so we can watch ours in private. Everything was about Reggie. He provided and Peggy pampered him, chronically anxious she'd lose him to some floozie with a convertible. When Mr. Zhaxybayeva's elegant widow drove the Buick in for servicing, Peggy fumbled her game-night food prep. "What's the matter with you?" Reggie demanded. "Why'd you burn the sausage rolls? Wrong time of the month?" This explained any female failing. On the rare occasions I mustered the courage to call him a selfish prick, he concluded it must be the wrong time of the month.

When other people's parents die I watch them grieve, thinking that must be nice, to care. Maisie, my former Walmart associate in Lingerie, was close with her mother and still talks as though the world ended when she did. It was a messy, painful and complicated death. Maisie, red-eyed, pushed around carts of bras for reshelving. "I'm getting all emo," she'd say. I couldn't take my eyes off a sorrow I couldn't imagine feeling.

"Esther!" echoes from somewhere in the woods.

A small tousled boy, gripping the hand of his large tousled father, hops down the trail. "We've got to get a backpack to put *all* the guns in," the boy enthuses. "Dexter's bringing a rocket launcher."

I didn't want Pierce playing with guns, but Reggie said all little boys want to shoot things. Big boys too, apparently.

Peggy named my son after James Bond. I didn't care what they called him. I skulked around dreaming of suicide. Pierce didn't take well to formula. "Babies prefer Mommy's milk," Peggy informed me like I couldn't figure this out. "The doctor says we should get you a breast pump. Then I could put your milk in his bottle."

"What am I, a cow?"

"You always see the bad in everything."

His cries were in my head. Wandering high-school corridors, blocking out his wails with a Walkman, milk blossomed through my T-shirt. School work wasn't hard, I just didn't see the point of it. I tried to blend in with the Doc Martens, Buffalo Jeans and Nike crowd. I read crime novels, fantasizing about working in the criminal justice system like the foxy chicks on *Law & Order*, and nailing rapists.

The Bosnian cat lady is out front in her mini-nightie shovelling dirt around the yard. This landscaping project started when she moved in. She told me there are hills in Bosnia that she wants to replicate on this patch of dirt.

"You can't obstruct the walkway," I tell her. She stares at me like I'm a serf. "All the plants you plant"—I point to the vegetation spreading around us—"grow into the path. It's dangerous. Someone could trip. And the piled-up dirt makes the rain run down into the foundation."

"Your son was making noise last night," she says. "I could not sleep. God willing, tonight will be better."

"Lady, turn your stereo down, then we'll talk about noise." She doesn't react: a tactic of hers. You could shout in her face and she'd have the same dull-eyed, vacuous expression.

No sign of soldier boy in the apartment. I listen for death not knowing what it sounds like. "Pierce?"

Sometimes he dozes on my bed during the day. A quick recon reveals he's not there. Bathroom next; flick the switch and brace yourself. Not here either. Is he playing hide and seek? He loved playing it when I showed up at Reggie and Peggy's for booze and shelter. He'd squeeze his eyes shut and count down from sixty. "That gives you a *whole minute* to hide," he'd explain. Dragging my ass into a corner I wished, as usual, to be someone else. "Ready or not, here I come!" he'd squeal and charge around the yard. Sometimes, after a binge, I'd get the spins and black out. Eventually he'd pounce and I'd shriek. He thought it was a riot. "Did I ever scare Mommy," he'd tell Peggy.

"Pierce?" Beer cans and a half-eaten baloney sandwich litter the coffee table. Maybe he's gone out although, other than a house fire, I can't imagine what would make him vacate the building. When he first got back he pounded the pavement for work, but those days are long gone.

"Ready or not here I come!" I shout. The apartment door swings open.

"Are you nuts?" he asks.

"Where were you?"

"Laundry."

"Since when do you do laundry?"

"Since I remember to do it," he says. "You shouldn't have to."

"I don't mind. It's therapeutic."

"The Bosnian was coming on to me."

"I can't breathe."

"I'm serious. She's horny. Kept offering to help."

"How?"

"Measuring the soap, getting real close. She groped my ass."

"I have to go throw up now," I say.

"Maybe I should bend her over the dryer and fuck her brains out."

"Might make her stop complaining about the noise."

We've never discussed his sex life, or how he explains his Black penis. Maybe nobody notices in the dark.

He flops on the couch and grabs the remote.

"Please don't turn it on, Pierce. I really need some quiet. There's chicken strips and coleslaw. Do you want some?" Setting the food out, I regret stopping him turning on the idiot box because suddenly we have nothing to say. When he first moved in he'd ask how my day went. Days never went particularly well. Discussing world events lead to clashes between what he called my paranoid conspiracy theory and what I called his military-fucked mind. To this day he remains loyal to the Canadian Forces and would return to them in a heartbeat if they wanted him. The fact that he doesn't get disability, and was ejected before he could qualify for a pension, does not dent his dogged devotion.

"I'm guessing you didn't go out today," I say.

"You guessed right. We need beer."

I've been enabling him by doing the beer run, empathizing with his need for anaesthesia post-trauma. "We have to talk about that."

"What?"

"How it's always beer o'clock."

"That's rich, you lecturing me about drinking."

"The beer budget, Pierce. I can't afford it."

"Were you laid off?"

"Even with the job I can't afford a two-four a day. You need to get some kind of work." He applied for a zillion jobs online. When your only work experience is the military, you don't get many requests for interviews.

"Been there done that," he says.

"What about working at Chappy's? We need a disher."

"You're shitting me."

"You'd like it. It's secluded back there. No windows to secure. Nobody bugs you." Except servers screaming for cutlery, or cooks for plates. Dishers are low on the pecking order but essential. No dishes, no service. Fast dishers are quietly appreciated. Slow ones loudly cursed. "I can train you," I say, like I have the time. "And maybe, after a while, we can move you up the line."

"I don't get why this is a problem now," he says, tugging at his T-shirt. "I've been drinking cheap beer for months. It's not like it's Heineken or something."

"You've been drinking more and more cheap beer for months, and we've been getting poorer and poorer. Reggie and Peggy's pensions don't cover all their expenses."

"Why don't they just fucking die."

They didn't recognize him the last time they saw him. Even after I explained who he was they looked unconvinced. "Our grandson is a soldier," Reggie said, pointing to a framed shot of Pierce in uniform before his first deployment.

We sit at the rickety little table under a darkening cloud.

"Do Grandpa and Grandma know who *you* are?" he asks.

"They've never known who I am."

"Cute. I mean do they recognize you?"

"Sometimes."

"Is the house worth something?"

"Maybe if a developer dozes it and builds a monster home."

Our knees touch under the table. I pull back fast. His hands, tearing apart a dinner roll, creep me out, hands I never touch but can feel. People have always said he looks like me. I never believed them but see it now around the eyes, a weariness and a hardening. We've both seen too much.

"What's the pay?"

"Minimum. You'd start part-time. Whatever you make you can spend on beer. Just don't tell anybody we're related."

"Why not?"

"Nepotism." Not sure he knows what this means.

"You're ashamed of me."

Hmm, I can't say *If you freak out I may lose my job.* "Do you want more slaw?"

"I'm good." He leans back in his chair, tipping the front legs off the floor. The Bosnian thumps up above.

"Did you know," I say, to keep some semblance of communication going, and because I'm still a little buzzed due to the six lattes Daniel provided while practising latte art, "that the word jihad has nothing to do with violence? It's got to do with discipline and faith, loyalty, the personal struggle to reform society and your heart. Most imams talk about leniency, forgiveness and piety. There's nothing in the Quran about killing people of different faiths, it says all prophets must be honoured. Infidels are people of any faith who commit crimes."

"Tell that to the guy getting his head cut off." He drops his plate in the sink and returns to his station on the couch.

"Beheadings are totally contrary to the teachings of Islam. Most Muslims are as horrified by them as we are."

Pierce stares at nothing like it's something threatening but appears to be listening, offering me a rare opportunity to de-brainwash. "According to the Quran, men and women are equal. It's been misrepresented by fanatics, just like the Bible." I swallow a chunk of chicken. Noah asked us what our spirit animal was. I couldn't think of one but now I'm thinking snake. Chew my food? Don't got no time for that—too busy slithering around dodging bigger predators.

"What's your point?"

"I just think it's really sad that jihad has been made into a bad word. I mean, all this carnage started centuries ago with the Crusades, a hundred years of unprovoked raping and pillaging by the West. Then came Western industrialization, Big Oil, technologically advanced warfare and forced regime changes. It all adds up to brutal repression and collective humiliation."

There's a deafening stillness between us, probably similar to the one just before a blast.

"It makes me sick the way you take their side," he says.

31

"I'm not taking anybody's side. I'm saying violent crimes grow out of years of abuse. It's called dehumanization."

"Yeah, yeah, yeah."

"Righteousness in any religious faith is fucked up, Pierce. It's all guesswork anyway. How do we mere mortals know? But religious fervour makes enemies and we all know how badly we need those."

He closes his eyes to make me disappear but, caffeinated, I is on fire, as wannabe rapper Olaf would say. "Plus, when you're fleeing from hunger, deprivation, mortar and sniper fire, Allah or Jesus or Our Lord in Heaven make good road buddies. In a few years one percent of the population will own half the earth. That's a lot of fleeing for the remaining ninety-nine percent. Road buddies that don't require feeding will come in handy."

Pierce rubs his forehead, throbbing for alcohol, a torture I'm familiar with. I keep talking out my ass to offer distraction; pissing him off will keep his mind off the drink.

"Talking a hundo percent realness here," I elaborate, "if we exploit *all* the oil in the ground, we'll be dead. Maybe fundamentalist frenzies are an apocalyptic coping mechanism. Who knows, maybe we'd all feel better if we cut someone's head off."

"Would you shut the fuck up." He looks flummoxed, which is better than being sunken and closed in. The fridge knocks and gurgles, putting him on the alert.

"It's just the fridge." We listen to it for a few minutes, trying not to despise each other, or each other's beliefs, anyway. "If you come to Chappy's there's a busboy you might like. Slovakian, his English is pretty good and he always wants to practise. When things are slow we talk and I find stuff out. Like today he told me he was a lab assistant on a brain study. He wants to do more research like that here, get his PhD. It's kind of wonderful how he thinks he has his whole future ahead of him."

Pierce, his face flat, looks directly at me, which is unsettling because he rarely does. "Why are you telling me this?"

"I just thought you might like him. He's not much older than you, working a shit job in a country that doesn't speak his language, but he thinks he has a future."

"And you don't think he does."

"What I think doesn't matter. It's what *he* thinks that'll get him through."

"An inspirational story." Pierce clicks the remote.

"Please come to Chappy's with me tomorrow," I say loudly over a Pizza Pizza commercial. "Just try it out. See how it goes."

He's withdrawn again, inert. Best to go to my room and make the daily call to my parents, who rarely pick up due to the blaring TV.

"Who is it?" Reggie demands.

"It's just Stevie making sure you're all right."

"Of course we're all right."

"I'm buying you groceries in the morning. Anything special you want?"

"Marshmallow cookies and liverwurst. And licorice for your mother's bowels."

"Got it."

"You bringing me the bills?"

Old invoices from Chappy's make Dad think Reggie's Auto is still in business. He's happiest "doing the billing," or fixing cars in the living room. He bends over invisible engines, kneels to scrutinize invisible chassis, handling invisible wrenches. Peggy watches with the respect she has always paid him, probably also seeing the invisible cars and tools. Even Ducky, their petite Filipino personal support worker, plays the car repair game to keep the old man occupied.

"I'll bring the bills tomorrow, Dad. Sleep tight." I hang up and grab a pencil to scribble in my diario/logbook.

Wade, the evolutionary biology grad with boy-next-door good looks, returned a half-eaten club sandwich today. The customer said his Muslim friend couldn't eat bacon and had to make himself puke five times. The Viking roared, "It's not my problem some fuckwit orders something he can't eat!"

I said to Wade, "Did you point out that bacon is listed as one of the club sandwich ingredients on the menu?" Mr. Personality, a tip slut, would never cross-examine a customer.

"Can't we offer him some alternative?" he pleaded.

"Forget about it," Siobhan said. "He wants his money back. He literally had to make himself puke five times and doesn't want to eat anything. I'll give him a refund."

I took the untouched half of the offending sandwich to Gyorgi, who was unloading a bussing tray for Jamshed. If Michelangelo were around, the old queen would want to sculpt Gyorgi's mouth. His lips are almost girly but he has a strong jawline. We shared a cigarette, even though I quit. Gyorgi asked, "How are you, Stevie?"

"I'm fine, Gyorgi, how are you?"

"I'm fine also."
Sweet lies.

Because there is no beer Pierce mainlines caffeine, coughs and does his caged animal impression for hours. At 4 a.m. he starts vomiting. The Bosnian has her trash radio going. I venture out of my bedroom to widdle. "Drink water," I tell him.

"I think I got food poisoning."

"No you didn't. You're going through withdrawal. Also known as the DTs."

"Booze never makes me puke."

"It's *not* having booze that's making you sick. I know, I've been there."

"Where haven't you been?"

"All the fun places."

His lower eyelid twitches. He rubs his forehead.

"Want some Tylenol?"

"I'll just puke it up."

After peeing I collapse on the easy chair he's pushed against the front door. "One time when I stopped drinking," I say, "I saw mice scurrying up walls. That was after I woke up in Reggie's driveway with vomit in my hair."

"You're enjoying this."

"No."

"You have to get me beer tomorrow."

"Not a chance."

"Fuck you." He sits with his head in his hands. His biceps and forearm muscles twitch. The pop radio racket thrums through the ceiling.

"You've got the shakes," I say. "In forty-eight hours you'll be through it."

"And then what?"

"You'll start crying, for no particular reason. But you'll be sober."

"I'd rather be canned."

Can't argue with this, can't spew super positive Oprah reinforcement.

"A guy lost his dog in Warden Woods," I offer, to change the subject. "I'm thinking maybe the dog lost *him*. Finally Esther is free to romp in the wild."

A sucking pause. The soldier has left me again, gone wherever he goes, far, far away.

He scratches his arms. "What kind of headcase calls his dog Esther?"

"Maybe he named her after Esther Williams, the Hollywood swimming starlet. Boy, could she dive."

"Why are you being such a bitch about the beer?"

"Money. Believe me, I'm not trying to cure you. Do what you want with your own hard-earned cash."

"I want to fucking die."

Again, no point in arguing. I start to push myself off the chair.

"Don't go."

This is new, him not wanting me to buzz off. Not sure what to do with myself, where to put my hands.

"Listening to you," he says without looking at me, "is easier than what's in my head. Talk shit. I don't care what, just talk." He drops his head on his arms on the table.

"Okay." I try to think of something that won't make him want to fucking die. When he was little he asked me to tell him stories and I made stuff up about man-eating goblins gobbling each other by mistake because they only had one eye and couldn't see properly. Green and hairy, the goblins never wiped their slobbery mouths. Bits of human and goblin entrails dangled from their warty lips.

"How about the evolution of the peppered moth?" I say, gripping the easy chair's armrests as though readying for takeoff. "The peppered moth didn't used to be peppered a couple of hundred years ago. It was lightly coloured, which camouflaged it against the lighter coloured trees and lichen the moths rested upon. Then along came the Industrial Revolution and the pollution killed the lichens and blackened the peppered moths' trees with soot. So the lighter coloured moths were easily spotted by predators. Meanwhile the darker coloured moths flourished because they could hide on the sooty trees. Same moths but they evolved to a changing environment." Pierce doesn't move and I suspect he's either passed out or thinking I'm trying another one of my being-different-colours-doesn't-mean-you're-different lines or, more specifically, having a different-coloured penis doesn't mean you're different.

"Bad news for the lighter moths," he grumbles.

"Well, here's the thing. The twentieth century gets into swing and believe it or not, there's less pollution, or anyway, less soot, so guess what happens?"

"The darker moths get eaten."

"Correct. That's how they evolved into peppered moths. A mix of light and dark so they're camouflaged in both light and dark trees." What a good story. I bet that made him feel like evolving, like he doesn't want to fucking die.

He lunges for the toilet and vomits, flushes, rinses his mouth under the tap, leans against the bathroom door frame and stares at me. He has a deep-sea-fish look about him.

"If I close my eyes, I'm back in the fucking desert."

"So don't close them." Bass beat bangs from above.

Pierce crumples on the couch. "I'm not good at anything here. Everything I'm good at is over there. All this shit going down in Iraq and Syria. I should be there."

"They won't let you go back."

He stretches his arms upward as though feeling the air for something then rolls onto his side, curling his hands under his chin. He slept like this as a child. I'd watch him and marvel that a child of rape could sleep so peacefully.

"Talk at me," he murmurs.

"Okay." Hmm, what's a good topic at 5 a.m.?

"After World War I," I say, "what we call PTSD was called hysteria and considered unmanly. Freaked out soldiers were sometimes shot in the trenches. Figuring they better suck it up, soldiers zipped it, but their reaction to trauma showed up in their bodies. Snipers went blind. Soldiers who'd bayoneted men in the face developed facial tics. Men who'd knifed the enemy in the stomach got cramps and nausea. Soldiers buried by shell explosions became terrified of the dark. Because there was no scientific explanation for their suffering, the soldiers were considered weak and whiny."

I wait for Pierce to ask me what my point is and I try to think of one. "It just seems to me if we can't express psychic pain, traumatic pain, broken heart pain, it shows up in other ways, and we get seriously messed up with depression and anxiety and all the other stuff you're going through."

The Bosnian tromps overhead, beating a path from her couch to her fridge, back and forth, spooning cartons of yoghurt and feeding her cats.

"The point is," I continue, "soldiers get fucked up, have been getting fucked up since war was invented. And if you're already fucked up before you enlist, a war zone isn't going to make you better. So cut yourself some slack, Pierce. I'd be worried if you *weren't* fucked up. Think about the civilians over there, we're talking non-stop trauma. How do they get through? From their perspective, you soldiers are the lucky ones." Can't believe he's letting me ramble on like this, feeling sorry for the bad guys. I lean forward to get a closer look at him. He's unconscious, mouth gaping slightly, eyelids twitching—back in the desert.

FIVE

Peggy attacks Ducky, the personal support worker, with a plastic spoon.

"That's *my* Daddy!" Peggy screams. "Keep your hands off *my* Daddy! Whoop, whoop!" This has happened before when Ducky dresses Reggie.

"Mom," I say, "look! Marshmallow cookies!"

She shuffles in fluffy slippers to the dining room and snatches the cookies. The devoted wife, who spent fifty years watching calories to maintain her figure, has become a sugar junkie. "Have a look at the flyers, Peggy. I need to know if there's anything on special you want." I don't, but it keeps her occupied. She has always been keen on flyers and cutting out coupons. Irritable lineups formed behind us while Peggy handed over stacks of coupons to cashiers. I looked busy checking out the gum rack. I never use the coupons Peggy cuts out in jagged slashes.

Ducky manages to pull a sweatshirt over Reggie's head. The track pants prove a bigger challenge. Grabbing his argyle-socked feet, I fit them through the holes. "How's it going, Dad?"

"Did you bring the bills?"

"Of course. You have some signing to do. Did you manage to replace that gasket on the Lincoln? You had to special order that, didn't you?"

"The stinking dealership, always making trouble."

He despised the stinking dealerships and their corporate policies.

"I bet you gave them hell," I say.

"Those numbskulls know diddly about carburetors."

I place the old invoices on his desk and pull his cheque book from the drawer. As secretary, it's my responsibility to fill out cheques for him to sign. When he forgets how to write his signature, forging will be required. I broached power of attorney when they were slightly more cognizant. They accused me of trying to steal from them: a charge not unjustified. To support my alcoholism, I've stolen cash, jewellery, watches. Reggie only allows me to organize "the bills" because it's either me or direct debit. He's never trusted the stinking banks.

With them both distracted, I help Ducky in the kitchen. "Did Peggy hurt you?"

"No, no. She just gets jealous. My goodness." When Ducky says my goodness, *ness* sounds like *nuss*.

My mother is a large woman of Scottish stock. Ducky is 4'8" and easily mistaken for a teenager even though she has a teenage daughter back in the Philippines. "How's Angel?"

"Good."

Ducky sends most of her meagre earnings home to support Angel and Ducky's sister, who looks after her along with her own brood. Ducky is the family success story, the sibling who made it out. Her relatives want her money more than they want her. Which is why she hasn't been back in six years. If this distresses her, she hides it well beneath a cheerful demeanour. She never mentions the father of her daughter, which suggests there isn't a legitimate one. Having a child out of wedlock among Catholics could not have been easy. Maybe she supports her family as penance—like I support my parents.

We haul the groceries to the kitchen and start unpacking them.

"Your father needs diapers at night now."

This doesn't surprise me as more shit stains have been appearing on the sheets. "I'll get some." Although how Ducky will convince him to wear them, never mind getting them on and off, is beyond me. Panic flares as I realize she might expect me to do it. "Anything else you need?"

The day will come when Ducky can no longer manage my parents. Every few months they're reassessed by a supervisor to determine if they can continue to live on their own.

"Please explain to your mother that I am not Mr. Many's girlfriend," Ducky says. "My goodnuss, last night she hit me with a dishtowel." If Ducky reports this kind of abuse to her agency, we will lose her.

"I'm so sorry, Ducky. Did she hurt you?"

"No, but she shouted at me, called me names."

"I'll talk to her."

Peggy never shouted. Reggie and I shouted at her, and each other. Now all those years of tightly sealed jealousy and suspicion are spewing out of her in shrieks and tears. She didn't cry openly once during my childhood. Like Pierce, she jammed it all inside. Now, when she weeps, Reggie pats her shoulder and says, "Don't cry, missus, you're scaring the living daylights out of me." As always, it's about Reggie, not Peggy. He hands her Kleenexes and she plugs herself back up.

Bob locked himself out of his office and is in mine. He saw a fruit fly swimming in his Feeling Soothed Peppermint, Ginger and Fennel tea and sprayed his entire office with chrysanthemum insecticide. The spray, although organic and non-toxic, burned Bob's throat and eyes. He quickly escaped, slamming the door. With his keys locked in his office, no one has been able access the dry storage room.

"Since when is the dry storage room locked?" I ask. It's never locked; kitchen and house staff go in and out of it all day—for napkins, jam packets, takeout supplies and condiments, straws.

"It has come to my attention," Bob says, "that certain items are missing."

"What items?"

"Food items."

"You're saying somebody's stealing?"

"I did not say that."

"What are you saying?"

"I'm not at liberty to say."

"Then why say anything?"

The billy goat snorts and adjusts his Chappy's ball cap. "The undeniable fact remains that those men are dreadful and a nuisance. What's in that gruel they eat anyway? The fridge is crammed with stuff that looks like vomit."

"That's Indian food—dal, curries. They don't like our food, which is why I'm sure nobody is stealing ketchup."

"You need to be telling your staff they can't keep food in our fridge. It could cause cross-contamination."

"It's in plastic containers, Bob. Plus you keep telling them 'No eating!' They work in a kitchen, they should be able to eat a couple of spuds."

"That's exactly why you lack leaderships skills. You're too permissive. You need to be growing your leadership skill set."

Helga blasts in wearing studded Cat Woman boots. "Why's the dry storage room locked? I need saltines."

I open it, and Bob's office. It stinks of chrysanthemum.

He hovers outside the door. "Any fruit flies?"

"You said there was only one, and no I can't see it."

"You need to be making sure the dishers pick up the rubber mats near the sinks and mop underneath. Fruit flies *breed* in damp."

"What I need to be doing is mixing ten litres of gravy." I scoop powder into the mixer.

"Fine, be negative." The old goat glances around in a fruit fly frenzy. "I need sugar. Is there any of that Triple Chocolate Loaf left? I hardly slept last night, I was so stressed. You don't know what it's like."

I turn on the mixer in an attempt to drown him out.

"You look sick," he says. "And too skinny. Are you on the paleo?"

"I don't diet, Bob. Anxiety is the secret to skinnyness. And I *do* know what it's like. If you want, I can give you a crash course in exhaustion management."

Helga struts up. She's only five feet tall and often declares, "You're just saying that because I'm short." The big boots compensate for her lowly stature.

"I have to bev a table," she announces, "and all Daniel's doing is practising latte art."

"Talk to Siobhan," I say.

"She ran over to Shoppers for tampons."

Bob does his billy-goat yelp. "I don't need to hear this." He covers his ears and heads for the cake fridge. "Don't forget there's a *mandatory* meeting for all restaurant employees at three."

I decide to have "a family emergency" at three. Mandatory meetings are Desmond's brainchild. A self-described "hands-on" district manager, I've never seen his hands on anything except his iPhone and the clipboard he slaps against his thigh while detailing our failings. He monitors staff for signs of sloth, theft, drug abuse or underworld activity. Once a KM himself, he has crossed over to the other side—corporate as opposed to human. Mere mortal cooks and servers aspire to satisfy customers. Management aspires to satisfy Corporate, a Sisyphean task. Desmond's mission is to make money for Corporate, which exists in an office tower downtown although none of us has ever seen it. Desmond hangs around Chappy's doing nothing to ensure no one else is doing nothing. Slow times are excruciating. We drag out each little chore because if Desie or the Bobster catch us in an idle moment, they'll give us something far nastier and pointless to do.

Back in my office/closet the hypoglycemic shakes set in. The stench of Pierce's puke permeated the dugout this morning, making breakfast unappealing. If he doesn't start taking in liquids to replace electrolytes, he'll black out. I dashed to the convenience store for Gatorade and left it on the coffee table. He was face down on the couch again, unresponsive to a shoulder nudge. People drown in their own vomit. I nudged him harder. "Fuck off and get me beer," he grumbled. Sometimes I think I'm daring him to kill me.

"Knock knock," Daniel says. "Surprise!" He sets two lattes on my desk. "Which do you like better, bae? The heart or the leaf?"

I stare at the coffee swirls in the foam, unable to detect a difference. "They're both nice."

"The Bobster likes the heart. I'm serious, pick a fave." He starts to sneeze. "I'm so allergic. This hot guy I met last night is a vet tech, totally covered in animal dander." I choose what might be the leaf.

Siobhan joins us. "Is Desmond literally going to sit in the dining room all day?"

"Oh my god, oh my god, oh my god, Desie's here? How thrilling. I'll make him a heart latte." Daniel bustles out, leaving both lattes. I down one then the other.

Hands on hips, Siobhan says, "Desmond is making Helga take all the desserts out of the display case and clean the shelves. Meanwhile a busload of seniors headed for Niagara Falls just pulled in. They're going to want the Traditional and the Superscramble." Breakfast specials ordered minutes before the cut-off time of eleven infuriate the cooks, who have cleared away the homefries, bacon and eggs to make room for the lunch menu. Seniors order breakfast because it's cheap. A tour bus seats fifty people. That's a lot of scrambled. No question I'll be pitching in.

Siobhan tugs down on the pleather mini sliding up her thighs. "Can't you get Desmond off our backs? He's literally taking up a booth in Helga's section."

"I am the kitchen manager, Siobhan. You are the house manager.

Manage it." I squeeze past her and grab a hard-boiled egg from the pile Praveen is peeling and snake-gulp it down. As the seniors' orders stack up, I fry bacon strips worrying, as usual, about what's making Pierce drink himself senseless. Presumably relentless, debilitating shame for something he either did or witnessed. When he describes the atrocities over there, he portrays himself as an innocent bystander. Can a soldier be an innocent bystander in a war?

To avoid the mandatory meeting, I visit Maisie, my former Walmart associate in Lingerie, at her house that doubles as a daycare. On the way I spot a *Lost Little Dog* sign taped to a street lamp: *Terrier bulldog mix, female, adult, brown and white, short haired, answers to Esther, please call Ern Lockraw 416-694-6645.*

I feel sorry for Ern but sing a quiet song of freedom for Esther.

Preschoolers scoot around Maisie's kiddy-worn furniture while the TV pumps background noise. We drink coffee at her crayon-stained kitchen table. "It's a strug," she says. "He says to me, 'You better check yourself before you wreck yourself.' I'm like, who's he to talk?"

Unsavoury men find shelter at Maisie's. Initially grateful, they treat her well until they figure out all she understands is abuse.

"Then he says to me, 'Bitches need stitches.'"

"Ah," I say, "he's a poet."

"Here's the ish. I don't want him going all aggro in front of the kids. It's bad role modelling."

Role modelling is new. She's been attending group therapy for victims of childhood sexual abuse. The group leader, according to Maisie, is dece (short for decent) and talks about choices and how important it is to make the right ones—like it's all laid out before us and we just have to pick door number one, two or three.

"It's a bad sitch. He got laid off because he missed so much time after stepping on a nail."

"That's no reason to let him hang around doing bad role modelling."

She picks at a muffin. "I should never have left Walmart."

We used to split a box of Krispy Kremes and eat them in the parking lot. Watching the sun slink behind the squiggle of trees at the end of the plaza, we shared a feeling of accomplishment because bras, camisoles, thongs and panties had been wrangled.

"At least it was a job," she says.

That's where they get us. At least it's a job. What we endure in the name of a job seems limitless. Soon we will be grateful that newly introduced child labour laws provide job opportunities for Junior. "We're so lucky the sweatshop is in Canada," we'll enthuse. "They'd have built it in Bangladesh if it weren't underwater."

"I miss my mom," Maisie says.

I nod but don't understand missing a mother who let an uncle step in after the husband took off. An uncle who took Maisie for ice cream then made her suck his cock. Penetration came later, always after ice cream. The uncle said she made him do it, and that if Maisie told anyone he'd tell them what a dirty little slut she was. She tried to eat her troubles away, downing bags of chips and, of course, ice cream. Ultimately, the uncle called her a fat whore and left her alone.

When she confessed this, she couldn't stop crying and said she was ashamed. I came as close as I ever have to telling someone, other than my counsellor in cherry red cat-eye specs and matching lipstick, the whole truth about my rape; how I too was ashamed and felt partly to blame. But I couldn't form the words, didn't see the point—we are all alone in our solitary confinement. Talking about it just makes it more real, more important. When I tried to explain this to my counsellor, she pushed for a play-by-play of the rape. "At any point," she asked, "did it feel good? Did you enjoy it?" She believed Herr Freud's conjecture that women possess a natural masochism. She cited a criminologist who claimed women have "a universal desire to be violently possessed and aggressively handled by men." When she quoted his theory, "The victim is always the cause of the crime," I quit counselling.

Maisie wipes yoghurt off a toddler. Her ability to care for other people's children, has freed her from minimum wage penury. Yet she continues to pine for Walmart and seek the company of abusive men.

"Why do you want a man around, anyway?" I ask. "You can date, just don't let him sleep over." Her one-year-old crawls towards her, howling his insatiable need. Maisie scoops him up and bounces him on her bosom, cooing baby talk. The Peggies and Maisies spend their lives fulfilling the needs of others. And when they are no longer needed, the Peggies and Maisies can't remember who they are, or were. Not that I know who I am, or was, but I sure don't need someone telling me who I should be, a.k.a. Wolf. Ah, those days spent pretending to be a homemaker, cleaning and dimming the lights to hide missed dust bunnies, spending weekends roaming Home Depot in search of reno supplies, offering my womb during ovulation. Deluding myself that a wanted baby might heal my wounds. The victim is always the cause of the crime.

"I should go," I say.

"Why? You just got here."

"It's Ladies' Night. It's going to be busy. Lots of chicken Caesars. Catch you later."

I'm halted by a posse of miniature dogs and a chain-smoking dog walker. The critters crowd the sidewalk, sniffing urgently at a picket fence. On the other side of the fence a bulging woman, in turquoise velour, stops raking leaves to admire the dogs. "Aren't you nice little doggies? *My* little doggies are away. Can you smell them? You can, can't you? Oh yes you can. They'll be so sorry to have missed you. Would you like some treats? Shall I get you some cookies?"

We have a regular, Mrs. Flood, who orders mozzarella sticks and mouths baby talk through the window to her miniature dog tethered to a trash can. She even throws it kisses. Before paying her bill, Mrs. Flood exits briefly to ask Baxter, the dog, if he wants a burger. If Baxter says yes, we're ordered to prepare it rare for him. The kitchen staff, raised in countries where dogs are considered unclean, treated like dogs and in desperate times eaten—certainly rarely permitted alive in houses, let alone kissed and cuddled or named Baxter—take turns watching Mrs. Flood through the hutch, their expressions a blend of bafflement and revulsion. They giggle when Baxter takes a dump and Mrs. Flood bends down to collect his turds. In the Western world, it is only a matter of time before domesticated animals join their owners at tables in restaurants. Servers will be required to complete e-learning to interpret doggy and kitty requests. Pet Specials will be introduced, stooping and scooping listed in the front of house task binder. Let's hope Gyorgi will have found his way to a brain lab before then. Doubtless I'll still be at Chappy's, prepping the kitty caviar.

A funereal aura pervades the kitchen: mandatory meeting fallout. Corporate instills fear of layoffs to increase productivity. That the staff produce less, resenting every second of their labour, does not register with the untouchable office tower. Corporate knows there is an endless supply of low-wage workers to chew up and spit out.

With my office/closet door closed, I drop my head on my arms on my desk like my son does in the dugout, hoping he hasn't blacked out or drowned in puke. Can't phone him, he quit paying for it months ago, and has no friends to notice his silence. At first there were occasional calls from Greg Lem, also in Logistics, whose vehicle was caught in a Taliban ambush and struck by a rocket. Greg, the sole survivor, was peppered with shrapnel and suffered blast-induced brain injury along with damage to his pancreas. Daily, when shaving, Greg picks pieces of metal out of his face. He requires eight to ten needles of narcotics every twenty-four hours to control his pain. Like Pierce, all he wants is to stay in the military. When Greg Lem stopped calling, I asked Pierce why he didn't call him. "He's totally fucked," he said.

"What's totally fucked mean in this context?"

He swilled more beer, shrugged and said, "He's not the same guy."

"What's changed about him?"

"He's totally fucked."

Pierce isn't the same guy either. Not that I knew the other one.

SIX

The mandatory meeting topic was theft—time theft and property—as well as illegal drug activity. Desmond warned that Corporate can order a locker search at any time. Anyone caught stealing, or using drugs, will be dismissed and criminally charged. Corporate is installing security cameras throughout Chappy's to maintain surveillance on staff at all times. These cameras will be accessible to Desmond via his laptop.

This Halloween I'm coming as Joe Stalin.

Daniel, shaken by the police state, hastily reapplies Swagger High Endurance in my office/closet.

"Daniel, why are you doing this here?"

"It's not safe anywhere else. I don't trust anybody—like not even Bob. Maybe he's a mole."

"I thought you liked Desie the party boy."

"He's gotten so Darth Vadery, like what's up with that?"

"Absolute power corrupts absolutely."

"Bob is totally supplicant around him." This is a big word for Daniel. "I always pegged Bob for a top, but now I'm thinking he's a bottom. I'm always telling him I'm worried *I've* been pegged for a bottom, and there he goes supplicating himself to Desmond. Do you really think they'll dock our pay if they see us standing still on the cameras?"

"Anything's possible."

He pulls what looks like a lipstick out of his pocket. "See this? It's mace. Any time some guy tries to finger me again, he gets it in the eyes."

"Might be hard to do if you're a bottom."

"I'd just squirt it over my shoulder." He demonstrates the ease of this manoeuvre with the lipstick. "So, bae, who do you think is stealing from the dry storage room?"

"Nobody." I did notice some shrinkage and suspected it was Gyorgi stuffing his pockets with saltines and jams, maybe even ketchup for watery tomato soup back in the apartment with the Slovakians. The theft was so minor I didn't worry about it. Now I'll have to talk to him before he gets arrested and deported.

"Like, who would steal that stuff?" Daniel says. "It's not like it's cake or something fun." He checks his hair on his phone again. "What do you think about the alleged drug activity? Can they really do random testing?"

"Probably."

"Oh my god, oh my god, oh my god, they'd have to watch us pee."

Siobhan barges in. "What the fuck, Daniel, a tournament literally just showed up. They want the Pitcher Special. Get your lardy ass out there."

"There you go body-shaming me again. That's discrimination." Off he huffs and she hangs around my desk while I call the plumber and lock-smith. Our back door lock is jammed in lock mode, making deliveries challenging. What with earbuds, kitchen noise and Conquer's classic rock, the driver has to hammer on the door to be heard.

"Personally," Siobhan says, "I think Desmond has the drug problem. Have you seen his pupils? Literally dilated."

"His eyes are dark brown. How can you tell if his pupils are dilated?"

"When he's in my face about 'customer care,' literally all I see are his drugged-out pupils."

Stonewalled by voicemail, I leave more pleading messages.

"Does Bob know you're calling tradesmen?" Siobhan studies her aqua acrylic nails. "He'll go ballistic when he finds out."

The phone rings. It's not a tradesman but a sales rep wanting to set up a meeting. "Not a good time," I say, googling plumbers.

"I'm so upset about Edvar." Siobhan leans her butt on my desk. "He refused to pick me up from the blood donor clinic. I told him three weeks ago I was giving blood and needed him to take me home. So I call him from the clinic—I'm literally passing out—and he says, 'You'll be all right.'

I tell him I'm dizzy and can't walk. They wouldn't let me leave for two hours, that's how weak I was."

"Maybe you shouldn't give blood."

I try another plumber, talk to an English-challenged woman, explain the urgency. She assures me that Shakthi, the plumber, will call me right back.

"He got me knives and forks for my birthday," Siobhan says, "and told me I shouldn't share cutlery with my roommate because she's Somalian and dirty and I'm like, gee, so sorry I literally bought you a $200 outfit from Club Monaco for *your* birthday."

Shakthi calls. I'm stunned, breathless, my heart swinging around my ribcage. He says he can snake the drain this very afternoon. I hang up before he can change his mind. Siobhan, with one hand on her pleather mini, appears to be waiting for me to offer advice. So I say, "Speaking of South Americans, there is a South American orchid that makes itself look like a bee so male bees will fuck it. Imagine that, looking like an orchid one minute then switching to bee mode to get pollinated. Pretty trippy, as Helga would say."

"If she talks about Connor's dick one more time, I will literally vomit."

Connor, Helga's latest Tinder hookup, has a large penis. Apparently Helga has to grip it with both hands when she sucks on it. To enhance our understanding of what's involved in fellating Connor, she has mimed the required massage/sucking technique. She says Connor's penis is so long she can feel it "touch the back." We all checked out Connor on Facebook. He looks like a girl. "Connor just has to say 'sex,'" Helga tells us, "and I'm wet." I miss talking about the weather.

Praveen scrambles in looking more like a startled bird than usual, pulling the hairs on his forearms. "They all want the Club Sandwich Deluxe," he gasps. "The *whole* tournament. Chef says he's no assfuck sandwich maker."

"I'll be right there."

The introduction of touchscreens to the resto biz, where fingers are greasy, sticky or just plain wet, was an act of short-sightedness. There is no room for fine tuning with touchscreens; it all whips by so fast you have no choice but to shout special orders to cooks deafened by earbuds and classic rock. Consequently the mashed arrives without gravy, the dressing not on the side, and the servers have hissy fits. Multiply this by a tournament of Club Sandwich Deluxe eaters and Pitcher Special drinkers, all demanding white or brown plus mayo on the side, and you are buried in chits, fighting to keep your head above the kitchen's grease-coated walls and slippery/ sticky floors. Amazingly, just when you thought you were taking your last gasp, survival instincts kick in and it's ride or die in a club sandwich marathon starting with the required three pieces of toast throwing off the logistics of using a four slice toaster. Next, the absurdity of the club sandwich: labour intensive to assemble as the three pieces of toast, chicken, bacon, lettuce, tomato—cut into four triangles—are bound together by four toothpicks. No easy feat—nimble fingers are required, not Praveen's nervous digits. Tareq, at the fryer station, grudgingly follows my orders to assist but Conquer, no assfuck sandwich maker, ignores our travails while finishing up his Sudoku. Within minutes we are low on stock on the line, requiring me to skedaddle repeatedly to the prep fridge while frying endless bacon strips. We run out of toothpicks and Jamshed, the slowest man alive, is sent to find more in the dry storage room. King Bob, through all this, is in his office staring at his phone to determine if one of his pupils is smaller than the other, indicating a stroke. He complained to Daniel that *nobody* is on his side at Chappy's, and that when he woke up this morning his left arm felt numb—but also kind of like painful from the inside—and he thought maybe he'd fallen asleep on it, or that the pain could be a symptom of a stroke or a heart attack. He cornered me briefly while I was drain-fishing pre-rush. "Why weren't you at the mandatory meeting?" he demanded.

"Family emergency."

"What family emergency?"

"It's a private matter, Bob."

"I have family emergencies all the time and you don't see me missing *mandatory* meetings."

He has never mentioned family. Daniel divulging that *Love Story* is Bob's mother's favourite movie is the first I've heard of her. On his days off Bob shops at Dollarama. I can't picture him with a mom, pop and sibs, only alone in his apartment surrounded by Dollarama trinkets.

"Cutbacks," he declared, "make *preventing* time theft a top priority."

"What about cutbacks causing wage theft? These people support families. You can't just cut their hours to meet some bullshit bottom line."

He clutched his chest. "The French Onion Soup must be giving me heartburn. I better take some Tums." He scuttled off.

Wade drifts in, stinking of pot. "Are there more clubs coming?"

"What's it look like?"

"It's just that the tournament guys want their sandwiches served at the same time. Like, they want to eat them together."

"Do you see forty-three toasters here?"

The university grad looks around for forty-three toasters.

"Do the math, genius. To serve them simultaneously we need forty-three toasters."

Siobhan speeds by. "Where's Bob?"

"Having a heart attack or a stroke in his office."

"The homeless guy's here again, taking up an entire booth."

"So serve him."

"He just orders coffee and literally a hundred refills."

"That's because he's homeless."

"He smells disgusting."

"That's because he's homeless. They don't have showers."

Siobhan does her jazz handsy thing to signal exasperation. "We can't just let him *sit* there."

"Why not?"

"What if he starts shouting about duct cleaning again?"

Duct cleaning terrifies the homeless man, causing him to shout intermittently, "I don't want duct cleaning!" or "No duct cleaning!"

"Tell him if he leaves after his next refill, we won't clean his ducts."

We feed the tournament—all ten teams—then prep for Ladies' Night, the most reviled night of the week. When inebriated with Ladies' Night cocktails, the female customers turn catty and loud while scouting Tinder for potential hookups. When matches are made and the Tinder duds show up, hormonal static fills the air and waitresses become targets of abuse for minor errors. The waitresses take their frustrations out on kitchen staff, who hustle to manage special orders spun out of control due to the ladies' diet requirements. Food is sent back repeatedly and, when reheated in the microwave, described by the ladies as fossilized. After prep, I am determined to strike camp before they arrive.

The prospect of questioning Gyorgi about cracker theft coats me in seaweedy dread. How's he supposed to like me, smile at me, if I accuse him of stealing. We cross paths in the dishpit and I ask him to come to my office for a chat. The chat line is Bob's. That I resort to such a lame line indicates a need to grow my leadership skill set.

Clearly surprised and anxious, Gyorgi stands awkwardly in my clos-et—a trapped majestic animal. I'd offer him a seat but there is only one and I'm on it. I stand to level the field but he is so tall, I feel like a child. Better to rest my tush on the desk Siobhan-style and attempt to look casual. Can't take my eyes off him, and the Frankie Valli tune "Can't Take My Eyes Off of You" whispers warnings in my head. Being in a confined space alone together is new. I can feel his breathing and know he fears being fired.

"I was just wondering," I say, "have you been going into the dry storage room at all?"

He crosses his arms, burying his fists in his armpits. He won't look at me, making me yearn for his hazel gaze glowing with brain researcher intelligence.

"You have to go in for dining-room supplies," I point out. "But there's no other reason, is there?"

A stinging silence. Within seconds someone will scratch at my door.

"I take crackers," he says, looking at the floor. "Ketchup also. And jam."

All I want is to put my arms around him, press my face into his chest and murmur, "Don't worry about it, take all you want." Instead I say, "Okay, well, maybe you shouldn't do that. Any food going to waste you can have, but please don't take the crackers, ketchup and jam."

"I'm sorry," he says. "Please, I need job." He looks at me but it's different. We are no longer allies.

"You still have the job. You are an excellent worker and I'm going to talk to Siobhan about letting you work on the line."

The clouds part and sun spills around him. "Thank you. I never take crackers again."

Jamshed, the slowest man alive, bursts through the door breathless, as though he has run 10K. "The plumber is here! For real!"

Shakthi wobbles like a penguin. It's impossible to imagine how that low-hanging girth and those stubby legs will allow him to get down on all fours for drain exploration. I continue chopping romaine for chicken Caesars, keeping an eye on Bob's office door which, fingers crossed, will remain closed for the duration of the snaking adventure.

Praveen leads Shakthi to the drain. They're both Tamil, and a whole new Praveen gushes forth, full of vim and vigour and—here's the shocker—confidence. He converses animatedly in Tamil about our plumbing tribulations, demonstrating my plunging technique. Shakthi nods sagely, with one hand on his chin. All this communing takes time and

I want to shout "Hop to it!" before Bob recovers from his latest medical crisis, but I sense that interfering would rob Praveen of his moment. After much discussion, while I grind peppercorns in the spice grinder, Shakthi retrieves plumbing implements from his truck and begins to snake the drain. We hear it belch, gurgle and fart. Even the Viking is transfixed by Shakthi's snaking abilities as he twists and turns his bulk in unison with the metallic snake. Much slimy debris surfaces: soggy bread crusts, lemon rinds and a sock. I look around at my staff for signs of the sock's ownership, but they all stand mesmerized. It is this awed silence that draws King Bob from his office.

"*What* is going on here?"

Shakthi, in a Zen state, pays the billy goat no heed but Praveen immediately relapses into startled-bird mode.

Bob stamps his feet and jerks his arms. "I said *what* is going on here?"

"What's it look like, Bob?" I ask.

"It looks like you acted without my authority."

"It's not the weekend. You said we couldn't call a plumber on weekends."

All the South Asians, except Shakthi, back away from Bob to resume Ladies' Night prep. The Viking plays solitaire on his phone.

"Bob," I say, "the drain was completely blocked. He pulled a sock out of it."

"A sock!" He hits a high note with "sock." "How did a *sock* get down the floor drain?"

"I guess it slipped off somebody's foot."

"Ha ha, very funny. How did it get through the grill? Someone must have removed the grill and stuffed the sock down it." Bob's already tense body stiffens. This is where Jesús would say, "Become a noodle, boss," and Bob, taken aback by the love of Jesús, would relax slightly in an attempt to become a noodle. Jesús loves everyone and everything, which is why his absence leaves us skulking around, mistrusting ourselves and each other. Without Jesús to tell us, "I *love* yusse!" or "I *love* it!" we feel loveless.

"Is this some kind of joke?" Bob demands, turning purplish, possibly due to heart failure. "This is unacceptable and completely unprofessional. We can't have socks lying around higgeldy-piggeldy." His voice climbs higher and his arms jolt from his sides. "This sock belongs to someone here and that someone better step forward!" He grabs tongs and picks up the soggy sock, thrusting it at us. "I demand to know whose sock this is." Olaf and Wade stand frozen by the hutch, poised to input touchscreen orders.

"If you refuse to cooperate there will be consequences. I will *not* tolerate *insubordination*!"

Smiling beatifically, Shakthi withdraws his snake. "All clear," he says. "No more problem."

"You hear that, Bob," I say. "No more problem. Isn't that wonderful?"

"I'm calling Desmond."

"I already did."

"What?"

"Desmond okayed the service call." The look on Bob's face belongs to a child at his no-show birthday party. "It's all good, Bob. All taken care of. Have a piece of Chocolate Mousse Bonanza Cake, we just got it in." I signal to Praveen to get the cake and put my arm around Bob's shoulders, guiding him back to his office. "And Daniel is dying to make you a tree latte."

Siobhan storms in from the dining room. "The homeless man literally shit in the booth!"

"Iconic," Wade says.

Siobhan does the jazz handsy thing. "I can't believe you make me serve him. That's it, no more. Serve him yourself."

We're not sure who she's talking to. It can't be me, the KM, so it has to be Bob the GM, although he's retreating, shit-phobic. Siobhan covers her face with her hands. "I'm not going out there until somebody cleans it up."

"Siobhan," I say, "you are the house manager. Get a busser to do it." This means Gyorgi, and no way am *I* ordering the majestic animal to clean up shit. "This is not my department."

Siobhan fulminates into sobs, turning her face to the wall as if it's a shoulder to cry on. Tareq's eyes glom onto her buttocks as her pleather mini rides up her thighs. Bob takes cover with his Chocolate Mousse Bonanza Cake while Olaf and Wade hop about pinching their noses.

"Da bro legit pulled his pants down to drop da load," Olaf informs us, gleefully. "In total realness, on da banquette, three feet from dem interior decorators. They was talking wallpaper and didn't notice nothin'."

"Solid work," Wade says.

"Would one of you go and clean it up?" I ask.

"No way, cuz," Olaf says. "Not in da job description. Dudes, where's my spag and meatballs, yo?"

Siobhan makes heifer snorts and squeals. Her boohooing probably has more to do with Edvar's insensitivity than the homeless man's excrement.

"Oh my god, oh my god, oh my god, it smells like poop out there," Daniel says, tree latte in hand.

Then my knight appears, armed with rubber gloves and a bucket, his single earring sparkling under the fluorescents.

"Not to worry," Gyorgi says, and out he goes to save the day.

Trying to decide which style and size of diaper to buy Reggie, I ponder the homeless man's indiscretion. The fact that he pulled his pants down to defecate on the banquette brings the accidental element into question. But why would he soil his own nest? Did the coffee refills streaming through him create an unstoppable urge and, rather than shit his pants that he is unable to wash, he shat on Chappy's faux leather upholstery? What was he in his previous life—a manager in a duct-cleaning conglomerate that kept acquiring and merging until there were too many managers and our man was informed by a pantsuited woman in HR that "we don't feel you're happy here"?

Without a toilet to call his own, he shits where he wants.

Before facing soldier boy at base camp, I pull out my pencil and logbook, sit on my mossy stump in Warden Woods and try to endure with grace like a tree.

For years I stopped walking if I heard footsteps behind me. I'd duck in door-ways or between parked cars until people passed. I see this in Pierce. The blast of an IED can cause blood to swell in the brain, stretching and breaking vessels. The grey matter bleeds and withers, misfiring the fight-or-flight response—the sensor wired to keep us alive. Pierce is completely paranoid. He sees a bump in the road, it's a bomb. He can't disassociate the memory from the emotion. It's replayed over and over. Story of my life.

Presumably survivor guilt chokes him any time he tries to crawl out of his personal hell. This is familiar. Eleven days after my rape, a fourteen-year-old was gang-banged and abandoned behind a dumpster. She died of internal bleeding from the repeated penetrations. I don't know if it was the same four-some—they were never caught—but I've always felt it should have been me dead behind the dumpster.

Rustling in the bushes triggers my fight-or-flight response. A small, short-haired, brown and white dog scampers towards me then stops still, with the frightened stare of a movie star caught by paparazzi. A grass snake dangles from its mouth.

"Esther?"

The dog's ears prick up.

"Esther, is that you?"

Clearly alarmed at being recognized, she emits a low growl—dogspeak for "Don't tell Ern!" Esther unchained. Snake in mouth, she darts back into the woods.

SEVEN

The emergency vehicles outside my crappy stucco triplex are visible from two blocks away. I've been preparing myself for this, focusing on the upside, debating whether or not there is a downside. For him, I conclude, it would be tragic: a young life cut short, blaggablagga. On his last tour, when he went back to die because being dead there was easier than being alive here, I became fatalistic about the whole deal. Whatever happens, happens. Then it didn't. He came back even more nuts. Now The End beckons again, and moist fall air turns to swamp sludge, impeding my progress to the flashing red lights, suddenly impossibly far away. Neighbours gather around the vehicles, bonding over someone else's tragedy.

It is not a tragedy. It is for the best. No more vomit, no more fights, no more beers and DTs, no dishes to clean but my own. Defeated by the autumnal bog, I slump on a lawn while memory flashcards my maternal inadequacies. The small boy switching on the nightlight, not because he needed to find his way to the toilet but because he feared he would be forgotten in the dark. Sitting very straight in his Teletubby PJs, tugging at them like he now tugs on T-shirts, he'd make me read Dr. Seuss's "The Kaverns of Krock." "And you're so, *so, SO* lucky, you're not a left sock, left behind by mistake in the Kaverns of Krock! Thank goodness for all of the things you are not! Thank goodness you're not something someone forgot."

I abandoned him this morning, again. I have exploited the rape, used the catastrophe to stop feeling and thinking, to avoid taking responsibility for my many intimate acts of destruction.

When I see the body wheeled out in a white neoprene bag, adrenaline kicks in and I charge the last half block to the gurney but am stopped by a wide cop. "What do you think you're doing, ma'am?"

"That's my son."

"Your son?" He has a handlebar moustache. I try to push past him but an even wider cop blocks my path, their combined bulletproof vests making them impenetrable.

"That's my son! You can't take him away until I see him." What am I seeking, closure? Never believed in it. It's delusive, the false hope that we can deaden our living grief.

"Your name, ma'am?" the moustached cop demands.

"What's my name got to do with it?"

"To determine your relationship to the deceased." He hooks his fingers in his belt. They smell bad, these cops, like fast food.

"Tree. His name's different from mine. Many."

"Many what, ma'am?"

"Many, his name is Many, Pierce Many."

"This is not Pierce Many, ma'am. Take it easy. This is not your son."

Men in dark suits and ties slide the body into a black van.

"Do you live here, ma'am, with your son?"

"Yes." So he's alive? So I should rejoice?

"That wasn't your son, ma'am," the cop says. "You go in now. We'll take care of things out here." Cops never take care of things, they bully and maim and let you die in the street.

Pierce waves cheerily behind the glass door. He did not commit suicide, is not leaking shit and piss. A gust of what might be relief knocks me off balance. A bulletproof vest offers an arm I avoid, lurching towards my son. He swings the door open, smiling like he's won a prize.

"Well hello," he says. "You missed quite the party."

"Who's in the bag, the Bosnian?"

"The Bosnian called 911, identified the body, was really chills about it. Apparently she IDed all kinds of corpses back home."

"Who was it?"

"Mr. Winsome. His dog was howling so I checked it out, jimmied the door."

Our heroine appears on the landing in leggings, mounds of flesh jiggle beneath hot pink spandex. "God willing, he will rest in peace."

"How long has he been dead?"

"Days," Pierce says, cackling. "Surrounded by eggshells."

"It's not funny, Pierce."

"What's not funny? Old guy kicks it after eating a couple dozen eggs. Not a bad way to go."

No doubt he's seen worse.

"Can we keep the dog?" he asks, looking twelve. Winsome's white-whiskered black lab stands at his feet, wagging his tail tentatively.

"No way." Ever since Pierce could talk he's been asking for a dog. Reggie forbade it—dirty mutts, he called them.

"Someone's got to take the dog," Pierce says. "It's not like Winsome had relatives."

I look at the Bosnian. "Why don't you take it? Or are you strictly a cat person?"

She stares past me at the hound nuzzling Pierce's thigh.

"Pierce," I say, "how do you know Winsome had no relatives?"

"Amina says nobody ever visits."

"Amina?"

"He was always alone," the Bosnian says. "The dog is Benedict."

"Ben, cool." Pierce crouches and lets the dog lick his face. This is too much.

"Why didn't the police take the dog to a shelter or something?"

Pierce scratches behind the dog's ears. "I said he was mine."

"Okay, that's not happening. Amina can take the dog. Maybe it'll eat her cats." I slam the door to the dugout. We've been breathing dying and dead air. How did we not notice? The old man used to plug up his tracheotomy hole with his finger to force cigarette smoke into his lungs. We stepped around each other in the laundry room. My efforts at small talk were met with three responses: "Maybe," "Not so much" and "Maybe not so much." If I managed to get Winsome talking he never said *I* but used *we*, as in *we* were all in this together. And now he died alone, died for days, and we didn't notice.

On the other side of my door the Bosnian and Pierce chat cozily. Maybe he can move into her place, with the dog. All my touchy-feely, remorseful thoughts dissipate because my son is drunk. Time to search the dive, check all the usual places: toilet tank, broom closet, garbage can, under the sinks. The bottle of Captain Morgan is wedged between the vanity and the wall, half-full. I consider taking a slug, or two, or three. Sitting on the toilet lid, bottle in hand, I work at remembering why this is a bad idea. It takes awhile—a slide show of vomit-soaked years avoiding reflective surfaces for fear of what would stare back at me. Twist off the cap, have a sniff. Never was a rum drinker, except in daiquiris. Where did he get the bottle? Off the dead man? A dead man's rum for a dead man because that's what he'll be if he keeps this up. What do I care. I want to be unchained like Esther.

While Mr. Winsome was dying for days, important facts were revealed at Chappy's.

1. Helga uses anal plugs to expand her anus to make it more hospitable for Connor-who-looks-like-a-girl's large penis.

2. Siobhan only needs three dresses if different people see her when she's wearing them (she keeps a list in her phone about who saw what when).

3. Wade requires weed to sleep soundly. Without cannabis, when the evolutionary biologist eventually nods off, he has weird dreams, like the one where his whole family—except his little brother—got eaten by a great white shark and his phone turned into a baby.

4. Siobhan and Edvar did shrooms before rollerblading and the hallucinogen hit Edvar an hour before it hit Siobhan. She had to pull the Brazilian bombshell along by his belt while he spaced out about the infinite cosmos.

I pour the rum down the sink, inhaling its aroma, hoping for a buzz. No noise up above, not even trash radio.

5. Wade, in a pot fog, expounded about sexual selection in animals. The males have to strut their stuff, displaying their feathers, horns, antlers and other attributes, or perform alluring mating rituals or calls, to win the females over. Male peacocks struggle to fly with their weighty, awkward plumage. Brightly coloured show-off male birds make easy targets for predators. Elks with impressive antlers labour to lift their heads. Male animals suffer to be sexy. Meanwhile, male humans schlep around with pants sagging off their asses, gaming or watching porn on their phones while female humans expand their assholes, laser pubic and butt crack hair, and rotate dresses.

Time for Swiss Almond Fudge Cake, stolen from the cake fridge. When you're treated like a criminal, you act like one. Bent over the little rickety table, forking it in, I hold a small memorial service for Mr. Winsome. "May you rest in peace," I say, making the sign of the cross with my fork. "*I* remember you, even if no one else does. Or should I say, *we* remember you."

Pierce pushes open the door. "You talking to yourself again?" He heads for the bathroom and the disappeared Captain Morgan, groping around quietly then frantically. "Where'd you put it?"

"You stole a dead man's rum."

"He won't be drinking it. Where is it?"

"Down the drain."

"You're fucking kidding me."

"Try some Swiss Almond Fudge Cake."

"I fucking hate you."

"Right back at you. Why don't you go see your girlfriend. A fuck for a beer. Do Bosnians drink beer? Vodka?"

"You fucking cunt."

"Whoa, where's all this hostility coming from? Try becoming a noodle." Jesús's other favourite phrase is "Don't worry about it." He doesn't pronounce the *t* so it sounds like don worry about it. "Don worry about it," I say.

"What the fuck does it matter to you if I drink?"

"Not sure." I hold the fork in my mouth, sucking the icing off it. If he strangles me now I'll miss Wing Night and can join Mr. Winsome in the land of white neoprene body bags. *We* could be together.

"You said if I got a job, I could buy beer."

"Correct."

"So what's wrong with drinking rum I found?"

"I appear to care about your liver."

"For fucksake, I was shaking so bad I couldn't even start a toilet paper roll. I sat on the can for half an hour trying to start it."

"That's called detoxing. It ends when you are no longer toxic. Now, thanks to Cap'n Morgan, you'll have to go through it all over again. He died a terrible death, by the way, due to the bottle."

"I feel fine. Look." Pierce holds out his hands. "Rock steady."

"Are you aware that, by caving to your addiction, you are risking a seizure or a cardiac arrest? Shortly you will be sweating and puking your guts out all over again."

"No way. I can hold my liquor."

Yeah, yeah, yeah, I'm so tired of lies and vomit. We all know who gets to clean the toilet. "I'm going out," I say, because I can't stay here. With two dead bodies in one night, the crappy stucco triplex will make headlines.

"Take the dog," he says.

"Forget it."

"He needs to shit and piss. Amina gave him some chicken necks."

"Chicken necks?"

"She makes soup with them."

"Get Amina to walk him." But then he's there, old Benedict, looking up at me imploringly, eyes clouded blue by cataracts, completely clueless as to why his master died on him.

"Where's his leash?"

The mutt squats to poop and yours truly forgot a plastic bag. I look around for the dog shit police. Benedict's hind legs tremble with the lengthy effort. The pooch needs fibre. Time for kibbles, not chicken necks. My ass vibrates. It's Conquer.

"Do you want to talk about what happened today?" he asks.

"Nah."

"Bob's losing it."

"You just noticed that?"

"We should go over his head."

"Feel free. I'm very tired, Conquer."

"He's flipping out in front of staff. Somebody's got to tell him to get a grip."

"That somebody isn't me."

"As KM you're responsible for what goes on in the kitchen."

"Remember that next time you start giving orders."

"Are you telling me you're going to let it go?"

"Life's about letting go, bro. I'm very tired, gotta go."

"Where?"

"Did you check the steak stock? Please tell me you took them out of the freezer. It's the twelve-ouncer tomorrow."

"Like I don't know that."

"If I'm late, make sure Praveen takes the boxes of wings out to thaw."

"Why would you be late?"

"It's . . . complicated."

"You sound out of it, what's going on?"

"Oh, well, if you must know, a man in my building's been dead and dying for days, my son's hit the bottle again and may become comatose, and *we* are walking a constipated dog." A sticky pause, might as well hang up.

"Do you want me to come get you?"

"What?"

"You can't go back till he's sober."

"Oh he'll never be sober."

"I'm coming to get you. Where are you?"

"Forget it. I'm not getting in a confined space with you."

But I do, and feel unexpectedly safe in his rust-bucket pickup. One thing about Conquer, he shows up and sticks around. He may be KKK, but he's steady. Baby shoes dangle from his rear-view. "Whose shoes are those?"

"None of your business. Like your son is none of my business."

"Deal."

"Who was the dead guy?"

"A nicotine addict."

"You knew him?"

"Barely. The dog is his."

"Have you eaten?"

We stop at a Swiss Chalet, tether the hound to a spindly tree and order quarter chicken dinners. The mutt looks up every time the restaurant doors swing open, no doubt hoping to be reunited with Winsome. If I had the energy I'd cry a little inside about this.

Conquer critiques the menu, the servers, the decor, the food then asks, "Who do you think put the sock down the drain?"

"Nestor the Nicaraguan union man, of course."

"Why didn't you tell that to Bob?"

"What's the point of telling anything to Bob."

The Viking tears meat off a leg with his teeth. "We need another cook on grill."

"I'm interviewing one tomorrow. Just to fill in till Jesús comes back."

"*If* he comes back."

"I'm seeing him tomorrow. Downloaded a bunch of lucha extrema for him. Did you know that Mexicans toss thumbtacks into the ring? Keeps it lively."

Conquer chews sombrely, and you can see why the girls go for him. You can lean on the guy. "Is he white?"

"Who?"

"The cook you're interviewing."

"Oh get over it, hard-on. Tareq highly recommended him, and Tareq's the best cook we've got."

He grimly cleans his fingers in a finger bowl. "You coming back to my boat?"

"What a funny joke."

"You can't go home till your son settles down and that won't be tonight. I'm not coming on to you, trust me. You need sleep. I'm being practical."

"Always the Scandinavian."

His yacht's cabin smells of mountain man and waitresses. "Do you ever actually float this crate?"

"Needs repair."

"And your aunt doesn't mind you living in her driveway? Is that even legal?"

"Want some fruit water?" He holds up a plastic pitcher with an inner perforated pocket for fruit. "Pineapple." He points to the chunks of yellow fruit.

"You mean you cut up fruit to stick in the pitcher pocket?"

"Does that surprise you?"

"It just seems kind of . . . time-consuming."

"Time is on my side." He pours me a glass.

"Yummy."

"I know all kinds of tricks."

"Spare me. We should give the dog some water."

We sit outside on the bow. Benedict sprawls on the aunt's lawn, exhausted from the day's events. Dead leaves skitter around the boat.

"Are you staying on at Chappy's," I ask, "with the totalitarian regime?"

"I'm looking around."

Suddenly life without the Viking feels untenable, but I can't admit this, can't look needy, must accept that I will be left behind, striving to please the cat and dog customers, urging Bob to become a noodle.

"Where's his father?" Conquer asks.

"Whose father?"

"Your son's."

"Oh. Don't know."

"Don't know or don't want to know?"

"Both."

"Is that what made you a manhater? What he put you through?"

"A manhater. Hmm. Seems a bit extreme." Somebody's partying a few yards over. Drunken, callow laughter pierces the soft air above the aunt's flower beds.

"So you don't hate men?"

"Not sure 'hate' is the appropriate word. More like when faced with a male, the question that springs to mind is *Is the fellow capable of higher function?*"

The Viking snorts and pulls out a cigar.

"Didn't know you smoked."

"Just cigars."

A dog barks somewhere in the hood and geriatric Benedict hauls his ass up to defend the territory. "It's okay, pooch," I tell him. "He's nowhere near your turf."

We listen to the partiers, the distant dog, hurtling cars, a lurching bus. Something needs to be said before our incompatibility becomes impossible to ignore. Conquer puffs on the stogie: lord of the manor.

"Wade told me about a scary-looking deep sea angler fish," I say. "It lives at the bottom of the sea, up to a mile below the surface. Females are a metre long with huge heads and crescent-shaped mouths filled with sharp, translucent teeth. They can swallow prey twice their size. The males are much smaller and incapable of higher function. A horny male latches on to a female with his teeth and gradually fuses with her, connecting with her skin and bloodstream thereby losing his eyes and all his internal organs except the testes. A female carries six or more of these deadbeats on her body."

The Viking squints into the distance. Smoke billows from his Nordic lips. "Males become parasites."

"Correct."

He stubs out the cigar on his workboot. "Remind me never to ask you on a date. I'll sleep in the house. The cabin's yours. The sink and toilet work, just go easy on the water supply." Off he strides and it's just me and weary Benedict under the stars.

I feel surprisingly energized, having slept surrounded by Viking and waitress secretions. A rooster crowed at dawn. The aunt's Italian neighbour breeds chickens, Conquer told me while handing me a bowl of homemade granola.

"You mean you actually made this from scratch?" I asked.

"Does that surprise you?"

"It just seems kind of . . ."

"Time-consuming."

"But time is on your side."

"You said it." He legged it back to his aunt's, striped bathrobe flapping.

After dropping the hound at the dugout, I head for my parents'. Peggy answers the door shrieking. "He's got a woman in the house!" She shuffles back and forth in her fluffy slippers, clasping and unclasping her hands. "He's no good. He's a no-good two-timing bastard." She stops, stalled by a brainwave. "I want a divorce."

We hear Ducky's consoling murmurs as she dresses Reggie in his bedroom.

"Mom, he hasn't got a woman in the house. That's Ducky, your personal support worker. She's here to look after you."

"I don't need looking after." She's smeared fire engine red lipstick on again.

"Ducky just helps out a little."

"We don't need helping out. *I* look after Daddy. He's *my* Daddy." My mother has always called Reggie "Daddy," maybe because hers was a write-off.

"Peggy, look what I brought. Mini chocolate bars. It's almost Halloween. You want to be ready for the trick-or-treaters."

Peggy grabs the bag of candy bars, tears it open and unwraps a KitKat, her favourite food. "What are *you* going as?"

"What?"

"On Halloween." She looks truly curious, her crazy red lips forming a questioning *O*.

"Joe Stalin."

"Who's he?"

"A murderer."

"I think I'll go as a gypsy. I'll tell fortunes."

Ducky appears with Reggie in tow. Peggy throws her KitKat at her but misses.

"Mom, please don't do that. This is Ducky, your personal support worker."

"I want a divorce!"

"Now calm down, missus," Reggie says.

"Get that trollop out of my house."

"Oh my goodnuss," Ducky says.

"Mum, she's your employee. She works for you."

"She works for *him*. Don't think I don't know what's going on around here." All those years turning a blind eye to Reggie's philandering, and now she knows what's going on around here. Squeezing her pillowy body into a corner of the couch, she starts blithering.

Reggie hastens to console her as fast as his calcified joints will let him. He sits beside her and pats her shoulder. "No need for that, missus. You're my one and only, always have been. No need for that."

I signal Ducky to join me in the kitchen. "How long has she been like this?"

"She wouldn't let me in the house. Your father had to open the door, my goodnuss."

"Here's a key." I take the spare out of my wallet and hand it to her, terrified she'll refuse it and say she can't handle my parents anymore. "And here are the diapers. I hope they're the right kind." I hold up the diapers like a kid displaying a school project, desperate for an A.

"Those are fine," she says, poker-faced, and I know she's thinking about the money required to provide for her daughter she hardly knows.

"What do you want me to clean?" I ask. "Is the bathroom dirty?"

"He soiled his sheets again last night. Please do the laundry."

"You got it. Anything else you need, just holler." Holler is Ern's word and feels apt. Hurrying to Reggie's bedroom to strip the bed, I note the demented lovers embracing awkwardly due to Peggy's girth and Reggie's arthritis. Not sure which one is the parasite.

EIGHT

"He was negging me," Helga says re Connor-who-looks-like-a-girl. "He goes, 'Your mouth is really small but kind of cute, I guess.'"

"What's up with that?" Daniel says. I'm forcing them to clean the break room. "That's, like, a totally backwards compliment. I hate that."

"He only says those things to me because I'm short."

Am I the only one to comprehend that Helga's mouth is insufficiently large for Connor's penis? At least if she dumps him she will no longer have to endure anal plugs.

"He's garbage," Helga concludes.

"So, bae," Daniel says, "does this mean you're back on Tinder?"

"No way, too many pervs. I'm trying OkCupid, it's less rapey. And I'm saying straight off I'm not interested in a one-night stand. When guys message 'hey, what up?' I say, 'Only message me if you have good taste in stuff and like short girls with small mouths.'"

"Slay, girl, slay," Daniel says.

"I tell them I'm not, like, looking for The One, but not rando sex either. Like, these gross married douches keep messaging me and I'm like, I will not be your side piece."

"Shots fired."

"They're garbage."

This morning, Jesús was uninterested in lucha extrema. Drained by pain and blurred by opiates, he watched *Rumores*, his wife's top telenovela. When I asked how he was doing, Jesús spoke of Dolores on the soap opera as though she were a close personal friend. Dolores came from a poor family, Jesús explained sadly, and was sent to work for a rich man who had a son, Alvaro. Dolores and Alvaro fell in love, enraging the rich father who wanted Alvaro to marry a girl from a wealthy family. When Dolores got pregnant, Alvaro believed that the child was his brother Ernesto's.

"Why would he think it was Ernesto's?" I asked.

Jesús shrugged as though that's just how things work in Latin America. I talked about Chappy's, told him we missed him and couldn't wait for him to return.

"You'll find somebody," he said.

"I don't want to find somebody. I want you to come back." At this point Dolores, in labour on a narrow bed in the servants' quarters of the rich man's mansion, was screaming in agony.

"You'll find somebody," Jesús said. I didn't admit I was already interviewing a cook.

After popping the baby, Dolores ran out into the street with the infant. "Poor girl," Jesús said. "She don deserve that."

"How are Rosa and the kids?"

Engrossed in Dolores sobbing on a park bench beside an old woman selling empanadas, Jesús seemed not to hear me. I leaned over his shoulder to read the subtitles.

"I have no money for food," Dolores told the old woman, "only this baby boy."

"What a beautiful baby," the old woman said, stroking the head of the infant. "What is his name?"

"Fernando," Dolores said tearfully. "Take him if you want him." She held the baby out to the old woman. "Take him. I can give him nothing."

"No!" Jesús gasped, covering his mouth with his bandage-free hand. The old woman put the baby in the basket with her empanadas and the credits rolled. Jesús shook his head, muttering, "Ay cariño, mi amor," then flopped back on his pillows, emotionally spent. The burn unit beeped and hummed around us. We could hear intermittent shrieks. Last visit, the matronly nurse explained that the screaming was due to severely burned patients requiring daily re-dressing to prevent infection. The place smells like pus and burnt pork.

"How long before they let you go home?"

Jesús shrugged. "If I go home, is too much work for Rosa. I'm no good with one arm."

I considered saying something brilliant like lots of people manage really well with only one arm, but thought better of it.

Jesús stared at the ceiling tiles. "It'd be really nice if one thing went good today, you know, just for some variety."

I tried to think of something good that might happen, to either Dolores or Jesús. Behind a curtain a patient moaned.

"Well, I should be getting back," I said. "Call me if you need anything."

"Don worry about it."

Both Daniel and Wade are in my office.

"Boys, what are you doing here?"

"It's the only private place," Daniel says. "They might have put cameras up already."

"They haven't put cameras up."

"How do you know? Wade says hidden cameras can be the size of dimes."

"Too many spy movies, Wade."

The genius pinches his love handles. "Am I getting fatter? I have to smoke less pot, it's giving me the munchies."

"Out of my office." I shoo them out with the recipe manual. We have to make mashed potatoes from scratch because the bags of frozen didn't show up in a shipment. Supplies missing from my carefully placed orders is not unusual with Corporate in a cost-cutting craze.

Conquer, cussing behind the chargrill, inspects the steaks laid on wax paper overnight to age.

"Get the potatoes on the boil," I tell Praveen, who looks mortified at the prospect of mashing pounds and pounds of potatoes. "It's no biggie. Check the manual and follow the steps." He pulls on his forearm hairs. Tareq fits an earbud in the hole where his ear used to be. Nobody's dared ask Tareq what happened to his ear back in Bangladesh but, from the bits of torn skin surrounding the hole, it appears his ear was chewed off by an animal, human or otherwise.

"Tareq, you have to help Praveen peel potatoes. Now." He gives me his who-the-fuck-are-you-white-skank look. "I'm serious, mashed is the priority." Baked is already on. I taste the Moroccan vegetable soup, check the gravy texture. Bob trots in from the dining room, all flushed and girly.

"That semi-regular sexy jogging guy is checking me out again," he says. "I bet that's why he keeps coming back." He peeks through the hutch at the semi-regular sexy jogging guy. "He's got nice legs but I just don't know if I can handle a relationship right now. Like, I'm so exhausted. I clean here all day then have to go home and clean my place." *What* is he talking about? He never cleans here.

The baby shoes dangling from Conquer's rear-view can only mean he has a kid somewhere—a kid he wants to remember but can't talk about. They were pink. I picture a mini Viking girl with golden tresses.

"I woke up this morning," Bob says, "and thought for sure I was dying. Like, I was so sore everywhere, even my mouth hurt, and my legs and arms. I should probably go to Emerg and get some medication for my neck." He rubs his neck.

"Good idea," I say, adding more cherry tomatoes to the salad station and pulling out wilted greens.

The Bobster, arms folded behind his back in Captain Bligh mode, declares, "Oh, and don't think I don't know someone stole my owl plushy. When we get cameras in here, there'll be no more of these shenanigans." He grabs his chair and climbs on it, hindered once again by too-small skinny jeans. He claps his hands in quick succession to get our attention. "Who stole my owl plushy?" Earbudded and intent on prepping for the twelve-ouncer rush, everyone ignores him.

"Bob, we're in a crisis here. We have to make mashed from scratch because no frozen was delivered."

"Excuse me, *I'm* in a crisis. Snowy has great sentimental value and I expect him to be returned immediately." He claps again, waves his arms and stamps his feet. "Attention, *all* staff! Whoever took my owl plushy will be fired unless it is returned *immediately*." The crew look up briefly before resuming prep. "Fine!" Bob shouts. "Maybe I just won't submit your hours this week. If my owl is not returned by Friday, maybe I'll just forget to pay you. I can't do paperwork without Snowy, and *payroll* is paperwork."

Siobhan bustles in. "A cook's here for a job interview."

"Now?" I ask. "He's not supposed to be here till three."

"Well, he's literally taking up an entire booth, so get on it. We've got the Lions Club codgers coming."

Rinkesh Bhagat wears gold rings and chains and tells me repeatedly that he can cook "like never tomorrow." His cursive on the application form is illegible. In my office—to make way for the Lions—I offer him the chair, which Rinkesh gallantly refuses. We both stand as I enquire about what stations he's worked at what restos. He peppers his replies with "Right on," "Same to same" and "Please and thank you." As I attempt to conceal my desperation for a new body on the line, Rinkesh twirls the rings on his fingers and smiles as though he is harbouring a deep, dark secret: presumably why he was let go by his previous employer.

"Let me be clear," I say. "It is absolutely crucial that you know how to work *all* stations and have experience on chargrill. I want a vet who won't burn high-cost items like steaks."

"Right on. Please and thank you."

Dwelling on the reason for an applicant's termination, in my experience, is counterproductive. Kitchens are high stress; people get fired for stupid reasons in the heat of the moment—beyond the usual theft, not showing up, mouthing off, etc. Asking for references is pointless because competitors give good references to lousy cooks to screw competitors.

"I can't promise long-term work," I say. "We're short a cook due to an injury, but when he recovers, he'll be back on the line full-time."

"Sure, right on. Please and thank you." He spreads his ringed fingers and pats the air as though it needs consoling. "I cook like never tomorrow."

Praveen, distraught, bursts through the doors to display a lumpy spoonful of mashed potatoes. "I followed the steps in the manual. It didn't work."

Rinkesh Bhagat takes the spoon from Praveen and examines it closely. "Need melted butter and milk."

"You know how to make mashed from scratch?" I ask.

"Like never tomorrow."

"You're hired. Starting now. Praveen, suit him up."

While they hit the spuds, I get going on the mushroom gravy, onion crisps and Cajun dry rub. We need more potatoes, but I can't spare anyone on the line for a supermarket run. I ask Siobhan if she can loan me Gyorgi for half an hour.

"I like how you think you can just nab my staff whenever it suits you." She's still miffed because I'm not suitably sympathetic about her Edvar struggles. "Don't for one second think you can pull rank on me," she says. "Let me remind you that I literally have a diploma in Hospitality and Tourism from Algonquin College."

"Oh, I never forget that, Siobhan, and it's very impressive. The thing is we're having to make mashed from scratch, and you know how the Lions love mashed with their steak. Those duffers believe fries cause heart failure."

She covers her face with her hands, looking like she might boohoo again. "Edvar says he wants to go to Nepal to become a Buddhist monk. He's just saying that to make me back off about that slut. I told him going to Nepal to be a monk is literally a cop-out."

Gyorgi, carrying a bussing tray, tries to slip past her. "Gyorgi," I say, "would you mind going to the store for some bags of potatoes?"

Siobhan throws up her hands. "Fine, steal my busboy."

"He'll be back in ten minutes," I say, handing him a twenty I'll have to beg Bob for later. Our hands touch over the exchange and I feel a little sizzle. Not good. He's at least ten years my junior.

Bob, increasingly unglued, hobbles towards us. "I just barfed in my office after eating two pieces of Very Berry Cheesecake."

"I really think you should go to Emerg, Bob. You look a little wan." He looks no more sickly than usual but, with orders coming in, I want him gone.

"Aren't these adorbs?" Daniel asks, holding up animal-shaped key chains. "They're filled with hand lotion. Bath & Body Works, best store ever. Don't you just love the hippo? Try some."

"Daniel, we're in the middle of a rush here."

"Don't be poopy. I was going to let you choose one but if you're going to be mean, forget it."

Olaf grabs the hippo and sniffs it. "Coconut. M-mmm, I rate dat, I rate dat so hard. I need three Heineken and a glass of red, dollface." He pockets the hippo, flips his luscious blond curls and swings back to the dining room.

Daniel flaps his hands. "He knows just which buttons to press."

Siobhan, who's been checking her phone, presumably for news of Edvar, snaps into action. "Get your lardy ass behind the bar, Daniel. We've literally got fifty crabby old men out there."

"Stop fat-shaming me, bitch, or I'll file a complaint with the Human Rights Commission."

"Both of you," I say, "get out of my kitchen."

While Tareq and Praveen work on the mashed, I tend the fryers.

"Bob took off for Emerg," Conquer says. "Did you talk to him yet?"

"I'm hoping he'll be hospitalized."

Helga yanks up her Cat Woman boots and touchscreens an order. "If this customer's steak isn't rare, he's going to go apeshit."

Conquer ignores her. They had a fling awhile back but presumably that ended with all the Connor activity.

Praveen offers me a spoon of mashed that is undoubtedly the best mashed potato I have ever eaten. Rinkesh smiles and pats the air again with his bejewelled fingers. Something good did happen today, but I can't tell Jesús because it would mean I found somebody, as he predicted.

The rest of the afternoon passes gloriously without incident, the only disruption being that Gyorgi can't enter through the back door due to the faulty lock and earbud-deafened staff. Consequently he lugs the bags of potatoes through the dining room packed with Lions Club geezers who can't get enough of Rinkesh's mashed. They order sides upon sides and Rinkesh manages it all with calm, as though this task were expected and to be graciously performed. Graciousness is not something I associate with kitchen work and I find myself gawking at him frequently. While he multi-tasks like never tomorrow, his eyes meet mine and smiling—revealing a gold tooth—he pats the air consolingly.

"Talk to Bob when he gets back," the Viking says. "Or *I* will. I'm done with him losing his shit in front of staff."

"Just pretend he's not there. That's what I do."

"If that cumdumpster screams in my direction one more time, I'm out of here. I'm no fucking third-worlder."

"Isn't Rinkesh amazing?" I ask. "Did you try his mashed?"

"Fuck you." He knows I'm subtexting that first-world aggression can be replaced by third-world graciousness.

"I'll talk to Bob," I say, only because I don't want the billy goat scaring away Right-on Rinkesh. He and Tareq, who looks less murderous while chatting in Bengali with Rinkesh, smoothly deliver order after order. All this peace and harmony enables me to prepare bakery and dairy orders, being graciously firm with reps about problems with quality, pricing and timing. At my desk, contentedly spooning Rinkesh's mashed, I even have a moment to check last year's figures to see how busy it was. Corporate gets hysterical when sales are down from the previous year. Since the world collapsed into an unending recession for the working poor, sales rarely go up. Excuses must be made for what might have affected the numbers: ice storms, earthquakes, floods, wild fires, terrorist attacks, nuclear fallout.

But Daniel and Wade, also spooning mashed, crowd into my closet to gripe about credit card debt. "I just tell myself it's not happening," Daniel says.

"Boys, eat in the nice clean break room."

"Wade says there's a hidden camera in the clock."

"There is no camera in the clock."

"The latest technology," the university grad insists.

Daniel flaps his hands. "Oh my god, oh my god, oh my god, we figured out who took Bob's owl."

"I already know."

"How can you know?"

"I know everything."

"She does," Wade concedes.

"So, bae, who is it?"

"Olaf."

"Classic Olaf behaviour." Wade looks at his phone and sighs a boytoy sigh. "The Algerian's texting me again."

"I thought you blew her off."

"Must be the language problem. She says, 'Do you like me or not?'"

"Text 'not,'" I suggest, trying to squeeze past Daniel to open the door.

"She wants to meet up. Guess she wants an in-face rejection."

"Out of my office, now." I yank the door open with force fuelled by Rinkesh's mashed.

"Bae, you have to do something about Olaf and the owl or Bob won't do payroll."

"Send the rapper back here." I grab the daily log and record the Shakthi plumbing expense, also noting that yours truly had to pay for potatoes and scrubbies. Getting petty cash off Bob—the only one with access to the safe—will not be easy, particularly if I don't locate his owl plushy.

As soon the gangsta waiter, born and bred in high-society Rosedale, is in the door I say, "Where's the owl?"

"Now hold up," Olaf says. "I was jus' jokin' around."

"You won't be laughing when you miss a pay period."

"Dat cat is, like, some kind of *way*. I don't wanna throw shade on da dude but he's always on my ass about 'image.' Like, at first we was totally in sync, catching feelings, right, because we was both hipping *Destiny*. Then I make level twenty-eight and he's stuck at eight and he's, like, making uncool comments and saying I'm super high on myself or whatever."

Destiny is an online video game they both waste hours playing. "You *are* super high on yourself, Olaf."

He flips his blond curls. "He's been legit whacked lately, man."

"Where's the owl?"

"Now hold up."

"I'm not holding anything. And speaking of holding up, I thought Siobhan told you to wear pants that don't sag off your ass."

"Don't rag like my mom, fam." He points to the black jeans hanging below his hips. "Dis be dope. In total realness, dis be da realest me. Dis is how I *do*."

"In total realness, where is the owl?"

"It's my bad, I get dat, but don't go hating on me for dis, cuz."

"I won't hate on you if you return the owl immediately. When Bob returns, I expect the owl to be on his desk."

"What you sayin', girl? I can't go in da bossman's cave. It'll blow my cover. What if *you* put it back? Are you down?"

Hmm, hadn't considered the logistics of returning the bird. "Put it under his desk so it looks like it fell off."

"No way is I goin' in there."

"You went in there to steal it."

"Dat's a totally different scene, fam."

"Fine. Get me the owl."

"If you inform, I will deny."

"Deny all you want, cuz."

"It's just dis be my life right now, yo. Like, I can't lose da gig." He hitches up his dope jeans.

"You should have thought about that before you took the owl."

"I figured everybody would go ham on da joke, yo. I mean, come *on*, dat bro's, like, high-key flexin' on us, you know what I'm sayin'?"

"Get the owl." My ass vibrates. I don't recognize the number but take it to break up the sesh with the rapper.

"It's me," Pierce says, wheezing like an old man. "I want to apologize."

Drunks always apologize before getting shit-faced again. "Whose phone are you on?"

"Winsome's."

I shove Olaf out and close the door. "You stole a dead man's phone?"

"He can't use it. It's old, a flip. Are you coming home?"

He's never referred to the dugout as home or asked if I was coming there. "After work."

"I dreamed you were a corpse. On the couch."

"I'm never on the couch. That's your territory."

He sounds like an old man because drying out over and over again takes a toll on the nervous system. When the liver can't process any more alcohol, you black out, the stomach bloats, the legs get skinny. Between drying out sessions I was up in the middle of the night having just-a-few glasses of Pinot Grigio to help me sleep—more like pass out—for a bit. Result: fitful hours of nightmares and sweats.

"Did you feed and walk the dog?"

"Amina let it out in the yard while she was gardening. Listen, I've got cash. I tightened and oiled Amina's hinges. She paid me twenty bucks. Can you pick up a twelve-pack? I'll pay you back."

This explains why he's apologizing. "Pierce, *you* can pick up a twelve-pack when you walk the dog." I end the call. The gangsta returns, producing the owl from somewhere in his saggy jeans.

"No ratting on me, 'kay, cuz?"

"It's missing an eye, Olaf."

"No way. It's winking."

"No. A glass eye is missing. Where is it?"

"In total realness there be only one eye."

Never having looked closely at the owl, I don't know if he's lying. "Go away."

On the owl's breast it says *A Word to the Wise, Sharing Is Caring*. I unlock Bob's office and toss the plushy under the desk.

NINE

Jesus Christ's son is behind Chappy's scrounging for food again. She's wearing her usual fishing vest, pink ear muffs and American flag scarf. I hand her a bag of day-old dinner rolls. Gyorgi's leaning against the wall, looking James Dean–ish, finishing up the mashed I gave him, and I badly want him to forgive me for telling him to stop stealing. If he offers me a smoke, or a haul on his smoke, I will suck the poison deep into my lungs.

Jesus Christ's son makes gremlin noises and bluff-charges me, stopping a head-butt inches from my face. "You're His favourite."

She's told me this before and made it plain she considers me undeserving of His love. When I asked her why I was Jesus Christ's favourite, she said, "*You* know." When I explained that I didn't know Jesus Christ had a son—or that his son was, in fact, female—she glared at me like I was disdainfully ignorant and cursedly ungrateful.

Around Jesus Christ's son, I regress into the loathsome creature that sought hootch and shelter at Reggie and Peggy's. Jesus Christ's son seems to sense this, nodding knowingly and making disapproving clucking noises while checking out the bag of rolls. "You're His favourite," she grumbles before trudging off.

Gyorgi offers me his cigarette, which I grab like oxygen.

"If she is son of Saviour," he says, "for why is she so unhappy?"

"I think it's a sibling rivalry thing, even though I'm not really her sibling. I suspect she's an only, actually. I mean, I can't believe Jesus had more than one kid. When would he have the time?"

"Between miracles."

"Yeah, maybe if he was good at time management. Bob tells me *I* need to be working on my time management."

Not sure if Gyorgi—staring off in James Dean mode—is following my English. I try to come up with an un-Chappy's-related game changer. "Do you think convenience is killing us?"

He looks at me. "I'm not understanding."

"Everything's so easy now. Nothing requires much effort, not even killing hundreds of thousands of people, heck, you waggle a button and cities burn, pull a trigger and shred thirty people. A technologically advanced age means minimal effort can produce maximal results. Seems to me it's killing us."

He nods, suggesting he's catching my feelings but there's no way to be sure.

"Making hard things easy," I say, "means we do them without thinking, destroy entire species, rainforests, lakes, oceans, each other. Easy peasy." I pass him the cigarette.

"Convenience is killing us," he repeats slowly, and I realize you don't tell a young man, on the threshold of a career in brain research, that the human brain is accelerating our extinction. Maybe, like Daniel, I should say, "Jokes! I love you!" or, "We'll make it all better, bae." Instead I prattle on. "Thanks for getting the potatoes. Aren't the mashed delicious?"

"Sure."

He hands me the cigarette. "You finish. Me back to work."

And then it's just the killjoy smoking—even though I quit—savouring a tumorous buzz. Go me.

I drop the butt and grind it into the tarmac.

Wing Night prep begins. Fortunately, Conquer remembered to get the crew to pull the boxes from the freezer first thing. We start frying them up—it's called blanching—cooking them forty to fifty percent. Next the undercooked wings go into a super-sized beer tub. Blood and fat congeal, the blood thickening into pinkish gelatin while the fat mixes with the hardening fryer oil. Placing basket after basket of semi frozen wings into the fryers renders the oil useless for anything else. The water causes the hot oil to boil, foam up and pop, making holding your hands over the fryer risky. We've all been burned but Rinkesh, with heavily scarred forearms from working a tandoori oven, is fearless and scoops wings into the baskets like never tomorrow, dropping them in the fryers and letting them cook just enough to turn whitish. "Right on!" he cheers when they're ready, lifting the baskets and, with a swash-buckling motion, dropping them in the beer tub. "Bucket of ice, please and thank you," he says to Praveen, who fills buckets with ice to dump into the tub to halt the cooking process. As the super-sized tub fills with wings, water, blood and grease, the cooks' whites turn slaughterhouse pink. Conquer, too haute-cuisine for lowly Wing Night, prepares the occasional mid-afternoon order. Mostly he plays solitaire while the South Asians and I toil, slipping on layers of grease forming on the floor. Praveen sets the stainless steel mixing bowls of wing sauces on the few remaining clear surfaces. I spice up the Extra Hot with jalapenos, mustard and chilies. It is to this controlled chaos that King Bob returns, presumably from Emerg, and stands before us with arms outstretched at his sides. Huffing and puffing, he circles his arms.

"What are you doing?" I ask.

"Qigong breathing. The hot intern showed me. He says he gets panic attacks all the time and controls them with qigong."

"That's great, Bob. As you can see, we're in the middle of Wing Night prep."

"We should all be doing qigong," he says, apparently hyperventilating while circling his arms. "It balances yin and yang so our energies can protect us from other people's energies."

"Nice. Maybe later."

"Jordan's going to specialize in psychiatry. We totally need more gay shrinks. He's into mind/body stuff, like, not a pill pusher. He talked about the importance of passion and purpose and doing what you love. Some people search their entire lives, he said. Some gain remarkable skills and talents only to think, I'm great at this so why don't I feel successful? Well, I *am* successful, but Jordan thinks I struggle too hard to stay disciplined. He says I have to prioritize, that the challenge I'm facing is that there are so many things I'm passionate about that I struggle to decide what to do first. And all of this affects my yin and yang on a molecular level."

Conquer, behind Bob, circles his index finger at his temple and mouths, "Talk to him!"

"Jordan says," Bob continues, "when you love your work, it's like peeling an onion. There's always more layers to discover and explore. When you hate your work it's also like peeling an onion—but all you find are more tears."

"Well said." I wipe bloody hands on my apron. "Bob, can we talk more about this in your office?"

The first thing he notices is the owl under the desk. He grabs it and clutches it to his breast before taking a good look at it. "Who stole his eye?"

"Whose eye?"

"Someone *blinded* Snowy. What kind of disturbed person would do that?"

"Maybe the eye fell off. Did you look on the floor?"

"Glass eyes don't just drop off. Someone, some *sick* person, tore it off and they're going to pay." He starts for the door, which I block.

"Bob, don't go out there. You can't keep freaking out in front of staff. It undermines your authority."

"I am not freaking out."

"Standing on a chair, clapping and shouting and stamping your feet looks like freaking out."

"I'm passionate about my work, Stevie. I'm not like you, this isn't just a *job* to me. This is my life." He presses the owl to his chest again.

"We all appreciate your commitment to Chappy's, Bob, but would Jordan recommend standing on chairs and shouting at staff? He might consider that counterproductive and disruptive not only of your yin and yang and molecules, but the staff's. We need you to steady us, Bob. We count on your leadership to help us discover and explore the layers of our onions. Without your guidance, all we find are more tears."

He sighs deeply, the responsibility of our mental health weighing heavily on his shoulders, and sits at his desk, carefully setting the owl beside his monitor. "That may well be, but it doesn't justify stealing and blinding Snowy."

"Well, the fact is, as I'm sure Jordan would agree, when people's yin and yang are unbalanced they feel threatened and lash out in irrational ways. You're a very intimidating presence."

He nods gravely, considering the extent of his power.

"I'm sure Jordan never shouts," I add. "According to the Buddhists, who also speak metaphorically of onion peeling, shouting is a sign of weakness." I'm making this up.

Siobhan pushes the door open. "Desmond's literally replaced whipped cream squirt cans with plastic baggies of cream we have to squeeze with both hands."

Bob, contemplating his molecules, doesn't respond, so I say, "Is that a prob?"

"Are you kidding me? Like a server has both hands free to squirt whipped. Bob, you have to talk to him."

Bob stands and resumes huffing and puffing and circling his arms.

To fill the insanity void, I say, "Maybe Des thinks baggies are more environmentally friendly."

"It's got nothing to do with the environment," Siobhan says. "Desmond thinks staff are trying to inhale nitrous oxide from squirt cans. I like how he's always accusing us of 'drug activity' when anybody can see he's literally on dexies."

Bob slowly lowers his arms. "Siobhan, I just returned from the hospital. This is not the time."

"With you it's never the time where Desmond's concerned," Siobhan snaps.

Thanks to Daniel's loose tongue, we all know that Bob considers Desmond "fearsome and powerful, which is kind of a turn-on." He frequently checks Desie's Instagram, @theblackatlas, where Desie posts gym selfies and videos of himself manfully handling dumbbells and straddling stationary bikes.

Bob points the hairy digit at Siobhan. "*You* need to be paying closer attention to the goings-on of your staff."

"And you need to grow a pair." She exits, slamming the door.

"I bet *she* stole Snowy. I'm going to write her up to Corporate."

"For what? You have no evidence, Bob. Snowy fell behind the desk, you just didn't notice because you've been so overworked with paperwork and all that cleaning. Rest here. I'll get Daniel to make you a nice decaf heart latte. And we got some of that Coconut Cream Rapture Pie in. After all your hard work, you deserve a little rapture."

Reggie will not let Ducky remove his dirty diaper. Somehow she got it on him but can't remove it easily as it's pull-up rather than tearaway. Marooned in feces, the grump won't budge from his bed. Peggy, incensed about the trollop in the house, charges around with her Swiffer duster.

"Dad, you have to change your diaper. It's like underwear, you have to change it every day." The room stinks of shit. "Dad? You'll get a rash if you don't get out of those pyjamas and put on regular underwear. The diapers are just for nighttime."

"Who gave you the right?" he demands.

I have no right, and no choice but to bear witness to his decline. When I see the impoverished and demented elderly in the streets, I wonder where their children are, and how they could let this happen to their parents. But watching my parents' circumstances worsen, I suspect a time comes when it's you or them because they'll take you down with them, trash what's left of your life just as they trashed the beginning. In between trashings, you were free of them—an adult making your own choices and mistakes—but now you're back in the bungalow attempting to communicate with minds missing circuits.

In the resto biz, faced with jammed freezers, appliances, cabinets, doors, we use brute fucking force. My arms, strong from years of pounding chicken breasts, are too powerful for my withered father. I hug/lift him into the bathroom, suppressing my gag reflex. Ducky whips off his pyjama bottoms while he's in transit screaming like the fatally wounded. Peggy too starts squalling and thwacking me with her duster. I sit him on the edge of the tub and Ducky cuts the soiled diaper off him. Feces spills on the floor which Peggy immediately steps in. With my free arm I push her out the door and lock it, knowing she'll trek shit all over the house. "Whoop! Whoop!" she shrieks, pounding on the door. "You leave my Daddy alone! He's *my* Daddy!"

When Reggie's fist strikes the side of my head, I resist the urge to swat back because Ducky might report elder abuse. I grab his wrists and look into his watery eyes, trying to locate him in there. But Reggie has left the building. There is only shit, piss, delusions and paranoia left in the sack of bones before me.

"Time to calm down, Mr. Many," Ducky says. She holds out her palm, revealing an Ativan. "Let it dissolve under your tongue, Mr. Many. It will relax you. The doctor said you should take these when you are agitated, remember?" He bats the pill out of her hand and regales us until his breath is spent and he can do nothing but wilt on the edge of the tub, only remaining upright due to my restraining hold.

"Can you put him on the shower stool so I can hose him?" Ducky asks.

I step into the tub and hoist him onto the stool that Ducky holds steady. His penis, a wrinkled worm, dangles and I marvel at the suffering it has caused and can only hope it provided some pleasure. Not for Peggy, judging from her dour expression when I walked in on them one rainy Sunday afternoon in search of my Etch A Sketch. Seeing him sprawled naked over her I thought something was wrong. "Knock before you enter!" he shouted. "Close the door." I did and sat at the kitchen table sipping Kool-Aid. Minutes later they came out of the bedroom acting as though nothing had happened, as did I. Our whole lives together we have acted as though nothing has happened. Even now as I clean up his shit, pick up the rejected sedative and dissolve it under my tongue, we pretend nothing has happened.

On my mossy stump in Warden Woods, breezes kiss my face. The day's scraggy edges, blunted by the Ativan, soften. "Esther?" I call several times, proffering a handful of Benedict's kibbles, but there is no sign of her. Who needs kibbles when you can eat snakes?

Sedatives make you notice details that normally speed by unappreciated. The fungi growing at the base of the stump—fleshy eruptions of mauve, green and cream—look extraterrestrial. In bygone days, after a few glasses of sedating wine, I'd go to the free night at the AGO and become engrossed in how paint was applied to canvas or board, bringing my face close enough to the paintings to alarm the guards. Pen and ink drawings I'd zip past sober entranced me with cross-hatching. The down side of tranqs in any form has always been the after-effects and, of course, addiction. My Cinderella moments in the castle always end in a moat full of shit. Even the single Ativan will sink me in a few hours.

A greasy-haired troll of a man squats at my feet. "You look like a movie star."

With my fight-or-flight response curbed by the drug, I remain stuck to the stump. The troll touches my knee, leaning into me. "I am Spanish. You like Latin lovers?" He reeks of beer. I try to stand but he grabs my hand. His teeth are brown around the edges, his incisors longer than the front ones. "Don't be scared, señorita." He slides his free hand between my legs. A swift, if drug weakened, kick to the shins causes him to tumble backwards and I clamber, doped, through trees no longer allies but obstacles in my path. I listen for the Spaniard as I have listened for assailants for years. The terror returns at warp speed, and I try to imagine what it's like for my son to fear constantly for his life.

Pierce is not in the dugout, has gone out finally, doubtless in search of intoxicants. "Good luck with that," I grumble, locking the door. His keys are on the coffee table. If he returns potted, I will not let him in.

The TV offers distraction: a news item about a pet hotel by the airport. A $199-per-night all-inclusive package comes with poolside suites, organic treats for Rover from the mini bar, a swag bag, plus cuddle time. Also offered are heated floors and flat-screen TVs. Spa services cost extra. The day lounge is abundant with doggy toys, slides, hoops and balls as well as a special area for senior dogs requiring quiet time and orthopedic beds. An outdoor doggy splash pad is under construction, and a smaller wing for cats. Penthouse pet suites come equipped with video chat, providing jet-setters with long distance quality time with their fur babies. For an extra fee, owners can electronically dispense an organic treat through an opening in the wall. All slumber rooms come with fleecy dog mattresses and a large screen TV hooked up to Netflix because most dogs are TV conscious and need entertainment.

One in five children in Canada lives below the poverty line. Just sayin'.

I turn off the TV and lug my tranqed ass to the bedroom to scribble some fragments.

An OkCupid dud described Helga's cat as "a generic tabby." "Are you negging my cat?" Helga demanded. The dud apologized for using "generic," and they agreed to watch Ghostbusters *at his place.*

Siobhan said, "You're literally going to his place on your first date?"

"I deep-Facebooked him. Ghostbusters *is both our totally favourite movie and bourbon our totally favourite drink. Pretty trippy."*

An allergic reaction to eyelash extensions has put this hookup on hold. Helga worries that the reaction will compromise the effects of her Botox injections.

"You use Botox?" Siobhan, an old-fashioned girl, enquired. "How old are you, twenty-five?"

"It's preventative," Helga said. "Everybody could use a little Bobo."

Hammering on the door jolts me alert despite the Ativan.

"Mom?"

He never calls me Mom. It's because he's tanked.

"Let me in. I forgot my key."

That's what you get, laddy, for banging the Bosnian for beer. Don't bother me. I'm done with ploys intended to loosen my anti-drinking regulations. A Spaniard took liberties with me today, my boss thinks he's an onion, and I had to clean up my father's doo-doo. All of this despite being

Jesus Christ's favourite. Besides, my drug-bludgeoned body cannot rise from this bed.

"Mom, I'm sorry. I've been an asshole."

The OkCupid dud (Bryan-with-a-y) manages an Enterprise Rent-A-Car and owns a condo. His financial solvency makes him a prime dating candidate. Plus he told Helga she was really pretty. Bryan's a bit pudgy and losing his hair, but Helga says it's best to not always go for hot guys who sleep with randoms. They're garbage.

"Mom, please let me in." He pounds on the door. "Come on, let me in."

"Go fuck the Bosnian!" I shout, surprisingly loudly for a stoner.

"I already did. It was like fucking a sewer."

"You obviously got some bevies out of her."

"Cointreau. That's all she's got left. It's making me sick."

"Go puke in *her* toilet."

"She's disgusting, stinks of cats. I had to watch her eat an entire bowl of cold spaghetti."

"Not my problem," I say.

"She's a fucking nutjob. Please don't make me go back there."

Wade told me the government is shooting wolves dead from helicopters, blaming them for the dwindling caribou population, not human encroachment on BC's interior forests. Predator kill programs increase reproductive rates in wolves, destabilizing pack structure, resulting in more predation of caribou. Starvation and getting shot at make the wolves fuck like crazy to keep the species going.

The Spaniard was wearing a sweatshirt with a wolf's head on it. I was about to mention the chopper slaughter when he slid his hand between my legs.

More drunken pounding on the door. With just the Bosnian in the building—no Mr. Winsome to disturb—I scream until my throat burns then shove my face into a pillow. I hear a forlorn sound, a howl—Benedict on the other side of the door voicing his sorrow and infinite losses. I open the door for the dog. The souse lumbers in after him.

TEN

Chappy's kitchen is silent except for heavy breathing. Bob has my staff stretching their arms out from their sides. "Circle as you exhale," he commands, pointing to his mouth and making blowing sounds. Next he moves his arms as though doing breaststroke. "This is called Bear Swimming in Ocean."

Conquer is nowhere in sight and the lunch rush is pending.

"Bear Swimming in Ocean," Bob intones, doing breaststroke.

I find the Viking behind the bar, knocking back a Jack on the rocks. "What are you doing?"

"Balancing my yin and yang."

"I was counting on you to oversee lunch prep."

"Don't count on me for nothin', baby." He starts pouring another one.

"I have to charge you for that," Daniel says. "Corporate's *weighing* the bottles now. And Desmond's making me measure every single glass of wine, like I'm incapable of eyeballing six ounces. He's turned so Darth Vadery it's depressing."

"Conquer, I need you on the line."

"Not till yoga's over."

Back in the kitchen the guru stands on the chair. "To freak out," he explains loudly to the earbudded, "means to be, or cause to be, in a heightened emotional state, such as that of fear or anger."

"Bob," I say, "can we speak privately, please?"

He shushes me with the hairy digit. "I'm explaining the difference between a Freak Out and a Sense of Urgency." He turns back to Rinkesh, who smiles and pats the air with his bejewelled fingers. Praveen, Jamshed and Tareq look like they'd rather be watching wrestling.

"In business," Bob continues, "a Sense of Urgency refers to the ability of leaders to drive activities in the organization to meet important windows of opportunity. A Sense of Urgency is vital to success."

"Right on!" Rinkesh cheers. Olaf and Wade, transfixed by Bob's oratory powers, hover over the touchscreen.

"Bob," I interject, "we are currently experiencing a Sense of Urgency about the Butter Chicken Burrito special."

"As you can see," Bob says, gesturing grandly around the kitchen, "we need to optimize our Sense of Urgency in order to remain competitive in the marketplace. Poor performers will *not* be tolerated."

"Orders coming in!" I shout. "Get to your stations. Bob, you might want to write these helpful tips on memos for the break room. Right now, we have to get back to work."

A hunch tells me Rinkesh is an experienced chicken picker and can strip a dozen birds like never tomorrow. I steer Tareq back into curry prep and Praveen into the tuna and egg salads. Tonight is Build-a-Pasta Night, meaning we'll have to prep and portion multiple twenty-pound boxes of spaghetti, linguine, fettuccine and penne.

"Conquer, get your ass in here, we've got orders for Banquet Burgers."

After checking and rotating stock, I sit in my closet and marvel at how I lizard around the black holes surrounding me like I have a plan when all I'm doing is avoiding the holes. Within seconds someone's knocking on my door. "What?"

"It's Gyorgi."

The one person I don't mind seeing. "Sorry, didn't realize it was you. Come in." He looks scared I'll hit him. "What's wrong?"

"Bob gave me this. I am not understanding." He holds out a sheet of paper.

I recognize Bob's mutant handwriting. *WRITTEN WARNING*, the letter begins, *Regarding biosterous behavuior that could laed to destruction of proprety. A Chappy's employee was seen on securty camera kicking the wheelchair access lever just outside the dining room. After veiwing the footage I, Bob Kidd, have concluded that it was Gorgi Klek. Gorgi you are bieng isseud this WRITTEN WARNING as a direct result of this behaviuor. It is important to note that we are renters of this biulding and as such are expected to abide by the rules. Respecting poeple and proprety is part of the Chappy's value system. As one of our busboys, it is your job to uphold these principels while on duty. This is your first written warning and I hope your last. If this behaviuor is not immeditatly corrected, more drastic steps will follow. I appreciate your time and attention to this matter.*

Who has time to study the security footage? Maybe Desmond when he isn't posting selfies on Instagram.

"Gyorgi, did you kick the wheelchair access lever?"

He nods. "Because of potatoes. I carry potatoes."

"Right. Did you explain this to Bob?"

"He says I am not to use dining room entrance."

"Did you explain that the back door lock is busted?"

"He says no excuses. Does letter mean I lose job?"

"No." I resist an urge to wrap my arms around him.

"I worry he feels hatred to me."

"He's like that with everybody. I'll talk to him."

"Please don't ask for me to use front door."

"I won't."

"I need job."

"I understand. I will take responsibility for this. Please don't worry." We stand awkwardly, repelling magnets. I reach across the currents between us and give him a man pat like I'm a coach and he's a downcast player.

Daniel bursts in with blue hair. Gyorgi, crowded out, squeezes past him. "Don't worry about it," I say again.

"I'm not," Daniel says. "I lo-ove it." He pulls out his phone to admire his hair. "Siobhan says it's unprofessional but I mean, excuse me, I saw Gaga at the Bluesfest and her hair was, like, *blue*, so that snooty bitch hussy might want to reconsider who she's calling unprofessional."

"But your hands are blue, Daniel, not just your hair. You're a bartender, with blue hands." I google locksmiths.

"It'll come off eventually. It's just a rinse." He twiddles spikes of blue hair. "Have you noticed Wade gets foam in the corners of his mouth when he smokes pot? I've been totally on edge with all this surveillance going on and that manwhore is, like, so chills about it and I'm thinking, Why can't I be more like him? Then I realize he never gets fussed because he's stoned all the time."

With a Sense of Urgency, I leave voicemails for locksmiths. Praveen pokes his head in. "Bernie's back!"

"What do you mean 'back'?" Bernardo, the Colombian, left without notice a couple of months ago. We assumed his disappearance was narcotic related.

"He's helping with the nachos." Praveen pulls on his forearm hairs. "A *whole* baseball team is having Hearty Nachos and the Pitcher Special."

"That's your cue, Daniel."

Bernardo works the line as though he never left it, energetically sprinkling sliced olives and grated cheddar over corn chips. I stand a few feet from him, waiting for an explanation. He pretends not to notice me.

"You can't just show up when you feel like it, Bernardo. We're not your wife."

"Miss Stevie, I didn't see you there. How you feelin'?"

Bernie is unusually short for a male but has a flock of women, besides his wife, tracking him. In spiked heels they scour the kitchen for him, leaving wafts of perfume in their wake. When I shoo them out they cuss in Spanglish and flip hair in my face.

"Are you volunteering today, Bernardo? Because last I looked, you weren't on payroll."

"I still work for you, Miss Stevie, but I had to go to Colombia. My mother, she sick."

"And she's all better until the next time you leave town." Bernie sells merchandise he gets cheap (or steals) in Buffalo: phones, SIM cards, cigarettes, watches, headphones, jewellery. "Whatever you want, I find," he tells staff who place orders and eagerly await Bernie's return, crowding the break room as he sits like Santa, reaching into his backpack for shiny items. I put up with this because it adds sparkle to their daily grind, but going AWOL for two months is pushing it. Whatever his excuse, it will be a lie prefaced with "To tell the truth."

"You haven't been working for me for the past two months, Bernardo."

"To tell the truth, it all happened so fast, my mother, she sick, and a friend of mine needed help with shippings."

"Shippings? You mean shipments. What were you shipping?"

"School buses. The yellow ones. Chicken buses. My friend gets them at auction for, like, five hundred bucks and sells them for two grand in El Salvador. There's no buses there so people ride school buses."

"You're telling me you've been driving school buses to El Salvador for two months?" This is so far-fetched it might be true.

"Yes, Miss Stevie. And helping my mother. She sick."

"Why did you stop driving buses to El Salvador?"

"My wife. She worry is too dangerous. She want me to save money to take the kids to Disney World."

In the mini UN that is Chappy's kitchen, the only dream is the American one. Whether El Salvadorian, Tamil, Eritrean, Bangladeshi, Pakistani, they're all chasing the resource-draining, unsustainable dream of the house, car and Disney World.

We had a regular, Brody Flynn, who'd attained the American dream then ditched Mrs. Flynn, the house and kids. Brody specially requested that I grill his steaks and would stick his head through the hutch and say, "Are we having fun yet?" Flattered by his attentions and enticed by his wallet, I agreed to go out a few times. Brody was a consultant hired to make businesses more efficient. Your stock's down? No worries, just fire five thousand workers.

Following a $400 meal, I once asked Brody, "Be honest, is anything better after a takeover?"

"Everything's better after a takeover." He held the door of his Merc open for me.

"Like what? Name something."

Behind the wheel covered in dead animal skin Brody mentioned banks, grocery, hardware and restaurant chains, real estate franchises, funeral homes, drugstores, pharmaceutical giants. None of it translated to good times for Joe Public.

"Seriously," I said, "as soon as I hear the word 'merger,' I know quality is going to go down and prices up, and workers are going to get shafted."

He shrugged. "I just look at the numbers. Just like you look at steaks. It's a job."

"Ah, the Nazi war criminal excuse." I got out of Brody Flynn's German car. Two thousand years of civilization has reduced us to numbers.

Speaking of which, Desmond emailed and wants to meet up to discuss numbers. I usually make excuses to avoid meet-ups with Desie, but I need him to okay the locksmith service call.

Siobhan sticks her head in. "Where's Bob?"

"No idea."

"A homeless guy's literally passed out on a banquette. If he shits on it, I will scream."

"Is it the duct cleaner?"

"Different guy."

"Well, if he's passed out, chances are he won't shit. Just let him sleep."

"A customer's complaining, says the homeless guy is gonzo."

"Is the homeless guy bothering the customer?"

"Would you want to eat beside a stinking homeless person?"

"Talk to Bob."

"I can't even find Bob. I'm literally concerned for my personal safety here."

"Because of an unconscious homeless man?"

"What if he turns violent?" She's testy today because Edvar's gym is hounding him about his direct debit bouncing. He owes them for five months, which means, according to Siobhan, he'll literally never get a decent credit rating.

An irate man with a gut hanging over his plaid shorts, obviously a tourist because of his *I LOVE TORONTO* T-shirt, blocks my doorway. "There you are," he says to Siobhan. "If you think we're paying for a meal we got to eat beside that shit pile, you've got another thing coming."

"Sir," I say, "you're not allowed back here. Please return to the dining room."

"Not till you get that nutbar out of here."

"We'll take care of it. Please return to your table."

"Take care of it *now*!"

"I'm calling the police," Siobhan says.

"No you're not," I say. "Both of you, return to the dining room and I'll take care of it." The tourist looks ready to plug me, but Rinkesh and Tareq, clutching knives, stand on either side of him. Rinkesh smiles and pats the air with his free hand in the direction of the dining room. "Please and thank you, sir," he says. The two small brown men escort the large white man to his table. I follow, grabbing and wrapping a burrito.

It takes several nudges to wake the homeless man who panics, no doubt fearing persecution. "It's okay," I say. "Here's something to eat. No charge, but please take it outside. We need this table." He looks young under the matted hair and beard, probably had potential not so long ago, like Gyorgi.

Wade told me about disoriented penguins who, instead of marching to the sea with the other penguins, head in the opposite direction to certain doom in the mountains. Disoriented penguins, after well-meaning humans redirect them back to the sea, turn around and resume their march to the mountains. Maybe they're not disoriented but know something the other penguins don't. Same with the disoriented homeless man. "Thanks," he says, taking the burrito and plodding towards the doors.

"Sorry for the disturbance," I say to the Pitcher Special baseball team, the burrito and burger eaters, and the tourist now sitting with his fry-gobbling wife and tweens.

"You is on *fire*, girl," Olaf tells me as I grab a loaded tray he should have removed and return to the kitchen. My Bangladeshi bodyguards deftly handle orders as though nothing out of the ordinary has happened. That they were there for me, watching my back—knives in hand—provides an unfamiliar feeling of safety. Weird that Conquer's boat and Chappy's kitchen provide sanctuary from the dugout and the bungalow, two places I once called home. Talk about disoriented and heading for certain doom.

ELEVEN

Desmond appears while I'm parboiling pasta. "I'm a little pressed," he says.

"Of course, just let me finish up here. It's Build-a-Pasta Night, always a bit of a strug prep-wise." It bothers Desie that I'm a hands-on manager, undaunted by the most humiliating tasks. For this reason I always make him wait. Oiling the pasta takes a couple of minutes, then weighing the portions as per Corporate's instructions.

Desmond slaps his clipboard against his thigh, checks his phone then says, "Get a prep cook to do that."

"Oh, actually, we've been short-staffed and are only just catching up."

No doubt cutting labour costs is on his agenda. DMs receive bonuses when they cut staff. In my closet I offer him the chair. He sits, lays his clipboard and phone on the desk and leans back, clasping his hands behind his head. His Paco Rabanne cologne causes a headache to blossom over my right eye.

"I really appreciate all the good work you do," he says, which means he's about to kick my ass. "Keep in mind I was a KM once so I know what you're dealing with. The fact is this Chappy's has the highest labour costs in the chain." He's talking fast, probably due to the dexies.

"Desmond, we have a higher turnover than any other Chappy's due to movie theatres, tour buses and tournaments. The downtown stores don't have parking or a local mall."

"In that case your numbers should be up. Don't make excuses for poor management."

"Do you mean Bob? Because you can't mean me." I stare at him like I stare at Pierce, daring him to kill me. What Wolf called my "strained bitch face" snaps into place, masking my jangling insecurities.

Desmond drums his fingers on my desk. "You need to cut hours, Stevie. I come in here and see people standing around. If there's downtime, you can cut hours. There's way less prep with pre-cut stock."

"Not *way* less, Desmond. And, frankly, pre-cut means less fresh, less flavour, and more plastic packaging to contend with, which takes time. The Pickle Barrel *advertises* that their veggies are fresh cut."

"I'm done with you playing the Pickle Barrel card." He checks his phone. "Cut hours, Stevie. Keep in mind, if *you* don't do it, I'll get Bob on it. He told me you hired another Paki."

"I hired a Bangladeshi named Rinkesh, and he's the best cook we've got. Don't think of him as a new hire, he's just filling in for Jesús. And we lost a disher to the feds so we'll need another one." Diversion tactics and flattery usually derail the cost-cutting argument. "By the way, Desmond, your task binders were a fabulous idea. My staff refer to them constantly. Oh, and I keep meaning to mention that the back door lock isn't working properly, bolts shut no matter what. We miss deliveries, and one of our busboys was forced to come through the dining room with the potatoes."

"The Russian who kicked the handicapped lever?"

"He's Slovakian, actually, and an outstanding worker. He felt terrible about entering through the dining room, but he couldn't get in the back door because of that darned lock. The good news is I found a locksmith who can fit us in. He's coming this afternoon." This is a lie but who's checking. Bob, bless him, pushes open the door.

"Guys," he says, "I just found some positive workplace initiatives online I'm going to pin up in the break room." He reads slowly due to his dyslexia. "'Don't talk *about* other people, talk about the cool things they're doing, e.g., 'I hear Chad invested in a start-up. How exciting. I wonder what they're working on?' or 'I can't believe Angie won their business back. I'd love to know how she did it.' Or, 'Kristy developed a new sales channel. Let's ask her how she leveraged that.'"

"That's v. exciting, Bob," I say. His crazy spells don't faze me but Desie seems a little uneasy, clutching his clipboard, possibly to use as a shield.

"I have a fabulous positive workplace initiative," I say. "How 'bout we not see customers as numbers? They're real people with real needs and I, personally, experience a *real* sense of fulfillment satisfying those needs." Shove that up your Corporate arse and smoke it.

Desmond flinches. "Have you given any thought to Chicken Month?"

Oh, please, not Chicken Month. "Of course."

"And?"

"We'll need three or four new types of chicken breast prep. I was thinking about a smoker. We could rent one for the month." Suggesting added expense for innovation causes Corporate to panic and back off, briefly, about unavoidable expenses like labour costs. "How 'bout we do something with fresh basil, some kind of chicken pesto special. What about a chicken pesto wrap?" Fresh herbs translate to extra cost. "I was in the Pickle Barrel the other day—"

"I said quit with the Pickle Barrel card."

"Des, you tell me to keep an eye on our competitors. Seriously, I was just amazed by the number of items they had on the menu, in fact it was more like a *book* than a menu. Each station must have a lot more menu items to remember and execute compared to Chappy's. Bigger overhead too, keeping all those items in stock. Pretty impressive." Desie's on his phone checking out the Pickle Barrel's menu.

"Each station must have super experienced staff just to get the food out," I add, noting inwardly that this would be a KM's nightmare. "The prep's got to be enormous even if stuff comes in packages. We're really lucky we can get by with low-wage staff with minimal experience."

Still riveted to the phone, Desie says, "Bob, have you talked to the servers about upselling?"

"Definitely. Especially the desserts. I told them to tell customers every day should be cake day."

"Good, good. Servers need to understand it's showtime out there. No standing around chitting the chat, we want them *upselling* the specials. Stevie, keep in mind you should be ready for that."

"I'm ready," I say, not knowing how you upsell an entree—*would you like an entree with your entree?* And why do I have to keep this in mind? My mind's already crammed with Build-a-Pasta Night prep, and Chicken Month and, btw, where's the baguette order? We need to cut and butter garlic bread pronto. My hand's on the doorknob.

"I think it's really important," Bob says, clearly annoyed I stole his shine with my excellent positive workplace initiative, "that we emphasize when you love your work, you don't gossip about the personal failings of others. You talk about their successes because you're happy for them, which is also a sign you're happy with yourself."

"Bob," I say, "I haven't heard anyone gossiping about the personal failings of others."

"You tell yourself that if it makes you feel better. Not *one* single person here asked me about my vacation in Saint Maarten. You'd think you'd all be happy for me, but oh no, not so much as a 'did you have a nice time?' or 'gee, nice tan.'"

His vacation was months ago. On his return he looked orange. Siobhan concluded he didn't literally go to St. Maarten but sat in his apartment popping tanning pills. We decided it was best not to ask questions.

"How did that go by the way?" I ask. "Wasn't it hurricane season? Were you on the Dutch or the French side?"

Unable to answer these questions, he appears to be hyperventilating again. Time to Swim like Bear in Ocean. "Des," he splutters, "I'm enforcing a rule that no one goes on break without the manager's authorization, unless the manager is not on duty, like with closers."

"Bob," I say, "*I'm* a manager, all they need is my permission."

"You are the kitchen manager. You have no authority over house staff. Don't think I don't notice the little goings-ons in your office with house staff."

"What goings-on?" Des asks sternly.

I shrug. "They like my office for some reason."

"House staff should not be in your office," Des says, as though my closet is a hive of criminal activity and, of course, substance abuse— house staff crowding in shoulder to shoulder, snorting whipped cream canisters.

"That's what I've been telling her all along," Bob insists. "Them fraternizing in her office undermines my authority. Nobody here likes me and it's because of *her*." He points the hairy digit.

"Excuse me?"

"You talk behind my back. She turns people against me."

My phone rings. It's a locksmith. I pretend I'm confirming the appointment. The heavily Greek accented Nektarios Armatas seems a little bewildered as we haven't previously spoken, but he agrees to come anyway. Mission accomplished.

Wade told me female penguins prostitute themselves for rocks because rocks are a prized item in Antarctica. The female will approach a male rock owner, have sex with him then take off with his rock. This brings to mind Helga and Bryan-with-a-*y* swilling bourbon while quizzing each other on *Ghostbusters* trivia. With every incorrect answer, not only was another shot obligatory but the removal of a clothing item. In no time they were both naked and smashed, rolling around in the Enterprise Rent-A-Car manager's condo.

"How did he rate?" I ask.

"A four."

Siobhan, the old-fashioned girl, says, "You literally took your clothes off in front of a total stranger?"

"He wasn't a total stranger."

"She deep-Facebooked him." I point to the ketchup and vinegar bottles that require refilling. "Aren't you two supposed to be topping up condiments?"

"I'm confused," Siobhan says. "Didn't you postpone the date because of the eyelash extension reaction?"

"Yeah, but Bryan was super horny and I really wanted to watch *Ghostbusters* on his widescreen. The cortisone brought the swelling down."

"Are you going to see him again when he was literally a four?"

"Four's not that bad. Could've been a zero."

She'd be better off prostituting herself for a rock.

My knees hurt. Woodpeckers have spongy cartilage behind their beaks to absorb the impact from ramming them into trees. I could use some of that in my knee joints. My ass vibrates. It's Ducky. "A girl was here," she says. "Twice now, looking for your son. Do I give her your number?"

"What's she want?"

"She's a little crazy."

"What kind of crazy?"

"Like from drugs maybe. She didn't believe me when I said he doesn't live here anymore."

"Did Peggy or Reggie recognize her?"

"Peggy thought she was Hilda Wurm. She told me not to let that floozie in the house."

"Hilda Wurm died of thrombosis." Hilda was one of Reggie's squeezes. Possibly the current floozie is related, which would explain the resemblance. Question: do I want a Wurm floozie to have my phone number? No. But what if the druggie continues to harass the already harassed Ducky, giving her more cause to quit? "Call me if she shows up again and I'll talk to her. Do you need help with Reggie's diaper?"

"Yes. And please make him stop unplugging everything. My goodnuss."

"I'll try." The old man unplugs appliances, convinced if there's a blackout and the power suddenly comes back on, the appliances will explode.

"Your mother keeps crying for no reason," Ducky says.

"She didn't cry for years. She's making up for lost time."

My counsellor concluded that I suffered anxiety because I never had a strong emotional attachment to my mother. When I reminded her that I suffered anxiety because I was gang-raped, the counsellor shook her head and said it began earlier, that I feared abandonment as a child. Which is true. I always worried my parents would leave me behind in a mall or get killed in a car crash. If they weren't holding a game night at our house, they were at somebody else's. I'd make sure to get the name and phone number of the hosts and, if my parents stayed out late, would sneak past the babysitter and dial the number. "Is missus or mister Many there, please?" This precociousness, cute when I was seven, became irritating when I was thirteen. "What's the matter with you?" Reggie demanded. "It's not like we're on a boat to China." I couldn't sleep until I heard their key in the lock and the drunken fumbling as they readied for bed. If I didn't have a strong emotional attachment to them, why did I experience separation anxiety? "It's *because* you didn't have a strong emotional attachment to them," the counsellor explained. "You never felt secure in their affections. You never felt loved."

Which was true, but lots of kids despise their parents and siblings. All those happy families on TV, what a crock.

When I gave birth Peggy turned all warm and cuddly. Not with me, of course, but with Pierce. Her baby talk made me want to clock her. No doubt I was bleeding inside. You don't notice when you're chasing the next buzz.

Wade and Daniel, with a Sense of Urgency, drag me to the break room to show me the positive workplace initiatives printed out by King Bob, and pinned to the notice board.

1) You think about what you will say, not how you will say it.

2) You don't worry about hidden agendas or politics. You trust your team members—and they trust you.

3) You see your internal and external customers not as people to satisfy but simply as people.

4) You enjoy your time at work. You don't have to "put in time" at work and then escape to "life" to be happy. You enjoy life and you enjoy work. You feel alive and joyful not just at home but also at work. When you love your work, it becomes part of your life.

Below this, in Bob's felt-markered hand is *MIANTIAN A SENES OF URGENY AT ALL TIMSE.*

"I feel better after reading that," I say.

"What does internal and external customers mean?" Daniel asks.

"Maybe an internal customer is a parasite," Wade suggests. "Like a tapeworm. That's going around. People get them from kissing their dogs."

"Speaking of a Sense of Urgency," I say, "shouldn't you two be on the floor?"

Wade slumps on a chair. "I'm totally wiped. I hooked up with a smoker three days ago and still feel sick." He rests his feet on the remaining chair and sighs a beleaguered boytoy sigh.

"Back to work, boys. Now."

The garbage bag filled with staff's random crap remains in the corner. I grab it and take it out to the dumpster, forgetting that the back door will lock behind me. Crossing the parking lot to use the front entrance, I'm approached by a whiskery old man in a green ballcap that has *MY NAME IS BILL* printed on it.

"What's my name?" he asks.

"Bill."

"Wrong," he replies jubilantly. "My name's Alvin." He dances a little jig then taps his ballcap. "The birds come back and so do the birdbrains." I have no idea what Alvin's hidden message is, and the headache over my right eye is splintering into my skull. "He was wearing boots up to here," Alvin says, pointing mid-thigh, "and he said, 'Ooooh, sooo continental.'" He dances another jig as Jesus Christ's son reaches into the garbage bin. Cornered by nutters, I make a beeline through the dining room, knowing my grubby whites will be caught on the surveillance camera.

I order Bernardo to clean shrimp then look around for the Bangladeshi dream team. They're in the break room slapping their arms and legs in unison with Bob who shushes me with the hairy digit. "We're bringing our energy up," he whispers, "making it open and circulating." He starts swirling his arms. "Find a nice harmonious rhythm. This is called Embrace Tiger, Return to Mountain."

"I need my staff, Bob."

"They're entitled to balance their energy." He swoops his arms. "This is called Harness Tiger, Return to Mountain."

Siobhan pokes her head in. "The locksmith's here."

Nektarios Armatas has a ring of white hair around his head and bushy black eyebrows. He handles the lock with precision while talking non-stop about his six children, doctors and lawyers and engineers married to doctors and lawyers and engineers. Nektarios has seventeen grandchildren destined to become doctors and lawyers and engineers. First generation, he arrived in Halifax with no English and worked as a farmhand, then a factory worker, moonlighting as a locksmith's apprentice until he saved enough to start his own business. Now all his kids are living the American dream in Canada. His wife died years ago, probably of exhaustion. "I tell my grandchildren, study hard," Nektarios says. "But they don't want to work hard. Kids today, they're soft. Wimpy wimpy."

As he dismantles the lock he repeats, "Study hard," and begins a conversation with, I presume, an invisible grandchild who doesn't want to work hard. "Wimpy, wimpy," he chides then adds in a whiny voice, "*If* my marks are good enough, Grandpa." Nektarios wags a finger at the invisible grandchild. "*If* shouldn't even be in your vocabulary."

Ah yes, the hard-work-pays-off doctrine. A tough sell in the outsourcing economy. I don't dare tell Nektarios about the engineering and law grads waiting tables. No med grads as far as I know. The robotics industry isn't quite there yet. Maybe, in ten years, I'll be ordering Dr. Armatas to top up the ketchup bottles.

"All fixed," Nektarios says. "You try."

The lock works. I track down Bob doing Buddha Holding Up the Earth solo. Rinkesh and Tareq, their energy open and circulating, are back to Build-a-Pasta prep.

"I need a cheque for the locksmith, Bob. Remember? Desmond okayed the service call."

"Then get *him* to write a cheque. I'm not letting you call service people willy-nilly. You can't fool me like you fool all your little friends." He wags his digit at my staff. "Don't think I don't know about your scheming. Well, that's over." He resumes Buddha Holding Up the Earth, and I forge his signature on the cheques I hide in my office. Given my current circumstances, going to jail for fraud might offer a welcome change of scenery.

Peggy has Reggie trapped in his polo shirt.

"She was trying to change him," Ducky explains, "and forgot to undo the buttons. She won't let me help, my goodnuss."

Reggie, hooded by the polo shirt, jerks his arms. "Leave me be," he pleads, but Peggy keeps tugging at the shirt, forcing his head down.

"Mom, you have to undo the buttons. His head is caught in the shirt."

"You leave us alone. We were doing just fine before you started interfering."

Ducky scratches the eczema on her hands that has flared since she started caring for my deranged parents. "Mrs. Many shouldn't be changing him all the time," she says. "If he drips one drop of juice on his shirt, she changes it."

Peggy never allowed Reggie to look like a car mechanic. She made him wear rubber gloves on the job and leave his coveralls at Reggie's Auto. To and from the shop she suited him up like a banker. She despises his current polo shirt and track pants combo and repeatedly irons the shirts he never wears.

"Mom, why do you keep changing his shirt? It just means more laundry."

She continues to tug on the polo shirt even though Reggie has crumpled into a chair, headless. "I can't let him go out like that."

"Can't let him go out like what? You think anyone's going to notice a tiny stain? Besides, who's watching?"

"That horrible woman for starters," Peggy says. That horrible woman phoned 911 when she saw smoke billowing out the kitchen window the day Peggy melted the electric kettle.

"Carmella Schmurlich is not a horrible woman," I say. "She saved your lives. You're lucky she keeps an eye on the place." Carmella wears bright pink lipstick to match the pink floral patterns in her coordinated tops and bottoms. In recent months, she has become disabled for some undisclosed reason. She roars around on a motorized wheelchair, saying howdy to everyone and waving at passing cars. Phone in hand, she has her eye on the beat.

"That horrible woman's got nothing better to do than gossip," Peggy says. "I can't go out the door for two minutes without her gabbing about it. And she's a flirt. Any time Reggie mows, out she comes."

"That's not flirting," Reggie protests from under the polo shirt, "that's conversation."

"You can't pull the wool over my eyes, mister."

"Settle down, missus."

"Don't you tell me to settle down. I want a divorce!"

With Peggy distracted, Ducky pulls the shirt back down over Reggie. He looks wasted. He will die first, worn down by Peggy's bulk and hysteria. She will go on for years, thriving on KitKat bars and marshmallow cookies, watering plastic plants, ironing Reggie's shirts, accusing me of treachery and lying and stealing, maybe even of murdering Reggie. I will have to care for her because no one else will. "Peggy, look, I picked up some Smarties. Remember at Easter you used to leave a trail of Smarties for Pierce to follow on the egg hunt?" Usually hungover, I'd watch him gobble handfuls of Smarties and chocolate eggs. Buzzed on sugar, palms smeared with candy dye, he'd grab at me, hoping I'd act like a mother. Now, when he calls me Mom, is he still hoping I'll act like a mother? I have no idea how to do that.

Wade has acquired a rescue lovebird and showed us a picture of it nestled in his hand.

"It looks like a parrot," Daniel said.

"It's too small for a parrot, dingus," Helga said. She'd deep-Facebooked Bryan-with-a-*y* again. His status update said he is in a relationship with Tess Mutch. This info torpedoed Helga into super upsetness.

"'Tis a bit much about Tess Mutch," Wade said.

"Bae, consider Bryan cancelled," Daniel added.

"Total garbage," Helga concluded.

Stroking his phone displaying the pic of the lovebird, Wade said, "I sleep with her in my hand."

I looked for indications that he was stoned. "You sleep with the bird in your hand? Aren't you afraid of crushing it?"

"Her. I'd never crush her."

"That's so sweet," Daniel said, readjusting his apron over his girth. "Seriously, that's the cutest thing I've ever heard. Man and his lovebird."

"Doesn't she fly away when she's out of the cage?" I asked.

"She can't fly anymore. She's blind."

"Oh my god, oh my god, oh my god, that is so tragic."

"How do you know she's blind?" Helga asked.

"She smashes into things and doesn't respond to visual stimulus."

"I'm going to start crying now," Daniel said.

The lovebird might be an excellent riffing fragment: A bird in hand. Love is blind. Loving a blind lovebird equals blind love. Who needs love when you've got a blind lovebird in hand. Blinded by love you smash into things.

Bob came in to pin up more magic-markered missives: *Claening and keeping busy is the only optoin. Maintian propre higeine to prevent unsihgtliness. Do not stand still unless serving a customer. Customer Service is a must. Sense of Urgency is a must. Days off are negotiable with 2 weeks in advance. Unless you have a good excuse, do not ask for a day off. All food must be piad for. 50% discount is avialable for employee food and drinks (please cash out before consuming).*

Next he rotated his waist and swung his arms causing his hands to alternately slap his lower back and abdomen. "The spot between the kidneys is the door to life," he advised then pointed to the microwave. "*That* should be kept clean at all times."

Crunching Smarties, Peggy points to Reggie, limp on the couch. "He's a no-good two-timing bastard. Don't think I don't know what's going on around here, mister. I want a divorce!" Reggie holds up his hands in a help-less gesture I've never seen before and doesn't resist the diaper. As Ducky helps him into the Depends, he leans on me for balance. This docility unnerves me, so I take the garbage to the curb where Carmella Schmurlich wheels speedily towards me. "Howdy! Just the person I wanted to see. A woman's been looking for you."

"I heard. Was it Hilda Wurm's granddaughter?"

"Oh no, not that slatternly soul. A respectable woman. The wife of a soldier who was in Afghanistan with your son. A sweet little thing." Carmella swigs coffee from her thermos mug. "She's at her wit's end. Her husband's hallucinating and whatnot. She's hoping your son can help type-thing. I said I'd give you her number." She hands me a crumpled note with *Greg Lem* tidily printed on it and a phone number. "My Wesley was never the same after he came back." Wesley Schmurlich volunteered to go to Viet Nam and returned with what was called 'operational exhaustion.' Cirrhosis killed him years ago. All I remember about Wesley was he had a limp and a stammer, although he rarely spoke as Carmella did the talking for him.

"Do you know Greg Lem?" she asks. "His wife's a sweet little thing."

"I'll give Pierce the message." Greg is the Logistics guy who picks pieces of metal out of his face when shaving and requires eight to ten needles of narcotics every twenty-four hours to control his pain.

"Nobody thinks about the wives," Carmella says, waving at a passing car. "The husbands come back completely changed and everybody expects the wives to take care of them. I hardly slept for twenty-eight years, Wesley was so disturbed. Nobody took care of *me*, it was always poor Wesley this and poor Wesley that. Nobody takes care of the wives. You should help that sweet little thing. She looks fit to be tied."

"I'll give my son the message." I don't let on that Pierce is fit to be tied himself and in no condition to help type-thing. Fit to be tied—another excellent riffing fragment: Fit to be tied to what? A stake? A cross? A bed? A bomb?

TWELVE

"I didn't drink all day," Pierce says.

"Congrats." He's doing his caged animal impression again, pacing and bouncing from one foot to the other. Astounding these swings from manic nervous energy to catatonic stillness. "Don't wear out the floor," I say, handing him Greg Lem's wife's note. Pierce stares at it for a nanosecond then shoves it in his jeans pocket, his face, as usual, revealing nothing. When he was four he hugged fire hydrants. I had—still have—no explanation for this.

"Are you going to call him?"

No response, just more angsty shoulder hunching and bouncing.

"Did you ever meet his wife? Apparently she's a sweet little thing."

"Tara."

"Somebody actually called their kid Tara?" I do my Viv Leigh impression: "Oh Rhett, I love ya, I've always loved ya." Then my Clark Gable: "Frankly, Scarlett, I don't give a damn."

"Shut up."

"I've got to bake something for my writing group kaffee klatsch. Any suggestions?"

"Like I give a shit."

"Brownies maybe." I search the cabinets for baking squares; there should be some, my last brownie binge was only a few months ago. I made them for solider boy because he used to love them. He ate one. I ate six and offered one to Winsome in the laundry room. "We find them very tasty," he said, taking two more. Oh Winsome, if only we'd admitted how sad and lonely we were. We could have gorged on those brownies together, shared our out-of-body experiences, our moments of disconcerting disconnectedness. The DDs we call them.

Watching Pierce do a perimeter check, I feel a case of the DDs coming on, along with the usual hankering for a glass of wine. Heck, I'd slug down anything, but a crisp, cold, dry Chardonnay from the sunny valleys of Northern California would go down real nice right now. *We* would find it very tasty.

I melt chocolate and butter for the brownies, enjoying the prospect of slinging cellulite onto the yoga moms' thighs. I've never figured out the yoga thing, why people twist themselves into pretzels. We had a yoga-obsessed alcoholic at Chappy's who drank our house plonk. She'd show up around eight—all breathy from a hot yoga session—and sit in a booth downing glass after glass, staring glassily at the TV. She'd order a soup or salad to make it look like she was having dinner, not hiding out in a craphole where she could chain-drink incognito. She tipped well. Servers welcomed her in their sections because she was low maintenance but ran up a considerable bar tab. I never saw her look inebriated until the day she was made redundant due to restructuring. She showed up early in a pencil skirt and blazer, not her usual yoga garb, and ordered a Caesar with no croutons, dressing on the side. Through the hutch I watched her down three glasses of plonk in record time. Somehow her order got screwed up and her romaine arrived coated in dressing and topped with croutons. She reeled to the hutch and vented her fury. "Fucking place, fucking losers!" she railed. I assured her we'd prepare her another salad, but she resumed slurring about the fucking place and the fucking losers. "Do you know what I *mean?*" she said. "Am I making myself *clear?*"

"Absolutely," I replied.

"Fucking assmunchers," she said, and I realized the losers she was referring to were her former associates. "Fucking ass-licking opportunists." She never came in again, was probably ashamed of having revealed her inner drunkard. I missed her. She'd been an inspiring presence for me; an active alcoholic who didn't look like a drunk, who had a good job and pencil skirts—the drunk I aspired to be, not the strumpet who puked in garbage cans, backpacks, cabs.

Pierce sets up the bottles in the windows, barricades the door with the easy chair and resumes panther pacing.

"Try sitting down," I suggest, "just to switch it up a bit."

Now might be a good time to ask about the fire hydrants, like, what could that possibly signify: no mother therefore he hugs fire hydrants—something he can rely on. "Stop pacing, Pierce. You're driving me nuts."

"Get me beer and I'll stop pacing."

"Nice try. What's up with your Bosnian squeeze? Out of Cointreau?"

"Fuck you." He hurls himself on the couch and channel surfs.

"Hope you didn't get some disease off her or her felines. Tapeworm's going around. Speaking of diseases, where's the dog?"

"What do you care?"

"I bought him a Frisbee."

"What the fuck for?"

"To play with. Go fetch."

"He's too old for that shit, he's not going to want to run around."

"How do you know? *I'm* old and I like playing Frisbee."

"He's passed out on your bed."

"You let him on my bed?"

"He needs a soft mattress."

The mutt's snout is pushed under my pillow. He looks up through the cataracts. At least he's not smashing into things like Wade's lovebird. "Do you want to play Frisbee later?"

Helga messaged Tess Mutch that she had been to third base with Bryan and was doing Tess a favour by informing her that Bryan is a piece of garbage who screws around. Tess read the message but did not reply. Possibly she already knows about Bry's indiscretions and is focusing on his financial solvency and condo.

Helga concluded that Tess Mutch is a doormat. "No way would I put up with that shit."

"Now hold up, fam," Olaf said, "in high-key realness, anybody coulda posted dat slander about da BF, you know what I'm sayin'?"

Daniel wrapped a protective arm around Helga. "Bae, you are so a woman spurned. There is no wrath like that of a woman spurned. Shakespeare said that. He was gay but totally got women."

"It was Congreve," Wade said. "Nor hell a fury like a woman scorned."

"Was *he* gay?" Daniel asked.

The servers were crammed into my closet, dodging imagined hidden cameras. Wade showed us a Vagankle on his phone.

Daniel gasped. "It's a foot with a vagina in it!"

"A usable vagina," Wade said. "The silicone's moulded from real women, so the feet have detailed skin texture."

We stood agog, blinking our incomprehension.

"It's for guys with foot fetishes," Wade clarified. "It's like a pussypocket except it's a foot."

Pierce bounces into my bedroom. "Can I use your phone?"

"For what?"

"What do you mean for what? It's a phone."

"It's *my* phone."

"Fuck off."

I toss him the phone. "Call Reggie and Peggy while you're at it." That's not going to happen.

After his hugging-fire-hydrants period, Pierce became a bear-child, growling and mauling. I'd be having an in-body experience, shakes, spins, nausea, and an inability to become ambulatory. Nothing to be done but lie here, I assured myself, grateful for the familiar forced confinement of a hangover. But a bear-child kept mauling me.

Benedict slides his rump off the bed and sits at my feet, fixing me with his half-blind purple gaze. "I need to take about twenty Advils for my knees," I tell him. "Then we'll go play Frisbee."

Knocking back pills, I attempt to eavesdrop on the Greg Lem phone conversation but Pierce has positioned himself as far from me as the micro apartment will allow. I grab high-fibre doggy biscuits to offer as rewards for fetching the Frisbee and a plastic bag for resulting doo-doo. The pooch's ears prick up when he hears the tinkle of the leash, and he clacks across the linoleum. As soon as I open the door, soldier boy says, "Get me beer and I promise I'll sleep."

"What a funny joke. Take the brownies out when the timer beeps."

The Bosnian is out front staring at her plants. It's like she thinks they won't grow without her constant supervision. Occasionally she bends over and fondles something leafy, shoving her thunderous ass in the air, exposing the gelatinous folds beneath the mini-nightie. Lately she's taken to wearing a touque over her greasy hair, bag-lady style.

It's hard to feel at ease in a world where foot fetishists spend $175 U.S.

on Vagankles. During my active alcoholic years, I spent an inordinate amount of time gauging whether or not the patrons of the liquor stores I frequented were also active alcoholics. Now I'll be sussing out the active Vagankle users.

"Like, what kind of pervball does that?" Helga demanded.

"A pervball afraid of real vaginas," I suggested.

Daniel flapped his hands. "Oh my god, oh my god, oh my god, real vaginas are sooo scary."

How do you clean a Vagankle? Shove Q-tips into those hard to reach toes?

In the park Benedict sniffs the asses and crotches of other dogs, one of which has a bloodied sanitary napkin in its mouth. The assorted dog owners pretend not to notice while exchanging deets about the endearing habits of their fur babies. I try to deduce if any of the dog men are Vagankle users, or furries—another deviant culture Wade felt we should know about— humans dressing in animal costumes and going bestial.

"How do you know all this garbage?" Helga asked, yanking up her Cat Woman boots.

Wade shrugged so I said, "He majored in evolutionary biology."

But it is hard to imagine how shoving your penis into a silicone vagina inside an ankle moulded from real women, with detailed skin texture, would provide a sense of self-worth. Because a sense of self-worth is what we're all after—being able to get up in the morning free of self-loathing and tell our messy reflections, "It's just you and me, kid, but hey, we can live with that."

Does a corporate power lurk behind Vagankle production, possibly the same one producing five-pound military drone spy machines? When Pierce told me about these all-seeing, omnipresent, privacy-invading intel gatherers, I said, "What a mindfuck for the folks rushing to bury their dead between air raids. Smile, you're under surveillance." Pierce told me Afghans call drones "wasps" and are so accustomed to being watched or targeted by unmanned flying machines, some no longer run for cover when one buzzes overhead.

I toss the Frisbee for the hound. "Go get it, boy," I say. He doesn't. I retrieve it and toss it again. "Come on, Benedict, go fetch." It's fluorescent yellow; surely he can see it. One more time. What a throw! This chick's still got the moves.

Ah, those drunken days at the beach, tossing Frisbees in cut-offs and bikini tops, comparing myself to the other skimpily clad hotties and, of course, never measuring up. But what I lacked in looks I made up for with no-limits sex, telling myself being permissive equalled being liberated. Not that I enjoyed any of it. The desire to be desired was more powerful than the desire to desire. Helga states with pride that she "delivers great sex," and that "two dicks in twenty-four hours" is not uncommon for her. She has "friendships with benefits," which is what her relationship with Connor-who-looks-like-a-girl was until Helga made the mistake of telling him she wanted more than hookups, that she had "feelings" for him. Despite all the cavalier sex talk, the poor girl just wants a boy to love and cherish her. Cherish yourself, I tell her.

The pooch trots after my expert toss this time, holds the Frisbee in his mouth and lies down.

One of the yoga moms has chemo brain. "It's my chemo brain," she says apologetically when forgetting something. My fellow writers and I know about her breast cancer treatment from the fragments she writes in her pretty bound notebook. Her chest has been left concave after a double mastectomy. She is delaying breast reconstruction, a multiple stage process requiring the insertion of tissue expanders and, later, implants. "I just want to heal," she says. "Women get sick from those implants." Only one of her breasts contained a tumour but Maya didn't want to take any chances. No amount of sleep frees her from chemo fatigue, but she has no regrets. She's young and hopes to live a long life. I cry a little inside when she writes about her fears for her children; how they will manage without her if the treatments fail. She pens her nightmares about her daughter. The child rushes around looking for Mommy. "I want Mommy! Where's Mommy?" Katie cries, and Maya can't comfort her because she's not present in the dream, just watching from somewhere, "the other side, I guess," she tells us. The yoga moms nod sympathetically but are repulsed by Maya's bloated chemo belly and wish she'd stop riffing about the side effects of the toxic meds intended to keep her alive that feel like they're killing her. She didn't show up a couple of weeks ago and one of the moms—with pop-up tits—said, "It's terrible, but I don't know if I can handle her writing about her phantom breasts again." The other moms murmured agreement but I said, because someone had to, "Really? I find her compositions enlightening. I had no idea phantom breasts got cold, and ache, and feel wet. Who knew that phantom breasts drip? The reality of this stuff needs to be known, it's not like in the movies—all about getting skinny and bald. Maya has permanent neuropathy in her hands from the chemo. They burn 24/7. Her eyebrows won't grow back. She pees six times a night because her bladder's scarred from the poison they dripped into her."

Suffocating silence followed until Noah ambled in, his leather man purse slung over his shoulder. "Sorry I'm late," he said, fondling the scruff on his chin. "Does anybody have a Kleenex? I think I might be coming down with something." All the moms, eager to please the passionate poet, offered Kleenexes. With Maya and her suffering forgotten, the moms kvetched about how hard it is to get good recipes for bourbon chicken or Kansas City barbecue sauce off the net.

My park bench is now surrounded by dog owners discussing canine ages, breeds and the lovable things doggies do, like snatch muffins out of people's unattended bags. I attempt a benign expression while two miniature dog owners gripe about online dating fatigue. "I'm so bored with the same old questions," the one compulsively fondling her braid says.

"I hear you," her nail biting associate responds. They're both wearing fluorescent orange runners. The yoga moms also wear fluorescent runners—must be another fashion trend I missed. I buy white because food splatter looks so good on them.

"Last week I tried going to a bar," the braid fondler says. "You always see that in movies, people meeting in bars. So I sit at the bar and this not-too-hideous guy comes over, and I'm thinking, Okay, maybe this bar stuff actually works. Guess what he said?"

The nail biter takes her fingers out of her mouth. "'Hey girl, 'sup?'"

"He says, 'Where's your boyfriend?' I say I don't have one. He says, 'A pretty girl like you should have a boyfriend.'"

"That's fried, like, that's such an old man's line."

The braid fondler notices me. "Is that your dog with the Frisbee? He's cute, like, really old, but still cute in an old kind of way."

"He's available, if you want him. No charge."

Both girls stare at me as though I've said something heinous and depart, picking up and kissing their miniature dogs, possibly contracting tapeworms.

"Did I ever tell you about the night I quit drinking for real, or anyway, the day after the night?"

Pierce doesn't object so I press on. "The day before the night had been pretty rough because I'd decided to cut back on drinking. Not stop entirely, of course, just not touch the stuff till five. Being hungover, I stayed in bed to counteract the spins and shakes, distracting myself from my need for alcohol by thinking about houseplants and why they died on me."

Pierce is on his second brownie; odd that this pleases me when they're supposed to be fat fodder for the yoga moms. His knees bounce under the rickety table, causing it to rattle like we're at a seance. I haven't enquired about his call to Greg Lem, am waiting for the opportune moment.

"In my expert view at that time," I continue, "abstaining till five meant I wasn't an alcoholic. The fact that I couldn't stop thinking about drinking or trying to remember things I'd said and done blotted the previous night didn't dampen my conviction that I was *not* an alcoholic. By the time five o'clock rolled around I was feeling mighty proud of my self-control and consequently looking forward to some well-deserved Saturday night partying."

Pierce starts on a third brownie.

"So I hit the town and meet this Australian, all craggy and tanned, tossing back martinis—straight up with a twist—and I'm thinking, How sophisticated. So we get talking and it turns out he's a hard-drinking reporter in town for some convention. He's writing a piece on refugees and it's getting to him, which justifies the martinis. He orders me one, and then another, while talking about migrants crammed onto rubber dinghies and drowning or dying from exposure, dehydration, or throwing dead babies overboard, or making it to refugee camps only to live in shit and garbage, and the whole time I'm getting divinely smashed on hard stuff. At one point I put my hand on his shoulder to comfort him, and he kisses it. How romantic, I'm thinking, I mean who kisses hands anymore? Accepting the dinner invite was a no-brainer. I had an old beater car then, was DUI on a regular basis, so we drove to some Thai place, drank a bottle of Shiraz, finished up with Rémy then got back in the beater—only he drove this time—and ended up at his hotel near the airport, where, you'll never guess, he had a bottle of duty-free J&B. By this time I was syrupy and completely convinced I'd found my soulmate in Crocodile Dundee. We got in the sack and performed the usual hydraulics. Next morning he was on a plane and I had no idea where my car was. Like, none. I didn't even know where Mississauga was. The obvious parking choice was the hotel lot, which I stumbled around before staggering through the surrounding streets. All the houses and lawns looked identical and the sun was broiling my frazzled noggin. I collapsed under a sprinkler until the hairy-bellied homeowner yelled at me to get off his fucking lawn."

Pierce flicks brownie crumbs from his fingers. "Is there a point to this story?"

"The point is I was really scared. So scared I stopped drinking for real."

"You want a prize?"

"I thought you might like to know why I quit."

"Nope."

"I went through exactly what you're going through, Pierce. The sickness was with me for *days*, the nausea, the feelings of powerlessness. Everything in my life was the same—shit job, shit relationships. None of it was going anywhere unless I quit drinking and took it on, dealt with it."

"You dealt with me real good."

"I didn't think you needed dealing with."

"Is that your excuse? You are such a useless piece of shit mother."

"No argument there." I wait for abuses to rain down on me.

"What happened to the beater?"

"The hotel had it towed because Dundee didn't get me a pass for it. I had to pay for the towing plus the impounding fee."

He rubs his eyes. "I used to hope that car was in our driveway because it meant *you* were there. Beats me why I gave a shit."

Kerplunk. I squat in a puddle of shame while he flops on the couch. This feeling that everything I say and do is wrong brings back Wolf sensations. I couldn't even dress right.

"I don't get why that made you quit drinking. Sounds like your usual night out."

"Way worse. The whole experience was so humiliating and demoralizing—out of control. The guy at the reception desk, and the thug at the pound, treated me like your regular skeezy alky, and all that time I'd been thinking I was a sophisticated social drinker."

In a tube dress? It's impossible to walk in a tube but Wolf decided I looked "gorgeous" in it. We went to his sister's wedding on a goat farm where my Wolf-selected stilettos sank in the dirt while my tube dress wriggled down my chest, determined to expose a nipple. Goats, chewing, watched unimpressed. Wolf's sister appeared, fresh and pretty in a simple white dress and I wondered why he set me up to be such a spectacle. "Did you want me to look like a hooker?" I asked when we got home and I was trampling the wretched garment.

"You would have looked stunning if you'd stood straight."

"It was sliding off me. How could I stand straight, I was too busy hanging on to the thing so the goats wouldn't eat it."

"You're determined to look masculine."

"Excuse me?"

He was down to his Calvin Klein skivvies, the cut of every muscle visible. "You dress like a man, Steve. I'm trying to bring out the feminine in you."

"Is that right? Well, if slutty dresses equal feminine, quit trying."

Pierce has slipped into catatonia, is lost in the desert or cratered mountains. As always, I try to imagine what he's seeing. He told me the major highway in Afghanistan—appropriately named Highway 1—circles the country, skirting the Hindu Kush mountains, forcing Logistic troops onto secondary dirt roads. The Afghan dust chokes electronics, clogs fuel and oil filters, wears down metal parts. Vehicles break down, leaving soldiers stranded, available for ambush.

In an effort to bring Pierce back to the dugout, I continue gabbing. "Helga, one of our waitresses, said she got so drunk she and two guys used a handicapped washroom at the same time. She peed in the toilet while the gents piddled in the sink. The trio washed their hands together in the urine-coated sink then went out for more tequila. A while later they were all three back in the handicapped can urinating in unison again. It was pretty trippy, Helga said."

"Spare me stories about your sick friends."

Aha, he is listening. "They're not my friends. I have no friends."

"No surprise there."

"Unlike yourself, Mister Social."

"Fuck off. I'm sleeping."

"You don't sleep. Speaking of friends, did you talk to Greg?" I feed Benedict from a lumpy bag of dog food.

"He's totally fucked."

"That's already been established. Can you be more specific?"

"His brain damage makes him hallucinate and shit. He's delusional."

"That's not unusual for someone with PTSD."

"This is different. He can't put memories together. Like with Tara. He thinks she's screwing around. Chunks of time go missing in his head, like he thinks she's gone out when she's been there the whole time. His short-term memory is messed up. When the docs test him to see if he can remember a series of words, he can't and it makes him feel stupid, so he takes it out on Tara. She's scared he's going to kill her. He used to smoke, now smoke makes him sick. She has to smoke outside or he goes nuts."

"Has she contacted Veteran Affairs?"

"Like they give a fuck. All they tell Greg is not to think about who he was before the blast, that he should concentrate on who he wants to be now. Accept the new you, they tell him."

This is where moral injury sets in. The soldier, feeling betrayed by the military, ends up betraying his loved ones—maybe even killing them.

"The docs tell him he shouldn't trust everything he sees. Like, he thought there were goats under his bed and kept chasing them out. Then he thought goats were drinking out of the toilet and decided one had a bomb in it. The docs say this is minor given the extent of the injury, and that Greg's scans are looking better than expected. He's not slurring words and his headaches aren't killing him anymore. To keep the VA happy the docs say he's doing great, but *they* don't have to live with him. He throws a fit if his shirts aren't ironed. Tara even has to iron his jeans. And he's wearing faggy clothes, like girly colours. Sometimes he wears Tara's clothes, stuff that stretches."

Hard to picture a soldier squeezing into girly clothes.

"Greg was the coolest guy I ever met. I wanted to be like him, *be* him." Pierce's ribs heave slightly. He's crying noiselessly like the fevered boys in the trenches with rotting feet, terrified of being found out, labelled coward and, ultimately, shot.

"During World War I," I say, not knowing how to help but determined to try, "they called PTSD Disorderly Conduct of the Heart, insisting the condition had to do with the heart being disorderly. Like it could be that simple. The soldiers' hearts were broken because they'd thought they were fighting for their country when in fact their government gave zero fucks about soldiers and ordered them to charge into machine gun fire. You and Greg weren't even defending your country. No wonder your hearts are disorderly." He stiffens as he always does when I criticize the military. "It's okay to cry, Pierce."

"Go fuck yourself."

Benedict meanders over to the couch and rests his snout on the upholstery inches from Pierce's head. Soldier boy rolls over and ruffles the pooch's fur and I pray, even though I don't believe in God, that the dog can save him.

THIRTEEN

Ashley Shutt's state-of-the-art kitchen is the size of my entire apartment. The yoga moms, distressed that the Parliament Hill shootings mean Canada isn't terrorist-proof, nibble on bits of celery and cauliflower while discussing ISIS beheadings. Noah has a cold and repeatedly snots into Kleenexes that Ashley provides saying, "You poor boy."

Nobody's touched my thigh-enhancing brownies.

"ISIS are subhuman," Ashley says.

Jean Jabs adjusts a strap of her sports bra. "They're raised to devalue human life."

"Actually," I say, "one of the decapitators was raised in Britain. North London to be exact. He was newly converted."

The yoga moms look at me with suspicion, swishing Merlot in their glasses.

"Seriously," I say, "let's talk Christendom. All those Catholics and Protestants killing each other during the Reformation, meeting violence with violence, raising sons in a culture of hatred. Finally, after a hundred years and thousands of deaths, the Catholics and Protestants go, 'Gee, maybe we should just try to get along, you know, tolerate each other.'"

"Islam does not teach tolerance," Jean Jabs—who no doubt has studied the Quran closely—declares.

I help myself to another mini quiche. "Well, you know, it's not like some of my best friends are Islamic extremists, but you have to wonder how *we* would feel if a superpower invaded our backyards and started telling us what to do. I mean, brutal repression and humiliation caused by Western industrialization, missiles, drones and fighter jets doesn't spell happy place."

Maya, of the phantom breasts and chemo brain, says, "America has delusions of postcolonial grandeur."

"They're selling arms to the Saudis," I say. "Why? Because the Saudis are buying. Mass murder keeps the economy going. Too bad there's no trickle-down effect."

"Canada," Maya says, "even sells fighter jets to the Middle East."

"And armoured vehicles to Sudan's military," I add. "Go us for profiting from brutal civil wars, supporting armies that massacre, rape, loot, arbitrarily arrest and use a scorched-earth strategy on civilians."

A belch of discomfort. Noah sneezes and snots.

"You need a rum toddy," Ashley Shutt tells him.

"Speaking of violence," I say because being surrounded by liquor makes me stroppy, "a UN report says one in three women experience physical assault, one in ten is forced into sexual acts and in over thirty countries it's legal for husbands to beat their wives."

"Most of those stats," Jean Jabs assures us, "come from the Middle East, Africa, South Asia, Latin America and so forth."

"Interesting you'd say that, because the report said eighty-three percent of girls in the U.S. between twelve and sixteen experience sexual harassment in school."

"I worry for my daughter," Maya says. "It said on the radio a woman is raped every one hundred and one seconds and beaten every nine."

Ashley Shutt dabs her glossed lips with a napkin. "I can't believe you two actually remember those numbers."

"They're memorable," I say.

Our hostess hands Noah his toddy and we all watch him sip, then Ashley says, "These brownies are to die for. Who made them?"

I raise my hand and, for an instant, it looks like she might spit brownie at me.

Maya pulls her sweater wrap tighter. "It's sort of depressing. I mean, with all the online porn and everything. It's teaching our sons the wrong things."

"What can you do?" Barb Funk says, her stock response when faced with "negativity." Barb teaches high school and has surrendered to the students' addiction to smartphones. Apparently online porn is very popular with the boys. Whenever I ask Barb how she is, she says, "Good, good, not so bad." She plans to retire to Florida, has a condo there and—when faced with Canadian bureaucracy—says, "This would never happen in Florida."

"'Think occasionally of the suffering of which you spare yourself the sight,'" I say. "Albert Schweitzer said that."

Maya holds up her glass. "To Albert."

I only know Albert's quote because it's on a sign outside a local church. But I try to appear as though I have infinite profundities tucked inside me. The sad truth is I want people to like me. Why, then, spout negative bilge? I intended to behave at this event, even dressed up, shedding my T-shirt and dirty jeans combo for clean jeans and a Mediterranean-blue blouse festooned with tiny seashells—a girly shirt that Greg Lem might enjoy. "My mother used to press flowers," I say to lighten the mood. "Do any of you press flowers? It's a little weird. First you kill the flowers by cutting their stems, then you squash them in a book."

"When I was a little girl in Normandy," Monique of the blue hair says, "I pressed flowers. It is not killing the flowers but making them last forever."

"What a nice way of looking at it," I say, trying to sound positive.

When the yoga moms compare their kids' swimming levels, I wander into the vestibule to stay out of trouble. I got an email this morning from Ted Cockpurse in Advertising, who told me that Wolf had "passed." On the bus over here I tried to process this. Ted Cockpurse wanted to know if I'd attend the informal gathering of friends and family to share memories of Wolf. On his last night, Ted informed me, Wolf spoke fondly of me. "I think he'd like you to be there," Ted said, and I couldn't disagree more. But I get weary of being a party pooper so I said I'd try to make it. Still, none of this has sunk in because Wolf can't really be dead. He eats right, exercises right, dresses right, decorates right. There's nothing wrong with Wolf. Except that he thinks he's straight. Since our messy parting, I've fantasized about running into Wolf on the street and impressing him with how I've pulled my life together. I picture myself in a stylish leather jacket, even though I don't own one, and Italian leather boots, even though I don't own any. He had a thing about quality leather. He'd run his hands over the murdered animal's skin and say, "The quality's there." I imagined him running his hands over *my* leathers and saying, "The quality's there."

But he's died on me. Thyroid cancer, which I thought was curable. Apparently he *was* cured but it came back. All this time he's been dying a painful death and I didn't know it, didn't feel it. Just like Winsome. We plod through the detritus ignorant of each other's suffering, wailing in operas nobody wants to hear.

"Hey," Noah says.

"Hey."

"Nice house."

"Big."

"Don't let them get to you."

"Who?"

He jerks his thumb towards the kitchen. "The bourgeoisie."

"Oh, no worries, I'm used to being the little match girl." We both stare at what looks like a vomit-inspired abstract painting.

"Are you an alcoholic?" he asks.

"Excuse me?"

"You get fidgety around wine, can't stop looking at it."

"Really. Huh. Well, yes, I'm an inactive alcoholic. And what a clever boy you are."

"I don't drink either."

"You just drank a toddy."

"To be polite. Didn't finish it."

"So what's your excuse for not drinking?"

"Don't like the taste."

"Nobody drinks because of the taste."

He shrugs. "It's all vinegar and rubbing alcohol to me."

I've never met a creature like this. "I thought all poets drank."

He snots into one of Ashley's Kleenexes. "I like your shirt. Nice seashells."

"Well thank you." I try to think of something complimentary to say in return but Wolfish words of caution restrain me: *you need to be careful how you talk to people, you need to tone down your strained bitch face.* How unjust that he's gone and the strained bitch is still offending.

"Hey, Noah, do you want to go to a memorial service with me? I mean, it's not really a service, it's just an informal gathering in a café the deceased used to frequent. There might be some free biscotti or something."

"Who's the deceased?"

"An ex."

"Could be interesting." He frequently refers to things being potentially interesting. Unlike the rest of us, he sounds genuinely interested. "Why do you want me to go?"

"Back up. I don't actually know these people. I mean, his family a bit, but I don't think they like me. I wore a slutty dress to his sister's wedding."

"Then why go to the memorial?"

"Not sure. To convince myself he's dead."

"There you are," Ashley says and drags the poet back to the kitchen. He mouths, "Text me."

I spot clutter on the Shutts' foyer table. Mess in the mansion, how unexpected; some loose change—I pocket a toonie—then, under crumpled receipts, I discover an owl figurine. One of its eyes is closed and printed on its breast is *SLEEP IS OVERRATED*. I slip it into my backpack because it is a must-have for Bob.

Maya almost catches me at it. "I shouldn't have eaten those shrimp thingies," she says.

"Shellfish can be a gamble."

She falters slightly and sits at the base of the grand staircase leading to grand bedrooms with ensuite baths. I sit beside her to steady her. She puts a hand on my knee as though it's an armrest.

"People liked me better before," she says.

Before the cancer she means, or more to the point, before she talked about the cancer.

"Well, nobody has ever liked *me* before or after anything," I say. "I wouldn't worry about it."

"They seem really far away, those women. Waaaay over on the other side. Of my cancer, I guess."

"The great divide between the well and the sick."

"Crazy, right? When any one of them could find out tomorrow they've got a fatal illness." She slumps against the bannister and fondles the sizable diamond on her wedding finger. "My aunt died two days ago. Without drugs or any visible disease. All the house-call doctor said was there must have been something nasty going on inside her."

"He actually used the word nasty?"

"He did." She stares at the vomit-inspired painting. "Meanwhile I'm going through brutal treatments. It's sort of nuts. Maybe I should just go au naturel like Auntie."

"Did she have kids?"

"No."

"Maybe it's easier to let go without kids."

"Auntie looked almost translucent before she passed, like she was becoming her skeleton. That must be all we feel in the end—what's in our bones."

My ass vibrates, which is unusual after eight. Normally, Perry Meeker, the night manager, keeps Chappy's operating relatively smoothly as it's mostly the bar crowd ordering finger foods. But if it's a blockbuster movie night, there can be problems.

"Auntie fretted more than anyone I've ever known, always needed people to do things for her. Then she figured out how to die all by herself."

Not sure what to say here. "Bravo for her. Sorry, I have to take this call."

Perry Meeker is a Loretta Lynn groupie, drives all over the U.S. to attend her concerts, pays big money for meet-and-greet tickets and regularly posts selfies bending down so his grinning face is level with Loretta's corpse-like one. In the shots Perry appears ebullient but the coal miner's daughter, with dead eyes and a fixed smile, looks body-snatched in her sequined gown. During one meet-and-greet, on her hundredth birthday or something, Perry presented Loretta with a cake decorated with his pics of the two of them. Apparently her response was "You're crazy."

"The ordering system is down," Perry tells me. "I'm going bananas."

"Just take handwritten orders from the servers."

"I've been doing that, but I can't keep things straight with all the attitude coming at me about the *It's the Chicken at Chappy's* T-shirts. Staff refuse to wear them because they don't want to pay the five bucks."

The *It's the Chicken at Chappy's* T-shirts were Perry's brainwave to promote Chicken Month.

"Please, please, please, Stevie, can you come in and take over the board? You're so good at turning a bad situation around by getting up to speed on the orders. I'll owe you one." He already owes me plenty, but I don't want disgruntled kitchen staff. And it's a good excuse to vacate Ashley Shutt's.

Perry Meeker never shuts up about his dogs, Emmy and Oliver. Whenever I ask him some Chappy's-related question, he'll tell me Emmy cried when the awesome new vet left the examining room to get Emm's meds and that, as they were leaving, Emm tried to drag Perry back into the vet's examining room. I didn't know dogs could cry but Emmy does frequently. Perry admits he is a little overprotective of her but, he says, "You know how crazy I get when it comes to Emm."

To avoid Perry and dog blather I enter via the back door, repaired by Nektarios, and see immediately that the line is short-handed because Bob sent someone home after the dinner rush to cut labour costs. I take over the board and get up to speed on the orders, giving the cooks direction on what to put up next. The night crew, mostly part-timers, are reluctant to reset and clean after rushes and consequently are continually playing catch-up. I call Bernardo, knowing he wants to get in my good books. He says, "No worries, Miss Stevie, I'll be there in twenty," which means an hour in Colombian time.

"Bernardo is here," he announces when he shows up in a mere forty-five—no doubt to impress me. "Hello, good-looking. How you feeling, Miss Stevie? You are so calm. Not like Mister Bob, what's up with him? He won't let us drink Coke no more."

"What?"

"He says no more free drinks. We have to pay." Bernardo checks the steam table. "We low on mashed?"

"I just got an order in."

"I don't see none defrosted."

I grab a bag of mashed from the walk-in freezer, pull a couple of inserts out of the steam table, drop the bag of mashed into the hot water, turning it over with tongs until it softens enough to squeeze some potato out of the bag and into the microwave. "Voila," I say. "Mashed."

"You are amazing, Miss Stevie, one of the fastest cooks ever."

"Quit sucking up, Bernie, I'll put you on the schedule. Can you take over here?"

"No worries."

When things run smoothly in my kitchen I feel good, like I'm doing something with my life. If only Wolf could see me now. I text Noah the deets re the memorial. He replies, "Coolio."

"Miss Stevie, why does Mister Bob hate POCs so much?"

"Hate what?"

"People of colour. Mister Bob hates us."

I could explain that racism is about needing someone to blame, that hating is easier than loving, and that a Colombian should know this, given what the Spanish conquistadors and U.S. imperialists did to the indigenous people of Latin America. Instead I slip into the billy goat's office, set Ashley Shutt's owl figurine on his desk and scribble *Bob, you da best!!!! From your loyal kitchen staff!!!!*☺ on a piece of Chappy's stationary. If King Bob feels appreciated, he may repeal the Coke ban.

Once the blockbuster rush is over, Perry Meeker beckons me into the dining room. This might be an opportunity to get him onside about replacing the crap ice machine. If we both kick up a fuss, Bob might take notice.

"I'm super excited," Perry says. "Fifteen days before Loretta month begins. Three shows in two weeks in *six* states. Forty-five hours on the road—here's hoping the body cooperates." Perry has a bum knee that swells when he drives for days to see Loretta. "I'm taking salmon oil and it's pretty much taken away the necessity for cane usage. I guess the top-hat and monocle will just look silly now. Ha."

"Listen, Perry, Siobhan and I have been running into problems with the ice machine."

"Bill Natural Sources, Alaska Deep Sea Fish Oil Omega-3, 1,000 milligrams. You should try it, Stevie. Bob says some days you're practically limping."

Initially I thought Perry had a hearing problem because I'd say something like, "We're low on creamers," and he'd tell me about an awesome organic cheese Emm totally loves. But then he'd respond appropriately to a server's order, and I'd deduce that I was not making myself understood so I'd rephrase: "Perry, we're almost out of creamers. Did you notice this?" And he'd tell me that poor Buffy, his Corolla, had her first body damage and he was super glad he bought the two-dings-covered insurance package.

"And," I persist a little louder, "Daniel says the espresso machine is being finicky. None of this is really my department, but it should be brought to Bob's attention. The frappés sell big with the tournament crowd."

Perry's thumbs are busy on his phone. "I really wanted Dolly Parton tix, but the first few rows are two grand regular price with meet-and-greet. Dolly's way pricier than Loretta."

I try a new tactic. "I got a dog."

He looks up as though I've just been teleported. "A dog? What kind?"

"A lab. Black."

"Oh labs are great. Boy or girl?"

"Boy. Well, he's an old man in dog years."

"Is he a rescue? Emm's a rescue, which is why she can sleep through anything. She learned at an early age to shut down to avoid seeing and hearing traumatizing things."

"Well, Benedict may be traumatized because he watched his former owner eat many hard-boiled eggs then kick it. He lay dead for days while Benedict howled."

Perry places his hand over his heart. "That is incredibly sad. He's probably got PTSD and should be seeing somebody. I have a great therapist who helped the pups with anger management."

Perry took a course in pet CPR that required he practise blowing into the snout of an electronic CPR training dog. Apparently, when performing breaths on large canines, the rescuer closes the dog's mouth and blows into its nose. For small dogs, the rescuer blows into the mouth *and* nose. No wonder tapeworm's going around.

"I never heard how Pet Day with Santa worked out last year," I say, trying to hold his attention.

"Oh it was super awesome. Emm walked up the ramp and sat right beside Santa and put her chin on his lap. Ollie took a little longer to warm to him. He can be a little skittish." Perry holds out his phone to show me the pup pics with Santa.

"Cute. Perry, I'm a little worried about Bob. He's been shouting at staff."

"Oh here's a good one. Aren't they precious? My babies."

Sherry Fish, the night floor manager, returns empty pitchers to the bar. "Sherry," I say, "have you been having trouble with the ice and espresso machines?"

"They suck." Suck is a popular word with Sherry. She frequently says, "I suck at everything." Which may be true. Siobhan complains that the Fish bitch literally doesn't know how to close.

"See what I mean, Perry?" I say. "You really need to talk to Bob about the ice and espresso machines. And maybe caution him about losing it in front of staff. It's not good for morale. Are you enforcing his Coke ban?"

"Bob uses elderberry syrup from Germany in his Mai Tais. I prefer Jamie Oliver's recipe."

"Jamie Oliver sucks," Sherry says. "He's so judgey about everything." She points at me as though trying to place me. "A woman was here looking for you. I said I wasn't sure if you worked here anymore."

"What woman?"

"I don't know. She had a kid with her."

"What did she want?"

"A job maybe. She looked out of it."

"Did she leave a name?"

Sherry grimaces at her order pad. "The frat boys want three more pitchers. FYI they're complaining the steaks are emaciated and the fries too sparse."

"They actually used the words emaciated and sparse?" Perry says. "How scholarly."

"Did the woman leave a name?" I ask again.

"I didn't talk to her. The kid tried to run out but the woman grabbed her. The kid started screaming and punching."

"It was quite the scene," Perry adds.

"I also need two cosmos," Sherry says.

"Okie dokie, artichokie." Perry's bartending expertise has increased the collegiate activity at Chappy's, bringing up the numbers, which is why Corporate disregards his incompetence as a night manager. I thirstily watch him mix vodka, Cointreau, lime and cranberry juice, and decide that sliding onto a bar stool is preferable to going home to sonny boy the quitter. He didn't use to be a quitter. Driving convoys despite sleep deprivation, gastrointestinal torment, lice, he kept going, his eyes scanning for signs of trouble. If he spotted a potential bomb, the convoy stopped and waited for EOD to check it out. A sitting target, Pierce felt his heart slamming his ribs, his body thrumming, his brain zapping, but then they'd get rolling again and he'd be back on auto.

"We can't find anyone to wear the chicken suit," Perry says. "I'd have thought spending a shift in a chicken suit would be like a day off. All they have to do is hand out flyers."

I've been trying to forget about the chicken suit.

"The kid was Black," Sherry tells me.

"What kid?"

"The kid with the woman. Don't think it was hers. Anyway, the kid kept trying to leave and the woman kept screaming at her. The girl didn't react. Maybe she's deaf or something."

"When Oliver got an ear infection," Perry says, "he went deaf for three weeks. Emm was so miffed he wasn't listening to her, she ate all his food. Can I get you anything, Stevie? It's on me. How 'bout a Moscow mule? Are they ever tasty."

He doesn't know I'm an inactive alcoholic. It's one of those do-I-or-don't-I moments you see in movies, where the alky hero broods over his untouched glass of whiskey, then walks away from the bar.

"Set' em up, Joe," I hear myself say.

"Oh isn't that a dandy song? Nobody could sing it like Old Blue Eyes."

"I never understood the blue toupee though." I watch Perry's hands magically mixing.

"All crooners had to have hair in those days. Bald wasn't sexy back then."

"But why a *blue* rug?"

"Superman's hair was blue. I'm going to make this a double because you saved my ass tonight."

"Okie dokie, artichokie."

FOURTEEN

Right up to the moment the first drip hits my tongue, I'm rationalizing my behaviour: it will be different this time, I won't end up in a pool of vomit because I've proved I don't need the stuff. Four years and eight months of *proof.* Clearly I can control my drinking. Given the psychotic soldier in the dugout, the delirious oldies in the bungalow, the madness of King Bob, the demise of the Wolfman, surely I deserve *one* Moscow mule. And it's so obvious once I take a mouthful and swallow half, sucking hard on my tongue, pressing it against the roof of my mouth to prolong the sensation of the liquor warmly coating my throat; so obvious once I'm swishing the double like mouthwash, blowing my cheeks in and out to taste the lime, ginger beer and vodka with every molecule, that this calming of my shaky stack of cards is the right thing to do. How wrong I was to ban this gentle friend, this delight to the taste buds, from the quagmire that is my life. How absurd to *never* sip from the bottle of happiness when one has proven oneself capable of *not* drinking. One cocktail, whoopty fuck! Prison awaits, let's have a last Moscow mule. "Thank fucking god," I yawp, startling Perry Meeker. "It's scrumptious," I clarify. "Gotta love those Russians."

Accustomed to the adulation of bar flies, Perry merely nods and tells anyone within hearing distance about the growth on Oliver's chin that required testing the day the mutt's testicles were cut off.

"He was so adorable before he went into the O.R.," Perry elaborates, "stressed out but such a good little munchkin. I was afraid he'd start crying when I had to leave but he just jumped over the bins and wiggled off with the tech, didn't even look back. Mr. Oliver just loves his awesome new vet. Ha."

I reverently hold up my glass. "To Mr. Oliver."

Funny how everything feels warm. I didn't realize I was cold. My free-floating anxiety drifts skyward. Balloons of worry vanish into the blue. The niggling whispers of self-doubt quiet as the pace of everything slows. Tensions keeping me upright release and, lo and behold, I'm still standing—actually sitting on the bar stool—appreciating its cushy faux leather gently supporting my beleaguered buttocks. The bottles behind the bar sparkle soothingly as my sprawling concerns fade. Gentle currents caress me, washing away regrets. All those plans destined to fail no longer matter. Whatever happens, happens. Hit me again, fuckers, I am invincible.

"Guess you really needed that," Perry says, nodding at my empty glass. "Want another one?"

Another one?

"I've got to use the ladies."

A large dump slides easily out of me, another indication that the bevvie is therapeutic, purging the passive wickedness within. While I wash my hands, the mirror assures me I don't look that bad, even a little sexy; flushed but that adds colour to the vampire complexion. And my jaw isn't clenched—no strained bitch face—even my eyes look relaxed. Can eyes relax? I don't mean the skin around them but the eyes themselves. They look like camel eyes, all droopy and unfussed. Strap a hundred pounds on my back and send me into the desert, I can take it. I hold my arms up over my head forming a *V*—a TED Talk advised this makes us strong—and say, "I got this."

Corpses left in the sun bloat and putrefy. Eyes bulge, mouths stuffed with swollen grey tongues gape. The skin detaches and slides around in your grip. If a body bag ruptures in transport, the skin tears with it and rotting blood, fluid and organs leak out. "It's just flesh," Pierce told me, knocking back Buds.

Bartholomew, a barfly looking for love in all the wrong places, bought my third double Moscow mule and gazed at me like I was some kind of wonderful. He told me the stories behind his tattoos: the death of the first wife, his inability to conceive with the second. The robed figure on his forearm had a face but no eyes, "because I believe we all wear masks." The dragon spanning his other arm was just because Bartholomew liked dragons. The compass between his shoulder blades symbolized moral guidance. The falling star on his calf represented his loss of faith due to his first wife's torturous death and the second's inability to conceive while enduring invasive procedures until she fell into a bottomless depression. "It was like she left her body," he said.

Bartholomew bought another round for the road. A modest single, I insisted—it wasn't like I needed it. We made out in his Volvo. All it takes is seven vodka shots.

It was like I left my body. It was just flesh.

I hear soldier boy stumble and cuss on the stairs and surmise he's been banging the Bosnian for Cointreau. He fumbles around the kitchen, slamming cabinets and drawers and I want him gone, out of my life, back to war—any war—that gives his life meaning. I'm done with this shit.

When dinosaurs roamed the Earth there were no trees, only ferns and moss to nourish the dinosaurs. After the dinos expired, some ferns got feisty and developed bark, growing bigger and bigger, evolving into trees. Deciduous trees producing fruit the birds ate spread faster than the conifers because the birds shat seeds near and far, and bees buzzed around pollinating the blossoms. The poor old coniferous trees feebly dropped their cones at their feet and hoped for the best.

In Warden Woods, a pushy Japanese elm shoves its branches into the big fir beside it. Why doesn't the fir defend its territory? It's spiky and should be able to hold its own against a scraggly elm that's leafless for six months. There's a big chunk missing from the fir where it's been accommodating the bossy elm. This is how I feel, cowering in my room, obliging a bully because all I know how to do is drop a few cones and hope for the best.

He raps on my door. "Are you in there?"

I pull my branches close.

"Where's the dog?" he demands.

I'm shaking so hard I drop a couple of cones.

"Where's the fucking dog?"

"I let him out."

"What do you mean you let him out?"

"In the yard. To shit. Since you don't walk him."

"You can't just let him out. He'll get lost. He's almost blind."

"You should have thought of that before you banged the Bosnian."

"I can't fucking believe you. It's like you're jealous or something."

The Crocodile Dundee reporter was in Sarajevo during the war and stumbled onto a rape site where women were dead and dying, with broken bottles between their legs. "The birds were singing," he told me. "Over the carnage."

I fling my door open, suddenly determined to defend my personal carnage. "You sicken me. What you will do for alcohol sickens me." The anger I spit at him is the anger I feel towards myself. "Do you wear a condom when you fuck the sewer?" Bartholomew didn't. How stupid am I?

"None of your fucking business."

"Oh, it is my business because if that screwball gets pregnant, I'll be the one paying for the abortion."

"She's too old to get pregnant."

"Is that what she told you?"

"What are you writing in that thing?"

"None of your business."

"If you write about me, I'll fucking kill you."

"Relax, you're not that interesting."

"Go find the dog."

"*You* find the dog."

"I'm not going out there."

"Then the dog won't be found."

"Why are you doing this?"

"Because I'm tired of cleaning up after you, Pierce. I'm tired of your freak-outs. I'm tired of worrying about you."

"You never worry about me."

"I always worry about you. Non-stop worry."

"Bullshit." He looks directly at me for a change, presumably to figure out if I'm lying. "You're drunk."

"No I'm not."

"Yes you are. I've seen you drunk my whole life. You're on my ass about a few beers, meanwhile you're fucking loaded."

"Do you know any other adjectives or adverbs besides *fucking*?"

"I fucking hate you!"

"I fucking hate you back!"

The Bosnian stamps on the floor. Limbered by the super-sized mules, I charge up the stairs and pound on her door. She opens it, no doubt expecting the gigolo. I lean in close. "If you give him one more drink, I will rip your tits off." She maintains her usual stunned expression and tries to push the door closed, but my chicken-pounding arms force it open. "Understand? No more alcohol for my son or I'll smash your face into bricks." I wait for her to fight back, pull a knife. A knife would be welcome—something tangible.

"I call police," she says.

"Really? Are you even legal? What are you exactly? A sex worker?"

Then the howling begins and Pierce rushes to open the front door. He's on his knees hugging the dog like he used to hug fire hydrants. "It's okay, boy," he says over and over. The fluorescent yellow Frisbee lies at the mutt's feet. This distraction enables the Bosnian to slam the door, leaving me and the soldier loathing each other. So exhausting.

"I'm going to make some chicken noodle soup."

Shaking soup out of a packet was something this drunk mom could do. Pierce would sit on one of Peggy's kitchen chairs, swinging his legs, so happy Mommy was doing something normal.

Not this time. He stays by the front door with the dog. It's a pileup. I should fold but no, in minutes I take a cup of soup to him and a Milk-Bone for Benedict.

"Thanks," Pierce grumbles. When I sit on the stairs, he adds, "You're going to watch me eat?"

"You're not eating, you're sipping. Be careful, it's hot."

We hear a chopper, not unusual in our sketchy part of town, but he looks around like it might swoop down on us. The dog chews carefully, is probably low on teeth. "Do you remember Hilda Wurm?" I ask.

"She died, didn't she?"

"Yeah, did she have a daughter?"

"What's it to you?"

"Some woman keeps trying to track me down at Reggie's and now at work, if it's the same woman. Peggy thought it was Hilda. Since Hilda is no longer with us, I thought it might be a relation."

"The old bag had an apple tree in her backyard, was always giving apples to people."

"How neighbourly."

"They had maggots in them. Peggy threw them out, but Mrs. Wurm made apple sauce with them. It tasted all right. We ate it, maggots and all. It was the only way we got ice cream out of her."

"Who's 'we'?"

"Me and Sophie."

"So there is a daughter. What's she look like?"

"It wouldn't be her. She moved to Regina for some nursing job.

Speaking of moving, the junk removal guys came and emptied Winsome's apartment. He had a piano. They had a fuck of a time getting it down the stairs."

"I never heard Winsome play piano."

"Maybe he stopped before you moved here."

"Why stop?"

"Why not? Who gives a fuck."

We do, *we* give a fuck, and would have listened while Winsome played piano, experiencing disconcerting disconnectedness. An avalanche of sadness buries me as I picture the old man with the tracheotomy hole peeling hard-boiled eggs, no longer playing piano.

The Bosnian cranks her stereo. What crimes against humanity has this damaged woman witnessed/committed? Crocodile Dundee told me he saw buckets of heads in Bosnia, and children nailed to walls. What does the cat lady know of what one human will do to another? And why hasn't that knowledge made her more human rather than less?

"There was a picture of a Syrian kid in the paper," Pierce says. "All by himself in rubble, holding a couple of plastic bags."

"What's your point?"

"Kids are dying. I should be over there."

"Doing what exactly? After hundreds of years of tribal feuds and sects hating, blaming and killing in the name of honour and shame, how does dropping bombs help?"

No answer.

"Air strikes kill children, Pierce. We murder more children than ISIS, we just don't show it on YouTube." I blow on my soup to cool it. "Fun fact: of the past 3,400 years, humans have been entirely at peace for 268 of them, or just eight percent of recorded history."

"How do you remember this shit?"

"Managing a kitchen." My exceptional ability to remember facts and figures was the first thing Stan, the KM who hired me, remarked on. "Lordy, lordy," he said, watching me mix steak sauces from memory on day two. Stan wasn't from the American South but when he said "lordy, lordy," it sounded like "loady loady." And when he said "now looky here, looky here," it sounded like "now looky heah, looky heah." He reminded me of Foghorn Leghorn, the big rooster on Bugs Bunny.

When I visited Stan in the hospital, he was jaundiced from liver disease. "Don't come back," he told me when I said I would. "Now looky heah, looky heah," he said. "You staring at me doesn't do me no good. You all look after my kitchen. Call me if you need some talking to." I did call him, pretending to need guidance, yearning for him to say "loady loady." He sounded weaker, then more weak, then stopped answering the phone. I was too scared to visit. The last time I called, the phone line belonged to another patient.

A fly buzzes. I swat it with rolled-up junk mail. Blood attracts flies. In blistering heat, wounds are covered in them.

"Guess," I say, "the estimate for the total number of people killed in wars throughout all of human history."

"Fuck off."

"150 million to a billion. An expensive way to slow population growth."

Not sure why he isn't escaping to the dugout—the Cointreau maybe. And I'm emboldened by vodka. Two drunks riding the last of the fizzle. "Would you be willing to wear a chicken suit on weekends in November? You could spend your wages on beer. All you have to do is hand out flyers."

"Are you fucking nuts?"

"We can't go on like this, Pierce. You living off me. I can't do it."

"You never could do it. It was a miracle if you remembered my birthday."

"Here we go."

"Birthday after fucking birthday I hoped you'd show up."

"I'm sorry. I've said I'm sorry."

"Talk is cheap. Make up for it now. I need help now."

"Not the enabling kind of help."

"I fucking hate you." He hugs the dog. A train toots in the distance; somebody's going places.

"Did you know," I say because something must be said, "that elephants can recognize themselves in mirrors? Although it beats me how a human can know if an elephant recognizes itself. What do the elephants do, pull out a comb, adjust their trunks?"

Clinging to the mutt, Pierce is only listening because Benedict won't budge, is knackered from his night out, his tongue lolling.

"Did you and Sophie have a thing?" I ask.

"A thing?"

"She has a child. Four or five years old."

His military-trained face remains a closed door. Just like Emm, Perry Meeker's traumatized dog, the soldier shuts down.

"Just asking," I say. "Thought you should know about it, in case there's any chance it's yours." I wait for him to ask if it's a boy or girl, which would indicate a curiosity that might indicate culpability. But he only ruffles the dog's ears.

"Do you feel like discussing the nature of evil?" I ask.

"I feel like you should sober up."

It *is* the mules making me mulish, empowering me to continue my deprogramming efforts.

"ISIS tween recruits aren't evil, Pierce. Like you, they just want to believe in something, and it's easy to believe killing bad guys fixes things."

He has never recovered from seeing child combatants. During his teens he was a camp counsellor and adored children and was adored in return. Distrusting children, fearing they might be hiding guns or bombs, or sending signals or acting as decoys, was impossible for him. Children had to be visibly armed to qualify as bad guys.

I sip soup. "Emma Goldman said, 'All wars are wars among thieves who are too cowardly to fight and therefore induce the young manhood of the whole world to do the fighting for them.'"

"Who the fuck is Emma Goldman?"

"A pacifist and anarchist from a hundred years ago."

"That's relevant."

"Yeah it is, because she lived through two wars she believed the state had no right to start. There are 2,200 homeless vets in Canada, Pierce. That's how carefully the CF looks after its soldiers."

"You don't know shit about the CF."

"I know they train people *not* to advocate for themselves, to obey orders without question, then expect them to integrate with the general public. I know that this year alone sixteen Afghanistan vets committed suicide."

"I'm done fucking listening to you." He lifts the dog carefully, cradling him in his arms, and carries him to the dugout.

"Why does it bother you that you *didn't* kill anybody?" I ask his retreating back. "You should be glad you didn't kill anybody."

"You don't know shit about what I did." He slams the apartment door and locks it. My keys are inside. How fortunate that I still have my logbook and pencil.

Bartholomew told me he missed the old days when he didn't give a fuck about mass stupidity. I asked why he gives a fuck now. He wasn't sure. I suggested maybe he was stupider before—that I certainly was—and that maybe, before, we didn't notice the mass stupidity because we were part of it. Bartholomew considered this, running his fingers over his cloaked figure tattoo with no eyes. "Deep breaths," he advised. Hammered, we breathed deeply. Perry Meeker pointed at an old lady and gasped, "She could be Loretta's identical twin sister. Even the hair!" Having scored Dolly Parton tix, he was euphoric. "Eight years of waiting is over!" he cried. "It's Dolly time. This will be my nineteenth time seeing her. I'm such a backwoods Barbie. Ha."

Bartholomew has neighbours who play sixties folk music, smoke weed and quarrel nightly on the balcony. After screaming at each other, they play guitar and sing. This morning the joint-sparking, squabbling and hootenanny went on until five. Bartholomew opened his balcony door and yelled, "Shut the fuck up! It's five fucking a.m." The folkies played "Blowin' in the Wind" before going inside. While reenacting his show of testosterone-charged balcony aggression, Bartholomew became energized. Conflict enlivens our world, fools us into thinking something important is going on when it's just the same old, same old. Different monkey, same organ grinder.

Conflict does not enliven me. It chisels my resolve. To do anything.

I knock on the door to the dugout. "So tell me what you did over there, Pierce. How am I supposed to know shit about what you did if you don't tell me?" One of my many fears is that he committed rape. One in four women in the military is sexually assaulted. And raping girls, even little ones, is not a crime in Afghanistan. It dishonours the girls but not the rapists. Dishonoured, the girls are sold or enslaved or murdered, often by their own families. Out of respect for the culture, Coalition forces pretend this isn't happening. The uncomfortable question is, do Coalition forces rape little girls? It's not beyond the realm of possibility. UN troops molested displaced children in Haiti.

I knock once more, harder, and when he doesn't respond, rage that should swell inside me and bust out instead recoils, contracting my muscles until I'm so scrunched I can hardly breathe. I sip air and deep-Facebook Sophie Wurm on my phone. Her profile hasn't been updated since May 2012. Posted are selfies of Sophie scantily clad. Straw-coloured hair hangs over her face and she wears red lipstick and big sunglasses. In one shot she sports bunny ears. She maintains the same pouty expression in all the selfies. Also posted are party pics. There is no sign of a nurse's uniform or a child. Why hasn't she posted anything since 2012? Did she die in Regina, OD on fentanyl?

Conquer calls. "Did you talk to him?"

"Who?"

"Bob."

"Of course."

"And?"

"I'm locked out of my apartment. Soldier boy locked me out."

"Why?"

"We had a fight."

"What about?"

"We're both active alcoholics. And we hate each other."

"Right. Okay, well, stay where you are. Don't provoke him. I'll be there in twenty." He hangs up over my objections.

When ants start a community, they build a nursery then a graveyard. They anticipate more births than deaths. Ants are optimists. It takes them 125 milliseconds to determine if another organism is an ant. If it's not an ant, they don't start a war. They march back to their communities.

On convoy it's not a question of if you'll get blasted, but when. Suicide bombers smile or offer flowers before detonating. So you distrust Afghan hospitality. Insurgents fly colourful kites as signals. Whenever Pierce saw kites he got pant-shitting scared.

What's left after the fear is gone? When we're charred hollow inside, what keeps us standing?

Conquer put blueberries in his pitcher pocket. The water tastes of summer.

"Why do you have a basket of rubber bands in your boat?" I ask, because he's not talking. I sense his disapproval. His square lower jaw juts slightly in front of the upper. The Viking rescues me because I can't rescue myself. This reminds me of Wolf. Old patterns.

"Do you remember Stan?" I ask.

"Of course."

"He pulled me from the dishpit. Taught me everything I know."

"You were teacher's pet. He called the rest of us dipshits and ne'er-do-wells."

"I went to see him in hospital. It was weird because there was nothing to say, really, outside Chappy's. I said I'd visit him again, but he told me not to come back."

"*I* visited him a bunch of times."

"When?"

"Before he died."

"He let you?"

"I didn't give him a choice. He had nobody."

"But, I mean, you just showed up at the hospital even though he told you not to?"

"I brought him thermal socks. His feet were cold."

That I didn't have the courage to do this, to show my devotion despite Stan's objections, reactivates a seething inner loss. I grab a rubber band and stretch it between my fingers.

"He talked about you," Conquer says. "Was worried you wouldn't be able to handle the takeover. All the corporate shit."

"How wrong he was. I am one corporate animal." The rubber band snaps.

"What did Bob say?"

"Bob is taking an online course called Discovering Inner Pathways to Success. He is learning about the importance of empathy and understands that he needs to be more empathic, only he keeps saying 'emphatic' because, as you know, he's dyslexic."

"Tell me about it. Last week he saw a truck in the parking lot with Geek Squad on it and wanted to know what a Greek Salad truck was doing outside Chappy's."

"Conquer, it's time you learned to appreciate the upside of Bob. Imagine if we had a real general manager giving real orders—a corporate manager we couldn't ignore."

In a Viking quandary, he savours blueberry water. I need a shower to get Bartholomew off me, to become fully sober, to manage my regrets about deserting Stan all yellow and bloated with cold feet; Stan who didn't call me a dipshit or a ne'er-do-well. Who told me I did whiz-bang jobs. Why couldn't I interpret that "don't come back" meant come back and bring me thermal socks? Why do I cave so easily?

"I wish my son didn't hate me," I say.

Conquer shrugs. "Kids hate their parents."

"Your daughter hates you?"

"She wants to become a divorce lawyer and skin the likes of me."

"Doesn't it make you sad that she hates you?"

"Of course." He stares gloomily out a porthole.

"Do you ever try to make her not hate you?"

"How?"

"By doing something nice like getting her socks if her feet are cold."

"Do you do that for your son?"

"Too scared."

"Copy that. She scares the shit out of me. I stay out of her way."

"Maybe that's a mistake."

"Maybe it is." He drinks the last of his blueberry water and sets it on the counter by the tiny sink. "You want to shower? Use the one in the basement, down the stairs on the right. Be quiet about it. Don't wake my aunt. She had a big bingo night and needs her sleep. I put clean sheets on the bed." He's gone in a blink and it's just me in the sanctuary of his creaking boat.

Stan only watched movies with happy endings. He'd check online summaries to make sure the movies' endings weren't sad.

You know when you're thinking you're lost—as usual—then someone says something and you realize they're more lost than you, but you don't want them to be more lost than you so you don't let on that you know they're lost? Stan was lost but I didn't let on that I knew. I didn't want to go back to the hospital just like I don't want to go back to the dugout.

Just like I didn't want to know Winsome was suffering from disconcerting disconnectedness, eating hard-boiled eggs and no longer playing his piano.

When elephants lose their teeth, they can't eat and slowly die. I will be funnelling purée into Reggie and Peggy long after their teeth are gone. Yesterday Peggy told me there was a picnic and "the teddies were all dressed in blue blue blue." Then she said there were terrorists on the roof.

I'd rather be a toothless elephant.

Afghan soldiers wear flip-flops and not the assigned boots because they're too hot. They eat stewed goat and drink tea with sugar cubes. Some of them have more than one wife. If Pierce had caramels, he gave them to the Afghan soldiers. The men in flip-flops, carrying guns, adored caramels.

Pierce told me everything over there gets glazed with fine opaque dust. Even the dead. He told me he was tired of seeing mutilated bodies. But he went back, wants to go back. Kind of like the drink; we're tired of it, charred by it. But set 'em up, Joe.

FIFTEEN

Conquer's aunt's house smells of potpourri and rotting fruit, which induces my first tsunami of nausea. I make it to the shower and stand under it but there's not much water pressure. A hangover is already clawing at my skull and the spins are pending. This is a condition I understand. It's real and will pass. I lean my forehead against the shower stall with relief because this I can handle.

The room tips as I step out of the stall, causing me to grab the towel rack, which crashes to the floor. The walls shift but I manage to get my head over the toilet bowl before the retching begins. My body, alcohol-free for four years and eight months, rejects the poison with punishing power. Knocking on the door sounds far away in another galaxy and not the purgatory I have tumbled into. And I think of Maya, so brave, galaxies away, welcoming chemical weapons into her veins because she wants to be there for her children, and here am I poisoning myself because I don't want to be there for my son.

"Stevie?"

"Sorry."

Conquer pushes the door open, bumping my leg as I kneel on the tiled floor. He grabs the towel that fell from the rack and throws it over my shoulders. Gripping the toilet bowl like a chunk of a sinking ship, I gush puke. Conquer closes the door gently and I hear voices; I've woken the aunt after her big bingo night. In seconds the door is nudged open again by the legs of a metal walker with yellow tennis balls jammed on its feet.

"Get it all out," says a voice belonging to the Big Bad Wolf disguised as Little Red Riding Hood's grandma. "There's nothing for it but to spew your guts out, girly, then you'll feel better." Unable to lift my head from the bowl, I feel a blanket being tucked around me.

Naked under a comforter on a scratchy couch, a chiming grandfather clock jars me into sickly awareness. I try to lift my head but can't, so roll my eyes around and note that my phone, pencil and logbook are on the coffee table. On the wall is a ship painting and a framed photo of a young blonde woman wearing a graduation cap and gown. Porcelain shepherdesses and grand ladies in feathered bonnets crowd the mantlepiece alongside Lindt bunnies. Conquer's aunt, hunched over her walker, waters the tropical plants by the window. As she turns my way I pretend to be asleep.

"Good. You've come to," the wolf growls. I hear the tennis balls slide on the hardwood then the clump of the back legs as she moves crab-like across the floor. "Any friend of Billy's is a friend of mine."

Billy? Oh right. William as in Conquer.

"I'm sorry I broke your towel rack," I murmur.

"Bah, don't worry about that. Billy'll fix it. He doesn't want you going to work tomorrow. Says he'll look after things." A chair creaks as she sits on it. "I was a cook once myself, second cook at the college. Those kids loved my sloppy joes. And my meatballs. You know the secret? A sprinkle of sugar. There's a glass of water beside you. Don't lift your head. Sip from the straw. Go ahead, right beside you on the coffee table. You need to hydrate to get rid of that pounder. Bah, I used to hate those. It's like your head's in a vice some jackass keeps tightening."

I reach for the water and glug it into my charred innards.

"That's the stuff. You want some Vicks VapoRub on your temples?"

"No thanks."

"Just let me dab a little on either side." And she's up and hauling her spindly self towards me. "I use Vicks for everything and never get sick. You ask Billy. He gets colds so bad he's stuffed up and coughing for weeks. Not me." Her fingers on my temples feel soft as feathers.

"Where are my clothes?" I ask.

"Bah, don't worry about those. Billy put them in the washer."

Billy handling my naked body *and* my dirty underwear. Loady loady.

"It's daffy what you're doing," she says. "I used to make moonshine from white California grapes. Kept it in the cellar. Then I got diabetes. Had to quit. Still miss it though. When the sun hits the trees in the evening I miss my moonshine."

"I should get my clothes and go."

"You can't even stand up, girly."

She's right. I gingerly sink back into the scratchy couch.

"Olivia," Billy in his bathrobe says, "you're supposed to be sleeping."

"And miss this? I haven't had this much fun since I backed the Chevy into that jackass's fence."

"When you don't sleep, Liv, you fall. If you fall you break something. Then you'll be bedridden and never able to get up again."

"Bah."

"Conquer, did you put my clothes in the dryer?"

"I did, boss. Go back to sleep. Sleep it off. Come on, Olivia. Don't fuck with me."

"Now, now you know how I feel about that word."

He lifts her into the hallway, walker and all, while she tells him to stop fussing.

Billy wiped vomit off me. If I cared, this would be embarrassing. The grandfather clock ticks.

Billy returns. "It stinks in here. She must've got the Vicks on you."

"It's currently burning my skin off."

"You can't sleep?"

"On this sandpaper couch, with Grandfather tick-tocking my life away? When will my clothes be dry?"

"When the dryer stops. Relax. Liv says you can't even stand." He sits on the La-Z-Boy. "You still dizzy? Close your eyes."

I do but there is no peace behind the shutters. "Why is your aunt so lively? How old is she?"

"Eighty-seven."

The thought of living that long causes the vice to tighten on my head.

Conquer pushes the La-Z-Boy into the reclining position. "Olivia's outlived her entire family—sisters, brothers, even her daughter. All that death makes her value time. The days go by too fast, she says. She googles all the places she's never been. Spends hours on my laptop, sightseeing. She calls it her magic carpet."

"Does she ever leave the house?"

"Fuck yeah. She's nuts about classes at the community centre. But she failed her last driving test so she's dependent on me and cab drivers who shaft her. She's a mess, seriously, don't be fooled. I moved my boat here because cumdumpsters showed up to clean her eavestroughs and got her to write a cheque for a thousand bucks. The neighbour with the rooster told me they came back to do 'yardwork' and charged her another five hundred. She won't admit it, but those fuckers must have scared her. Now she tells scammers, 'You'll have to talk to my nephew. He's in the boat,' and they buzz off."

"Why don't you tell her to stop answering the door?"

"That's like telling her to stop breathing. She's not like us. She wants to know about everything."

"Why don't we want to know about everything?"

"I want to know about getting laid, but that's about it."

"You might want to get a Vagankle."

"A what?"

"It's a silicone pussypocket shaped from a real woman's foot with real skin texture."

"I'll put it on my list for Santa."

I can't see his face without turning my aching head but his plaid slippers twitch in my peripheral vision. "I used to want to know about stuff," I say, "wanted to know what happened next. Now I can pretty much guess what happens next and it's not pretty."

I'd guessed Conquer was slumming in his aunt's driveway, not protecting her from cumdumpsters. "Is she mentally competent?"

"As long as you don't get her talking about pedo priests or ancient philosophers. Drink some water."

"How did her daughter die?"

"Some rare disease nobody's supposed to get. She's the blonde in the graduation gown. I was jealous of her because she had looks *and* smarts. When she started wasting away I stopped coming around, couldn't handle it. Liv did it all."

"Where was her husband?"

"At the Legion. Then he got pneumonia and slipped in the bathroom and the crud in his lungs stopped his heart. Liv found him dead. Never talks about it. They didn't get along. So, the last one standing plays bingo and takes classes."

"What kind of classes?"

"Community centre stuff. Watercolour painting, tai chi—she manages some version of it with one hand on her walker. And she gardens, gets out there on her hands and knees, digging up dandelions, planting tulips, putting chicken wire over the bulbs so the squirrels can't get at them. She's unstoppable. She may look skinny, but what's there is stringy muscle. Are you sleepy yet? You should sleep. I'll head over to Chappy's in a few hours, tell Bob you're sick."

"I can't stay here."

"You don't have a choice, boss. Sleep it off. She makes the creamiest Cream of Wheat you'll ever taste."

"Go easy on my staff."

"I'm always easy." He switches off the light.

I lie with eyes wide open listening to the clock, running out of time.

The sound of explosives wakes me. "Is it too loud?" the wolf disguised as Little Red Riding Hood's grandma asks, adjusting the volume. "Didn't mean to disturb you, but I like to keep up with what's going on. Do you watch the news?"

"I used to. Then my son came back from Afghanistan and freaked whenever he saw war coverage."

"Why's that?"

"He said it was like he was back over there and he didn't want to be over there."

"Where did he want to be?"

"Not here. Now he says he wants to be in Iraq or Syria."

"Bah."

"Surrounded by death, he feels alive."

"He isn't the first and won't be the last. Mr. Tolstoy said to get men to stop war you'd have to drain the blood out of them and fill their veins with water." She turns the TV off. The rooster crows. Grey dawn seeps behind the curtains.

"I can't fry pork chops for him anymore," I say. "He says it smells like burning human. He used to love pork chops. It was something I could do right." Pork chops and real mashed potatoes with green beans. Suddenly the fact that I can never again perform this simple task for him causes a surge of DT tears. They're not real tears because I don't really care, don't really want to cook for him, clean for him, look after him.

"That must hurt," Liv says.

"Not really."

"Looks like it hurts."

I can't stop sniffling, am having an out-of-body experience. I spot my clothes folded neatly on the coffee table and start to slip them on under the comforter.

"Have some Cream of Wheat before you go," Liv says. "It's delicious with a sprinkle of cinnamon and sugar."

While she pushes her walker to the kitchen, I finish dressing and try to stand. Bad idea. I sit back down, notice a photo on the side table of a blond boy holding a fishing rod. It's Conquer as a tween believing he will catch a fish, wanting to know about much more than getting laid, and I feel cripplingly mournful because he is not that little boy anymore, just as I am not the little girl who believed she'd find romance like in Peggy's Harlequins.

Back Liv comes with a steaming bowl wafting cinnamon. I've never eaten Cream of Wheat: we were a dried breakfast cereal family—flakes with cold milk, day after day after year.

She sets it on the coffee table then reaches for a Kleenex box on the shelf behind her. Her ability to twist and turn while gripping the walker is impressive. She yanks out some tissues and hands them to me.

"Thank you." I mop tears and snot off my face.

"Eat up. I poured milk on it to cool it."

Liv's Cream of Wheat is the most heavenly food I have ever eaten. Like Baby Bear, I spoon it all up.

"Feeling a little better?" she growls.

"A little. Thank you."

"You don't need the drink, you know. I thought I did, was tippling when no one was looking. Then, living alone, I could tipple all I wanted, but I got sick of the pounders. You don't need it."

"I haven't touched the stuff for years. It was a mistake."

"Nothing's a mistake. Everything happens for a reason. What happened to you?"

"Excuse me?"

"What made you a drunkard? Something always happens. There's all kinds of little reasons then kaboom, something big triggers it."

"Oh, well. Kaboom. Yes. I know what you mean." I take in a breath as though about to dive underwater then say, "I was gang-raped."

All these years I've kept it battened down and all of a sudden I let it fly in the face of an eighty-seven-year-old mother who watched her daughter waste away. A widow who found her dead husband in the bathroom.

She's looking right at me, her electric blue gaze shining light into dark corners. "Gang rape would do it," she says.

My discomfort at having exposed my body and trauma to a stranger propels me off the couch. Gurgling shame aside, I have a job to do and somehow, with logbook and dead phone in hand, I shuffle past Conquer's boat onto the street before realizing my wallet is locked in the dugout. I could once more impose on Liv and ask to use her phone to call Billy. And, doubtless, for no reason I can understand, the Viking would come to my rescue. I couldn't stand this.

The wind whips me like nettles and the sidewalk seesaws as though I am at sea, the walls of waves seemingly endless. The you're-fucking-up-again voice bellows in my head and I vomit Cream of Wheat over my freshly laundered clothes. Revolted pedestrians step around me zigzagging like your regular wino.

After what feels like hours I stumble into Warden Woods and bury myself in leaves. The ground feels steady beneath me despite the world relentlessly turning. No one will find me here.

Pierce loved covering me with leaves. I'd lie down because it was easier than standing and he'd scoop armfuls of leaves over me, giggling wildly, until I was completely submerged. "You're invisible," he'd squeal, and I'd wish I was. If I dozed off, Pierce would charge at me and I'd scream, causing him more delight. It was so easy to please him. Why didn't it feel easy?

Stan used to say, "Skip the hoping and start the coping." If I lie here, quiet and still, maybe a coping mechanism will kick in. But in seconds the free-floating anxiety swoops back into my chest and sad shame takes root. "Deep breaths," Bartholomew advised. Dried leaves tickle my nostrils and make me sneeze, which miraculously opens air passages. I roll onto my side in a fetal position like the burned soldiers Pierce had to straighten out.

He won't tell me what he did over there because what he did is unspeakable.

Deep breaths. Mother Earth stoically supports me. She copes with drilling, burning, poisoning, healing as best she can, bursting forth spring after spring. Her powers of endurance inspire. My suffering is infinitesimal.

Pushing myself onto my knees, I'm charged by a miniature dog.

"Esther!"

She holds my wrist loosely in her mouth, apparently considering if it'll be as tasty as a snake.

"How are you, Esther? Did you know Ern misses you?"

Her ears prick up but she does not release my wrist.

"I won't tell him I saw you if you don't want me to. Frankly, if I were you, I'd stay in the woods at least until the snow flies." Her inquisitive brown eyes don't leave my face. "In Ern's defence, I've heard that when you love someone very, very much, you try to control them because you're afraid you'll lose them. I've never loved anybody so can't speak from experience. But I think Ern gets a little overprotective because he loves *you* very, very much. Maybe, if you decide to go back, you can set new boundaries, establish that you need some personal space. I know I do. My son moved back in with me and, to be honest, it's been really, really awful. Which is why I'm here with you." She lets go of my wrist and sits back, eyeballing me, tilting her head. "You look wonderful, by the way. You really do. The wilderness suits you, but it'll get tough in winter. A nice doggy bed by the rad might be welcome." I try to pet her but she darts into the brush. Poor Ern. Poor Esther. If only they could talk to one another. Like I can't talk to Pierce.

The door is open but he's not on the couch. I check the bathroom and laundry room. His debris is everywhere: dirty plates and cups, Kleenexes, clothes humped on the couch and floor. When he first came back he maintained militaristic order and complained about my "crap." He has regressed to slob. The place smells of locker room but feels larger without him clinched on the couch or panther pacing. He wouldn't have gone outside so, presumably, he's banging the Bosnian. I listen for noise above but only hear her usual tromp from the TV to the fridge and back. So he's gone, so who cares. Bugs are crawling in my veins. I need a drink. Stop. Open the fridge, swill OJ. Charge your phone so he can call you if he's in trouble. Wait a minute, what do you care? The post-binge edgies keep me moving, picking up his junk and stuffing it in a garbage bag.

Benedict, on my bed, looks up as though he's been waiting for me and does the tail wag.

When a teenager detonated his vest on a snowy road, his burned and twisted body parts scattered. The stem of his cervical spine, blasted high in the air, plopped to the ground in front of Pierce's truck, its fibrous strands spreading against the powdery white. Where the boy had stood, only a blackened circle remained.

"Where were you?" He looms large in the doorway.

"What do you mean, where was I? You locked me out."

"I didn't lock you out. You were drinking soup in the hall."

"I knocked on the door, Pierce. Several times. You did not open it."

"You needed to sober up. It wasn't like I was locking you out."

"That's funny, because usually when someone refuses to open a door it means that person is locking the other person out."

"Not all fucking night. You were gone all fucking night, what was I supposed to do?"

"What you usually do. Secure the perimeter, pace, wrestle ghosts on the couch."

He leans against my door frame, his head low. "I haven't seen you tanked for years. I can't handle you drunk anymore."

"You were canned too, sonny boy."

"I didn't let you in because I was afraid I'd hurt you, all right? I was scared I'd fucking kill you." He looks straight at me for a second then heads for the kitchen and pops open a Bud.

I follow him. "Where'd you get beer?"

"Tara. She came and got me. Greg's nuts. He thinks she's thinking about other guys all the time. Dirty stuff. He accuses her of dirty stuff." He takes a long haul from the can. "This was a guy with a can-do attitude, nothing stopped him. And his smile was like, it made you smile no matter what. Tara says he never smiles anymore."

I start doing the dishes. "Was he glad to see you?"

"I couldn't tell. He says back home he feels like he's watching a movie of himself. Nothing's real. It's like whatever he does, no matter how risky or stupid, the consequences don't affect him because it's just a movie. The shit he's pulling with Tara, it's a mindfuck. He's bored so he takes it out on her. All he wants is to go to Iraq. That's all he ever talks about. He watches helmet-cam footage all day."

The survivor of a Taliban ambush, who picks pieces of metal out of his face when shaving, who requires eight to ten needles of narcotics daily, who wears his wife's clothing and sees goats stuffed with bombs under his bed or drinking from the toilet, continues to yearn for war. It's a devotion that is self-destroying and unsustainable, like loving the bottle. There's nothing to say as I watch my soldier self-medicate.

"I'll wear the chicken suit," he says. "Make sure they fucking pay me."

Dog people crowd the park. I stand to one side pretending to be absorbed in my phone. A Kabul stray had a plastic bottle filled with dirt tied to its tail. Pierce couldn't understand why someone would do that to a dog. He said its body communicated suffering, shame and uncomprehending sorrow. Tooth marks on the bottle and nylon cord indicated that the dog had chewed at the weight it had been forced to bear. The dog snarled when Pierce tried to remove the bottle. He distracted it with some beef jerky and, while the emaciated dog gobbled it up, cut the cord with a penknife. The dog followed him around for hours then abruptly turned mean and tried to bite him. In self-defence, Pierce hit it with a bucket. The dog's whimpers still live in his head.

The soldier's body, like the dog's, communicates suffering, shame and uncomprehending sorrow.

Trudging home, I notice trick-or-treaters emerging in superhero costumes. Tonight's the night crappy Chappy's staff are expected to dress up and party. Bob, Daniel, Desmond and Conquer will be imbibing, possibly causing irreparable damage to my lineup. It is my duty to protect them.

The Bosnian, in her pink spandex leggings, squats out front with a pumpkin. She never carves the thing—that would require too much effort. Every year she sets the gourd on the front stoop for me to trip over. After Halloween she leaves it for the squirrels to torpedo. By December the pumpkin is transformed into orange sludge I slip on repeatedly.

As I walk up the path she looks away, gripping a plastic bowl of hard candy. A little boy cop skids up to inspect what's in the bowl. "What're those?" he demands.

"Candies," the Bosnian says. "Good."

"My mom says to only take wrapped stuff." He charges off, his cuffs tinkling behind him.

"Try candy bars, dipshit," I say, comforted by Stan's word.

My Halloween costume of choice, when required, is oversized Elton John sunglasses that hide most of my face. I dig them out of the closet.

"Why the fuck did you put all my stuff in a garbage bag?" Pierce demands.

"Because I'm tired of picking up after you." My DT shakes aren't visible, I don't think, although my guts jumble shame and fear. Maybe he'll slug me. I kind of want this—physical injury to obliterate the psychological.

He pulls his crap out of the bag and tosses it on the couch. I stealthily open the front door.

"Where are you going?"

"Chappy's. There's a party after closing."

"You're going to get shit-faced again."

"Bite me."

"Don't stay out all night."

"Don't tell me what to do."

He scratches his arms. "I don't want to be alone all night again." For a nanosecond he is the little boy not wanting Mommy to go. And for a nanosecond I almost don't.

SIXTEEN

Daniel, the happy hooker, is squeezed into a red dress/mini muumuu, with dangling earrings, fishnets and stripper heels. He twirls the pearls around his neck and purrs, "Honey, it's trick or treat and I'm all out of candy bars."

Wade, with a horse head on his shoulders, complains that he's "going to suffocate in this thing." His T-shirt says *SET YOUR PUSSY FREE.* He's "wiped" from a challenging threesome last night.

Helga, the flower, flutters in a green onesie with pink and yellow petals poking from her hairband, waist and hips. She got potted last night and was groped. Siggy Moretti, a Tinder catch, gave the groper a left hook to the jaw. "Nobody's ever protected me before," Helga told us with wonder, displaying Siggy the protector on her phone. He looked twelve. Wade said in a little boy voice, "Can Siggy come out to play?"

"You're garbage. Like, when have you ever defended a woman?"

"*I'm* the one needs defending," the studmuffin said.

Rinkesh, in a turban and guy-liner, repeatedly holds up three bejewelled fingers and says, "Three wish." Possibly a genie.

Desie on dexies, sporting a black fedora, a short-sleeve shirt rolled up to the shoulders and a thin silk tie, is Bruno Mars, a famous pop star I've never heard of.

Bob, in Lululemon togs, shows off his skinniness. "It's impossible to look fat in four-way stretch," he says. With sweatbands on his wrists and forehead, he just looks like Bob. Sucking in his gut he announced, "I'm a hot yoga instructor."

Siobhan, black corseted, also in fishnets, wields a whip. Edvar is expected to make an appearance as Humphrey Bogart but is delayed due to the blast he's having at a party courtesy of his fitness club. Siobhan had one of her mini-meltdowns over this. Apparently Edvar has been massaging people in the weight room.

"What's he mean by 'people'?" Daniel asked.

"Guys who work out there," Siobhan said. "Like, if they have a strained muscle or something he massages it."

"Only guys?" Wade asked.

"Of course only guys. He wouldn't go around literally feeling up women."

"As I suspected," Daniel said, "he's a closet case."

"He's South American, lardy ass," Siobhan countered. "South American men aren't uptight about touching each other."

"You tell yourself that, bitch, if it makes you feel better."

Jamshed, the slowest man alive, has a single feather poking up from a pink hairband he borrowed from his niece. He told me he is an "Indian" for real.

Praveen stomps around with his arms stretched in front of him, his Michael Jackson skin smeared with black and white face paint. Fake blood trickles down his cheeks.

Olaf, in a muscle shirt with a black and white bandana on his head and a crucifix dangling from a gold chain over his golden chest hair, tells me he's "legit Tupac, da rap legend." He points at my oversized sunglasses and says, "Is you shakin' da po po?" I ignore him and sit with Princess Leia, a.k.a. Sherry Fish, the night floor manager, at the bar. No free drinks, but Desmond mixed up a tub of pinkish punch laced with pure alcohol. Weird that he insisted on this party when Corporate outlawed staff fraternization. Wade's theory is Desie wants us to think he is not Corporate's puppet. Daniel thinks the closeted Black Atlas just wants to get laid. Desie's church lady mom was in again trying to fix him up with "a nice girl." He lives with his mother, which may make exploring his sexuality challenging.

Perry, eye-patched in a pirate hat, asks if we "mateys" want anything and I say "no thanks" while my pores scream for vodka.

"This party sucks," Sherry Fish declares.

"The pups got me up before seven to go walkies," pirate Perry tells no one in particular. "Mr. Oliver bolted, flipping Miss Emm onto her back and into a giant pile of mud *while* she was defecating. It was still dark. I stepped in dookie three times because of asshats who refuse to pick up after their dogs."

Tareq, in a Superman T-shirt, grabs Princess Leia's hand and pulls her into the group of dancers bobbing and jerking their arms to a techno beat. A few South Asians collect in a corner with yoga instructor Bob, following his Bear Swimming in Ocean instructions. They appear to be getting along swimmingly, possibly due to the *Sleep Is Overrated* owl figurine. I checked Bob's office and noted it was well displayed alongside Snowy, the one-eyed owl.

Conquer appears from the kitchen with a witch, who shimmies into the dance crowd. He takes the stool beside me. "Cool shades."

"What are you supposed to be?"

He points to chicken blood on his whites. "A serial killer." He waves a glass at Perry who swiftly pours him another Jack on the rocks. The Viking glances at me. "You look like a loaf of crap."

"You guessed my costume. What a genius."

"Did you hear your Pakis quit washing their uniforms to protest the *It's the Chicken at Chappy's* T-shirts? They'll only wear 'em if they don't have to pay for 'em. Maybe where they come from they don't mind being dirty."

"Conquer, once in a while I think you're all right. Then you say something stupid. My staff are not all Pakistani. Some are Sri Lankan, some are Bangladeshi, some are Punjabi, some are Tamil. Only ignoramuses like yourself assume that all brown-skinned people are Pakistani." My determination *not* to drink is making me contemptuous.

"Don't be that guy," Conquer says.

"Excuse me?"

"Irritable alky."

I swill club soda, hiding my bile behind the glass.

The Viking grunts. "I sure miss the good old days when all that mattered was booty and booze. How was the nineties for a ball buster like yourself? *My* nineties was one big party. Sure loved those raves. On acid, I was one too-sexy-for-you dancer."

"No need to overshare."

Olaf, tipsy on pinkish punch, does his version of gang signs, his fingers forming inverted peace signs. "Y'all gotta gangsta fucked up, you feel me? Dat's how we get down, you know what I'm sayin'?"

"I don't know what you're saying," I say.

He points at Conquer and me. "Is you dawgs settin' up for some double trouble?"

"Please stop talking."

More gangsta jabbing. "My soul's intact, I'm where it's at."

"Dawg, put yo' eyeballs back in yo' head," I snap, which stumps him.

Conquer nods towards Bob and his followers. "The old boy's lush, been calling everybody pal. Your brown friends gave him an owl."

"How thoughtful of them."

"He was stalking fruit flies with chrysanthemum spray again."

"Classic," Wade says. Someone cranks the stereo. Time for the ball buster to retreat as my staff seem to be doing just fine lubricated. Retreat where? Back to the dugout and soldier boy?

Conquer cricks his neck. "Don't you want to know how we managed without you?"

"You've mistaken me for someone who gives a fuck."

"We ran out of prepped stuff, thanks to the slacker closers. You got to get Bob on those fuckwit part-timers to restock." We watch lush Bob lead the crew in what looks like Raccoon Climbing out of Dumpster.

Helga the flower and Siobhan the dominatrix lean against the bar. "I even bought lingerie for him," Helga says. "Red."

"You literally shouldn't have told him about your feelings," Siobhan says.

"Connor said he has feelings too, but that he doesn't want to date. Then he shows up at 2 a.m. wasted and says he's sick of being just friends-with-benefits, he wants us to date. This morning he says he doesn't want to date, that he only said that because he was drunk and I shouldn't have believed him. I said, 'That's intellectually confusing for me.'"

"He's literally using you," Siobhan says.

"He's garbage," I add. "Well, it's been fun, guys, but it's time to round up the buffaloes."

In the kitchen I do damage control, scrub, restock, slice and refill, thankful that the health inspector didn't choose today for an ambush. The toil mildly diffuses the sensation that I just ran down a tunnel and slammed into a wall. I grab the stack of *It's the Chicken at Chappy's* T-shirts in Bob's office and shove them in a garbage bag, intending to hide them in my closet to distribute gratis when the king is otherwise engaged with qigong. But Gyorgi is asleep on the floor by my desk, vampire fangs and an empty punch glass beside him. I quietly shove the T-shirts behind the filing cabinet, pull out my chair—careful not to bump him—and complete my staff's e-learning to spare them the dreaded *YOU HAVE FAILED TO MASTER THIS ASSESSMENT* pop-up. Logging into the system is easy since I assigned the passwords. I click box after box in module after module with Gyorgi at my feet. Unconscious, free of hunger and worry, he looks ten years younger. His head rests on his rolled-up jean jacket, which suggests he is no stranger to sleeping on floors.

Bob opens my door, a grinning lunatic. "Did you see what my kitchen pals gave me?" He shows me Ashley Shutt's owl. "They just *love* my positive initiatives. Being more emphatic when stressed is so life-affirming." He looks down. "There's a busboy on your floor."

"Yes," I whisper, "he's napping."

"Is that appropriate?"

"He's really beat. I'm letting him sleep because an empathic approach to life keeps my mind clear and focused. I've been catching up on my e-learning and finding it really rewarding."

"And you're writing in the logbook. That is *so* going to improve your time management."

"It so is." I close my logbook/diario. "Since you're here, can we talk about the convection oven? I'm a little concerned because it's been over-heating and shutting down during rushes. I checked the fuse and the breaker. I can't keep wrapping the fuse in tin foil to get the oven working. It's time we got Mitch in to take a look at it."

"Aaaah!" Bob covers his ears. "Don't even mention that horrid little man. He is dreadful and a nuisance."

Mitch, an unshaven, blue-collar old-timer, yells at the cooks, calling them shitgoblins for not maintaining equipment, or not getting him in early enough to maintain them himself.

"Mitch may be dreadful and a nuisance, Bob, but he knows his stuff and is way cheaper than the corporate guys. We've been making do with the prep oven but that means the cooks have to run offline to bake then run back with the finished food. As you know, a lot of appetizers and entrees go in for baking so there's no real workaround option."

Bob adjusts his sweatbands. "I appreciate where you're coming from, Stevie. But try to see where *I'm* coming from. Respect is based on the awareness that everyone's opinion matters. We've already gone over the set number of service calls covered in the gas appliances plan."

"The convection oven is electric."

"Whatever, you'll have to wait till next month."

"Which starts tomorrow, when we've got the prime rib special, not to mention the Chicken Month fajita and sizzler plates."

"This is not the time."

"It *is* the time, Bob, because we require the oven for the World o' Chicken menu. I'm calling Mitch in the morning. I'll give you a heads-up when he's coming so you can stay in your office and get some of that work done you say you never have time to do. You won't even know the dreadful nuisance is here. The good news is I've found someone to wear the chicken suit. He'll start next weekend. And once we're through Chicken Month, I can train him for the dishpit then move Jamshed up the line."

"Fine, fine, fine," Bob says emphatically, pirouetting back to the party. I check the sleeping boy. Still out.

Pierce couldn't get over how the Afghans' chai was plain old Lipton tea. Why would they touch it after what the Brits put them through? And he couldn't get over how many Afghan children wore the same clothes summer and winter—thin cotton shirts and pants, no hats or gloves, usually barefoot—trekking through snow and ice, oblivious of the cold, enduring because that's what Afghan children do.

Before Pierce became agoraphobic, he'd hang out at a McDonald's where a homeless man nursed a small coffee for hours. When Pierce offered him food, the homeless man declined. He wore three overcoats over three blazers in all weather. One day he pulled a small flashlight from a Dollarama bag and struggled in vain to pry open its stiff plastic packaging. Abruptly he turned to Pierce and said, "Can you open this?" Pierce used his keys to free the flashlight and handed it to the homeless man, who thanked him politely then attempted to switch the flashlight on. "No batteries," he mumbled. The resignation in his voice and body was total, Pierce said. This desperate man had scraped together enough change to buy the flashlight, had even paid the extra dime for the plastic bag to ensure no one would think he was stealing, only to discover that batteries were not included. Pierce theorized that the man had intended to use the flashlight to spot attackers at night. "He just sat there," Pierce said, "like people sit in bombed-out villages. They don't know what to do, where to go."

This is how I'm feeling.

"Excuse me," Gyorgi says.

"You're awake."

He pulls himself into a sitting position, looking cornered.

"It's okay," I say. "Sleep here whenever you want."

"I drink too much."

"Me too."

"I don't drink."

"Me neither." I shrug. "Stuff happens."

He picks up his fangs and glass. "I go."

"Please don't. I mean, you don't have to."

He looks at me, into me. "You want cigarette?"

"Sure."

We sit on the tarmac beside the dumpster. Alcohol-impaired, he fumbles with the matches.

"Here, let me." I light the coffin nail and offer it to him.

"You first."

I inhale the poison like my pulmonary health depends on it.

"You used to smoke?" he asks.

"A long time ago."

"Like drinking."

"Yeah."

"Can I have a question?"

"Sure."

"Why you drink and smoke today?"

"I didn't drink today, actually. It was last night." I stare into the shadows unable to justify my appalling behaviour, even to myself.

"Stuff happens," he suggests. Due to the punch, his English is more laboured than usual, his Slavic *s*'s slow, his *k*'s heavy. "Jesus Christ's son tell me my mother is sick because she not pray to Jesus to save her liver. I worry, use up phone card to call my mother. She not sick."

"Yeah, well I wouldn't take what JC's son says too seriously."

"She ask what I did for Jesus today."

"What did you say?"

"Light candle."

"Did you light a candle for Jesus today?"

"No, but she go away."

"I'll try that next time she head-butts me." We pass the cigarette back and forth. Traffic hisses and rumbles. "I put chairs out here for kitchen staff but someone stole them. I've asked Desie for a picnic table because no one could make off with that easily."

"Desie does not want for us to sit. He is like police, always finding excuse for to punish."

"You've had trouble with police?"

He stares at the cigarette pinched between his fingers. "In Slovakia police break doors, kick us, beat us, give us electric shock."

"Why?"

"I am Roma," he says as if confessing a crime. "Police my father. Not sure which one—my mother not sure. When I am born in hospital they sterilize her without permission." He laughs a drunken, strangulated laugh. "After that, no one want to marry her." He glances at me as if to check for my reaction, then looks away. "I tell no one this. Why I tell you?" He shakes his head.

All I know about the Roma is that they're persecuted gypsies, considered criminals by many. Tinkers outsourced by cheap third-world manufacturing.

"I do not look Romani. I live here with Slovakians. If they find out I am Roma they throw me out." He flicks ash onto the tarmac. "I will do everything what is necessary for my mother. But I am tired of lie."

"Okay, well this is Canada. You don't have to lie here. No one cares what you are here." I'm not sure this is true anymore but it's a good line.

He stares dejectedly at a fuzzy horizon.

"Seriously, Gyorgi, nobody cares here. You do great work. You will do well here. In brain research."

He manages to stand. "I need drink. You?"

"No thanks."

"Finish cigarette."

I take it from between his fingers. The door closes behind him. I finish the smoke and return to my closet to google Slovakia. Last year the police raided the Romani settlement of Moldava nad Bodvou. Sixty police officers in balaclavas jumped out of twenty police cars and went house to house breaking in doors, smashing windows, demolishing furniture, beating people with truncheons, using stun guns and tear gas. The police claimed, "What we did was in order. The inadaptables demolished their own homes." "Inadaptables"—not even a word. Hard to believe the Roma demolished their own homes. In the photos the homes look like shacks.

Gyorgi is running from a kind of war, has witnessed what one human can do to another, like my son. And like my son, he is the product of gang rape.

Wade's at the bar, sans horse head, with foam in the corners of his mouth.

"Have you seen Gyorgi?" I ask loudly to be heard over the techno beat.

"Who?"

"The busboy. Sandy-haired, tall."

The happy hooker twirls his beads. "Oh my god, oh my god, oh my god, you are such a cougar."

"Daniel, why do you exist?"

He flaps his hands. "He's dishy. Get it? A dishy disher? But hopelessly hetero."

"I need to talk to him."

"You are such a human female." He points to a crowd by the condiment station. "That thirsty bitch hussy is so upset about her closgay gym queen BF she's acting out and making staff play spin the bottle. No wonder Edvar wants to be a monk."

I spot Gyorgi in the spin-the-bottle circle, looking drunker and sadder. A pussycat waitress coils her arms around his neck. Let's hope she has a bed he can sleep on.

I gulp soda and shove corn chips in my mouth while Princess Leia tells me about a customer who wouldn't stop bragging about his MEC equipment.

"What's MEC?" I ask.

"Do you live under a rock?" Wade says.

"It's Mountain Equipment Co-op," Sherry explains. "Really pricey meaning he must have a decent job. Anyway, it's slow on the floor so I listen to him blab about camping knives he bought at MEC that he loves sharpening with a whetstone. It takes him three nights to get them just right—it's a Zen thing, he says. Then I ask him what he does with the knives when he goes camping. 'Camping?' he says. 'I never go camping.'"

"Classic," Wade says.

"So when I bring him his bill he asks me out, and by this time I'm thinking it's a little creepy buying all those camping knives, sharpening them then never going camping, but I don't want to piss him off because I need the tip. So I say, 'Sorry, but I've got a boyfriend.' And the guy goes, 'You're breaking my heart,' and I'm like, 'Fuck you.'"

"Did he stiff you?" Daniel asks.

She nods. "People who shop at MEC suck."

"Bernie's gone Bollywood," Daniel says, observing Aladdin/Bernardo dancing raunchily, gyrating his groin. Daniel takes a pic of Aladdin with his phone to send Bob. Daniel and Bob share stalking shots of "hot" human males.

"Are you a dog or a cat person?" Sherry asks no one in particular. "A Japanese lady was feeding cake to her Pekingese with a fork. I thought sugar was supposed to be bad for dogs."

I see Gyorgi trying to disentangle himself from the pussycat.

Wade yawns. "What this place needs is an underwear-on-backwards day."

"My mother wears her cardigans backwards," I say. "She insists they're easier to put on that way."

"Iconic," Wade says.

The pussycat continues to paw Gyorgi. I recognize sexual harassment when I see it and motor over to extricate the lost boy. "Allons-y, Gyorgi. Time to go."

"Where are you taking him?" the cat hisses.

"I need help in the back." I pull him to his feet, wrap his arm around my shoulders and half carry him like a wounded soldier.

"Don't do anything I would do," Daniel says, copping a feel of Gyorgi's ass.

Knowing we can't stay at Chappy's under surveillance, I haul the six-foot-plus gypsy out the back door. The weight of him is considerable. Already I feel it in my knees and worry we'll collapse on the pavement. We stagger towards Tim Hortons while he mutters in what I assume is Romani. Once I settle him on a chair, I get coffee and water and place it on the table but he doesn't touch it. I sit beside him and hold the bottle to his lips, admiring his strong jawline and bobbing Adam's apple as he swallows. His body knows what it needs and drains the bottle. Next up, the coffee. I blow on it to cool it which, of course, takes me back to the soup-in-hall episode with Pierce, and how I hate who I become around him; how I want him gone so I can be whoever I was before. A person like Stan who will die alone with cold feet.

"Sorry," Gyorgi says.

"Don't be sorry. I've been apologizing my whole life and it doesn't help, just gets annoying." When I hold the coffee to his lips, he takes the cup in his hands and sips. A man dressed as Satan stares at us disapprovingly. I poke my tongue at him and he looks back at his bumblebee companion. Which gets me thinking about bees. I tell Gyorgi they flap their wings to thicken nectar into honey, but I suspect he can't hear me over the commotion in his head. Possibly he's having night visions in which police beat him with truncheons.

Gyorgi's mother must be beautiful to have produced Gyorgi. Or the raping cop was beautiful.

We need to lose the word "rape" and go with assault with a weapon. When a man, woman or child is assaulted with a weapon, there's no doubt that the victim did not want to be harmed by a knife, truncheon, broom handle, etc. So why when a woman is harmed by a penis, is the rapist's defence that the woman "wanted it" or "was asking for it"? I did not want, or ask, to be penetrated in multiple orifices by four men. And yet, had I endured a police investigation and it was decided I had a case, and if the cops succeeded in arresting the rapists, in court I would have had to prove that I didn't want, or ask, to be assaulted. Whereas if the men had penetrated me with a knife, truncheon, broom handle, etc., all four would have been found guilty of assault with a weapon.

It's the ripping sound of fly zips that forever reverberates in my head.

"What you write?" Gyorgi asks.

"It's for my creative writing class." I close the logbook. "Are you feeling a little better?"

He shakes his head. "I don't know for why I drink."

"To dull the edges. We all do it. Do you want a bagel or something? It would help." I get up and order before he can refuse.

Gyorgi doesn't consume the bagel with his usual gusto but self-consciously nibbles. "My edges are not dull," he says.

"Maybe you didn't drink enough. I pretty much have to knock myself out."

He nods, absorbed in his night visions. "At police station they shout and hit boys, make us take off clothes and slap each other. If we cry, police laugh. They make us kiss each other. Police laugh. I not tell my mother. She always scared I be hurt because I look different from other Romani children. I do good in school. They take me from Romani children and put me with Slovakian, who feel hate to me. I do everything what is necessary to study and win scholarship. My mother want me to come to Canada for to have opportunity. She save money. Hard for her. Now I get trouble."

"Not trouble. All you did was kick the handicapped lever because the back door was locked."

"I steal. I never steal in Slovakia. Everybody think Roma steal. I never steal."

"You took some crackers and jam. No big deal."

"I worry for my mother. She live in container house. Four people to one room. Open market economy in Slovakia mean closed to poor people. I want to bring her here to live in nice apartment."

"You will." I don't believe this. I believe stuff will happen until Gyorgi is wearing three blazers and three overcoats and buying a flashlight at Dollarama. "How did your mother tell you she didn't know which policeman was your father?"

He looks at me like he's wandered into the wrong movie. "I'm not understanding."

"Here we call what happened to your mother rape."

"Sure."

"How did she tell you that? That you came from that?"

"Everybody know."

"That must have been difficult for you."

"I have mother. Some children don't have mother. *That* is difficult." He pulls out his wallet and shows me a photo of his mother who may be my age but looks a hundred. She doesn't resemble Gyorgi. He got his good looks from the cop.

His mother must see and feel the rapists in her son like I see and feel them in Pierce.

"I miss her always," he says. "Nobody protect her. Do you have child?"

"I do. A son a bit younger than you."

"His name?"

"Pierce."

"Pierce. Is nice name. He live in Canada?"

"In my apartment."

A blast of a smile brightens his face. "You are lucky. One day I bring my mother here and we live in so nice apartment."

I avoid his eyes and say, "One day."

SEVENTEEN

Returning soused Gyorgi to the Slovakians' crowded apartment is not an option. He might speak openly and forlornly about being Roma. Nothing for it but to take him to the dugout where soldier boy may be waiting to pounce. My hope is that Pierce is with the Bosnian, or chez Greg Lem, or catatonic on the couch engrossed in the war carnage playing behind his eyes.

Even with my keys I can't open the door because the maniac has pushed the easy chair against it. "Pierce?" Steadying Gyorgi with my right arm, I pound the door with my left. "Move the chair, Pierce. It's only me."

"Are you drunk? I'm not letting you in if you're shit-faced."

"I am stone cold sober. Don't mess with me." As soon as he moves the chair, I push the door open before he freaks over Gyorgi and locks us out again.

"Who the fuck is that?" Pierce points a pair of gardening shears at Gyorgi.

"The busboy who thinks he has a future in brain research. He needs somewhere to sleep, can sleep on the floor so no need to vacate your couch."

"Tara's on it. Be quiet, she hasn't slept in weeks with Greg being psycho."

"What's with the shears?"

"They're Amina's."

"So when Greg shows up because he thinks you're screwing his wife, you're going to stab him with gardening shears. That's excellent." I guide

Gyorgi to my bed and lay him down beside the pooch, who looks at me like it's time for Frisbee. "Did you walk the dog, Pierce?"

"Shhh. Keep it down."

"If you can rescue damsels in distress, you can walk the dog."

"I didn't rescue her. She came here. She's scared shitless."

"Call the police, get a restraining order on the guy."

"She'd never do that."

"She'd rather be dead, I guess."

"He put his life on the line for his country. No way she's calling the cops."

"Where is this?" Gyorgi asks, suddenly alert. "I go."

"You're in no shape to go anywhere. Get some sleep."

I sit beside him on the bed and lay my hand on his chest, feeling undesirable cougar desire tingling through me. "We'll go to work together in the morning."

"Whose bed is this?"

"The dog's. Go to sleep. Everything will be fine." His heart pulses into my palm. I should unhand him but instead start massaging his chest à la closeted Edvar.

"What are you doing?" the soldier demands.

"Comforting him. Go away. Check on Tara. And put the chair back in front of the door. I'll make some coffee in a minute."

Surprisingly, sonny boy obeys.

"Is your son?" Gyorgi asks.

"He is."

"Is okay I stay here?"

"Yes."

"Thank you."

"You're welcome. Go to sleep."

"I like dog."

"He's a fabulous sleeping partner. Dependable warmth."

"Where you sleep?"

"Don't worry about me."

"I stop drinking."

"Me too. Go to sleep."

The prospect of Greg Lem going postal and leaving our mutilated bodies to bleed out doesn't alarm me. My preference would be that he gash a major blood vessel so it's over in a minute. A crushed throat or punctured lungs would be brutal because I'd have enough blood but wouldn't be able to suck in enough oxygen, consequently I'd bleed out slowly. A tear in a blood-filled organ like the liver or spleen is nasty. It takes hours to die.

Pierce is back. "I thought you said you were going to make coffee."

"Don't you know how to make coffee?"

"You said *you*'d make it." The little boy seeking Mommy appears again: "you said *you*'d take me swimming," "you said *you*'d buy me ice cream," "you said *you*'d take me to McDonald's." I never remembered saying any of the things he said I'd said, probably because I said them during low rumbling anxiety attacks when I'd say anything to keep him from grabbing at me.

"Okay, I'll make it." I check out Tara on the couch, who looks fawnish—way too delicate to be carrying Greg's burden. "Does Greg know she's here?"

"Shhh. No."

"So what's he supposed to think when he finds her gone?"

"He may not. He took sleeping pills. If he takes three or four they usually knock him out."

"So the gardening shears are just a precaution?"

"Would you fucking lower your voice? Are you planning to sleep with the busboy?"

"Do I normally bring men home to shag?"

"You were feeling him up."

"I was comforting him. Anyway, it's none of your business."

"Which means you're going to shag him. How old is he?"

"Why does the age difference only matter if the woman is older than the man?"

"Do what you want. It's just a little disgusting."

"I can't believe you care. And btw, this is *my* apartment. I can canoodle with whoever I want. Sit down, you're in my way. Are there any cookies left or did you eat them all?"

"You and your cookies. It's like a love substitute or something."

"Damn straight, what's *your* excuse?"

"Shhh." He pops open another Bud.

"Why am I making coffee if you're drinking beer?"

"Want one?"

"Do you relish being retarded?"

"*I* can hold my liquor, unlike your pathetic bingeing self. I haven't had one since before Tara showed up."

"Yowsa, what self-control." I make the coffee because the activity stops me from entering into hand-to-hand combat with my son or curling up with Gyorgi and the dog. The thought of the gypsy waking to find the old broad beside him, fearful she expects payment for the overnighter in the form of a fondle, keeps me cranky in the kitchen. I eat one of the remaining chocolate chip cookies and hand Pierce the other. We sit at the rickety table chewing and watching Tara sleep. "She even looks a little like Scarlett O'Hara," I whisper.

"Shut up."

"Do you have a thing for her?"

"Are you nuts? She's my best friend's wife."

"So?"

"What's the matter with you?"

"What's the matter with *you*?"

The upside of house guests is it seems unlikely he'll strangle me with witnesses present.

"What's the why in your life?" I ask.

"What?"

"My manager is taking an online course to discover inner pathways to success and apparently figuring out your 'why' is key."

"What why?"

"Why you exist, I guess."

"Why do you?"

"Beats me. But you and Greg seem to think you should be with your comrades in arms. Why?"

"To save lives and help people, duh."

"Right. Well, here's the thing. You're too late. We should have helped the Syrians before climate change–driven drought wiped them out. Before crops dried up, forcing farmers to desert fields full of cattle carcasses. Before hundreds of thousands of families fled to the cities to compete for dwindling food supplies with hundreds of thousands of Palestinian and Iraqi refugees fleeing from war zones. That's when Syria asked for foreign aid and guess what? We didn't give it." Beneath his poker face a multiplicity of impulses rattle around. "So now we spend billions bombing the shit out of the place, and not feeding or sheltering the starving, displaced people. Don't you think things might have turned out differently if the international community had spent billions on helping those farmers get through the drought?"

He leans across the table and speaks to me as though I am mentally challenged. "Have you seen what ISIS does to people? Do you want me to show you some videos?"

"I know what ISIS does to people."

"They put captives in cages, drop them in pools and video them drowning. They burn men alive—"

"Pierce, I know all this, and it's horrendous. Actually there is no word to describe what it is, but we burn people alive too. It's called bombing."

"Oh fuck off with your libtard bullshit."

We finish our cookies looking at anything but each other.

Tara pushes herself off the couch, shivering like a dog emerging from a cold lake.

"Great," Pierce says, "you woke her up."

"I think I should go home," she says.

"Not on my account. Hi, I'm Pierce's mother."

"I know who you are. Pierce, please take me home. I don't feel so good." She hands him her car keys.

"He's been drinking," I say. "He shouldn't drive. He *can't* drive."

"I'm totally sober," he says. "And of course I can fucking drive."

"Are you okay with cars passing you?" Tara asks. "Greg thinks every Toyota is a suicide vehicle."

"I'm okay with passing cars."

"Really?" I say. "Since when?"

"Since I took Reggie's car out."

"Reggie's car broke down."

"Before it broke down."

Given Reggie's dementia, I have no way of verifying this. "It wouldn't hurt to have a coffee before you go. Tara, would you like some coffee? We're all out of cookies unfortunately."

"No thanks." She doesn't look at me, apparently despises me due to whatever Pierce has told her about me.

"I was very sorry to hear about your husband," I say.

"Yeah, well, life's a bitch and then you die, right."

"Something like that."

"Pierce," she says, "can you move the chair?"

He does and I awkwardly escort her to the front hall, where she turns on me, all tight and sinewy, and says, "I wanted a kid so bad you have no idea. Pierce is a great guy. You don't deserve him." She steps delicately over the Bosnian's pumpkin, and the great guy wordlessly follows her. As they pull out, I wave but they don't wave back and the pumpkin trips me up. I boot it across the yard.

I slide fully clothed into bed with the mutt and Gyorgi because I can't weather this blizzard of misery alone. Bare-knuckled anxiety pummels me, not only about Pierce's crazy driving, but about what happens when Pierce shows up with Scarlett O'Hara. Does Greg Lem have a firearm handy? In my mind his head becomes a grenade and his face the pin.

I smell constipated dog fart. "Are you awake?" I whisper. The hound nuzzles me. "Let's go."

Nobody in the dog park. I guide the mutt around with a flashlight. He busies himself sniffing dirt. "Have a dookie while you're at it," I tell him, checking for assailants, hoping for trouble, distraction. An almost full moon hangs so low in the sky it looks like it might tip over while casting shape-shifting shadows through the oaks. Oaks don't have it easy, Wade told me. Beech trees, sprung from berries stored in the ground by blue jays, suck up the water around the oaks' roots. Faster growers, the beeches eventually reach the oaks' height and spread their branches, blocking the oaks' light, causing a slow, decades-long death. I feel oakish around the son I don't deserve. He's growing above and beyond me, killing me slowly.

Gyorgi wakes me. "Okay if I shower?"

"Of course." He doesn't seem surprised I'm on the bed. Maybe back home he slept with dogs and strange women because there weren't enough beds.

"I take dog out already."

"Great. Thank you."

No sign of the soldier. I charge my phone and slide bread into the toaster. The dog trails me, waiting for vittles. "Did you poop while you were out with Gyorgi?" Benedict does the tail wag that suggests it's a possibility.

The six-foot-plus gypsy dwarfs my kitchen.

"Do you want scrambled eggs?" I ask.

"Sure. I can make for us."

"Great. Go for it."

Pierce—if Greg hasn't murdered him—will lose his shit if he catches Gyorgi scrambling. I bustle into the shower then hurriedly snake-gulp the eggs.

On the street Gyorgi pulls me out of the path of a speeding truck, keeping his hand on my lower back until we reach the curb. "Crazy driver," he says.

"When does your shift start? I have to stop by my parents'."

"Eleven. You?"

"An hour ago." I've ignored three Chappy calls already. I left a voicemail with Mitch, the blue-collared dreadful nuisance, begging him to service the convection oven asap.

"If you have nothing else to do, Gyorgi, you could come with me to my parents'."

"Sure."

"First I have to pick up groceries."

An extra pair of hands to cart groceries is a bonus. Gyorgi and I have our usual hopscotch conversation then, two blocks from the bungalow, I blurt, "I was raped. My son is the product of rape. Like your mother, I don't know who the father is. There were four of them."

Gyorgi halts, making me stop. He faces me, stricken, puts the bags down and hugs me. I stand stiffly as he breathes into my hair. "I don't want pity," I mutter into his jean jacket. "I want to understand what it's like to be a child of rape. I want you to tell me what it's like." He holds me tighter and we wobble slightly, unsteady in the tumult of morning rush hour.

"Excuse me," a stroller mom barks, trying to get by. Gyorgi releases me and grabs the groceries.

"Sorry," he says.

We walk on without speaking and I marvel at how I blew it. We were getting along fine until I dropped the rape bomb. In my head Peggy says, "Why do you always have to ruin everything?"

He stops at the parkette, sets the bags on a bench, takes my hand and guides me to sit beside him. He looks at me, into me and says, "It does not matter."

"How can it not matter?"

"Because it does not."

"It has to."

"My mother, she feel love to me. Like you feel love to your son."

"I don't feel love to him."

Gyorgi pulls me closer and kisses my forehead as though I'm a child too young to understand. He smells of my shampoo.

A little girl in purple sunglasses stands on my parents' front steps, clinging to the railing as though, if she were to let go, she would fall off the planet. Her skin is light brown and her dark wiry hair pulled into puffy pigtails. Tucked into the bow tied at the back of her pink princess costume is a busted plastic samurai sword. A pink plastic purse dangles from her wrist.

"Hello," I say. "Who are you?" She doesn't reply, only stares at me from behind the purple sunglasses.

Ducky pushes open the screen door. "I've been calling and calling. Your voicemail is full."

"Sorry about that. Who's this?"

"Where's my Daddy?" Peggy demands over Ducky's shoulder.

"In his bedroom, Mrs. Many." Ducky hands me a sheet of well-handled notepaper. "From the girl's mother."

Printed in a messy, childish hand, the note reads: *Fuck you for not answering my emails. Fuck your crazy grandparents. DO NOT call Child Services. You OWE it to her to protect her. If you put her in foster care she will get WORSE. Her name is Trudy.*

"What did you do with my Daddy?" Peggy squawks. "Where is he?"

"In his bedroom," I say. "Stop asking. Have you vacuumed today, Mom? You know how those dust bunnies breed." Peggy shuffles to the kitchen to wrestle her Dirt Devil from the broom closet.

"I'm guessing," I say to Ducky, "the author of this note didn't leave a number."

Ducky shakes her head and points at a stuffed plastic garbage bag and a pink Hello Kitty backpack. "She left that."

"I like your sword," Gyorgi tells Trudy. "What you use for?"

Trudy stares at him.

"Will you stay out here with her?" I ask him.

"Sure." As he sits on the steps, the child backs away, still gripping the railing. I take the groceries to the kitchen while unease torques inside me. Peggy drops the vacuum cleaner, snatches the package of marshmallow cookies from me and scurries to the living room to gum them. Ducky wearily picks up the Dirt Devil and fits it back into the closet.

"Is Reggie letting you help him with the diaper?" I ask.

"It's Mrs. Many who won't let me help. She thinks I want to marry him. You have to explain to her who I am again."

"I will. What was her reaction to the mother and child?"

"She chased them with her duster. Mr. Many went to his room to fix a car."

"So they have no idea who she is?"

"Mrs. Many thinks she's that floozie Hilda Wurm. All Mr. Many said was 'What's a Negro doing here?'"

Air wheezes out of me, a decompression that forces me to sit.

"You should call the police," Ducky says. "They will find the child's mother."

"Not much point in finding her if she doesn't want to be found."

"I wrote your phone number down for her."

"Did she say she'd call me?"

"She didn't say anything. It all happened so fast and Mrs. Many was very distressed, my goodnuss."

"What did the child do when her mother left without her?"

"She tried to follow but the woman kept pushing her away. She got in a car with a man and the child tried to climb in with her. I was scared the little girl's fingers would get caught in the door."

This is all too familiar—a child clinging to a departing mother.

"The little girl started punching and kicking. Her mother called her a crazy brat and slammed the door and they drove away."

"What did the kid do?"

"She sat on the lawn. Mrs. Schmurlich brought her inside, said she shouldn't be out there alone. Mrs. Schmurlich was going to call the police but I said we'd wait for you."

"Has the kid eaten anything?"

"She said she didn't want breakfast. She's waiting for her mom. She says her mom always comes and gets her." Ducky finishes unpacking the groceries while I sit with guilt lodged in my gut because if Trudy is Pierce's, she is the product of the product of rape. And if she is the result of a drunken romp in which Pierce forced himself on Sophie, she is the product of rape times three.

It doesn't matter.

Peggy starts singing "It's a Long Way to Tipperary," and I tune out because tuning in is beyond my current capabilities. I feel nothing below the solar plexus where my plastic heart pumps steadily, immune to the waif clinging to the railing.

"The child can't stay here," Ducky says.

"I realize that. How old is she? Shouldn't she be in school?"

"She says she doesn't go to school, she's almost five. They don't have to go to school till senior kindergarten. My goodnuss, she's tiny."

I take three chocolate bars from Peggy's stash and sit beside Gyorgi on the steps. Trudy watches the gypsy do tricks with a piece of string, stretching it between his fingers. I hold out the chocolate bars. "Pick one." Trudy grabs the Oh Henry!—Pierce's favourite. Gyorgi takes the Mars bar. Trudy's sunglasses slip as she looks down to unwrap the chocolate

"You want I hold your glasses?" Gyorgi asks. She hands them over without looking at him. It is when she peels the wrapping back as though it were a banana that I see my son at her age, sitting on these same steps, peeling his Oh Henry! as though it were a banana.

Stan used to say pure fate only happens to the very lucky or the very unlucky, and that the rest of us "monkeys in the middle" have to make choices that determine whether or not we "go to hell in a handcart." I don't know what a handcart looks like, or how us monkeys fit into it, but sitting on the steps, with the Dirt Devil Peggy must have hauled out of the closet wailing, I know this monkey has a fateful choice to make.

Trudy bunches the wrapper, apparently unsure what to do with it. I hold out my hand and she drops the wrapper into it then retrieves her sunglasses from Gyorgi. Before she has them securely in place, I catch a glimpse of her eyes—the same pond green as my son's.

EIGHTEEN

The minute I open the back door, Conquer combusts towards me with a bloody log of meat in his arms. "This shit is bone-in," he bellows.

"Yes." Grease-laden vapour swarms me.

"I said I wanted bone-free."

"It costs more."

"So I'm supposed to bust my balls hacking away with a boning knife?"

"Get Rinkesh to do it."

The walk-in fridge door swings open revealing the genie with an armful of lettuce. I point to the beef in Conquer's embrace and make sawing gestures. "Rinkesh, can you cut bone-in prime rib?"

"Like never tomorrow."

"Problem solved. You can take the T-bone out of your ass, Conquer."

In my office/closet Daniel rummages in his lotion bag and Wade shoves Dristan nasal mist up a nostril.

"There she is," Daniel says. "The thirsty cradle robber."

"Where's Bob?"

"Ever present and always watching," Wade says. "He wrote it on the schedule instead of his hours."

Daniel squirts lotion onto his hands, making my office reek of pineapple. "We're all super stoked about you and the busboy. He's such a snack. Just make sure he washes. Bob got crabs off a Hungarian."

"I am not sleeping with the busboy."

"Why not? I would."

"Why are you rejects in my office?"

"Wade just explained why I'm fat. It's because I'm a superior ape."

"Not superior exactly." Wade snorts Dristan up his other nostril.

"Millions and millions of years ago," Daniel explains, "Europe froze over first and the apes that came over from Africa had to endure famine longer than the apes that stayed in Africa. So European apes got really good at storing fat. Like, they evolved and didn't burn calories as fast as other apes. That's why my metabolism is slow. It's a fat preservation gene I inherited from Irish apes. My great-great-great-great-grandparents were Irish and came here to escape the potato famine."

Siobhan barges in. "There's literally an entire table out there on a zero-carb diet."

"Tell them to go away," Wade pleads.

"Like I can do that. Get out there, Mr. Personality, and make substitutions." She looks at her order pad. "One of them is allergic to mustard, chicken, bananas"—Wade plugs his ears as she continues—"peanuts, blue cheese, wheat, sugar and tannins." She shoves Wade out the door and turns to Daniel. "And you, lardy ass, have to find an Ontario wine for table six."

"Do not fat-shame me, bitch."

"He's not a lardy ass," I say. "He's a superior Irish ape. Scram, all of you."

With the door closed I phone Maisie, my Walmart associate in Lingerie. "How's she doing?"

"She's been hanging around the front door, waiting for her mom to come get her."

"What are you telling her?"

"I say, 'All I know is you're staying with us today.' She's super protective of her stuff, like, she won't let the other kids even touch her sword. She gets aggro and doms them then goes real quiet and kind of disappears. I sus she's got some ishes."

"Well, her mother abandoned her. She's bound to have some ishes. Did she eat anything?"

"I offered her a cheese sandwich. She said she makes her own sandwiches with butter and chocolate sprinkles. I said I don't got no chocolate sprinkles. She hasn't taken her sunglasses off. She's on the couch watching TV. Her chin's on her chest so she could be sleeping."

A Viking roar penetrates my door, no doubt Conquer's response to the zero-carb order. "I've got to go," I say.

"It's going to be a strug dealing with this kid, Stevie. If I were you, I'd call Children's Aid."

"I'm thinking about it. Text me if things get worse."

"I can handle her."

"Thanks for this."

Conquer waves a spatula around. "Tell the fuckwits to go to a fucking juice bar. I'm not doing any wheat grass and alfalfa sprout bullshit."

I look at the order. "Asparagus no-cheese omelets and garden salad with dressing on the side. Seems straightforward. Rinkesh, let's get cracking."

"Right on."

As I beat eggs, my skull feels porous.

Baby deer's white spots are camouflage. They can't run from predators like adult deer. Instead they drop to the ground and hide in the grasses and shrubs until their mamas return for them. This is what Trudy is doing.

"'Sup, fam?" Olaf says. "Y'all got some heavy shizz on yo' mind?"

"Please don't talk."

"Some lady say da 'salmon smells a bit off,' you feel me?" He holds the plate of fish in question in front of me. It smells fine. "Da lady say, 'It might be the oil.' She say she 'very particular about her oils.'"

"Just give her something else."

"What are you?" Mitch yells. "A fucking jumping bean?"

"No sir," Praveen says, fidgeting while the dreadful nuisance pokes around the convection oven.

"Mitch," I say, "thank you so much for coming."

While he grumbles about shitgoblins, I check Bob's office, expecting to find it empty now that he is ever present and always watching, but he's in there breathing heavily and circling his arms.

"Can't you knock?"

"Sorry. I just wanted you to know that Mitch is working on the convection oven as there is no way we can start the World o' Chicken menu without all the ovens up to speed. I thought you might want to stay in here for the duration."

"Well, you thought wrong. This is *my* restaurant, and I'm not staying cooped up because of some dreadful little man."

"Funny that you used the word 'cooped' as in chicken coop, as in Chicken Month, as in we're not ready for it."

"Ha ha. Someday, Stevie, you will learn that envy equals unhappiness and that if you embrace humility with no expectation of success, accomplishment will come naturally, unfettered by what others say behind your back."

"I'll look forward to that." I gently close his door and hover around Mitch, hoping he'll berate me and not my staff. Helga and Siobhan share BF grievances while eating leftover hashbrowns. Apparently an "acquaintance" messaged Helga and said she just wanted her to know she'd seen Connor being flirty at a party and that she had, in fact, seen him being flirty a few times.

"So I call Connor," Helga says, "and he says, 'What are you talking about,' like, about ten times then says it was a mistake."

"What was?" Siobhan asks.

"His flirtiness. He didn't apologize, just treated it like it was no big deal so I hung up on him. He didn't call or text for, like, three days, so I texted him. He texted back, 'You are the best thing that ever happened to me but I know nothing I say will make any difference.' Meanwhile he's trying to hook up with my friends. He's total garbage."

"Cheaters are literally the worst," Siobhan says, which makes me realize I don't know what the literal worst is, only that it gets worse, literally.

"Why don't you shitgoblins clean this thing properly?" Mitch demands. "Get out the vinegar and elbow grease. There's *piles* of buildup."

"The closers are part-timers," I explain. "Not keen on cleaning. Can you fix it?"

"I got to get parts from my truck." Mitch's van is his getaway vehicle come the apocalypse. He stores gallons of water and a big bag of rice in it and plans, when we're all killing each other over bread crumbs, to head for the hills. He says a man can live for a week on a cup of rice. I open the back door for him. Gyorgi, by the dumpster, hands me his cigarette. We smoke listening to Mitch banging and swearing in his van.

"Man is angry," Gyorgi observes.

"That's just his way. I was scared of him till he told me about his grandson's floppy-eared bunny. It's a nice story, do you want to hear it?"

"Sure."

"A lost baby duck wandered up from the river into Mitch's garage, and his grandson put it in the pen with the floppy-eared bunny to keep warm. The baby duck decided the bunny was its mother and followed it around the garden. When the duck was full grown, Mitch advised his grandson that the duck would be better off joining the other ducks by the river and living like a duck, not a rabbit. The boy tearfully agreed but couldn't bear to separate the floppy-eared bunny and the duck himself, so Mitch took the duck down to the water to paddle around with the other ducks. He tossed bits of bread for them and watched to make sure his duck was being accepted by the other ducks. When Mitch got up to leave, his duck followed him home to the floppy-eared bunny. This went on for days until Mitch took the duck in his van to the river. He tossed the bits of bread as far as he could and watched as his duck and associates all gobbled them up. Then he jumped in his van and drove around the corner, out of sight of the ducks. He got out and peered through the bushes to see if his duck was looking for him. He stayed there twenty minutes but the duck kept chilling with the other ducks." I wait for some sign that Gyorgi has understood my English. He hands me the cigarette.

"Is nice story."

"It just goes to show, sometimes the kindest people have crusty exteriors."

"Like you."

"Not really."

"Sure. You are floppy-eared bunny and little girl is your baby duck." He winks. "Finish cigarette. Me back to work." He holds the door open for cussing Mitch and follows him inside.

I call Maisie. "How is she?"

"Okay. I guess she likes animals 'cause her purse is full of them, all kinds: lions, seals, moose—she's even got a whale in there. She won't let any of the other kids touch them though, does the dom thing then goes all quiet like a turtle. Def a troubled kid. Anyway, quit phoning. We're all right."

Someone taps my shoulder. "Hello, good-looking. Bernardo is here. How you feeling, Miss Stevie?"

"Did I schedule you, Bernardo?"

"I believe so, Miss Stevie." He holds up a mug. "See my zombie mug?"

I check the schedule. "You're not on today, Bernardo."

"That's funny. I thought for sure I was." He holds out his phone. "That's me in Las Vegas in front of the Zombie Apocalypse store. *Zombie Burlesque* is the best show ever, Miss Stevie. You should go, you never take time off."

"When was this shot taken, Bernie?"

"A few weeks ago. Why? I look different?"

"A few weeks ago you were driving school buses to El Salvador."

"To tell the truth, we stopped in Vegas. So many pretty girls. Ay dios mio!"

"You know what, it's actually good you're here because there's cleaning to do."

"Oh not possible, Miss Stevie, my back."

"Kitchen work requires strong backs. If your back's bad, it's not possible for you to do kitchen work and you should go home."

After I set him up with Mitch and a bottle of vinegar, I mix up oil, salt, pepper, paprika and garlic salt then pull the prime rib's mesh and fat cap back and rub the mix in. Tareq's riveted to wrestling on his phone. I wave my hand in front of his face and he glowers at me. "When Mitch says the convection is good to go, unwrap the fat cap and mesh, put it in a pan with water, cover it in foil then bake for two hours. Got it?" Rinkesh, smiling over Tareq's shoulder, says, "Like never tomorrow."

"Towards the end of cooking time," I add, "take the foil off and let the fat cap crisp up. We want it cooked rare to medium rare, then you'll slice it and cook to order on the flaptop grill. Got it?"

Rinkesh nods. "Please and thank you."

I do a stock check, make sure we have what we need for the Yorkshire pudding au jus. The veg delivery doesn't look too rotten. I set up the prep then check back with Mitch and Bernardo. "How's the elbow grease? Will the oven live another day?"

"If the shitgoblins clean it right, it'll last years. They don't make 'em like this anymore. The computer chip ones are shite."

"Can you also take a look at one of the fryers? It's not thumping."

"If it's not thumping I can tell you right now the grease buildup is shutting down the pilot light. There's no flame to catch. You don't smell the gas because the hoods draw it out. Get the shitgoblins to clean it right and it'll work fine."

"Bernardo," I say, "since we don't need you on the line today, stick to cleaning with Mitch."

"But Miss Stevie, my back."

"Mine too, not to mention my knees. Want some Advil?"

"You don't want to be taking those pills, Miss Stevie, they're bad for the liver. My mother, she took all kinds of pills and had to get operated."

I look through the hutch to see if we're done lunch. The zero-carb table is still at it. Can't wait to hear what they order for dessert—apple crumble pie sans crust or crumble.

Siobhan and Olaf are in a spat. "Yo, quit slammin' me, bitch, you need to down low your attitude."

Siobhan jabs his chest. "And you need to get a brain."

Back in my closet, Wade taps urgently on the computer while Daniel fans his face with a menu. "Wade's lovebird ate salted peanuts. He's googling symptoms of dehydration in lovebirds. His roommate's dumb bitch girlfriend fed them to her. Everybody knows you don't feed salty snacks to parrots. Wadesy, you need a nanny cam, then you could keep an eye on Kiwi 24/7."

"If anything happens to her," Wade says, afflicted, "I don't think I can keep doing this shit. Seriously, all the shit I do, I hate it, but then I get home and Kiwi's there preening even though she's blind, and she's so happy once she senses I'm home, it's like none of the shit I do matters because Kiwi's there and she'll sleep in my hand and it'll all be okay."

"Wadesy, are you crying? Don't cry, sweetie. Kiwi's a smart little bird. I'm sure if she feels dehydrated she'll drink the water you left her."

"What if she's too weak?" Wade asks, the words catching in his throat.

"That's it." Daniel flaps his hands. "I'm getting that bitch hussy to let you go home."

"I can't leave. I'm broke. I need the hours."

"Your lovebird is more important than losing a few hours."

I stand in awe not only of Wade's show of feeling but of Daniel's desire to help him. Like a visitor from another planet, I admire the emotions of humans. The child that could be my granddaughter is alone in the world with a broken plastic sword and a pink plastic purse—going all quiet like a turtle—and I feel nothing.

"My legs are tired," she says.

"You're not used to walking?" Her stuffed garbage bag, slung over my shoulder, causes burning pain in my neck.

She stares at her feet in jelly sandals as she walks, her sword bouncing and her pink purse slapping her legs. "Where's my mom?"

"She wants me to look after you for a bit. Then I guess she'll call me. I can't call her because I don't have her number. Do you know her number?"

She shakes her head. "She doesn't hear it anyway if she's sleeping."

"She sleeps a lot?"

"Where are we going?"

"McDonald's. It has a PlayPlace, do you like those?"

"They're okay."

She eats her Happy Meal fries and tucks the free toy in her purse but doesn't touch the burger. I wait for her to hop off her chair and charge into the PlayPlace like Pierce did. McDonald's was balm for my scratchy existence—a safe haven where I could zone out. He'd knock on the glass periodically to make sure I hadn't forgotten him, and I'd look up, jam my face into a grin and wave. Oh happy days.

"Don't you want to play?" I ask.

"Is somebody coming?"

"Who would be coming?"

She lifts the bun off her burger then presses it back on. "I can bug off if somebody's coming."

"Nobody's coming. I just thought you'd want to play."

"Okay."

"Shall I hold on to your purse and your sword?"

"Promise you'll stay here?"

"I promise."

"Promise you won't go for a smoke?"

"I promise."

She tromps into the PlayPlace and disappears up a tunnel. The caffeine-guzzling snake immediately breaks her promise by getting another coffee, all the while keeping an eye on the climbing apparatus.

Assuming that "somebody" in Trudy's world is male, and that Trudy is expected to bug off when one is "coming," along with the fact that she hasn't asked who I am, suggests that the child is accustomed to being handed over to strangers. If Sophie is desperate enough to turn tricks to support her habit, Trudy must be an inconvenience. Yet Sophie is only now deserting her, presumably because Trudy is "getting worse." What will Pierce do when he sees her? Grab gardening shears? Loady loady. Fingers crossed he's still with Tara and Greg dodging goats stuffed with bombs.

Winston Churchill said war is the normal occupation of man. Is it normal for a soldier on a base near Las Vegas to remotely drop a bomb via a drone on a Syrian wedding party he's mistaken for an ISIS think tank?

One night Pierce skipped dessert and walked out of the mess tent to the crashing sound from a rocket's first impact, then heard the long drawn-out whine of the next incoming round. The second rocket streaked past and blasted the kitchen. Amid screams of the wounded, Pierce found his way back to the smoke-filled tent. There was blood, vomit, Red Bull cans, Tim Hortons paper cups, doughnut fragments and muffin wrappers. "I shouldn't have skipped dessert," Pierce said.

"What are you writing?" the princess asks.

"Notes."

"Why?"

"For fun."

"What do you write about?"

"Stuff that happens."

"Are you writing about me?"

"No. Do you want me to?"

"No way." She grabs her samurai sword and scampers back to the PlayPlace, where a gaggle of children scatter as though the bad guy has come to town. A trio of stroller moms look on in dismay.

A face loses colour a minute after a heartbeat stops. Eyes lose their shine after five and look filmy. Eyeballs flatten. The body feels flaccid, like boned prime rib. Pierce told me bodies feel heavier dead than alive.

A few hours later, rigor mortis sets in and the muscles contract. First the face stiffens, then the neck, hands, feet. Pierce used brute force to straighten the bodies out. After forty-eight hours, a corpse loses its stiffness due to bacterial decay.

"Excuse me, are you with that girl?" one of the stroller moms asks, pushing highlighted bangs out of her eyes.

"What girl?"

"The girl in the princess costume. We saw her talking to you."

"Is there a problem?"

"She's very aggressive."

"She's playing."

"She's actually threatening the other kids."

"With a busted and blunt plastic sword?"

"She could poke someone's eye out."

I rap on the glass of the PlayPlace, startling the kids. I point at Trudy then at a poster of a McFlurry and nod, licking my lips. She comes running.

The pumpkin is back on the front steps, cracked and chomped by squirrels, leaking goop. I boot it across the yard.

"What'd you do that for?" Trudy asks.

"So we don't trip over it."

"Who lives here?"

"Me." Jamming a lid on my simmering fear of the soldier, my plan is to act like I bring tiny girls home all the time. It's my apartment, I can do what I like. Let him connect the dots.

"Did my mom phone you yet?" she asks as I fumble with keys.

"Not yet."

The dog clacks across the linoleum.

"A dog!" Trudy squeals, throwing her arms around the hound's neck. I wait for him to bark or growl but he behaves as though it's perfectly normal to have a princess hanging off him.

"Pierce?" I call.

"Who's Pierce?"

He's not here. A cloudburst of relief plops me into a chair while the child engages in dogspeak. He is gone. This is what I wanted. Open space swells around me.

But he has no money, no phone, no clothes. Maybe he can wear Greg's, or Tara's.

"Is this your dog?" Trudy asks.

"Apparently."

"What's his name?"

"Benedict." All I want is brandy, a hot bath and bed. "Trudy, do you have pyjamas?" I try to look in the garbage bag but she snatches it, dragging it across the floor to the dog.

"Okay, *you* find your pyjamas. It's bedtime. Do you have a toothbrush?"

"Where do I sleep?"

"On the couch. I'll get some blankets, unless you want to use the sleeping bag."

"What sleeping bag?"

Pierce's sleeping bag, usually bunched on the couch, is nowhere in sight. Even his garbage bag of crap is gone. I check the bathroom for his toothbrush and comb. Gone. No note, nothing. For some reason this stings.

Trudy drags her garbage bag to the couch. "I won't make noise." She pulls a worn pink teddy from the bag, perches on the couch and holds out her hand. "Come here, Benny." The dog ambles to her and licks her fingers. I pull sheets and a blanket from the hall closet and lay them out for her.

"I'm just around the corner if you need anything."

"What's your name?"

"Stevie."

She draws the blanket around her and the dog.

"Do you want the light on or off?"

"On."

During the spring of 1945, the rape rate for U.S. Army forces in Europe was four times the U.S. civilian rate. Soldiers use rape to terrorize, demoralize, interrogate and infect. More and more I fear that rape is the unspeakable act Pierce committed in Afghanistan. Like father, like son.

Stan used to say, "Don't step into that bear trap." But I did. Do. From my bloodied bear-trap perspective we all feel insignificant and consequently act cruelly, to others and ourselves.

"It is what it is," Stan said about our suffering. He considered his delicate mother greatly wronged until he realized she needed the thug of her husband to feel delicate. "There was a symbiosis between them," he said. "I was outside it."

Which is how I felt about Reggie and Peggy, then Peggy and Pierce, and now Trudy and the dog. There must be a reason why I am the perennial third wheel—some withholding of my worthless self. "Don't get caught up in those weeds," Stan would advise, and he'd be right.

In a few years I'll be menopausal, biologically prepped to be grandma. Wade told me few species other than human live long past their child-bearing years. One exception is the female killer whale, who stops birthing in her thirties or forties but can live into her nineties, acting as a lifelong carer for her offspring, particularly her adult sons.

"Why her adult sons?" I asked.

"Sons need mothering," said Wade, whose mother regularly stocks his fridge.

"What about the daughters?"

"They're busy with their own kids. All adult males have to do is fuck, which isn't a 24/7 gig like raising baby whales."

So here we are, my adult son and his motherless whale daughter in need of care, and me evolutionarily programmed to provide it.

I check on her. She's so small the dog can curl up beside her on the couch. She did not change into pyjamas and has wound a hair tie around the mouth of the plastic bag to keep out inquisitive fingers.

Noah texts me for deets re Wolf's memorial. How comforting that he too is sleepless at whatever o'clock it is, pumping out the poetry while I scribble bilge. I reply, "Meet me at Warden subway at 6:15."

"Coolio," he texts back.

What to wear, something black? Digging around my closet, the paucity of Wolf-worthy garments disheartens. I settle on clean jeans and a boat-necked navy and white striped sweater I bought at a Gap outlet for no reason I can remember. Wolf loved what he called "true navy." "What you need is an elegant, tailored true navy blazer," he told me. We searched what I considered to be outrageously expensive stores until finally locating a true navy, tailored blazer I insisted on paying for and wore twice, both times feeling like a flight attendant.

I study the stripes in the boat-necked sweater. True or false navy?

The princess cries out and I rush to the living room. She quiets but talks gibberish in her sleep. Pierce did this—does this—and I wait it out, too spooked to offer comfort. The dog, startled awake, also watches her warily. In seconds, as with Pierce, the gibberish subsides and she tumbles back into restless slumber. Benedict, suddenly aware that he hasn't shat all day, hobbles towards me. "Now you want me," I whisper. "You have to go in the yard because I can't take you to the park with her here."

Plastic bag and flashlight in hand, I guide him out the front door and linger in the hall, keeping an eye on him while listening for Trudy. After what looks like painful squatting, the dookie is done and I bag it and drop it in the bin at the side of the building. I lead the dog back, tripping over the cracked and gouged pumpkin the Bosnian has placed back on the front stoop. What kind of loco gourd game is she playing? I lift the pumpkin over my head and, with a surprising surge of power, slam it into her weed patch.

NINETEEN

I wake to kitchen sounds: tap running, fridge door opening and closing, ditto drawers and cabinets. Hoping/fearing it is the whale son returned, I roll over and put one foot over the edge of the bed into a saucepan. Pulling it off my foot I call, "Pierce, what's a saucepan doing in my room?" A roaring silence. "Trudy?"

The princess appears, hidden behind purple sunglasses. "I was being quiet."

"You were, it's a small apartment."

"It's bigger than ours."

"Is it?"

"You don't have coffee."

"I do." Mumpish with a today-is-just-more-of-yesterday feeling, I follow her to the kitchen, open the fridge and point to a tin of Maxwell House. "Coffee."

"You don't have it in a jar? I put some in water and cook it in the microwave for my mom. Where's *your* microwave?"

"Don't have one."

"How do you cook?"

"On the stove."

She stares at the stove. "I can't cook with that."

"You don't have to cook."

"Why don't you have a microwave?"

"Radiation." I suspect she doesn't know what this means. "I prefer cooking the old-fashioned way. I see you ate some Shreddies. And washed your bowl and spoon. Good for you." A chair is pushed against the sink, presumably for her to stand on.

She retreats to the dog and couch while I sit at the rickety table, self-consciously spooning All-Bran and checking my phone hoping/fearing for a message from Pierce. Nada. Fuck him.

"Trudy, why did you put a saucepan by my bed?"

"Barf pot."

"Barf pot?"

"For you to barf in."

"Oh."

"It's easier than cleaning it up after."

"Right. Okay, well, I don't barf, so no need for the pot. I'm going to shower. Do you want to bathe or shower? What do you usually do?"

She doesn't respond, pulls a baby doll out of her garbage bag and lays it on the couch. "You stay put," she tells it. "Shut up and don't move. I got stuff to do."

This kid is haunted. Like her father.

She tries to haul her garbage bag to the doggy park.

"It'll be safe here," I say, admiring the pumpkin splatter on the Bosnian's weed patch. "We're coming back here."

Trudy stuffs the scolded baby doll into her Hello Kitty backpack. "Can I hold his leash?"

"Of course."

No canine crotches or asses present themselves to Benedict. Until Esther appears in a doggy jacket, on a leash gripped by Ern Lockraw. I can't breathe for a second, so aghast am I to see Esther in chains.

"What a cute doggy," Trudy exclaims, rushing over to her.

"She's friendly," Ern says as the child strokes Esther's ears. "See, she's saying hi." He unchains the formerly wild beast, who sits demurely while Trudy fondles her.

"Isn't that the dog that went missing?" I ask.

"She sure did, but she's home safe now. She came back to her daddy, didn't you, Esther?"

"How did you find her?"

"Somebody spotted her in Warden Woods, gave me a ding and I hoofed it over there."

"So the dog answered when you called her?"

"It took a fair bit of hollering and her favourite bickies. But she's a good girl, aren't you, Esther, yes you are, you're a good girl."

I stare deeply into the dog's eyes, trying to interpret her silence.

"Esther's a funny name for a dog," Trudy says.

"You think so?" Ern asks. "What would you call her?"

"Sparky."

"Sparky's nice. Maybe that can be her middle name. She sure is sparky."

Esther doesn't look sparky to me, but fed and warm. I try to telepathically offer my assistance should she choose to make a break for freedom again in the spring.

We return Benedict to the dugout and I call Maisie, who agrees to take Trudy. I insist on paying her. Maisie insists on giving me the hugely discounted rate of $20 a day. This I can manage now that I'm no longer buying beer and baloney for the soldier.

"Let's go," I say to Trudy.

"Where?"

"To Maisie's. Where you went yesterday."

"Why can't I stay here?"

"Because you're a small child."

"I'm almost five. My mom lets me stay home alone."

"I'm not your mom."

"I'm taking my stuff." She grabs the garbage bag.

"You don't need your stuff. You're coming back here later. Just take your backpack, purse and sword."

She drags the bag to the front hall.

"Trudy, you don't need to bring that. It'll be here when we get back."

It's as though she has gone deaf. She struggles with the heavy glass door.

"Trudy, leave the bag here. You can't carry it and I'm sore from hauling it around yesterday."

She manages to push the door open a crack and starts to wedge herself through. When I snatch the bag from her, she screams no ordinary scream but a practised high-pitched, eardrum-searing screech that's only interrupted when she gasps for air. Moms and kids on their way to school stare. Gripping Trudy's arm, I pull her inside but the caterwauling doesn't abate.

If I surrender and cart the garbage bag, my neck and shoulder will burn even more and I won't be able to pound chicken. Grabbing and shaking her, I understand how a parent can accidentally kill a child. But not even the shaking has a muting effect. All the emotions she has kept tightly wound since being abandoned unravel in this otherworldly ululation. The Bosnian, in her mini-nightie, scowls from the landing. "I call police!" she yells over the shrieking.

"You hear that, Trudy? Do you want the police to come and take you away?" Instead of quieting the child, the mention of police ups the volume. From my bloodied bear-trap perspective I recognize defeat. Let the cops take over. Let *them* send the princess into the foster care maze of horrors.

Nothing to be done but sit on the stairs and wait for the cruiser. The mutt, initially flummoxed by Trudy's outburst, starts to howl. I block my ears.

But the squalling ends as abruptly as it started because the child scrambles to the dog and puts her arms around him. "It's okay, Benny. Stop crying, Benny," she says over and over, and he does. The two of them remain in a huddle. The resulting quiet feels sacred. I hold very still and savour it.

Not only did Bryan-with-a-*y* unmatch Helga on OkCupid and block her "on everything," so did his GF, Tess Mutch.

"Tis too much of Tess Mutch," Wade said.

"I was just trying to help her," Helga explained re informing Tess that she, Helga, had been to third base with Bryan during their *Ghostbusters* binge. "*I'd* want to know," Helga said. "Like, that's how I found out about Connor. Some people just don't want to face the truth."

This made me ponder the leaky vessel we call truth, and how my truth is different from your truth, and my truth is different from Pierce's. And how Trudy's truth is expanding the margins of my mind with her knowledge of barf pots, "somebodies," and cooking instant coffee in microwaves for her puking mother.

On the upside, Siggy Moretti, Helga's protector with the left hook, has been dazzling her with his black and white photos of ice in a multitude of forms: river ice, cubed ice, shattered ice, black ice, ice storm ice, icicle ice. "He's totally an artist," she told us.

"Your ice prince has come," I said.

"Lick him up before he melts," Daniel advised.

"Just make sure he isn't a minor," Wade cautioned.

"You're garbage."

Kiwi the lovebird has recovered; consequently Wade is back to his overeducated, pothead self.

Desie, iPhone in hand, pushes open my office door. "Stevie, I'm a little pressed. Why aren't the World o' Chicken menus on the tables?"

"Because there is no chicken."

"What do you mean there's no chicken?" Possibly high on dexies, Desmond seems to be vibrating.

"I mean the delivery was missing a few items, like chicken, or anyway, enough chicken to serve up the World o' Chicken menu."

"That's impossible."

"Apparently not."

"The other locations have chicken."

"Aren't they lucky? But then they get first dibs while us burbanites have to make do with crap ice machines and two-hundred-year-old convection ovens."

"Spare me the attitude, Stevie." He slaps his clipboard against his thigh. "Don't get me wrong, I appreciate all the good work you do here but, keep in mind, Corporate is not opposed to sunsetting this location if the numbers don't pick up."

"Did you just use sunset as a verb?"

"You ought to be thinking about how to protect this Chappy's from downside scenarios and mapping out potential upsell opportunities. Corporate expects to see a strong rolling pipeline week to week."

This is unintelligible Corporatespeak. "Des, getting back to the chicken crisis, the reason we do not have sufficient poultry is that head office did not advise the supplier of the scope of the World o' Chicken promo. Pankaj, or Panky as he prefers to be called, was not given adequate time to stock up on fowl, so Corporate's favoured stores scored what Panky had in stock, enabling them to provide worlds of chicken while we, in the burbs, are short a few boxes. Consequently, as the menus hit the dining room, we ran out of bird."

"That may be so, may be so." Desie resumes slapping his clipboard against his thigh then aims his dilated pupils at me. "You see how you do that? You always find an excuse."

"No chicken is not an excuse, Desmond. It's a fact. Head office messed up, and the question only you can answer is, while Panky goes hunting, do you, in your shiny SUV, speed to Costco to buy frozen fowl? Otherwise there will be no World o' Chicken at this Chappy's till Panky comes through."

"Keep in mind that would drive up food costs and drive down your performance metrics."

"Like I said, your choice. We can deliver if you provide the birds." Time for diversion tactics. "Oh, by the way, great news, all the kitchen staff are wearing *It's the Chicken at Chappy's* T-shirts." I distributed them while Bob was in the dining room telling the semi-regular sexy jogging guy about his online course and that accepting the self and others—emphatically—allows everyone to be true to their inner selves.

"No point in wearing the T-shirts if there's no chicken," Desie snipes, thumbing his phone. "Bob tells me the goings-on in your office continue. House staff should not be in your office."

"I don't want them in my office."

"To your point, explain to them in no uncertain terms that their biggest opportunity for enablement is in the area of social selling."

"To what point? Did I have a point? Also, I don't think enablement is a word, Des."

Siobhan, bless her, pokes her head in. "Stevie, Chef's literally flipping out because a customer says she has a deadly allergy to gluten, so nothing she eats can come in contact with any wheat-based products, but Wade saw her eating a dinner roll. Do I tell Chef to go ahead and prepare the order as is or do you want to talk to the customer?"

"Hmm, that's a toughie. What do *you* think, Desmond? As senior management, you might want to take care of it. Or would you prefer I enter the dining room in my dirty whites?"

He contemplates the gravity of this mission. "Leave it with me."

He exits and Siobhan, heaving a drama queen sigh, leans her tush against my desk. "You won't believe what Edvar said to me last night."

I don't respond, not wanting to encourage these disclosure sessions.

"He said, 'We have to talk and it's a bad one.' He told me we can't do this anymore, his heart's not in it, it's not going anywhere and he doesn't want to date." She covers her face with her hands. "I'm literally heartbroken."

"I'm so sorry to hear that." I calculate how many chickens Desie will need to cram into his SUV to last the week, and think maybe he's right about me always finding an excuse—for being a lousy girlfriend, mother, daughter, grandmother.

"He did the classic 'can I give you a hug?'" Siobhan says. "Then he literally packed his stuff and left. Ten minutes later he texts saying he's sorry he hurt me and it's been great spending time with me and he wishes we could be friends."

Wade sneaks in. "Has Darth Vader left the building?"

Siobhan throws up her hands. "We're literally in the middle of a conversation here."

"Pretend I'm not here. If Darth sees me, he'll make me vacuum or something equally debilitating." He squeezes between the wall and filing cabinet to check his phone.

Siobhan wipes her crumbling mascara. "He texted that he confused having fun with me with something more. I texted back I'm literally emotionally confused because things felt like more than just having fun to me. I said I can't fault you for feeling differently but I didn't sense that at all. Then he texts he's going to miss spending time with me. Good night. Like, he literally said good night in a text."

"Iconic," Wade says.

"You're not supposed to be listening."

Wade shrugs. "Dump his Brazilian ass."

"That's easy for you to say, hot stuff, because you don't have meaningful relationships."

Wade makes a cross with his fingers. "Dear Lord, save me from meaningful relationships."

Siobhan sighs again. "I totally want a loving relationship but I'm starting to worry I'll never get one. Stevie, I'm serious, do you think I'm literally too anxious to ever find love?"

This is where I become an ask-hole. "Not at all. It might not be in the way you expect it, or in the timeline you want, but you'll probably find love."

Bob pushes open the door. "*What* is going on here?"

"Oh, Bob," I say. "How fortunate that you're here because we've been discussing meaningful relationships."

"Meaningful relationships?" He looks puzzled, as though the idea of relationships being meaningful is peculiar.

"Yes," I say. "We're worried we're too anxious to ever find love."

"Oh," Bob says, nodding sagely. "Well, if we all take a moment each day to gaze within ourselves and experience the beauty of our *inner* qualities, our love will grow and we won't need to impress others because our love itself will leave an impression."

Wade and Siobhan, silenced, behold our enlightened leader.

"That's really profound," I say. "Guys, sorry to break this up but there's prep to do if we're to fulfil our promise of a culinary world tour of chicken."

After hauling boxes of bell peppers and onions out of the fridge, I instruct Praveen to grill them for appetizers on the chargrill. "Roast them *before* you slice them." My ass vibrates and I assume it's Maisie telling me the haunted kid's gone aggro, but it's a number I don't recognize. "Hello?"

"It's me," Pierce says.

"Where are you?"

"On a pay phone."

"Greg doesn't have a phone?"

"Just Tara's and she left."

"Where did she go?"

"Didn't say. She's scared he'll come after her. Listen, I need money. Did you set me up for the chicken suit?"

"The gig's yours if you want it."

"I'm bringing Greg."

"No, Pierce, that's not happening." I step into the dry storage room for privacy.

"I need him to watch my back. It'll be fine. You won't even know he's there."

"No guns."

"Who the fuck said anything about guns?"

"Just make sure he isn't packing heat. And no PTSD freak-outs."

"He's fine when he's with me. He knows I've got his back. It's just we need food. Like, without Tara, we're running out of supplies."

"Go to the store and buy some."

"We're broke. I just thought maybe you had some leftovers from Chappy's. Sometimes you bring stuff home."

His use of the word "home" confuses me. "Are you coming back?" I ask. "Home I mean? You took all your stuff."

"Shit, I better go before Greg gets suspicious."

"Suspicious of what?" He hangs up. I wait for something to make sense like I do in the dugout when Pierce looks at me without seeing me, or when I talk and he doesn't hear me. Then suddenly he returns from the desert or cratered mountains or the morgue and says, "What just happened?"

Gyorgi opens the door. "You okay?"

"Okay."

"You want cigarette?"

"Please."

He gently places his hand on the small of my back, guiding me into the sunshine. I don't know how to interpret this physical contact, identical to the hand-on-the-small-of-back gesture he used to steer me clear of the speeding truck. Is he being protective, brotherly, fatherly? Do the Roma, like Latin Americans (according to Siobhan), hug and caress the way the rest of us nod hello? Which gets me thinking about meaningful relationships and how I don't have any. Maybe, like Siobhan, I am literally too anxious to ever find love.

We pass the cancer stick back and forth, our fingers making brief, charged contact. In my mind I hear Chet Baker croon about "the gypsy in me," and I think about Chet's blazing talent, heroin addiction and love gone wrong, and it all just seems so pointlessly uphill.

Jesus Christ's son, wearing big glasses that magnify her crazy eyes, traipses towards us, possibly to head-butt me. "If you were a girl I'd have called you Deborah, because that's my mother's name."

I step back. "The son of God married a Deborah?"

"Some choices were inappropriate," Jesus Christ's son admits. "Compromises were made. He is familiar with the situation."

"Would I have been a Deb or Debbie?"

She gives me a lengthy once over, determining my fate as a Deborah.

"I pray to Jesus today," Gyorgi tells her. "And light candle. Was good."

JC's son ogles him before grabbing the day-olds and trudging across the parking lot.

"Her glasses," Gyorgi says, "make her eyes look like sea creatures."

"Trying to escape her face."

Gyorgi smiles and passes me the cigarette. "How is your baby duck?"

"Troubled. I don't know how to talk to her."

"Maybe don't talk."

"Maybe."

"She is smart."

"How do you know?"

"She figure out trick I show her. She watch and figure out."

"She knows how to cook in a microwave. I get the feeling her mother isn't around much. Not conscious anyway."

Gyorgi nods as though this is no surprise, bringing to mind the poverty, cruelty and violence back in Slovakia, and how he—a product of rape—felt lucky to have a mother when other kids didn't. "Maybe she'll talk to *you*," I say. "She seemed to like you. Do you want to come over and hang with her? I have to go out tonight to a memorial, and I need a babysitter. I'll pay you."

"Sure."

Wade says most male birds don't have penises, and female birds have only one functional ovary. Copulation involves contact between their cloacae. They rub their private parts together. Female birds don't produce milk, which means usually there is equal provisioning from both parents. He showed me an ornithologist's vid of a Bermuda petrel's nest. One petrel patiently warmed the egg while the other flew around in search of food. When mom or pop returned, they carefully swapped places over unhatched junior. Equal provisioning—the secret to a better world.

Desie's back at my door. "You got servers in here?"

I close my logbook and look around. "Can't see any."

"You need to make them understand it's showtime out there. They can't go hiding in your office."

"Desmond, house staff aren't my responsibility."

"If they're in your office, they're your responsibility. Show them the task binders."

"Did you decide on what chicken action to take?"

"We're postponing the World o' Chicken menu at this location till the weekend. Panky says you'll have chicken by then."

"Excellent. I have a guy lined up for the chicken suit on Saturday."

"Good, good." He glances at his fancy watch. "I got to be downtown in twenty."

"You'd better hustle then. Don't worry about us."

I close my door behind him.

The thought of Pierce and Greg holed up hungry at Tara's—watching each other's backs, covering windows, blocking doors, checking perimeters—plunges me into disconcerting disconnectedness. I leave my phone on full volume in case he calls.

Afghan parents wrap their dead children in blankets and scarves. Those whose sons patiently stood while being strapped into explosive vests full of metal and ball bearings collect their child's remains in Glad garbage bags.

Conquer pushes open my door. "Olivia wants you to come for dinner."

"Why?"

"She likes you."

"Why?"

"Fuck if I know. What Liv wants, Liv gets. Resistance is futile."

"I can't tonight."

"Why not, you hooking up with the busboy?"

"I am not hooking up with the busboy. And his name is Gyorgi."

"Gyorgeous Gyorgi."

"Go away."

"Listen, we're all for it, didn't know you had it in you. Just don't marry him. They all want Canadian citizenship. So, tomorrow, Liv's. Seven."

"Only if I can bring a child."

"A child?"

"I'm looking after a child, as a favour. A friend's child."

He looks at me in that conquering way of his, no doubt suspecting I'm lying. "Liv loves kids. Seven. Don't be late."

If only, like enlightened Bob, I could discover my inner pathways to success, emphatically accepting my inner self, thereby allowing everyone to be true to their inner selves.

I will buy Trudy chocolate sprinkles and a post-Halloween marked-down princess dress at Walmart. This I can do.

TWENTY

Wolf's friends and relatives murmur in the café's courtyard while wasps, enjoying climate change–induced fall warmth, buzz over the mourners' wine glasses, dessert plates and flavoured lattes. Knocking back little bottles of Perrier, I keep my eyes off the vino while Noah sips camomile tea. Not only does the poet not drink alcohol, he does not drink coffee. How is he alive? He told me he makes fruit smoothies in the morning and, when he needs "a little lift" during the day, drinks a glass of chocolate milk.

Ted Cockpurse, resembling an aging catalogue model, asked me to consider saying a few words about Wolf. "It's open mic," Ted explained. "We're not reminiscing about him in any particular order, just as everyone feels it."

People have been feeling it about Wolf, expressing their devotion in somber tones. Twice, tearful women with smeared makeup, both named Jen, spoke reverently about Wolf's skills as a fitness coach and how knowing they will never again hear Wolf say, "Good job" at the gym causes them sorrow. A man with a paintbrush moustache, in bicycle gear, echoed their sentiments but pointed out that Wolf also excelled at his day job as a financial planner. Popping the mic on "profound," "professional," "proud" and "prophetic," all of which Wolf apparently was, the man with the paintbrush moustache, overcome with emotion, had to walk away from the open mic. The stout South Asian nurse, who was with Wolf at the end, took over and spoke of what "a most kind man" he was, and that "for an example to other patients he was most important."

On what was to be his last night, Wolf asked the nurse, whose name sounded something like Ankledeep, if she could give him something to help him sleep. "Wolfgang knew it was to be his last night," Nurse Ankledeep said. "I could see it in his eyes." What colour were his eyes? Strange that I can't remember.

Nurse Ankledeep said Wolfgang's mother, who had a brain tumour and an appointment with the Grim Reaper herself, only visited him in the hospital once and refused to discuss his impending death. "She would not let him talk of passing," Nurse Ankledeep said, "and this hurt him most hardest. Wolfgang wanted to make things right with her."

His mother was batty long before the tumour tangled her grey matter. Mama Wolf scolded him like a child for doing unseemly things like shacking up with an active alcoholic. Wolf defended me with minimal evidence. I'd hear him on the phone telling her about all the positive changes I'd made. "Steve's a different girl from when you met her, Mother." I didn't feel different, although I wanted to be—one of those androgynous, super-flex fitness instructors who got their carb-loading over by noon and sucked on cucumber slices the rest of the day.

When Wolf expounded about me to his mother and some of the friends currently swatting at wasps in the courtyard, he made me sound reborn. "Many people *say* they want to change," Wolf told them, "but, in reality, they don't want to change. Steve embraces change." He was Dr. Frankenstein and I his monster yearning for love. I coasted along because the current was strong, although keeping house, shopping for organic everything, producing gourmet meals and offering my womb via my ass became exhausting. If we did conceive, how would I muster the energy to look after baby Frankenstein? Each month, when blood stained my under-pants, I acted disappointed but was secretly relieved.

And here, in the courtyard, the acting continues. Nurse Ankledeep tells us that Wolfgang was determined to "have enough of information to finish his work. He had his laptop out and was working for clients on his last day, weak as he was. For an example to us all."

Really? On our last day propped up in hospital beds we're supposed to balance investors' portfolios?

The other mourners murmur agreement. Noah nods even though he never met the guy. Noah nods frequently. When one of the Jens sidles up to him, he nods into her glow. He leans towards people when he listens, as though he really wants to hear what they have to say, and maybe he does. Best to keep my bilious self in the shadows while I try to reconcile the prophetic fitness guru Wolf with the control freak closgay.

The last time I saw Mama Wolf was at his sister's wedding where I was hanging on to the tube dress while my stilettos sank in goat turds. If sister Joy recognizes me, she's not letting on. She's hugely pregnant with child number three.

"Why did you and Wolf break up?" Ted Cockpurse, the ageing catalogue model, enquires.

"Oh. Hmm. Why does anybody *not* break up? Inertia then, blammo blammo, one day you can no longer deny the fact you can't stand each other and off you go on your separate ways."

"That's odd. I think Wolf saw things differently. He told me you were 'the one that got away.'"

I snort, which is inappropriate, but Ted, slurping grog, doesn't seem to notice. "I was with him on his last night," he says, indicating how intimate he was with Wolf, "and he talked about how you two failed to conceive, and how it shook you to the core and broke your hearts. He said he worried you blamed yourself and never fully recovered. He didn't want that for you, he said."

"Didn't want what for me?"

"For you to think you were to blame."

"For what?"

"Your inability to conceive."

"Oh, you mean because he was firing blanks. Gotcha."

How callow of Wolf to share our infertility farce with the catalogue model. How dare he rewrite our domestic dysfunction into a tragic love story.

"Talking truth here," I say, stepping up to the mic intending to explain that, rather than face my femaleness, the guru humped me doggy-style. But Wolf's words of caution stall me. Instead I say, "Did you guys know he weighed himself daily? Maybe that's a thing with fitness buffs but he also kept careful track of *my* weight and wouldn't speak to me if I put on half a pound. He paid meticulous attention to his coiffure, skin and facial hair, which meant he paid meticulous attention to mine. I was waxed in places you don't want to think about."

No one interjects, which spurs me on in my truth-telling mission. "For those of you who remember him as a profound fitness coach and a prophetic financial planner, that's excellent. What *I* remember was a narcissist who spent mucho dinero on clothing, home decor and colognes—big bucks on colognes in his quest for his signature scent, the scent that would fool the world into seeing him as the manly man he wasn't. While fussing over menus, he'd look up when attractive men walked into the resto and not even notice similarly attractive women. Nothing wrong with that except that he kept playing the straight game with clueless damsels like myself. The uncomfortable truth is I was the prophet's beard. The man who coached you in squats was a closet twink, and if that changes your feelings for him you are shallow indeed."

Hugely pregnant sister Joy charges at me using the "bitch" word. I tear out of the courtyard, through the café and onto the street. I have freed Wolf as he could not free himself.

Noah catches up, a little breathless. The boy does not have my kitchen labourer stamina.

"That was interesting," he says.

"Not really."

"You should write about it."

"I already did, maestro. Long after humans have drifted into self-destruction, the new occupiers of spaceship Earth will study my chicken scratch, baffled that anyone could be that stupid." I steam through the subway turnstile and head for the eastbound platform. The poet can barely keep up.

"It's interesting how you enjoy rubbing people the wrong way," he says. "You do it in the writing group as well."

"I don't enjoy rubbing people either way," I say, worrying that maybe I do, that my contrariness is an attention grab.

The display says the next train is coming in five minutes. Conversation is inevitable. I slink onto a bench and try to silence the cacophony in my head.

"Why do you do it then?" he asks.

"What?"

"Upset people."

"I'm tired of lies." This is what Gyorgi said. I tip my head back against the wall and close my eyes because looking at Noah with his man bun and purse, nodding, is too much for me right now.

"Go on," he says, which is what he says in the writing sesh when we're struggling to get words out. The barnacled pause becomes unendurable so I say, "What never ceases to amaze me is how we, or anyway I, come up with rationales for my bad behaviour, or just remain oblivious because that's what humans do best. How else could we do what we do to each other and every living thing on this planet? We shut down our lie detectors so we can march—ignorant—into relationships, jobs, wars. I want to reactivate my lie detector."

"But Wolf didn't. Wolf wanted to be remembered as a straight man. You ruined that for him."

"He won't notice. And if his buds are homophobic, they weren't buds."

All quiet in the dugout except for the usual Bosnian background noise. Gyorgi's asleep on the easy chair, and the princess plus hound occupy the couch. I stand very still, not wanting to disturb them, but Gyorgi opens his eyes and smiles a smile so genuine I'm disarmed and don't know where to look because looking at him makes me pine for a youthful potential I can't remember having, and fear that his youthful potential will soon be trashed.

He nods at Trudy. "She is beautiful."

"Asleep. When she's awake she looks ready to fight."

"Like you."

I put the kettle on for something to do. "How was babysitting?"

"Good. We play cards. She learn fast. I show her to play Concentration. I give her cards for to practise." He points to a deck of cards on the table.

"Did she talk about her mother?"

"She says her mom not like games, not even checkers. Trudy plays checkers. One of her mother's boyfriends have board."

"*One* of her mother's boyfriends. Good lord. Did she eat?"

"She made chocolate sprinkle and butter sandwiches. Was good. How was memorial?"

"Oh the usual. Me pissing people off."

He pulls his head back slightly the way he does when he doesn't quite get what I'm on about.

"It was fine." I hand him a twenty. "Don't refuse. Buy a phone card to call your mother."

He slides the twenty into his jeans but shows no sign of leaving.

"Do you want some Sleepytime tea?" I ask. "It's supposed to help you sleep. It doesn't but who's checking."

"Sure."

I drop bags into cups, hoping he'll say something to indicate he thinks I'm a nice person because Noah, unintentionally, made me feel despicable. Pariah that I am, I like to think my intentions are good while I commit small acts of destruction.

"You are upset," Gyorgi says.

"My stomach's weird."

"Eat something at memorial?"

"Nah. It's being around people. I'm not good at hanging out and talking about whatever people talk about."

"Me also. Not good at hanging out. There is uncomfortable."

"I bet you miss brain research, labs, cutting up mice."

He nods slowly, remembering his glory days. "Is all connected. Your weird stomach and your brain. Can I have a question?"

"Go ahead."

"Was stomach weird before you piss people off?"

"Not sure."

He scrutinizes me like I'm a bug in a jar and he an entomologist. "In study we drop mice in water. They swim in panic then give up and roll on backs to die. We take mice out and feed them human gastrointestinal bacteria in broth. This change GABA stress receptor activity in mouse brain. Now when we drop mice in water they swim calm for many minutes. We take mice out and cut vagus nerve from GI tract to brain. We again feed mice broth and drop them in water. They panic like before. We learn that gastrointestinal bacteria affect nerve message to brain." He taps his temple and abdomen. "Is all connected."

"Did you make mice smoke cigarettes? Lung cancer and cigarettes are connected."

"Want cancer stick?" He smiles again and I feel my facial muscles lifting the old sourpuss expression into a grin.

"Let's do it." I grab the cups. "We'll stay near the window so we can hear if she wakes up."

Sitting on the concrete, leaning against the building, the planet feels steadier.

Gyorgi lights the cancer stick. "A man move in upstairs. Trudy and I walk dog, we come back and man talk to us while men move furniture."

"What's he like?"

"Is cowboy. Has hat. He was run over by Caterpillar tractor, had thirty surgeries. Do you know what is Caterpillar tractor?"

I pull out my phone and google it for him.

"That is big tractor," he observes.

"Yes."

"Also he fall off diving board onto half water, half concrete."

"Can he walk?"

"Is stiff. Also he had bad kind of meningitis."

"There's a good kind?"

Gyorgi shrugs. "There is bacterial or viral. Bacterial cured with antibiotics. Viral, no cure, you wait."

"Which kind did he have?"

"He didn't know, said it was bad and he nearly die, probably viral."

"So he's like a cat with multiple lives."

"There is more."

"You're kidding."

"Cowboy also had whooping cough without cough."

I start giggling, which feels unfamiliar and wonderful. "How can you have whooping cough without the cough?"

"Also he had flesh-eating disease." This gets Gyorgi chuckling, and I'm chortling so much I spill tea. We're sharing a joke no one else finds funny. We are the naughty kids at the back of the class delighting in our shared naughtiness.

"That's terrible," I say. "Why did he tell you all this?"

"He want me to know why he not go to job."

"Ah, another soul on disability. Our absentee landlord prefers permanently injured tenants with guaranteed income."

"Cowboy's name is Chester."

"Can't wait to meet him."

"He does not like communists. He think Slovakia still communist."

"A man up on world politics. Excellent laundry room discourse ahead."

Gyorgi hands me the cigarette. It's uncannily comfortable sitting here with the crappy stucco at our backs and the churning burb before us. Scarborough, the suburb that never sleeps. Somebody's always driving somewhere.

"Chester has rat. White with pink eyes, in big bird cage with different levels for rat to run around."

"I hope you didn't tell him what you do to rodents."

"He didn't have a question for me."

"Did Trudy see the rat?"

"She like it. Her mother not let her have pet. Chester says she can hold Tiberius sometime."

Two cars, with stereos cranked, stop at the light on the corner. The drivers, in testosterone overdrive, yell obscenities at each other and screech off, burning rubber.

Gyorgi takes the cigarette and flicks ash into the Bosnian's weeds. "What happen to pumpkin?"

"I smashed it. I'm hoping for a pumpkin patch."

"Good for racoons. I like this animal. They have no fear."

The quiet between us stretches, soft and warm like a blanket. I'm tempted to rest my head on his shoulder but feel this might be interpreted as a cougar move.

"Can I tell you nice story?" he asks.

"Please."

"My mother find baby pigeon on street. She bring to apartment and feed it water and oats. Pigeon decide my mother is his floppy-eared bunny. He follow her all over building. People call my mother pigeon lady. Pigeon grow big and shit, and people feel hatred to him. My mother worry they hurt Pavol. She ask me to take him to supermarket parking to meet other pigeons. She says if she go, Pavol will follow her home. I take Pavol to meet other pigeons. I throw oats and wait to see he is happy. I leave slowly, look back. He follow me, look at me like this." Gyorgi tilts his head and looks at me sideways. "I say, 'Pavol, you are pigeon, not little boy. You must be with pigeons. Go play with pigeons.' Pavol go like this." Gyorgi blinks several times then nods quickly twice. "Then he go back to pigeons."

"That is a nice story."

"Your little duck will find her way."

"My little duck screams like no creature you've ever heard."

"Why she scream?"

"Because I wouldn't cart her plastic bag of crap around anymore. I told her we were coming back so the bag could stay here. Did she let you look in her plastic bag?"

He shakes his head. "Maybe leave it alone."

"It stinks. Who knows what's breeding in there, probably bedbugs. And the whole apartment is covered in dog hair. It's my day off tomorrow, time for house cleaning."

"Where is your son?"

"He took off with a soldier buddy."

"Because of Trudy?"

"No. Before that."

"Your son look like Trudy."

"He does."

"He is lucky."

"I don't think he'd see it that way."

"You want I help?"

"With what?"

"Cleaning."

"No, why would you do that?"

"For fun." He looks at me, into me. "This is fun, no?" He smiles and winks. I smile and wink back.

"Yeah, this is fun."

It's not beyond the realm of possibility that Sophie is being trafficked. I've heard about "princes," the front men who seek out hapless girls in clubs, befriend them, learn their personal details, where they live, where their families live, then step back and let the traffickers take over. Along with making the girl drug-dependent, the traffickers threaten to kill her family if she doesn't comply. Did one of the "boyfriends" threaten to kill Trudy? Or to sell her as "fresh off the boat"? Did Sophie abandon her daughter out of fear that the child would be raped twenty times a day? This would explain Sophie's directive to Pierce to protect his daughter. If so, the abandonment was an act of self-sacrifice.

Wade showed us a photo of an emaciated polar bear. "They're eating each other because there's no ice to fish from."

I'd grown numb to images of starving polar bears adrift on melting ice flows, but bears eating bears was news to me.

"It would be kinder to euthanize them," Wade said.

He believes, come the apocalypse, the super rich one percent of the world's population will escape on private jets. The roads will be gridlocked with us ninety-nine percent on foot, skateboards, bicycles or in cars and motorbikes running out of gas.

"Where will the super rich go in their private jets?" I asked.

The college grad shrugged.

Daniel gasped. "Oh my god, oh my god, oh my god, what if humans start eating humans?"

The first time Pierce saw a civilian pickup truck with dead bodies piled in its box and blood streaming over the bumper, he threw up. The second time he looked away. The third time he glanced at it. The fourth time he forced himself to stare at the truck, feeling guilty and victimized at the same time. By the fifth time he understood there would always be more dead bodies, truckloads of them.

My phone rings and I answer hoping it's him, but it's Maya the cancer patient. "I didn't know who to call," she says. "It's sort of weird, I know, because we're not exactly friends, but you said to call if I needed anything."

"Of course. I can't sleep anyway. What's up?"

There's a hiccup of a pause then she says, "My husband's been cheating on me."

This doesn't surprise me given her mutilated breasts and chemo brain. "I'm so sorry. Cheaters are the worst." Helga's wisdom.

"I thought he'd just done it the one time because I was in treatment, but today he told our therapist it's been going on all along, for sixteen years—our whole marriage. He didn't look at me when he said it. He just went on about how we married too young and he'd started having sex late because his parents are Armenian and expected him to marry a nice Armenian girl. Then his grad date gave him a blowjob and he couldn't get enough sex, all kinds, he said. And he went into details about the perverted things he does with these women, and I'm crying and feeling sort of sick and he says, 'See, you'd never do any of that. I couldn't get that from you and I wasn't going to force you.' He acted like he was doing me a favour."

"He's garbage," I say.

"He didn't wear a condom with these women because he doesn't like the way it feels. I've always made him wear a condom. Meanwhile he was doing perverted things, *unprotected*, with these women."

"You don't need him, Maya."

"I'm scared to be alone with cancer."

"Being scared to be alone isn't a good reason for putting up with abuse. Where are you?"

"In the basement. Everybody's sleeping."

"Do the kids know anything about this?"

"No. He's a good father, sort of. I mean he loves his kids."

"He can move out and still be a good father."

"We can't afford it. Cancer's expensive. Nobody ever talks about that."
She starts sobbing and I lie back and stare at the cracks in my ceiling
knowing that betrayal is part of life. It's best to get hardened to it, even
expect it.

"*I* was the good Armenian girl," she says. "The virgin, but I didn't want
kids right away. I wanted to finish my thesis. One night he takes me to a
club downtown he used to go to before we were married. The music's really
loud and everybody's drinking and dancing and I just want to fit in, like,
not look like a nerd. So I drink too much and we go home and have sex
without a condom. Next morning I get him to drive me to the pharmacy
for the morning-after pill. I get back in the car, swallow it, and he says,
'Now we can get one more in without a condom.' And you know what's
pathetic? I let him fuck me, right then in the back of the car because I so
badly wanted him to want me."

"I've been there," I say.

"Really?"

"Wanting to be wanted. Getting banged in the back of cars. I did that
last week, actually."

"Really?"

"Yep, 'twas a Volvo, v. classy."

She laughs a little and I feel like maybe I'm helping.

"Who was he?"

"A dude with tats who bought me super-sized Moscow mules."

She laughs more. Never underestimate the curative power of laughter.

"Was he hot?" she asks.

"Nope. It doesn't take much once I'm bombed."

"When I'm bombed sex is sort of strange, like I'm not sure what's
going on."

"I think that's the point."

"Dick always made me have a couple of glasses of wine before sex."

"His name is Dick? Seriously?"

"His parents wanted him to have an Anglo-Saxon name. Richard. Isn't
bombed a strange word for being drunk? I mean, bombs destroy and kill."

"So does booze." Still focused on the cracks in the ceiling, I ponder
how long it will be before the Bosnian comes crashing through in her
mini-nightie.

"I've never been with anyone else. Just Dick."

Not sure what to say here. Do you tell a betrayed wife and mother fighting for her life, in pain, with a concave chest, to go out and get some of what Helga calls "good dick"? "Well," I say, "I've banged busloads and can't say it's been great."

"You're funny. You're different. It's fun talking to you."

This is the second time in three hours someone has used "fun" in reference to yours truly. Look at me go.

TWENTY-ONE

Kitchen noises alert me to the possibility that Trudy's having a snack at 4:23 a.m., or Sophie's traffickers have tracked down the pedo bait, or we're being burglarized. With a headache fracturing my ability to think intelligently, I grab a hairbrush to use as a weapon and stumble into the fluorescent cruelty of the kitchen overhead. Pierce is tossing cans of food into his army-issue backpack.

"Empty the fridge while you're at it," I whisper.

"Why are you whispering? You got the busboy in there?"

"Were you planning to leave a note? Dear Mom, thanks for letting me steal your food."

"It's not stealing."

"What is it then?"

"You're my mother for fucksake."

"Mothers are to be pillaged, are they? Keep it down, Pierce, you don't want to wake the Bosnian."

"Since when do you care about waking the Bosnian? You *do* have the busboy back there." He moves with military stealth to my bedroom. Pushing thumbs into my temples in an effort to squeeze pain out of my skull, I check to make sure Trudy's asleep. Pierce returns, grabs his Shreddies and stuffs them in his pack.

"Where's Greg?" I whisper.

"At the apartment. Why the fuck are you so worried about waking Amina?"

"Does Greg know what you're doing?"

"He took pills, should be okay till I get back."

"Oh, so you only rob at night, when he's asleep. Have you pillaged Reggie and Peggy's yet?"

"No, but thanks for the tip."

I look in my wallet. "All I have is a twenty."

He takes it. "I'll pay it back." He's already at the door.

"Where's Greg's apartment?"

"Birchmount."

"Birchmount's a long street."

"I told you, we don't want anybody coming around. Who's that?"

The princess, ready for a fight, hovers at the edge of the light.

"Trudy," I say.

"What's she doing here?"

"Sleeping. Go back to bed, Trudy."

She stares at him and he stares back. I wait for a bolt of recognition.

"Is my mom with you?" she asks him, grabbing her backpack, sword and garbage bag and dragging it towards the door.

"Trudy, your mom's not with him. This is my son. He just came by to pick up a few things. Go back to bed."

"What's a kid doing here?" Pierce asks.

I could reveal all, but then the progress he's made leaving the dugout, driving Tara's car without crashing it, watching Greg's back, returning to raid my kitchen, resolving to wear the chicken suit, all that progress may dissolve with the news that the waif is his. And Trudy is traumatized enough without being introduced to her dishevelled, thieving, likely rejecting father.

"I'm looking after her," I say. "For a friend."

"What friend? You quit having friends when you quit drinking."

"I'm doing Maisie a favour. My Walmart buddy."

"For how long?"

"What's it to you how long, you need the couch?"

"I want my mom!" Trudy screams. "You're lying! My mom always comes and gets me! You're lying! I want my mom!"

"That'll wake Amina," Pierce says, hooking the backpack over his shoulder and grabbing my All-Bran on the way out.

The caterwauling continues, combined with waterworks until, once again, Benedict begins to howl and the princess rushes to console him. I dash out front to see what direction the soldier took, but he has vanished into the night. Behind me someone clumps down the stairs, probably the Bosnian.

"Everything in order down here?"

I turn to see Chester, the cowboy flattened by a Caterpillar tractor.

"In order? Yes."

"I heard screams." He stands very straight like a marching band leader.

"Night terrors. The child staying with me. She has them."

"Is that so." He looks unconvinced while patting the bulging pockets of his grubby safari vest. "You're sure she's all right?"

"Quite sure."

"I used to walk in my sleep. Urinated in potted plants so I'm told."

"Really? Well, she doesn't sleepwalk, just screams. Sorry about that."

"No need for apologies. As long as she's unharmed." He fiddles with keys on a lanyard around his neck. "I just moved into the penthouse."

"Welcome to paradise."

He laughs slowly, like it hurts. "Lions led by donkeys."

I have no idea what he's referring to, and the grinding in my skull and the pulsing behind my eyelids makes me want to smash my head into the wall.

"Good night." I close the door gently, not wanting to be rude. Trudy and the dog are both conked out on the kitchen floor. I wrap the blanket around them.

The flukiness of it all.

Sexual intercourse occurs, a gazillion sperm squiggle towards the egg, the fittest one scores, two cells collide. And all the stuff in between birth and death feels random. We thrash about trying to find a reason for it, a logic. Why? All the things that happen, or almost happen, or never happen, make us who we are. The delusion of a planned life versus a haphazard one propels us to despair, abusive relationships, alcohol, drugs, prostitution, self-harm, suicide.

Trudy and I could so easily not have been born and yet here we are, mean-faced, distrusting one another, fearful of more upset in our already muddled lives. Our disorderly hearts—mine plastic, hers a twitching muscle—cannot endure more disarray.

Father and child stared at each other but did not recognize their shared DNA, did not see themselves in the other and thereby bond. They are just cells.

Tomorrow I will call Children's Aid.

She stands beside my bed, the worn pink teddy bear hanging from one hand, the pink plastic purse dangling from the other.

"What time is it?" I ask.

"I don't know how to tell time. There's no food. If you give me a purple bill, I'll go get cereal. Or a blue bill. I can buy Froot Loops with a blue bill."

I sit up, check the status of the headache: a little better.

"When *we* have no food," she says, "Yegor gives us money."

"Who's Yegor?"

"One of my mom's boyfriends. He bought me this dress."

"Okay, well, I don't have any boyfriends, but I've got a credit card, so let's go get us some grub."

I don't usually shop at convenience stores, but desperate times call for desperate measures.

"There's no Froot Loops," Trudi observes.

"There's Cheerios. Those are loops too."

She grabs the Cheerios. "Are there yoghurt tubes?"

"I don't know. Why don't you ask the lady?"

She marches up to the cash counter. "Do you have yoghurt tubes?"

The Korean woman, watering orchids in the window, points to an aisle. Trudy tromps down it, finds the tubes then marches back. "Do you have cheese strings?" The woman points to the cooler at the back of the store. Trudy trudges to it, opens the cooler and peruses its contents.

"Get milk for the cereal," I say. "What about orange juice, do you like orange juice?"

The kid doesn't bother to reply but returns to the cash with her carefully selected, heavily processed items. "Do you have granola bars?" she asks. The woman points down the cereal aisle. As Trudy's arms fill with nutrition-free food, she says, "You sure we got money for all this?"

"Yes. What about cheese slices. Do you like grilled cheese?"

"What's grilled cheese?"

Grilled cheese was Pierce's absolute favourite food. "It's a fried cheese sandwich."

"What's fried? You mean like KFC?"

"No, I mean in a frying pan. You fry things in it."

"You mean like KD?"

"You don't fry KD, you just blend the cheese powder and milk with the noodles."

She stares at me with mesmerizing force. "I don't fry."

"Really? Well, then, you're in for a treat. Gyorgi's coming over later. We'll make grilled cheese for him."

Just hearing the gypsy's name shifts her into high gear. She hops up and down. "Can we buy chips for Gyorgi?"

"Of course."

"Is he your boyfriend?"

"No."

"Can we get Dunkaroos for dessert?"

"Sure." Whatever Dunkaroos are.

Back at the dugout she pours Cheerios into a bowl and peels a granola bar like it's a banana. She feeds a chunk of it to the dog. I shower, allowing the water to pummel my skull, hoping to delay the return of the headache.

Clothed, I collapse on the bed, expecting the princess to appear with a demand because that's what children do. But she doesn't and I doze off. She wakes me with a cup of coffee, actually coffee grounds in hot water with milk.

"I stirred it."

"This isn't instant coffee, Trudy. It needs to be brewed. But thank you anyway."

"It's not my fault."

"Nobody said it was. Don't worry about it. I'll make my own coffee."

In a snit, she retreats to what has become her territory: the couch. She's spread her plastic animals across it, each animal tucked under a square of toilet paper. I pull the blue princess dress out of the Walmart bag. "I bought you another princess dress. Actually, I think this is Snow White. Or maybe it's a snow princess dress."

Trudy stares suspiciously at the dress.

"Do you like it?"

"Can I wear it?"

"Of course, here's the thing. I'm going to run a bath for you. You bathe, right? Or do you prefer showering?" She stares at me, her eyes hissing. "After you bathe, you can wear the blue dress and we'll wash the pink one."

"I don't have money for the machines."

"Oh, we don't need money for the machines. We have a laundry room right here in the basement. Do you want to see it?"

She nods, apparently thinking I'm making this up. I lead her out the door and around the corner to the laundry room. "See?"

"Where do you put the loonies in?" She's still gripping her pink teddy.

"You don't need loonies. The machines are free for the people who live here."

Her mouth scrunches as though she's scalded her tongue.

"I was thinking," I say, trying to sound casual, "that we could sort through the stuff in your plastic bag and maybe wash some of it."

"What if my mom comes?"

"She'll wait. It won't take long."

"She hates waiting."

"We'll give her something to eat. Does she like yoghurt tubes and granola bars?"

"She'll get mad."

"Not when she sees us put everything back in a fresh plastic bag. Anyway, let's start with the bath. Then you can put on the blue dress." She follows me to the bathroom and watches me turn on the taps. "You know what's really fun?" I ask, sounding brain damaged. "Playing with yoghurt containers in the bath. They're like boats. I'll see if I have any."

A search through kitchen drawers produces two yoghurt containers. Back in the bathroom she sombrely watches the tub fill. I drop the containers into it.

"Yegor swam with dolphins in Mexico," she says. "He put his hand in their mouths and made them sing and wave their fins. When he put his feet together the dolphins pressed their noses against his feet and pushed him through the water. Yegor says, if I'm good and don't make trouble, he'll take me to Mexico to swim with the dolphins." This sounds like empty trafficker promises.

"How do you think the dolphins feel about Yegor putting his hand in their mouths and his feet on their noses?"

"He made them flip too."

"Really? Well, I don't know about you, but I don't like being made to do anything, especially not flipping if I'm not in the mood."

"You know how to flip?"

"I can somersault. That's kind of like flipping."

"No it's not." She gives me the stink-eye. The dog ambles in and laps bath water. Trudy squeals with delight, reminding me of her father on the rare occasions I delighted him. Seeing Pierce in her pushes slow knives through me. I turn off the tap. "Here's a towel. I'll leave you to it. Call me if you need anything."

I google Children's Aid and stare at the website, leery of its bureaucracy. The site tells me I am "obliged by law" to report child neglect or abuse, but I'm no dolphin and not obliged to do anything. I save the number in my phone and rest my head on my arms on the table like Pierce, remembering him falling off his skateboard, yowling in pain. "Don't be a baby," I told him. He got back on the board with a bleeding knee, leaving a trail of spattered blood I only noticed when I opened my eyes. Tracking the blood, I found him on the pavement, leaning against a newspaper box, salty streaks of dried tears on his cheeks.

"Do you have any Kleenexes?" he asked. Peggy always had Kleenexes in her handbag for runny noses.

"Why would I have Kleenexes? Do you see a handbag? Carry your own Kleenexes."

I tried to walk away but an old woman with a drooping eyelid leaned over him. "He should see a doctor," she said. "The child needs stitches."

"Mind your own fucking business," I told her.

A bus pulled up and the old woman squalled at the driver, "This boy needs a doctor!"

"Come on, Pierce." I grabbed his hand and yanked him to his feet. We never held hands. It felt wrong. We got on the bus.

In Emergency six cops surrounded a psychotic man with a bleeding gash for a mouth. Vitriolic, he lashed out in all directions screaming at his demons. The cops pushed him to the floor and held his hands behind his back. A white coat gave him an injection. In minutes the man was quiet.

"Is he dead?" Pierce asked.

"Not yet."

Back then the goal was to die young. Self-loathing, alcohol and reckless behaviour would kill me. I was counting on it. The burden of my son's need for me was crushing. The rapists lived in him. I couldn't see the boy other people saw. And now the rapists live in the beautiful mean face of his daughter.

"You okay?" Gyorgi, crouching beside my chair, puts his arm around me. "Your door was open."

I turn into him and rest my forehead on the curve between his neck and shoulder.

"What's wrong?" he says into my hair.

I think about the suffering endured by this Romani boy, and the obstacles he has yet to face, and I can't justify blithering on his shoulder.

"I'm just tired. I've got to get Trudy out of the bath."

She's shampooing Benedict's head. The pooch, eyes blissfully closed, rests his jaw on the edge of the tub while she plays hairdresser.

"Wash yours too, Trudy. Do you need help taking out the hair ties?"

She shakes her head but makes no effort to remove the hair ties. The bathwater looks grey. Her hair should be washed with fresh water but I'm not up to fighting her over this. We haven't touched, remain strangers.

"You want I make coffee?" Gyorgi asks.

"Please. Are you hungry? My son took all the real food, but we've got Cheerios, yoghurt tubes and Dunkaroos." I sit at the table and watch the lanky gypsy navigate the tiny kitchen with ease; no doubt he was raised in small spaces. His jeans fit. In a world where men, young and old, wear pants hanging off their asses—revealing their boxers and hairy butt cracks—seeing a slender young man in properly sized jeans feels novel. I try not to stare at his nice ass or the lean muscles moving beneath his T-shirt. He chews a granola bar and smiles, making the old sourpuss smile. "What we clean first?"

"Because Trudy likes you, it will be your job to get her to empty her bag of crap so we can wash whatever's in there."

"Sure."

When he says "sure," it sounds like he means it.

"And her backpack," I add. "I saw her put a stick in there."

"Sticks are good." He offers me a piece of granola bar.

I take it and chew thoughtfully. "Did you know that the male palm cockatoo beats tree branches with a stick to attract females? Look." I pull out my phone and show him the vid of Mr. Palm Cockatoo doing his chick-magnet thing, spreading his black wings while clutching a stick with his foot and banging it into a branch, all the while skilfully displaying his red head plumage.

"Must drive girls crazy," Gyorgi says.

"Totally. Wade says the males develop this stick-banging skill because they live a long time and have nothing better to do than invent ways to impress the girls."

"Lucky girls."

"What I can't figure out is why human males, who also live a long time, don't develop equally impressive skills to get girls."

"They get money. Money gets girls."

"Is that why you don't have a girl?"

He picks up the deck of cards, shuffles then fans the cards. "Pick one."

I pick a card: five of spades.

"Put it back." I do and he resumes shuffling then—surprise, surprise—holds up the five of spades.

"You got me."

He smiles, making me smile.

"You hear that?" he asks.

"What?"

"Trudy singing."

We listen and sure enough she is singing "Twinkle, Twinkle, Little Star," aggressively so it sounds like the stars better fucking twinkle.

"She sounds angry," I say.

"She is angry. Without mother."

"Her mother is a drunk with multiple boyfriends. The one called Yegor says if Trudy is good and doesn't make trouble, he'll take her to Mexico to swim with dolphins."

"Yegor is Russian name. Does Trudy believe Yegor will take her to swim with dolphins?"

"Apparently."

A muscle in Gyorgi's jaw twitches. "There is danger. Don't let her go."

She appears wrapped in a towel, her hair a sodden mop, the dog at her side. "Can I have the blue dress now?"

"Of course." I hand it to her. "I cut the labels off."

"Thank you." It's the first time she's thanked me and it feels undeserved.

"You can change in my room if you like."

"I can't wait to show my mom the dress. Did she call yet?"

"No, but Gyorgi's going to help us with laundry and housecleaning. Then we'll have grilled cheese."

"Grilled cheese!" Gyorgi exclaims as though it is a meal fit for kings.

"And chips," Trudy adds.

He gasps his disbelief at such delicacies. "So good!"

She laughs a tinkly laugh and scoots to the bedroom with the dress. Gyorgi smiles at me, making me smile. We sip coffee. I try to remember feeling this comfortable with someone. I can't remember.

When Ducky calls distraught because Peggy accused her of stealing her purse again, I hustle to the bungalow, leaving the gypsy and the princess to houseclean. Peggy refuses to believe she loses things, insists that "people" steal them. She has never been a victim of a crime, yet her mindscape is swarming with burglars and prowlers. I sit her down at the table. Her cardigan is on backwards. "Peggy, where did you hide your purse? You don't need to hide it. When you hide it, you forget where you hid it and we all have to look for it."

"*She* took it. What's she doing here?"

"Ducky is here to help you. She doesn't want to marry Reggie. She's your personal support worker."

Peggy presses her lips together, indicating that, as usual, I don't know what I'm talking about. "Why don't you colour your hair?" she demands.

She has never approved of my looks, which mirror hers. What she didn't like about herself, she critiqued in me: hair texture and colour, eyebrows, nose, mouth, breasts, waistline, hips, legs, feet. When I turned thirty-six and began sprouting the occasional grey hair, she told me to go to the hair salon that has kept her Hollywood blonde for fifty years. She was a brunette in her wedding photo but soon after started bleaching it because she believed that gentlemen, specifically Reggie, preferred blondes. Judging by the wives Dad groped in our bathroom, hair colour wasn't a priority.

"When did you last have your purse?" I ask her. "Can you remember?"

"A man was in the house."

"Nobody was in the house. The doors are locked, nobody can get in."

"They look in the windows. I close the curtains but that woman keeps opening them."

"Your plants die if they don't get daylight."

This gets her busy overwatering her plants, including the plastic ones. Water spills onto the floor, sure to damage the hardwood. Ducky beckons me into the kitchen.

"What is it?" I ask.

"Someone was here."

"What do you mean?"

"Food is missing. From the fridge. All gone. Even Peggy's pudding cups."

"Are you sure she hasn't stashed things somewhere?"

"I looked everywhere. Even the basement."

"Then it must have been my son. He still has a key." I will kick his ass. "Peggy, did you see the man who took your purse?"

"*She* took it."

"No, Pierce came by and took some food last night. He's looking after a friend and needed some food and money. Did you see him?"

"Who?"

"Pierce. Your grandson."

"My grandson is a soldier."

"He was a soldier. Now he's back from the war."

"You've always been jealous of him."

"Did you see anybody last night?"

"Who?"

"Who might have taken your purse?"

"*She* took it."

"Ducky didn't take it. It was Pierce." I pull the chair out from Reggie's desk and find the purse on it with the forty dollars I give Peggy weekly still in it. She snatches the purse from me.

"Our grandson would never steal. He's a good boy. A soldier."

My credit card restocks their fridge and cupboards. While helping Ducky with Reggie's diaper, I learn that her sister's place in the Philippines slid down a hillside during an earthquake.

"I didn't hear about an earthquake in the Philippines," I say.

"The small ones don't make news."

Reggie, surprisingly compliant, murmurs quietly to himself as we fit him into his track pants.

"My sister needs me to send more money. Can you give me more hours?"

"Of course," I say, knowing I can't afford it. "Is your daughter okay?"

"They're staying with my cousin, five to a room. Angel doesn't like sleeping with the boys but there is nowhere else." Her closed expression reveals nothing about what "sleeping with the boys" entails, but we all know most child molesters are family.

"Work as many hours as you want."

I stop in Warden Woods and sit on my mossy stump to recharge before facing Trudy's menace. In love with Gyorgi, she'll resent me interrupting their activities. A hint of frost in the air suggests we'll have winter even if the polar bears don't. Sparrows sing and hop about. Wade says sparrows are lusty birds and frequently practice rubbing their cloacae. In spring, when the male sparrows' testicles descend, they repeatedly hop on female sparrows, causing a mix-up of eggs in the nests. Male sparrows can be serial monogamists, nesting with several females in succession, or bigamists, mating with two females at once. Sometimes females nest with their sons, then cheat on them with a neighbour. Infanticide is common. Sometimes a male who loses his mate will fly into another nest, peck the nestlings to death and mate with the female. Or he'll have two nests, one with a primary partner, whose nestlings he'll feed, and another with a secondary female he ignores. The spurned secondary female pecks the babies of the primary female to death, forcing the male to help raise her nestlings. They may sound and look pretty but sparrows are as violent and dysfunctional as the rest of us.

TWENTY-TWO

Approaching the dugout I am shamefully grateful to the unnewsworthy earthquake for ensuring that Ducky cannot leave us. How sparrow-minded of me.

The prince and princess are cleaning the kitchen. She stands on a chair wiping the counter with a J-cloth. Her wiry hair, freed of pigtails, has dried into an impressive fro. Gyorgi, on his hands and knees, scrubs the linoleum. They're singing "The Wheels on the Bus." I stand, agog, until Trudy notices me and stops singing. She drops her hands to her sides and stares at the floor as though expecting to be scolded.

"Guys," I say, "this is way beyond the call of duty."

"Yegor plays that," Trudy says.

"No, I mean, you don't have to clean so thoroughly."

"We like to clean," Gyorgi says.

"Nobody likes to clean, especially not other people's dirt."

"Look what we find in Trudy's backpack. All kinds of cool stuff." Spread on the kitchen counter are sticks, pebbles, remnants of sidewalk chalk, a skipping rope, dirty gummy bears, a Disney princess sippy cup, some pink ribbon, two plastic dinosaurs, a teething ring, a pony squeaky toy and some odd buttons. Trudy is a hoarder.

"Nice," I say.

Gyorgi squeezes the pony. "Trudy teach me new word. Squeaky. And cool song about bus."

"How 'bout the garbage bag of stuff?"

"After grilled cheese and Dunkaroos. *You* make grilled cheese. *We* have break. Right, Trudy?"

"Can we play War?"

"Sure. After we put your stuff in backpack."

War seems to be about having higher cards than the other guy till you've acquired the entire pack. Trudy bounces on her chair and swings her legs each time she scores one of Gyorgi's cards. He has taught her the value of jacks, queens, kings and aces. She is scarily competitive. Pierce had tantrums when he lost at Go Fish which I only played under duress when seeking booze and shelter in the bungalow.

The mail's arrived, oh joy, my Visa bill. I note the amount of credit left and start on the grilled cheese sandwiches. "When do you have to be at work?"

"Five."

"Siobhan has you on nights now?" She wants my hands off her busboy.

"Somebody's sick. Tomorrow I do double."

"That's illegal."

"I am illegal." He smiles at me, making me smile, which is preposterous given the precariousness of his situation. His student visa ran out months ago.

"I win!" Trudy announces.

Gyorgi clutches his chest as though she's shot him then says, "Want to help Stevie put out plates and chips?"

She hops off her chair and drags it to the cabinets, where she finds plates and a bowl for the chips. She knows my kitchen better than I do.

"You want coffee?" Gyorgi asks. He reaches around me for the pot and I resist an urge to fold into him.

"Bob showed me this exercise," he says, stepping back and, coffee pot in hand, swimming like bear in ocean. "Is good. Bob says qigong is helping him forgive his mother."

"He mentioned his mother?" Bob never mentions his mother.

"She want him to be straight and give her grandchild."

"Why did he tell you that?"

"Why not?"

"It's a little personal."

"I'm not understanding."

"It's private. Not something you want strangers to know about."

"What?"

"That your mother doesn't want you to be gay. That's personal."

"Maybe he need to tell someone. Even stranger." He spoons coffee into the filter basket and I conclude that Bob confiding his gay struggles to Gyorgi means that Gyorgi's gay, which explains the earring, his good personal hygiene, properly sized jeans, discomfort while being mauled by the pussycat at the Halloween party and evasion of my question about a girlfriend. That gentle laying of hands on the small of my back was a bro touch. My gaydar was obscured by the red mist of my lust. Go me for having feels for another queer. Ah well, I'm too old for sparrow behaviour. I serve up the cheese and grease and the dugout feels, what exactly? Cozy.

After we've made the place shipshape and laundered Trudy's dirty clothes, the gypsy leaves for work. The princess and I stare warily at each other—two castaways on an island.

"Epictetus was born a slave," Liv tells us. "Around 55 A.D. in Hierapolis."

"Wherever that is," Perry Meeker, my Moscow mule provider, says.

When I asked Conquer why Liv invited the dog man he said it was because Perry mixes a superb dry martini. "Olivia rarely drinks these days, but when she does, look out."

Liv and the Loretta groupie have already enjoyed a couple of martinis while exchanging doggy death stories so it makes sense they'd move on to ancient philosophers.

"Pamukkale," Liv explains. "In Turkey."

"Gosh, don't you just love their rugs?" Perry says. "But très pricey."

"Epictetus said," Liv elaborates, weighting each syllable equally, "some things are in our control and others not."

Conquer helps himself to scalloped potatoes. "You don't have to be dead for two thousand years to figure that out."

"Bah."

The snow princess has a wiggly tooth and keeps pushing at it with her tongue. She hasn't said much since having another screamfest on leaving the dugout because her mom might show up and find her gone. We left a Post-it on the door with my number on it.

Liv jabs her fork in the air for emphasis. "Epictetus said the only thing we can totally control, and the only thing we should ever worry about, is our own judgment about what's *good*."

"I don't get that," Perry says. "I mean how are we supposed to know what is good? Like, did he offer some guidelines?"

"If we hunger after money, sex or fame, we are destined to be unhappy. If we fear poverty, sickness and obscurity, we will live in constant anxiety and frustration."

"We do that anyway," Conquer says. "Pass the peas."

"Personally," Perry says, "I think fear and hungering after things is unavoidable. I mean, if you're human."

"Or a sparrow," I add.

"We all have moments of dread or anticipation," Liv concedes. "Being a stoic means questioning those moments—asking if they apply to things out of your control and, if they do, saying to yourself, 'It's out of my control, no point worrying about it.'"

"But how do you *know* it's out of your control?" Perry asks. "I mean, you always think maybe you *could* control it if you did things differently, or better, I mean."

Trudy pokes her tongue in and out of the gap beside the wiggly tooth. She hasn't touched her vegetables.

"According to Epictetus," Liv continues, "a true stoic will endure flesh wounds, broken bones, suffer losses and humiliations, but he will view each setback as an opportunity for learning and glory."

"Cool trick," Conquer says.

Liv waves her napkin dismissively. "The stoic relishes adversity."

I wonder if getting Trudy to eat some vegetables is beyond my control. Then I wonder why I care.

Ready for a refill, Liv hands her martini glass to Perry. "Epictetus said it starts with the little things that aren't worth much to you, like a bit of spilled oil here, a little stolen wine there. Instead of becoming outraged by these little things, you repeat to yourself, 'For such a small price, I buy tranquillity.' His point is that it's not events that disturb people, it's their *judgments* about them."

"Kind of like don't sweat the small stuff," Perry says.

I pry my eyes off the bottle of gin in his hand. "That's if you can figure out what the small stuff is."

"I hear you," Perry agrees. "Like, a lot of times you don't realize it's small stuff till it's over. I was furious with Mr. Oliver when he figured out how to open my kitchen drawers and promptly chewed the wooden handles on my steak knives. I was so mad, I put him on the balcony for three hours. He kept looking in the window and whining and barking but I just ignored him. Then later I thought, golly, I don't even like those knives. The varnish comes off the wood, which is unhygienic. Ollie actually did me a favour by forcing me to buy a new set. But I didn't realize that at the time. Meanwhile my poor baby was out in the cold for three hours."

"Having ingested the varnish," I say.

"So you made the wrong judgment," Liv sums up. "If you'd made the *right* judgment you would have been spared all that outrage, and Ollie wouldn't have suffered."

"Oh dear. Now I feel terrible."

"Bah, you're doing it again, choosing to feel terrible about something you can do nothing about, something that's past. Quit wasting time and energy and smarten up."

"Amen," Conquer says.

Her stoicism must be what enables Liv to go on despite the loss of her daughter, her husband and her mobility. She judged those events out of her control and saw no point in fretting about them. Tragic loss freed her from the chattels of attachment.

Conquer and I do the dishes while Liv kneels on the living room floor playing tiddlywinks with Trudy. Perry searches Liv's record collection for a Tammy Wynette album Liv thinks she might have bought last century.

Conquer squirts dish soap into the sink. "So, how's crushing on the busboy going?"

"It's not. He's gay."

"Who says?"

"Me."

"How do you know, did you ask him?"

"That's not something you ask."

"Why not? Just say something like, 'Which way do you swing?'"

"Is that how you did it in the nineties?"

"He doesn't look gay to me."

"How does gay look in your world?"

"It's a vibe."

"Ah, yes. A vibe."

"He's always watching you."

"That's because he's afraid I'm going to fire him."

Conquer stops washing dishes and faces me. "I get it. You don't want him to be straight."

"Why wouldn't I want him to be straight?"

"Because then you'd have to make a move."

"I don't have to do anything, and why are you so interested?"

Conquer rinses pans and stacks them in the rack. "Just curious to see if the busboy can go where no man has gone."

"Plenty have gone there, hard-on, just not you."

"And why is that? I'm pretty, I'm nice, I've got a boat, I put fruit in pitcher pockets."

Good question. Because Conquer *is* attractive in a craggy kind of way, certainly hotter than Bartholomew. Especially when he's scrubbing his aunt's pans and making sure she doesn't fall and driving her to the community centre for tai chi. There is something essentially decent about Conquer, and I'm feeling essentially unsexy due to my misreading of Gyorgi's bro touches. A roll in the boat with Billy might reboot the old self-esteem. But first, step back and be stoic about it. Consider the motherless child with the hissing eyes. What is the right judgment given that she is the grandchild of a rapist and completely dependent on Grandma Whale at this point?

"You're thinking about it," Conquer says.

"What?"

"Sleeping with me."

"Not exactly. Can I ask you a personal question?"

"I've got condoms."

"Congrats. Actually, I was wondering if you've ever been in a situation that got a little weird, and you found yourself forcing yourself on a woman."

"You mean date rape?"

"Something like that."

He makes a spitting sound without spitting.

"Seriously," I persist, "we've all been in situations where we've been floundering around on a couch. A part of us is up for the approaching act, the other part a bit ambivalent, but we keep going because it's expected and easier than stopping the procedure, plus guys can turn vicious when girls put the brakes on." I hold up a stack of dried plates. "Where do these go?" He points to a cabinet. I open it and slide the plates onto a shelf. "Speaking from personal experience, I've gone along with it because, well, I was too drunk to really care. But sometimes the guy starts getting aggressive and countering my 'I'm not really into this' with *Fifty Shades of Grey* talk and I realize if it comes to a fight he'll win so we might as well get it over with. Have you ever been in that situation?"

"In my world no means no. Even back in the nineties."

"But what if the woman is too scared to say no? And the guy's not really listening because his boner's about to explode, so he forces himself on her, only he doesn't see it that way because at first it seemed like she wanted it—I mean she got on the couch with him, so she must have wanted it. Getting back to Epictetus, the woman's judgment of the act would be different from the man's. She may see the situation as beyond her control and go all stoic about it. Meanwhile the man gets his rocks off and doesn't see his act as rape. As far as he's concerned, he made the right judgment."

Conquer leans on the counter and stares at me. "What is this about?"

"What?"

"Is this about the kid in there?"

"What do you mean?"

"Were you raped? Is she yours?"

"No. God no."

"She looks like you."

"She's Black."

"Half Black." His piercing blues skewer me and I'm tired of lies.

"She's my son's."

"Does he know?"

I shake my head.

"You going to tell him?"

I shrug. "He saw the child once but didn't twig. He took off yesterday to help a war buddy. I'm scared he raped her."

"Who?"

"Trudy's mother."

"What makes you think he raped her?"

"It's a hunch."

"Okay, that's fucked up."

"I don't necessarily mean *rape* rape, I mean the kind of rape I was just describing, that doesn't seem like rape until you look back on it and go, yeah, I really didn't want that. She said she emailed Pierce and he never replied. He never replied to my emails either, maybe he quit checking. He was so messed up by what he saw over there, civvy concerns seemed trivial. Anyway, between tours he never mentioned her."

"Doesn't mean he raped her."

Tammy Wynette croons "Stand by Your Man" and the wolfwoman

howls along. The snow princess appears in the doorway. "Liv says there's ice cream."

"Sure thing." Conquer opens the freezer. "Strawberry okay?"

Trudy nods. My phone vibrates. It's a local number. "Hello?"

"It's me."

"Where are you?"

"Home. Why aren't you here?"

"Pierce, you can't steal more food, I've got a kid to feed."

"I'm just borrowing soap and shampoo and shit. Tara took everything with her."

I duck into the bathroom for privacy. "If you steal from Reggie and Peggy again, you will make things so much worse. Please leave them alone. They're demented, robbing them makes them even more demented."

"Peggy said it was okay. Or anyway, she didn't stop me. She was talking about umbrellas for some reason."

"She didn't recognize you. She thought you were a burglar."

"No way. She knew who I was."

"Did she say your name?" I hear cars zooming in the background. He's calling from another pay phone. "Pierce, did she say your name?"

"No." He sounds disappointed.

"She thinks you're still a soldier in a war."

"Where are you, I hear music. Are you in a bar?"

"Why do you always think I'm in a bar?"

"Because you always are, or anyway, used to be. Are you with the busboy?"

"What's it to you?"

"He looks younger than me."

"You look older than you. Are you drinking?"

"I gotta go, just be at Chappy's on Saturday with the chicken suit. No way I'm going inside the restaurant. I'll put it on in the parking lot. 11 a.m. You won't see Greg but he'll be there."

"Does that mean he'll be in camouflage peering out of a dumpster with an assault rifle?"

"Just don't look for him. He doesn't want to be seen." He hangs up.

In the living room they're spooning ice cream and listening to Tammy sing about standing by your man when he's a jerk because he doesn't really mean it. I sit beside Liv on the couch and she pats my knee.

Perry drives us home, insisting the martinis he made for himself were half-strength. "It's an old bartender trick—look like you're imbibing so the drunks don't feel they're drinking alone." He nods at Trudy in the backseat. "She really should be in a booster."

His car smells of dog.

"Did I tell you what Miss Emmy did with cocktail weenies? We were at my cousin Hugo's. Oh my gosh, Hugo goes bananas over cocktail weenies, lord knows why. So he puts them out and we start watching *Scandal*, totally forgetting about the weenies. Well, guess who tossed them all over Hugo's condo? She didn't eat them, just *distributed* them. She does the same thing with olives. She herds them. Emm *herded* the weenies."

"What's herded?" Trudy asks.

"What shepherds do with sheep. So now Mr. Oliver's got stomach flu from Hugo's cat. The poor pup projectile vomited over my entire living room. Hugo's cat is always sick. The vet bills are astronomical. He got a parking ticket outside the vet's. I swear the ticket guys trawl around knowing we're in there with our babies. I keep telling Hugo to feed Felix raw, natural meals with no preservatives, grains, fillers or added water. That's all I feed Ollie and Emm and they never get sick."

Abruptly, the ride is over and it's time to get out of the car. I don't want to. I need Perry to fill the tetchy silences between the snow princess and me.

As soon as we're inside she looks for her mother. "Sometimes she leaves a note," she says.

"Well, she doesn't have a key to my place so she'd have to leave it in the mailbox."

"Can we look there?"

"Sure." My "sure" doesn't sound sincere like Gyorgi's. I unlock the box and lift her to see in it. She reaches in and feels around.

"I have to put you down, Trudy. My back hurts." She keeps groping in the box. When I put her down she drops her arms to her sides and stares at her jelly sandals.

"Did you check your messages?" she asks.

"I'll check them now." There are no messages but I hold the phone to her ear so she can hear for herself. Her strained bitch face remains unchanged.

"Okay," I say. "Bedtime. I bought you a pink toothbrush. Do you want to see it?"

She nods and follows me to the bathroom. I tear the wrapping off the brush, squeeze toothpaste on it and hand it to her.

"I need a chair." She drags a chair in from the kitchen and stands on it at the sink. I leave to give her some privacy. The dog regains consciousness and looks in my general direction. "Do you need to go wee-wee?" I ask him, grabbing the flashlight. In the front hall I listen for Trudy while keeping an eye on the mutt and call Jesús to check up on him. He's excited because a childhood friend found him on Facebook. "I thought for sure he was dead," Jesús says. "He made trouble in prison, like spitting at the guards, so they put him in solitary. Paco said the way he grew up, with all the gang violence, he was ice cold inside and hard-wired for solitary. He didn't miss nobody in there because he had nobody to miss. After getting out and being clean five years, he started thinking about a guy he met apple picking. They'd both done time and hung out together because they couldn't talk to none of the other pickers about prison. So yesterday Paco called the guy to ask how he was doing and, afterwards, Paco was like, 'Whoa, that was my first selfless thought. This must be what real people do when they miss somebody.'"

What real people do.

"I gotta go," Jesús says. "Rosa's here."

I guide the dog back inside. Trudy's on the couch with the blanket pulled over her head. Benedict hauls himself up beside her. She covers them both with the blanket.

"Good night," I say, ice cold inside and hard-wired for solitary.

TWENTY-THREE

Orchid subtribes require euglossine bees, and the bees require specific orchids. A male bee, attracted to the orchid by the smell of the substances he needs to manufacture his perfumes for mating, lands on the orchid bucket and scrapes the substances into pockets in his hind legs, but the orchid bucket's rim is slippery. Mr. Bee falls into the bucket and nearly drowns before spying a bee-sized hole in the side of the bucket. Carefully designed "stepping stones" in the bucket guide Mr. Bee to the hole. He tries to squeeze through but it's a tight fit, giving the orchid's jaws time to contract and trap the bee, ensuring that two pollinia are glued onto Mr. Bee's back. Once the glue is set, the orchid's jaws loosen and off the stud goes to land on a female orchid. The trapping and gluing process repeats, only this time the pollinia are scraped off to fertilize the stigma of the female orchid.

You'd think Mr. Bee would be traumatized by his near-death experience and avoid orchids. But, no, off he buzzes to repeat the entire process to procure eau de cologne to attract the girls, like humans repeatedly step into the lust trap or some other addiction, like money, like power, like war.

It's not screeching I hear but plaintive cries interspersed with whimpers. Approaching the couch with caution, I note that even the dog looks perplexed. We both stare at the child rocking from side to side, bumping Benedict, who shifts away from her. I sit on the easy chair waiting for whatever it is to pass but it doesn't, and Trudy begins to cry for Mama. Self-consuming rage percolates inside me. How could Sophie desert her child with no explanation, no warning, no hope? Oh wait. I did this.

"Where's Mama?" the child cries. "I want Mama!"

Benedict slides off the couch and clacks my way as though expecting me to do something. What? He sits at my feet and we both watch the tornado of desolation. Trudy's eyes remain closed, which suggests she is asleep. Does this mean it's okay to do nothing? Count. I did this when Pierce called after me as I was walking away from the bungalow. One, two, three. His pleas would become less frequent, and I'd hear Peggy consoling him.

A new outburst of Trudy cries for Mama coming from deep within and spinning outward with alarming force. In moments the Bosnian and Chester the rat tamer will descend and make threats. One, two, three. "Where's Mama? I want Mama!" She starts to tear at her hair. This is too much. I charge to the couch, pull her onto my lap and wrap my arms around her, not with affection but to restrain her bucking body. She head-butts, kicks and jabs. I try to square breathe—something Wolf taught me. You picture a square and breathe to the corners, counting to four during each breath. My ribcage expands into her tiny one and I think of Vikings wearing their dead mothers' ribs in their hair to protect them in battle. My ribs move rhythmically while Trudy's jerk and twitch. She smells of my shampoo, like Gyorgi. The three of us, scorched and wronged, are walking around smelling of active fruit ingredients. I picture active fruit playing tennis, jogging; a banana does a downward dog while I square breathe into Trudy's jagged sobs. I will not let go.

Then her ribs begin to move more steadily against mine, and her wails become mewls. The dog rests his chin on her lap and suddenly Trudy's laughing a fizzing, hooting laugh, stroking his head and ruffling his ears. I expect her to realize I'm not Mama and pull away, but she seems oblivious to me while kissing the dog and garbling dogspeak. Then, just as suddenly, she goes limp. I hold still, not knowing what to do. A Chappy's regular's athletic fifteen-year-old daughter died in her sleep. Seemingly healthy children can die unexpectedly. Maybe this wouldn't be so bad for Trudy, drawing her last breath while sharing affection with the pooch. He continues to nuzzle her and wag his tail while Bosnian background noise punctures the still air around us. Square breathe. Don't fret. The child feels warm and light, not heavy and cold like the dead that Pierce handled.

She was talking to the TV earlier, or the actors on TV. "You'd better get out," she told them, "or you're going to get in trouble." Later she warned the TV it better be quiet or "she'll get mad." Whoever "she" is. Presumably me as Mom's not around.

Her head rolls to one side but her breathing's steady. I ease her onto the couch and cover her with the blanket.

Brushing my teeth, I blink at Grandma Whale in the mirror. Usually mirrors are to be avoided because what's revealed is discouraging, but now I peer into Grandma's faded eyes, her face swollen with unexpressed emotion. She's been bashed by boats, gouged by propellers, tormented by man-made sonar, poisoned by his pollution, choked by his plastics, trapped in his dragnets and yet here she is grandmothering the only way she knows how, despite yearning to swim away from it all.

Sitting on the toilet, grief tugs at me. Not sure what for. Who I might have been had I not bought raspberry dazzle lip gloss that day, had I not walked across the mall parking lot but kept to the sidewalk far from the dumpsters, and worn baggy jeans instead of a spaghetti-strapped summer dress. I tried to ignore the foursome's catcalling and lewd comments because that's what girls do, walk on pretending to be unafraid while fear stiffens their gait.

I swallow three Advil and four back pills hoping the muscle relaxant will knock me out. Self-pity rises like sap, and my many wrong judgments circle. As my joints erode and my hair greys, the circles will get smaller and smaller, ending in death. Why bother?

Sensing Trudy standing beside my bed, I keep my eyes closed because I'm not ready for more of yesterday.

"Here's your cereal," she says.

"Thanks, but you don't have to bring me things."

"My mom always has cereal in bed."

"Well, I'm not your mom."

"Did you check your messages?"

"I just woke up."

"Can you check?" She hands me the phone.

"It's dead. We'll check later."

Her face registers nothing. The kid is skilled at not reacting. Whatever happened last night has left no crack in the mortar between us. Maybe experience has taught her that offering cereal, coffee and barf pots to Mommy will prevent Mommy from snapping at her. Maybe the child takes to men and dogs because women, in her experience, are unpredictable and lash out.

"Your shoes are on backwards," I tell her. She must have pulled the beat-up runners from her garbage bag. They look like boy's shoes, black and blue hand-me-downs that clash with Trudy's frilly pink socks.

"Those look a little big," I say. "Maybe you should tie them tighter."

"I don't know how to tie laces." She looks fiercely at the shoes.

"Do you want me to show you how? Or re-tie them for you?"

She's still holding the cereal that must be soggy by now. "Can we check the mailbox?"

"When we come home. The mail doesn't come until the afternoon."

"Where are we going?"

I take the bowl and spoon All-Bran mush into my mouth to please her. "I'm going to work. You're going to Maisie's."

"Do I have to? I could stay here. I won't make noise."

"Trudy, you're too young to be left alone. I know your mom allows it but it's not okay in my book."

"What book?"

"Why don't you like Maisie's? There are other kids there, toys, snacks, TV. Why don't you want to go there?"

Her arms drop to her sides and she stares at the oversized shoes.

"Is it something the other kids said? Are they bullying you?"

She shakes her head.

"Okay, well, I've got to get ready for work. If you switch your shoes, I can tighten your laces."

She bends down and pulls at the laces, making knots. "It bugs me when I want to play by myself and they want to play with me."

"Just tell them you want to play by yourself. I tell people that all the time."

"What people?"

"People who want to play with me."

"Who wants to play with you?"

Good question. "Not play, exactly. But at work sometimes people come into my office when I don't want them to and I ask them to leave."

"Do they go away?"

"Sometimes."

"Not all the time."

"No."

She pokes her tongue in and out of the gap beside the wiggly tooth.

"How much does the tooth fairy give you for your teeth?" I ask.

"There is no tooth fairy. I only get money if Yegor's there. He gives me a toonie."

"Okay, how 'bout I give you a toonie?"

"When?"

"When your tooth comes out."

She looks straight at me. "Then can we go to Dollarama?"

"Of course."

Her shoulders lift slightly at the prospect of spending a toonie at Dollarama. She takes my half-eaten All-Bran to the kitchen. I hear her drag the chair over to the sink to wash the bowl. "Switch your shoes," I call after her.

A knock on the door causes her to hop off the chair and scramble to open it, no doubt expecting Mama.

"Hello, little lady." It's Chester.

"Hello."

"Everything okay down here?"

"Okay."

Cinching my bathrobe closed, I join them. "Good morning, Chester. What's up?"

"Well, I heard some commotion down here and wanted to make sure nothing untoward had occurred."

"Nothing untoward. As I explained, the child has night terrors."

"Fair enough." He fiddles with the keys on his lanyard. "Is that likely to happen nightly?"

"I can't say." His boots are unlaced. Maybe he got run over by a Caterpillar tractor because he tripped over his laces.

"I left my old place due to howling sled dogs."

Trudy sits on the floor to switch her shoes. "What kind of dogs?"

"Dogs that pull sleds. Dogs accustomed to the wilds. They were abused, ergo they howled all night long. When I complained to the owner, he threw beer bottles over the fence."

"I'm sorry to hear that, but Trudy doesn't howl all night long. It's a stage she's going through, and your understanding would be greatly appreciated."

He pulls a hanky from his safari vest pocket and polishes his glasses. What Gyorgi described as Chester's cowboy hat is a Tilley hat, wide-rimmed and sweat-stained. "My ex-father-in-law," he says, "was a herpetologist, kept all kinds of hissing creatures in his basement including

234

an albino boa constrictor and a crocodile. He told me if I wasn't nice to his daughter, he'd feed me to the critters in the basement."

"Nice."

"The albino boa constrictor was this thick." He makes a large circle with his hands.

"Amazing. The thing is, Chester, I've got to get to work."

"Upstairs he kept a black panther and fed it live rabbits. He told us never to play with the rabbits, you know why?"

Trudy pushes herself off the floor and checks her shoes. "Why?"

"Because black panthers eat rabbits. If you play with a rabbit, it makes you smell like a rabbit ergo a black panther will think you're his lunch. That cat took a bite out of my ex's face."

"Did it kill her?" Trudy asks.

"She was all right in the end, after some plastic surgery. But the black panther, my father-in-law shot him and buried him in the yard."

Trudy pushes her tongue into her cheek. The Bosnian, in her mini-nightie, gardening trowel in hand, descends imperially down the stairs.

"Hello again," Chester says. "You might want to cover up out there. It's supposed to rain."

The empress ignores him, steps outside and begins to dig, offering a view of her gelatinous ass and thighs. Chester looks back at me. "Is she all right in the head?"

"Definitely not."

Chester's phone rings. "Aha," he says, "the Bat Phone. Excuse me, that'll be Commissioner Gordon." He feels around for the phone in his safari vest.

"We'll leave you to it, Chester. So sorry we disturbed you. Have a nice day." I close the door. "Trudy, why don't you watch TV while I get ready?"

"That man has really long ears."

"He does."

"That lady should put clothes on."

"She should."

The night shift ran out of prepped stuff, and the slacker closers didn't restock, meaning instead of being ready for the lunch rush, we're still prepping garnishes, heating sauces and making soups when orders start coming in. No sign of the dynamic Bengali duo. I check the break room and find them buying contraband from the Colombian.

"Do you have to do business now, Bernardo?"

"Miss Stevie, they ask me, I can't say no. How you feeling today?"

More miscellaneous crap has accumulated where the bag of unclaimed crap sat for days. I grab the trash bin and stuff hair barrettes, paper cups, chewed pens, etc., into it, pull out the bin liner and sling it over my shoulder. Earbuds in place, Rinkesh and Tareq fiddle with their new techno gadgets. I snap my fingers in their faces. "On the line, now. We've got orders coming in."

"Right on," Rinkesh says. "Please and thank you."

I hold the door open for them before heading out to toss the bag of crap in the dumpster. Gyorgi, leaning against the building, passes me his cigarette. Seagulls peck at trash, cars drive in and out of the parking lot. The rain has stopped, giving the freshly watered world an unexpected feeling of renewal.

"Seagulls eat garbage but always look clean," I say. "How does that work? Their breasts are impossibly white. I can't wear white for ten minutes without getting dirt on it."

"Me also." Gyorgi and I admire each other's soiled whites. He smiles, making me smile.

"How are you today, Stevie?"

"I'm fine, Gyorgi, how are you?"

"Fine also. I finish reading *The House at Pooh Corner* to practise English. Is very sad ending."

"You mean when Pooh and Christopher Robin say goodbye?"

He nods. "Christopher Robin says he will not be doing Nothing anymore."

"Never again." I remember this bit, sitting on my parents' couch, absently picking a scab on my knee, feeling broken because Pooh and Christopher's fun in the Hundred Acre Wood was over.

"Christopher says they won't let him."

"Do Nothing." I hand back the cancer stick.

"Yes. Who are *they*?"

"Everybody. They want him to go to school, get a job, conform."

"What means conform?"

"Do what everybody else is doing."

"Pooh says, 'Promise you won't forget me. Ever.'"

"Yeah. Which kind of makes you think Christopher Robin will. Forget him."

Gyorgi flicks ash onto the tarmac. "Christopher Robin says, 'Whatever happens, you will understand.'"

"Then Pooh says, 'Understand what?'"

"And Christopher says, 'Oh nothing.' He can't find words for feelings. So he says nothing."

"I've done that."

"Me also." He looks at me and we say nothing.

Siobhan swings the back door open. "A smoke takes literally three minutes, Gyorgi, not ten. Get your cute ass back in here. Three tables need bussing."

He hands me what's left of the cigarette.

Wacky end-of-world weather blew unpredictable winds and seemingly horizontal rain at Trudy and me as we walked to Maisie's this morning. Discarded candy wrappers, chip packets, pop bottles and coffee cups whipped our legs. Come the apocalypse, while the one percent jet overhead, us ninety-niners will scramble over not only dead and dying bodies but garbage.

In Syria, starving people are scrounging for leaves and grass to fry in olive oil.

Trudy wanted to go to Liv's, insisted that Liv said she could visit anytime. We ducked into a convenience store to buy umbrellas. Trudy picked a kid-sized umbrella with princesses on it. For an instant she looked almost happy. We held the umbrellas like shields as we headed into the rain.

The good news is that Siggy Moretti continues to act like a gentleman, going so far as to buy Helga a diet Italian soda. "He respects me and treats me like a whole person," she said. Which begs the question, how do you treat half a person? Siggy not only photographs all forms of ice but writes "experimental lit." Helga showed us some of Siggy's experimental lit on her phone. Wade called it word vomit.

"You're garbage," Helga said.

Bob finally plucked up the courage to invite the semi-regular sexy jogging guy to his favourite juice bar. And Daniel had a decent hookup with a hot welder who has cats. Daniel spent the morning sneezing while lint-rolling cat hair off his Patagonia fleece. Ergo, as Chester would say, many windfalls of romance at Chappy's.

Daniel comes into my office to reset his hair, mussed from his activities with the hot welder. "So bae," he says, "what's up with you and the busboy?"

"Nothing. He's gay."

"Really? He looks so het."

"Looks can be deceiving."

Bob appears waving a bag of croutons. "*Six* croutons per salad, not eight. Speak to your staff. Corporate says only *six* croutons per salad."

"Bobsie," Daniel says, "is the cute busboy gay?"

"Which busboy?"

"The cute one."

"The Russian?"

"Slovakian," I say.

"Straight. I already asked him out."

"No way," Daniel gasps. "What happened to never mix business with pleasure?"

"My online course taught me in order to keep a constant hold on my inner peace, I have to let go of everything outer. Like, if I'm attracted to somebody, not to hold back. That's why I asked Ashton to the juice bar."

"Awesome," Daniel says, "but just because the busboy didn't go out with *you*, doesn't mean he wouldn't go out with somebody else. Like, I was totally shocked when Lake invited me to his place. I mean he's super buff from all that welding, but he says he's not into skinny guys."

"His name is Lake as in water?" I ask.

"His mom was a hippie. His sister's called Ocean and his little brother's called Pond."

Bob emphatically opens his arms as though holding a giant beach ball. "We all need to take a spiritual holiday inside ourselves, not away from life but away from the obvious."

Nobody knows what this means.

"Bobsie," Daniel says, "did you pick up the wine-scented candle at HomeSense I told you about? I bet Ashton would totally love it."

I discover one of Bernardo's brazen women in the dry storage room speaking heated Spanglish on her phone.

"You can't stay here," I say. "Salga, por favor. Vámonos." Very tall in her stilettos, she looks down her aquiline nose at me and struts out.

Bob's left a note in my office: *Stevei, do not resist change. Embrace it and find the path to internal transfromation and personal empowrment. Also, make sure your staff put only 6 cruotons.*

It takes time to count six croutons rather than toss a handful. I will not waste my staff's time by forcing them to count croutons.

Wade scuffles in and closes my door. "Abort mission, abort mission."

"What mission?"

"A corporate spy's been asking questions about the World o' Chicken menu. Tell Siobhan I'm throwing up or something."

Siobhan bangs the door open. "Get out there, hot stuff. You can't literally walk away from a customer."

"She's not a customer. She's Corporate's spy."

"How do you know?"

"She's interrogating me."

"So what, you know the menu."

"Not the World o' Chicken."

"That's not till tomorrow," I say. "You're not required to know that today. Just take her order and I'll make sure it's portioned to Corporate specs."

Olaf boogies in. "I don't mean to flex on you, fam, but Chef is straight-up losing his shit. Da customer say da pepper steak be rubbery, and he want gravy on da mashed, not da meat. Chef gotta dude up."

I head over to the chargrill and nudge fuming Conquer out of the way. "Chef, go take a holiday inside yourself. I got this."

"Dat's right, brosef, dat's how we get down."

Conquer makes a pistol with his hand, points it at Olaf's head and pulls the trigger.

"Seriously, Conquer," I say, "take a break and review the World o' Chicken prep. Big bird day tomorrow."

Safe behind the chargrill, I'm Buddha Holding Up the Earth, my energy open and circulating. The meat sizzles over the tiny yellow fingers of flame. I flip the steak, press down hard with the tongs and the flames jump up. Bob says I haven't found my passion. I'm thinking it's grilling animal parts.

Once the steak is plated, I speed to the dishpit and offer the rejected, barely touched steak to the gypsy. Working a double and pitching in as a disher because Jamshed—the slowest man alive—is late, Gyorgi probably hasn't eaten since grilled cheese and Dunkaroos yesterday. He looks dangerously tired, the kind of tired that leaves you standing in rooms not knowing what you're doing there. Maybe the Slovakians couldn't spare a bed last night. "Do you want to sleep at my place tonight?" I ask. "Trudy would love it. We'll call it a sleepover and make her a blanket fort. You can have the couch."

239

He looks at me to see if I'm serious. "Sure."

"I should warn you, she has night terrors. In her sleep. They're a little scary."

"I did this."

"What?"

"Cry at night. My mother said it was because I never cry in day. Don't be scared, Stevie. Everybody cry." He places his hand on the back of my neck. His bro touch feels firm on the point of most resistance. Tension softens under the warmth of his palm.

Olaf pokes his head in. "Dawg, I don't need you to wax my car but I straight-up need forks."

"Sure," Gyorgi says, grabbing a basket of clean cutlery.

"I'll cook something for us tonight," I say. "Real mac and cheese."

"What is mac and cheese?"

"Yummy. You'll see. Come over after your shift."

Siobhan reports that the pepper steak customer is literally thrilled with his steak, and Conquer is grudgingly back on task, allowing me time to carefully weigh and measure portions for the Corporate spy. Like I said, I got this.

TWENTY-FOUR

"Dick wants a trial separation," Maya says so quietly I press the phone closer to my ear.

"Are you surprised?"

I'm grocery shopping before picking up Trudy. Around me worn-looking people listlessly drop items into shopping carts and, for once, I'm not one of them. There's a spring in my step because I'm making dinner not for a war-damaged, embittered and resentful alcoholic son, but for a gay gypsy who swoons over grilled cheese. Wait till he tastes my baked mac and cheese with bacon and fresh basil.

"Our therapist thinks it's a good idea," Maya says. "I said how are we supposed to pay for two homes. That's when Dick dropped the bomb about moving in with one of the girls he has perverted sex with. I still can't believe any of this is happening. With my chemo brain, everything sort of doesn't seem real."

"Everything sort of doesn't seem real to me even without chemo brain."

"It's all too crazy, right?"

"All too crazy." Like the way Trudy stares at a wall, expressionless with her eyes half-closed, exactly like Pierce.

"Dick's picking up some of his things tonight and going over to Felicity's."

"How felicitous of Felicity to offer your husband shelter."

"I know, right? He says he'll break it to the kids."

"You might want to be there when he does."

"Really? I thought he should do that alone. I mean, *he's* the one leaving."

"If he does it alone, he might shit-talk you."

"Heavens, he'd never do that."

"People do all kinds of things we think they'd never do."

"Everything would be different if he'd just been honest about it from the start."

Maya reminds me of Anabel in high school who believed everything would be different if she had a boyfriend. I went to her Sweet Sixteen because I'd never been to one, hadn't been raped yet and still believed in romance. The partiers were making out on couches, floors, walls. Being the only girl not coupled up, I felt stupid and ugly and hid in the lilac bathroom until a hockey player pounded on the door to "take a leak." Back in the hall, the door to Anabel's foster parents' bedroom was open and boys were crawling all over the bed. Beneath them I saw Anabel's legs sticking out at awkward angles. Her skirt had been pushed up and her panties pulled down. Keith, the most popular boy whose girlfriend, Emma, was the most popular girl, had one leg out of his jeans and was straddling Anabel's face, pushing his penis into her mouth. She didn't resist but struggled to suck on it, her legs twisting with the effort. Keith got off her and Tristan, a boy with volcanic acne, shoved his penis into Anabel's mouth. Grotesque as it appeared, I thought maybe this was just something the popular kids did because Anabel wasn't crying out or trying to get away. Boy after boy skull-fucked her. She seemed barely conscious, presumably drunk, squirming with the effort required to suck and swallow. A week later I saw her making out with Tristan in front of the 7-Eleven. It seemed she'd got herself a boyfriend. In calculus, when I asked her if everything was different now, she shrugged without looking up from her worksheet.

"Dick keeps saying it's just a trial separation," Maya says. "I have to believe him, otherwise I'll just fall apart. I mean, I studied Greek tragedies so sort of believe in fate, like, whatever happens, happens. But this is different. Like, I thought I'd been hurt in every way possible, but this is different. You know what Sophocles said?"

"Didn't he say a lot of things?"

"He said love is like a piece of ice clenched in a child's fist. She wants to keep it even though it stings. She won't let it go."

I sniff some fresh basil and pop it in a plastic bag.

"When Dick said he didn't love me anymore, it was like I was that little girl gripping the ice. Oh heavens, my mother's calling. She thinks it's all my fault."

I know from Maya's writing fragments that her mother was raised under the shadow of the Armenian genocide. Even though Maya's parents and grandparents never spoke about the massacre in detail, they made sure Maya and her brother never forgot about it. "It gets hard to take," Maya said.

As does the hubby ditching the wife for a younger model. Lining up at the checkout with the worn-looking people, I try to be positive. "You never know, not having Dick around pining for pervy sex might be refreshing. Plus you don't have to get drunk and beg him to wear a condom."

"You're funny."

"Not really."

"Do you think you'll ever get married?"

"Nah."

"Why not?"

"Hmm, let me think. When around couples who've been together twenty-plus years do I say to myself, 'Break me off a piece of that?'"

"It might be different if you wanted kids."

"Maybe."

"The child, you know, is the reason for life. Some famous writer said that. I've got to talk to my mom. Can I call you later?"

"Sure." I try to sound like Gyorgi.

"It really helps, like, I can't talk honestly to people I know like I can talk to you."

Maybe we all need someone we don't know to talk honestly to. Although words can be slippery. Truth doesn't always stick to them.

At Maisie's, parents pick up their bundles of joy while Trudy, unresponsive to my calls, curls into a ball in a corner of the living room. Maisie exchanges small talk with the parents who complain about their struggles on a Caribbean cruise, waiting around to get through customs then waiting around for the shuttle to take them to the ship. "When we pulled into ports," a hair-gelled dad says, "the native hucksters were waiting for us. You gotta keep your hand on your wallet."

Maisie ushers the last of the parents out and joins me at the kitchen table. "Trudy's def got ishes. She had the kids playing prisoner today. She kept tying them up. They let her boss them around because she's older." She pulls Brandon, her toddler, onto her lap and hands him a cracker. "Did you call Children's Aid?"

"I saved the number in my phone."

"Call them."

Anabel was in foster care. Which may be why the boys pushed their penises in her mouth. No enraged bio dad would hunt them down.

"Seriously, Stevie, the kid's wrecked." She checks on Trudy. "She's still balled up. It's like she's in a trance."

"Think of it as meditation."

"I don't get why you don't take this seriously."

"Because, seriously, I don't want to traumatize her more." The wall clock ticks loudly, nudging uncomfortable seconds. "Does this mean you don't want her here?"

"I'm okay with it if the parents don't complain, but you need help with this."

"I'm getting it."

"From where?"

"A busboy."

"You're kidding, right?"

"Nope. Trudy likes him. And he's been traumatized himself. Seems to know how to be with her. Only the damaged can truly understand the damaged." This is why Greg Lem, loopy as he is, can help Pierce and vice versa. I checked the chicken suit. Wearing it, Pierce will have no peripheral vision, will survey the territory through a patch of yellow mesh in the chicken's neck. This is a soldier trained to scan the ground in a twenty-metre radius for any disturbance in the dirt that might indicate an IED. Scanning inside the chicken suit will be impossible.

"Have you told her you're her grandma?"

"Nope."

"Why not?"

"Too binding."

"Who does she think you are?"

"A stranger. She seems accustomed to being passed around."

Maisie brushes cracker crumbs off Brandon. "Do you think she's been molested?"

"Not sure. Why? Do *you* think she's been molested?"

"She kind of shuts down."

"Which means?"

"She could have been abused. You shut down so you don't feel it."

"Right. But isn't that a typical response to most kinds of trauma?"

In the living room, I curl up in a ball beside the princess and square breathe for a few minutes. "Guess who's having a sleepover at our place tonight? Your friend Gyorgi. We're going to make mac and cheese and play cards." She turns her head away from me.

"Did my mom phone?"

"No."

"Did you check your messages?"

"I did."

She faces me. "What about the mailbox?"

"We'll do that when we get home."

"Then let's go," she says as though I'm the one holding us up.

Male bower birds win females over by decorating bowers. In a vid one male collected little brown balls of deer dung and arranged them in his bower, while the other collected blossoms. They both waited days for females to notice. The deer dung began to sprout white fungi, destroying the smooth surface of the brown balls. A female bower bird, initially drawn to the deer dung, noticed the fungi and flew to the blossomed bower where she offered up her cloaca. The rejected male hurriedly tried to peck the fungi off the deer dung.

"What are you writing?" Trudy asks.

"Stuff about birds. Do you want to see what the boy bird of paradise does to impress girl birds of paradise?" I google the bird of paradise courtship dance in which the primarily black bird transforms himself into different shapes by changing plumage configurations.

"He looks like a ballerina," Trudy says.

"Watch his fancy dance routine." The bird of paradise performs acrobatic leaps and spins, making Trudy giggle. I show her other madcap bird courting rituals until she's chuckling so much she's rolling around on my bed.

"Check this out," I say. "The maypole bower builder weaves sticks around a tree and decorates it with crushed fruit and dead insects."

"Ew."

"And they do all that with just their beaks."

"They don't have hands."

"Aren't we lucky we have hands?"

"We can't fly."

Knocking on the front door gets her off the bed and running to see Mommy or Gyorgi. I don't recognize the voices. In seconds she's back. "It's the police."

"What?"

"The cops." She says this as though having cops at your door is oh-so-yesterday. "They want to talk to my mom."

"Why do they want to talk to your mom?"

"Hello?" a gruff male voice calls. "Is there an adult here?"

The cop is huge and bristled. His petite female partner looks chronically disappointed, her slit of a mouth tightened into a grimace. "Do you live here?" she demands.

"Yes." I don't invite them in.

"We've had a report of a disturbance at this address."

"Reported by who?"

"Your neighbour. What's going on here at night, ma'am? She's heard screaming."

"Nothing's going on. We're trying to sleep while your complainant cranks her radio. *She's* the disturbance."

"She says you're keeping a child here."

"What business is that of hers, or yours?"

"Ma'am, we're investigating a potentially dangerous domestic situation."

"According to who?"

"Who's the child, ma'am?"

"My granddaughter." Trudy's still in my bedroom, hopefully out of earshot. If the cops ask for proof we're related, I'll have no choice but to hand the child over, will feel justified in handing her over. Both cops scan what they can of the dugout for evidence of a dangerous domestic situation. The princess appears and leans against the wall behind me, clutching her pink teddy.

"A man resides here, ma'am," the chronically disappointed petite female cop says. "What's his name?"

"Pierce Many. He's not living here right now. He's at a friend's."

"For any particular reason, ma'am? Did he assault you?"

"Of course not. He's my son."

"Your neighbour heard him be abusive."

"Why is it that a neighbour can talk smack about my family and you guys take her seriously?"

"We have to investigate every complaint, ma'am," the huge cop says, sounding bored. But the small cop, whose name tag says *PC Pipit*, is starring in a crime show in her own mind, even has a notebook out. The huge cop checks his phone.

"She also claims," PC Pipit says, "that you've made verbal threats to her, along with racial slurs."

"That's ridiculous." I try to remember what I said to the Bosnian—something about ripping her tits off, maybe, or smashing her face into bricks. Nothing racist.

"You can be charged for making verbal threats, ma'am," PC Pipit says. "Consider this a warning. She says you damaged her pumpkin."

"You've got to be kidding."

"I'm not kidding, ma'am. That pumpkin was her personal property."

"On the front steps, which is property shared by all the tenants of this building."

"So you *did* damage her pumpkin."

"I did not damage her pumpkin." One thing crime shows have taught me: admit nothing.

Gyorgi shows up and immediately looks ready to bolt. "It's okay, Gyorgi, they're just investigating a neighbour's complaint. Nothing to do with you. Nothing to worry about." It sounds as though I'm hiding something. Around cops I feel guilty, for what is anybody's guess.

"Is this your son, ma'am?" Pipit demands.

"No. He's a friend."

"Your name, sir?"

"Why do you need *his* name?"

"We need all your names, ma'am."

"Why?"

"Your cooperation would be appreciated," the huge cop interjects. His tag says *PC Kruk*. The guns in Pipit's and Kruk's holsters and the truncheons in their belts appear super-sized in the narrow hallway. I'm vibrating, initially with anger but now with fear they'll interrogate Gyorgi and deport him. He stands defenceless, his arms limp at his sides, his eyes on his scuffed runners, like the little Roma boy waiting to get his ass kicked by the police.

Chester pulls his shopping buggy through the front door. "Hello, ladies. Well, well, what do we have here?"

"Do you live in this building, sir?" Pipit demands.

"I certainly do. In the penthouse."

The cops miss the irony. Pipit jots something on her notepad. "What's your name, sir?"

"Chester Coveyduck."

"Have you witnessed any disturbances?"

"Disturbances?" Chester, resuming his marching band leader stance, pulls his hanky from his safari vest and polishes his glasses.

"Noise," Pipit clarifies. "Screaming."

The fate of we three, smelling of active fruit ingredients, is in the hands of a man run over by a Caterpillar tractor, who had whooping cough without the cough and the bad kind of meningitis. He puts his glasses back on. "*I* haven't heard any screaming."

"We're investigating a complaint about domestic violence," Pipit persists. "Have you heard anything that sounded like a fight?"

"Not at all. Now the lady below me plays her radio all night long and that can be disturbing. With my polyamorous days behind me, I need my rest. You might consider having a word with the good lady about turning down the dial."

"There you have it, PC Pipit," I say, "your complainant is the problem. If you'll excuse us, I have a child to feed." I pull Gyorgi into the apartment. "Have a good evening, officers." I close the door. Gyorgi stands in the kitchen, visibly shaken. "It's okay," I tell him, putting comforting arms around him as he put his around me. "Stop worrying. I'm not required to let them in unless they're pressing charges. And the cowboy just blew the complainant's case." Although if Trudy keeps screaming the Bosnian will again summon her stooges. Gyorgi relaxes in my embrace and presses his face into my hair. This is our third hug and I'm astonished by how natural it feels, how well we fit. Maybe it's because he's gay and has nothing to prove, or because consoling hugs are common among the Roma. Then I feel a hardening in his jeans.

"You're not my grandmother," Trudy says. "Why did you tell them you're my grandmother? My grandmother's dead."

I break the embrace and Gyorgi pulls a set of dice from his back pocket, the bulge in his jeans receding. "Trudy," he says, "do you play with dice? Is fun and helps you count. I show you."

"And I'll get going on the mac and cheese. Trudy, do you like bacon?"

"You mean like bacon bits?"

"Kind of."

"Ew."

"I'll make yours just noodles and cheese."

"We play," Gyorgi says, sitting cross-legged on the living room floor and tossing the dice. Trudy kneels beside him. Benedict, on the couch, sniffs in their direction while a weakness in my knees unsteadies me. What just happened between me and the gypsy? Someone knocks on the door. Trudy runs for it. It's only Chester, holding the birdcage containing the albino rat.

"The little lady wanted to meet Tiberius."

"Thank you so much, Chester," I say, "for not mentioning the night terrors."

"Think nothing of it. I'm not keen on the fuzz myself. They go after the little guy because they can't catch the big one. Just like the tax man. Well, look who's here, my communist friend."

"Hello, Cowboy," Gyorgi says and Chester laughs slowly, like it hurts. Gyorgi seems completely at ease in his body, unfazed by his recent hard-on. Is this a Roma thing? Do they go around hugging at half-mast, whatever their sexual orientation? Maybe arousing each other is just something they do, like the French with all that kissing and topless bathing. Best not to think about it, better to grate cheese and invite Chester for dinner in way of thanks.

"I would be delighted." He arranges himself stiffly in the easy chair and takes the rat out of the birdcage. The princess squeals when he hands it to her. She holds Tiberius carefully with both hands, making me wonder if Trudy's ever been held carefully.

"Cute little guy, ain't he?" Chester says. My phone rings. It's not Chappy's so must be Pierce.

"What were cops doing there?" he demands.

"Are you spying on us?" I take the phone into the bedroom.

"What did they want?"

"Your Bosnian girlfriend is complaining about a domestic disturbance."

"What disturbance? Is that the busboy with you?"

"None of your business. Stop spying on me."

"I need gauze and shit. Greg cut himself. I stopped the bleeding but I need surgical tape and gauze. You always have that stuff because of work."

I dig around in my medicine cabinet. "When you say he cut himself, are you talking about self-harming or a suicide attempt? Because, in either case, you should take him to the hospital."

"He won't go. I just need to tape him up."

"Where are you?"

"Just leave it for me on the steps." He hangs up and I collect first-aid supplies, stick them in a Ziploc bag and put them out front. Looking up and down the street, I see no sign of the soldier. Back in the dugout, cheese melts in my double boiler and the rat scurries around the living room causing the half-blind mutt to sniff excitedly and attempt a few geriatric barks, although he doesn't budge from the couch.

"We've got to keep an eye on Tibby," Chester says. "He loves scooting under things."

Trudy, babbling ratspeak, trails Tiberius while the gypsy and the cowboy discuss man's quest for a cure for aging.

"There is surgical procedure," Gyorgi says. "Old mouse is surgically connected to young mouse and shares blood. In weeks, old mouse is young."

This gets me thinking about yours truly, the old mouse, wanting to connect to the busboy young mouse.

Trudy crawls under the couch after Tiberius. "Don't get stuck, little lady," Chester warns.

"There is naked mole rat," Gyorgi says, "that lives for thirty years. Is long life for rat. Researchers not understanding how is possible."

"Is that so?" Chester says. "You watch, that'll be the next big thing—humans shooting themselves up with naked mole rat cells. Would anyone like a glass of wine? I have some in the penthouse."

"Not for me," I grumble, badly in need of a splash of vino.

"Me also. No thank you."

My phone rings again. It's Peggy, hysterical and incoherent. Reggie's ranting in the background. "I'll be right over," I tell her.

With no time to fry bacon, I put the casserole in the oven. "Gyorgi, when the timer goes, turn the oven off and take the dish out, okay? Let it cool for a bit then serve it."

"You have to go?"

"There's some problem with my parents. Can you and Trudy entertain Chester till I get back?"

"Sure."

The bungalow's kitchen is awash with bubbles because Peggy poured Tide into the dishwasher. And she made what she insists is Kahlua ice cream pie, which melted all over the dining room table and floor. She stepped in the brown goo and is trekking it all over the house. I get her slippers off but it takes me an hour to clean up the mess with her flapping and squawking around me, and another hour to coax both senile parents into their separate bedrooms. I put them to bed fully clothed because I have no energy to wrestle them into sleepwear, and crush Ativan into two pudding cups. "Bedtime snack," I tell them. Peggy spoons it all down. Reggie lets me feed him a couple of spoonfuls then pushes my hand away.

"Dad, it'll help you sleep."

"Give it to the missus. She loves pudding." He lies back and stares at me. I have no idea what he's seeing, how I look to him, if he knows who I am. "The boy was here."

"What boy?"

"Needs a haircut. Take him to Tony." Tony was Reggie's barber, long since dead.

"Okay," I say.

"You been boozin'?"

"I haven't boozed for years, Dad."

"You'll die young the way you're going." This is what he'd say when I showed up with vomit in my hair.

I tuck the comforter around him and think of all the judgments he made about me that hurt. If we could see our parents' end at the beginning, maybe their judgments would lose their power. If we could see their lives before we were born, maybe what came after would make more sense. I want this for Pierce. Not that he love me, or forgive me, but that he understand why my judgments hurt.

Sitting on the bungalow's front steps where he sat, where I sat, where Trudy clung to the railing, I imagine him taping up Greg Lem in Tara's bathroom. Two soldiers left behind, shut down. The walking dead.

Soldiers don't use the word "died." They use tough-guy words like "offed," "zapped," "blasted," "greased."

Land mines are designed to severely injure, not kill. Adversaries want to burden each other with injured soldiers, not dead ones that can be left behind. A thirty-gram mine will blow your foot off or damage it enough to require amputation. You might get head or eye injuries from fragments. A 150-gram mine will shred your legs to mid-thigh.

What do you say to the soldier whose legs are blown off, whose face is raw with burns but who is conscious, snorting loudly, expecting you to save him when all you can do is hold compress bandages against his bleeding stumps?

Lions led by donkeys.

If Greg cut himself, intending suicide, he will likely try again. If he succeeds, Pierce will be even more alone, even more committed to acts of psychic self-mutilation.

His buddy Jake sat in corners with his back to no one. He'd say to Pierce, "If some fucker walks in here to shoot up the place, I'll see him. I'll know what to do." He'd make a plan: if the fucker comes in that door, I'll grab this bottle and flip that table. I'll break the bottle and go for his jugular. Jake had blueprints in his mind for every situation. His assailants could come from anywhere at any time, and he'd be ready. Despite all that planning and readiness, his final judgment led him to swallow all the meds the VA docs prescribed and to die in his mother's bathroom leaking shit and piss.

Sitting where Pierce sat watching for my old beater car, I know I must prevent him from making the same final judgment as Jake. Because he has a daughter who curls into a ball tight as a fist with her back to no one.

This is my first selfless thought.

TWENTY-FIVE

I don't rush back because I'm not ready for any of it: the possibly bisexual gypsy with the therapeutic touch, the screeching child, Chester the wine tippler, the Bosnian cat lady. All too much. They'll get along without me very well, which gets me thinking about Chet Baker again, singing about how he'll get along without you very well, and you know he won't. And Stan's in my head telling me what *happens* matters more than what me or anybody else thinks about it before or after it happens. "It's what we *do* that counts," he said, "not sitting around stewing about it." Which seems a good rule to live by if you know what to do, which I don't.

My feet lead me to Conquer's boat. Pressing my ear to the hull, I listen for sexual hydraulics. All quiet. Knock, knock.

"It's you." The Viking reaches an arm down to help me up the ladder. "Back for more."

"What exactly?"

"Grown-up company."

"Don't flatter yourself."

"Fruit water?"

"Don't mind if I do."

He pours me a glass. "Strawberry."

"Did you know that seven percent of Americans believe that chocolate milk comes from brown cows?"

"Doesn't it?" He lies back on his bunk. "You look worse than usual. Must be the kid."

"Probably."

"Where is she?"

"With the busboy. They get along like I've never gotten along."

"What's the busboy doing at your place?"

"Babysitting. He needs cash." I sit at the little fold-out table.

"And your son?"

"Bandaging his soldier buddy who cut himself."

"Badly?"

"He wouldn't say."

"When are you going to tell him he's got a kid?"

"Don't know."

"You have to tell him."

"I don't *have* to do anything."

The Viking broods.

"Listen, Conquer, can I let you in on a secret?"

"I hate secrets."

"Me too. But this is important."

"Why?"

"Because I might require assistance."

"What's in it for me?"

I try to think of something. "It may mean I won't get fired."

"What's it matter to me if you're fired?"

"They'll replace me with a micromanaging corporatetard KM who won't let you sling Jacks and tongue waitresses. You'll have to weigh and measure itty-bitty portions."

He sighs as Vikings do after a hard day marauding villages. "Shoot."

"Okay, well, here's the thing. My son is wearing the chicken suit tomorrow."

"You're shitting me."

"He needs the money."

Conquer makes the spitting noise without spitting and takes a long haul of strawberry water.

"Bob and Desmond don't know Pierce is my son. If he goes nuts, which I don't think he will, I don't want Corporate to know we're related. We have different last names. I think he'll be fine. He's been looking after this Greg guy who's way more nuts than he is. I just want to be able to call on you if I need help restraining him."

"Restraining him?"

"If he has a panic attack or something."

"Or something."

"My hope is if things work out in the chicken suit, I can get him in the dishpit and move Jamshed up the line, put him on one of the fryers."

"Jamshed is a putz."

"He just needs practice and training. He'll be fine."

Conquer folds his hands behind his head and stares grimly out a porthole. The Italian neighbour's rooster crows.

"Isn't it supposed to crow at dawn?" I ask.

"The yuppie couple on the other side are shit-crazed about solar lights. Their yard's littered with them. It confuses the bird."

"Makes sense. Electricity screwed up humans' natural rhythms."

"We were screwed up anyway."

"True." I sip strawberry water. "The mother of your daughter, did you know her well?"

"Who knows anybody."

"Good point."

"You think you know somebody then find something out that makes you realize you didn't know them at all. I loved her without knowing who she really was."

"Who was she really?"

"A bitch."

"Ah. You know that's a female dog, right?"

He stares out the porthole as though we're in the middle of a stormy sea, not a driveway. "We see what we want to see."

"Or don't want to see but expect to see based on previous experience. I mean, most situations are similar to other situations so we go, 'Okay, I get where this is going.' Seeing a new situation like a previous one makes it manageable."

"And predictable."

For some reason this gets me stewing about coffins, how the wooden structures we live in—that contain us—are no different from coffins. Conquer, lying in his boat, is already in his coffin.

"Your son losing his shit in a chicken suit will be a new situation for you."

"Lucky me."

He picks a strawberry out of a bowl, pops it in his mouth then passes me the bowl. "Olivia has this theory we go through life not really seeing what's around us or really knowing who's around us. And because we're shit-scared of what we don't know, we close our eyes to stuff."

Munching strawberries, we ponder our fear of the unknown.

"Is she still up?" I ask.

"Probably. Why?"

"Trudy claims Liv told her she could visit anytime. Anytime tomorrow would be good for me."

"Go ask her. Let yourself in. Save her dragging the walker to the door."

In her La-Z-Boy, reading a leather-bound opus, she looks up. "Were you in the boat?"

"I was."

She studies me over her reading glasses. "Are you and Billy an item?"

"Oh no."

"You don't trust him."

"Trust him? Well, hmm. I guess I've never been big on trust—trusting people and people trusting me. Personally, I think the trust word is over-used, like the love word. Nobody really knows what they mean anymore."

"Think they ever did?"

"Maybe. When talk wasn't cheap."

"Have a seat. Want a chocolate?" She holds out a box of Pot of Gold.

"No thanks."

The scratchy couch feels even scratchier with the wolfwoman staring at me.

"Does Billy know you were raped?"

"Nope. Nobody knows, except you and the busboy."

"The busboy, what busboy?"

"A Slovakian. He works at Chappy's."

"Why'd you tell *him*?"

"Not sure. His mom was raped. By cops. He's a product of rape."

"That's why you told him."

"Maybe." Suddenly I miss Gyorgi. Not sure why but there it is, a wallop of yearning. "He says it doesn't matter that he's a product of rape. He loves his mother and she loves him. Simple."

"Rape," Liv says, "is hate and fury where love should be. The male body becomes the weapon and the female body the enemy. I was raped by my husband for years, although I didn't realize it at the time. He'd want it, I'd let him have it. I got so bored with the whole exercise, I'd go places in my head."

"Where?"

"The supermarket, the cleaners. While he did his business, I was putting together to-do lists."

"Did you ever try to refuse him?"

"Girly, in those days husbands saw access to their wives' bodies as a right. If you kept your legs crossed, there'd be hell to pay."

Horrible to imagine Liv spreading her legs year after year, going places in her head, birthing a child, loving her, nurturing her then watching her waste away. Yet here the survivor is—more alive than any of us—welcoming the unknown, taking tai chi and painting classes, slaying bingo night.

"My love for my daughter," she growls, "has nothing to do with how she was conceived. Nothing to do with him. That's why your busboy loves his mother and she loves him." She peers at me over her glasses. "You don't believe me."

"I do."

"You don't, because you were gang-raped and had a son you couldn't love."

"Something like that." I point to the book. "What are you reading?"

"*The Odyssey*. What a mess that was."

"Journeys can get messy. Particularly when you're returning from a messy war."

"Particularly when you've lost all your men. He sets off in command of *twelve* ships, comes back twenty years later alone. He should be ashamed of himself. It says his soldiers perished because of their own recklessness, but I don't buy that. Soldiers obey orders. What kind of leader was he if he couldn't look after his men."

"Lots of leaders don't look after their men, or women. And feel no shame."

Liv eats a chocolate. "I think he's a crybaby and a liar."

"Lots of leaders are."

"And he cheats on his wife."

"Lots of leaders do."

"That's where they get us, isn't it?" Liv says. "We quit expecting anything good out of the idiots because they keep lowering the bar. Lies, lies, lies. This Odysseus fella gets all weepy with homesickness, meanwhile he's diddling Calypso every night for seven years. He's a half-witted, two-timing narcissist and I don't get why the gods keep helping him out. If I were them I'd leave him by the side of the road, let the Cyclops make a meal of him." She puts her book and glasses on the side table. "Tell me about that little girl. Billy told me she's your granddaughter."

"Right. But she doesn't know that. So please don't tell her."

Her electric blue gaze searches my dark corners again. "The love word," she says, "has no meaning for you because you haven't earned it. It's something you *earn*. And you can't control it because the person you love has their own rights and makes their own decisions. People think love falls into your lap. Bah. Love is work. A constant negotiation. That little girl goes places in her head because she doesn't know any different. You have to teach her how to negotiate. It's a collaboration, you have to respect her and pay attention. You're equals. Parents expect kids to love them just because they're their parents. It doesn't work that way."

"I don't expect anybody to love me."

"What kind of life is that?"

"A fine life. No complaints." She keeps staring and I try to think of a polite way to segue into babysitting.

"Where are the girl's parents?"

"Well, her mother abandoned her, and her father doesn't know she exists."

"That'd be your son who can't watch war news."

"Correct."

"Girly, there's nothing for it but to lay yourself open to rejection and abandonment. It's the only way to get feeling again."

"Who says I want to get feeling again?"

"Everybody wants to feel, they just forget how because they've been armouring themselves for so long. You're scared. Everybody is. Nothing wrong with that. Fear keeps us alive. But figure out that there's somebody more important to you than yourself. Once you figure that out, you'll be free." She keeps staring. I'm in her interrogation room and she's waiting for a confession.

"I've made mistakes," I blurt. "I keep making mistakes. With her. With him."

"Good. At least you're making something. Make some more."

"I don't know how I'm supposed to be with them."

"Don't be anything with them."

I avoid her eyes and stare at one of her shepherdess figurines, but he's in my mind, the little boy who didn't know what he'd done to make Mommy hate him. Just like Trudy doesn't know why she's been left behind. He used to crawl onto my lap. I didn't hold on to him and he'd slide off.

Conquer stands in the doorway. "Olivia, it's bedtime. Did you sort out tomorrow?"

"We haven't sorted anything."

"Actually, Liv," I say, "the reason I dropped by is Trudy told me you said she could visit anytime."

"That's right."

"Could I drop her off here tomorrow before I go to work? It might be a long day. We're starting a chicken promotion."

"Sure, bring her over. We'll get up to something."

"Thank you so much. Okay, well, I should head home."

"I'll drive you," Conquer says.

"It's okay, I'll walk."

"I'll drive you."

"Bah, let her walk."

Conquer places Liv's walker in front of her. "Beddy-byes."

"Don't fuss," Liv says.

Rain-soaked air seeps into my clothes and lungs, and the city's artificial light confuses me. Stone cold loneliness wraps itself around my bones. My phone vibrates.

"It's me," Pierce says.

"I figured. How's Greg?"

"Okay, he took some pills."

"Are you taking any?"

"Fuck no, somebody's got to keep watch. Where are you?"

"On the street."

"What're you doing on the street? It's late."

"Going home."

"Is the busboy with you?"

"Your preoccupation with the busboy isn't healthy."

"*Your* preoccupation with the busboy isn't healthy."

"Where are you calling from?"

"You shouldn't be alone on the street at night. It's dangerous."

This is new, his concern for my personal safety.

"Pierce, I've been alone on the street my entire life. Back off."

An ungainly pause careens between us, like when he was little and phoned me for no particular reason. He knew my number by heart. We couldn't think of anything to say. Our lives were too far apart. Like now.

"I watched this show about biological weapons," Pierce says. "Did you know the Romans used corpses to contaminate enemy water?" He's talking fast, either manic or caffeine buzzed. "And the Japs dropped rice, wheat, cotton and paper infected with plague on the Chinese. Plus they poisoned wells in Manchuria with typhoid, cholera and dysentery."

"Nice." Next he'll be compulsively testing our water supply. "Pierce, shouldn't you get some sleep? Big day tomorrow."

"Oh right. I meant to ask, am I supposed to talk to people?"

"Only if you feel like it."

"So I'm just handing out flyers?"

"Correct. I mean, you might consider waving to passersby. Be a friendly chicken."

"I'm not touching anybody."

"Why would you touch anybody?"

"Shake hands and shit. Like Ronald McDonald."

"None of that. Just politely hand out flyers."

"Got it." He hangs up and I know he'll panther-pace all night long, anxious about his day in the chicken suit.

Out of nowhere Desie's memo to house staff to "freshen" desserts with whipped cream drops into the old stew pot. How do you freshen an old dessert? A four-day-old key lime pie is an old pie. Like I'm an old mouse in need of freshening with whipped. Pierce is right, my preoccupation with the busboy isn't healthy. What happens to the young mouse when surgically connected to the old mouse? Does the young mouse develop sore knees, a bad back and a negative attitude?

Jesús filled me in on his soap opera. To please her father, Dolores married a banker she didn't love and popped another baby, a girl, Valentina, who grew up to be as beautiful as Dolores. Dolores convinced the banker to send their daughter to business school where Valentina fell in love with a young man studying marketing. She told her mother about him—how handsome he was, such a hard worker, so intelligent, so polite. "What's his name?" Dolores asked.

"Fernando," Valentina replied.

Fernando was the name Dolores gave the infant boy she exchanged for an empanada. Jesús, mortified, exclaimed, "Fernando and Valentina are brother and sister!"

Incest, always a complicated negotiation.

Liv found peace through loving her daughter, and maybe Billy. If figuring out somebody's more important than yourself is the ticket to freedom, Trudy might qualify. Not because she is important to me but because she has years and years ahead of her, and I don't want them to be the toxic waste mine were. This is not noble of me, or loving. It does not set me free.

The red-winged blackbird flies south every year, returning in perilous cold to stake out territory, attacking any bird or animal threatening terrain he defends for female blackbirds. He can mate and protect as many as eighteen female blackbirds.

Pierce, when he was seven, was dive-bombed by a red-winged blackbird. When I asked him if he remembered this he said no, which surprised me because he'd been terrified. Maybe he blocked it out, like he's blocked out whatever atrocious act(s) he committed in Afghanistan.

"You're back." Gyorgi leans against my door frame.

"I thought you were sleeping."

"I woke up."

"That's an impressive blanket fort you guys built. I'm guessing the dog's in there with her."

"You guess right. We take him to park. Meet dog whisperer."

"Really?"

"Dog whisperer can't whisper his dogs, Teddy and Bear, but can whisper strangers' dogs. He says Benedict is unmoored. What means this?"

"It has to do with boats, securing them with cables, ropes and anchors, so they don't drift away."

He slides his hands into his jeans pockets. "Teddy and Bear fight when dog whisperer is not home. Whisperer worries. I ask, 'How do you know your dogs fight?' I study animal brain and there is no way for how to observe consciousness. Is possible Teddy and Bear do not fight when whisperer is away, maybe whisperer project human consciousness and behaviour on dogs."

"I think that's pretty standard for pet owners."

Gyorgi nods. "For this reason houses in Western world are full of animals."

"They're easier to love than humans."

He stares down at a toe poking through a hole in his sock. "Police scared me."

"Me too."

"You did not look scared."

"I was. Trudy has to stop screaming."

"She did not scream tonight."

"That's because you're here. She doesn't scream when you're around."

He pulls the sock over his toe. "I'm not understanding for what reason I am here."

"You're helping me look after Trudy. Here's a twenty." He doesn't take it. I press the bill into his chest and he covers my hand with his. It feels warm.

I pull my hand away and tuck the twenty into his jeans pocket. "And *you* need somewhere to sleep."

"I don't want for you to pity me."

"I don't." The ugly truth is if I weren't an insecure grandma whale, I'd be all over him. Mistakes must be made. But suddenly I don't know what to do with my body, have none of the sexual prowess I display when disinhibited by booze.

"You didn't tell us what happened to the young mouse."

"What mouse?"

"The one surgically connected to the old mouse. Did the young mouse get sick or die? I mean, it must have been really scary for both mice to be stitched together like that."

"You are projecting human consciousness on mice."

"Did the scientists just leave the young mouse connected to the old mouse?"

"Scientists learn not to worry about mice."

"Because they believe mice lack consciousness."

He shrugs. "Without mice we don't learn. Want cigarette?"

We sit with our backs to the stucco. The Bosnian's pop radio drones above us.

"How was Chester?" I ask.

"Chester says humans are babies in the universe. He says by 2060 we will run out of resources on Earth for to sustain human life so will flee to other planets. It will be like *Titanic*. The rich will see iceberg first and tell musicians to play while rich grab lifeboats, leave poor below deck. The rich will float away while band plays on." He passes me the cigarette.

"Why specifically 2060?"

"He did not say. Maybe because of zeros. Zero is ordinal number between +1 and −1. Of no significance. Like poor people." A bus rumbles past. One of the Bosnian's cats scratches in the dirt, preparing to take a dump.

"When I was child," Gyorgi says, "I grow fast. My shoes too tight. I not tell my mother. She have no money for shoes. Sometimes poor women must use their bodies like credit card. I did not want this for my mother."

"I'm a little worried Trudy's mother is doing that."

The muscle in Gyorgi's jaw twitches. "With Russian."

"Yeah, or working for the Russian."

"If Yegor tells Trudy he will take her to swim with dolphins, she will go."

"I won't let that happen." I hand him back the cigarette.

"They want younger and younger girls. Men pay more for children."

"I know."

Teenagers on the sidewalk, drunken and disorderly, shout about fucking this and fucking that.

"Did you buy a phone card and call your mum?"

He nods.

"Is she okay?"

"Okay." He stubs out the cigarette, pitches the butt and stares after the teenagers, but I suspect he's not really seeing them. He is thinking about his mother, poor, vulnerable, without him.

"Are you cold?" I ask. "Should we go in?"

He shakes his head and puts an arm around my shoulders, which feels inexplicably right. I shift closer to him.

"I am unmoored," he says.

I wrap my arm around his bent knee, anchoring him.

TWENTY-SIX

King Bob left a Post-it on my desk: *The more you develope the habit of noticing goodness, the more your own sense of wellbieng rises.* He has a migraine today, is wearing his wraparounds and worried there's a tumour on his spinal cord. I suggested he go to the hospital to see Jordan, the gay intern soon-to-be shrink, but Bob said he has to be here for the first day of World o' Chicken. "Why?" I ask.

"What do you mean 'why'? I'm the manager."

"Of course, but I can look after things if you think you should get an x-ray, or something, of your spine to rule out a tumour."

"Corporate wants me to keep an eye on portion sizes." He watches Tareq with suspicion.

"That might be tricky with the all-you-can-eat buffet, Bob. You'll have to keep an eye on the customers going back for seconds and thirds. Siobhan says a Chinese tour bus just pulled in."

"Is it the one with the bosomy guide? She's into me. Don't tell her I'm here."

"I don't know who the guide is, Bob. The point is, with a tour bus arriving this early, we'll be going through a lot of chicken."

"It says on the flyers *While supplies last.*"

"Yeah, well, tell that to the customer coming back for all he can eat."

"Put out smaller plates so the greedy customers can't take as much."

"Smaller plates?"

"Dessert plates. And use teeny serving utensils so it's harder to scoop. Teeny plates and teeny utensils mean more trips to the steam table."

"Bob, I can't put out teeny plates and teeny utensils for a main course."

"There you go saying 'can't.' Do you have any idea how many times a day you say 'can't'?"

"Here's an idea. How 'bout you visit the tables going back for refills? Shame the greedy customers a little." I say this knowing he won't have the gumption to table cruise and, consequently, will retreat to his office.

On cue he winces and claps a hand on his neck. "It's in my cervical spine now. It started in the lumbar."

"That's terrible. Maybe you should take it easy in your office."

"I need you to post this positive initiative for me." He waves a sheet of paper. "Post it in *your* office, since staff seem to enjoy being there so much."

I post Bob's positive initiative. He must have found it online because it's spelled correctly. It reads: *Has one of your colleagues gone ABOVE AND BEYOND in their work? Did someone do something you APPRECIATE? Does one of your colleagues have a QUALITY you admire? IF YOU FEEL SO MOVED, TAKE A MOMENT TO SHOW YOUR APPRECIATION AND THANKS WITH A SMALL GESTURE OF KINDNESS. IT CAN MAKE ALL THE DIFFERENCE AND BRIGHTEN SOMEONE'S DAY.*

Wade stumbles in.

"Hey, Casanova," I say.

"What are you so chipper about?"

"Chipper? I hadn't noticed I was chipper." Maybe it's because the gypsy held me all night long and the pressure of his touch—deep, firm, gentle and responsive—released tensions that have been building for years. Wolf used to say I had rocks in my shoulders and kneaded them so hard they hurt. Gyorgi met my muscles' resistance with an equal amount of energy, allowing their grip to lighten slowly. There was nothing hesitant, forced, sharp or fast about how he fitted his body around mine. Or sexual. No boner pushing at my ass, no groping. Gay, bi, whatevs, I could use more of Gyorgi's careful, attuned handling. Good thing the dog ditched me for the princess, leaving plenty of room on the bed. Trudy rose early to toast waffles and did not scowl when I pointed out she had the too-big runners on backwards again, although she wouldn't let me untangle the laces. She said her mom leaves them tied so the shoes are easy to slip on.

"That makes sense," I said. "But if we get you shoes that fit better, you can learn to tie them yourself. With practice I bet you'll be able to tie laces in the same amount of time it takes to slip the big shoes on."

Unconvinced, she prodded the wiggly tooth with her tongue.

"Tying laces is fun," Gyorgi said. "Watch." He tied his with a flourish, causing Trudy to hoot her fizzy laugh.

Her hair defied my comb.

"That's why Mom puts pigtails in, so it doesn't get knotted."

"Do you like wearing pigtails?" I asked.

"They hurt."

"Then leave it loose."

"I like it like this," Gyorgi said. "Wild." He winked.

Wade pokes his head out of my closet, looks right then left and quickly closes the door. "Don't mind me, I'm just going to nap here briefly."

"Standing up?"

Daniel pushes the door open again and hands me a tree latte. "That bitch hussy just had a boohoofest in the break room because her super closeted BF changed his Facebook status to single. She tried to message him but he blocked her. So now she's on the rebound, getting all flirty with your busboy."

"I thought we decided my busboy was gay."

"The jury's still out," Wade says.

"Anyway," Daniel says, "she got hysterical because Edvar forgot to block her on Instagram, meaning she could see all his selfies with some hottie sitting in his lap. And what's up with the Bobster? He refused to open his door even when I made him a heart latte."

"Migraine. He wanted me to post this positive initiative for staff."

They both read the positive initiative.

"Time to die," Wade says.

"I think it's sweet," Daniel says. "A small gesture of kindness *can* make all the difference and brighten someone's day. It's the big gestures that open you up to abuse. Like, sometimes I'm too nice. Lake says I'm emotionally available, which he thinks is awesome, but he's worried people will take advantage of me. He wants me to see his psychic, Professor Bambo, for pointers on how to interrelate without getting emotionally abused. Professor Bambo helped Lake resolve all kinds of emotional problems, even the difficult ones like when his mom turned bipolar, and Pond decided he was a girl. Professor Bambo protects all his clients from evil spells and family problems."

"Aren't they the same thing?" Wade says.

"Did Lake explain the difference," I ask, "between interrelating and just plain relating?"

Siobhan storms in. "Get on the floor, you losers. We literally have an entire Chinese tour bus."

"It's buffet," Wade says.

"You still have to bev tables, genius. They're literally lined up for the do-it-yourself wafflemaker."

Wade groans and clutches his head. "Oh no, not the wafflemaker."

Servers dread the wafflemaker because customers don't know how to use it, even though simple instructions are posted on the machine. The actual cooking of the waffle takes two minutes but lineups due to customers decoding the instructions are inevitable, slowing turnover, resulting in fewer tips.

I herd the boys out and check the baked pasta with grilled chicken. "When the cheese is melted," I instruct earbudded Tareq, "transfer the pasta to a pasta bowl and garnish with chopped parsley, pepper flakes and black pepper around the rim of the bowl. Give me a sign that you understand."

He nods in that murderous way of his.

"Are you prepped for the Butter Chicken Burrito?"

He nods again.

The Thai, Cantonese and Mexican chicken prep all seems in order. "Make sure you flip the tortilla on the grill," I say, "three to five seconds on each side. Add only *one* portion of Mexican veggies to the centre of the shell. And don't forget the garnish."

Praveen is cutting slabs of chicken lasagna, portioning it by weight into single-serving sizes to be wrapped in plastic until needed. All pre-prepped supplies come wrapped in plastic that we unwrap, portion by weight, then wrap in more plastic. For the all-you-can-eat buffets, Corporate orders cheap ready-mades that come off the truck frozen in sealed plastic bags. Cutting labour costs using pre-prepped stock means using more plastic. Wade says by 2030 there will be more plastic in the ocean than fish.

"The Thai garnish," I tell the South Asians, "is a lime wedge and mint leaves. The Cantonese, just a lemon wedge. Hands up if you read me." They raise their hands. Rinkesh isn't on the line because he was the only one I could make presentable for the dining room. In a paper chef's hat and a rented white jacket too small to cover his gut, he is manning the buffet, smiling and patting the air with his bejewelled fingers.

Finishing up the All-American Chicken Pot Pie prep, I check my watch again: 10:56. Pierce may already be in the parking lot. Grabbing the bulky bag containing the chicken suit, I head out the back door. No sign of the soldier or his backup. Anxiety revs as I imagine the possibilities: Pierce drank himself sick and is lying unconscious. Greg flipped out and won't leave the apartment. Pierce flipped out and won't leave the apartment. They're both on Tara's bathroom floor gushing blood from self-inflicted wounds. Tara returned and Greg strangled her. Tara returned, Greg assaulted her with a weapon and Pierce intervened. All three are gushing blood in the apartment.

Then he appears on the other side of the Chinese tour bus, looking almost normal. He's even shaved his beard and put on a clean T-shirt that must be Greg's because I don't recognize it. I hand him the bag. "Where's Greg?"

"He's around." He looks in the bag.

"You can put it on behind the dumpster. I'll get the box of flyers."

When I return he's in the suit, the yellow mesh below the beak masking his face. "Can you breathe all right in there?"

"This is no chicken. It's got a crest. It's a fucking rooster."

"Is that a problem?"

"Just give me the box."

"Please stay in front of Chappy's. Don't wander."

"Why the fuck would I wander?"

"You might get talking to someone."

"I'm not talking to anybody. I'm a fucking chicken. Bok bok." He stays close to the building, sliding an orange-gloved hand along the wall as he creeps to the front, his yellow tail feathers bobbing. When he turns the corner, out of sight, I try not to care like I didn't care on his first day of school, or any of his first days of school. Sometimes he'd phone to tell me about a teacher or a classmate, and I'd want to hang up and run away. Now I can't run away and don't know if the revving anxiety is due to concern for him or my job.

Both rejects are back in my closet. Wade's talking about the bar-tailed godwit. "They migrate from New Zealand to Alaska, and no one knew if they did it without a stopover in Japan so they put a GPS on this one and she flew for nine days straight, didn't stop once." He holds out his phone to show me a brownish bird with a long beak. "Isn't she beautiful?"

"Beautiful. Aren't you supposed to be waiting tables?"

"Customers keep wanting water because of the Tandoori."

"Well then, you better get at it." I grab his elbow and steer him to the dining room where I check the temp and water level on the steam table. Stirring stews and sauces in the inserts, adding water, removing skin off the soups, I glance out the front window to spy on Pierce. He seems fine, walking back and forth, handing out the occasional flyer. When passersby refuse them, he doesn't appear to take offence. I feel a swell of something . . . pride?

Daniel flaps his hands. "Oh my god, oh my god, oh my god, there's somebody dressed as a chicken out there."

"A rooster," Wade says.

"Who is it?"

I turn over the starches. Rinkesh points to the empty egg roll bin. "Yes," I say, "get more out of the freezer. Please be quick about it."

"Like never tomorrow."

"There's that psycho kid again," Daniel says. "Talking to the chicken."

"What psycho kid?" I ask.

A boy of seven or eight, straddling a girl's pink bike too small for him, appears to be interrelating with Pierce. The sides of the boy's head are shaved. "He's got a haircut like yours, Daniel."

"It's called a fade and looks way cuter on me than that little savage. He's got no manners, is always interrogating customers. It's like he was raised by apes."

"Apes," Wade says, "have a strict code of conduct."

"What does the kid interrogate customers about?" I ask.

"The make of their cars, what they paid for them, where they got them, where they're going in them."

"Why is he on a girl's bike?" The ape child hops off the bike, drops it on the ground and pokes at the rooster. Pierce backs away but the little savage keeps at it. I wait for Greg Lem to charge the kid from behind the tour bus.

"He probably stole it," Daniel says. "I asked him once, 'Shouldn't you be in school?' He said he was taking the day off. When I asked where his parents were, he said, 'On the couch, looking at their phones.' Last week I saw him piss in the planter. Totally barbaric behaviour."

Pierce swats the kid with an orange-gloved hand.

"Did the chicken just hit the kid?" Daniel asks.

"No," I say, but the boy is holding his head and probably yelping, although we can't hear through the window.

"It looked like he hit him," Daniel says.

"Nah, he was just waving him away."

Pierce hands out more flyers and the kid gets back on the bike, flipping Pierce the bird. "See," I say, "it's fine, the little barbarian is leaving."

Daniel nudges me and whispers, "Check out Miss Slutty Hussy with your busboy. She's"—he makes air quotes—"'helping' him. Normally she'd never go anywhere near a bussing tray. The Russian's super hot. I bet he'd make serious bucks as an homme de la nuit. Lake did that before he got into welding."

Siobhan leans close to Gyorgi and puts an arm around his waist while clearing a plate.

"If you ask me," Daniel says, "there's something wrong with that kid."

"What kid?"

"The little savage. He's super aggro and his parents aren't dealing with it. Some people just shouldn't be parents."

I check the cold table, lift covers, stir salads. Seeing Siobhan grope my busboy has pitched me into a vat of tumultuous, unfamiliar feelings. Gyorgi smiles at the hussy and she smiles back, adding her flirty laugh. She pinches his cheek before shimmying off in her pleather mini. I feel weepy and droopy suddenly, pathetic. How old and stupid am I? Obviously Siobhan is better suited to him than this old mouse. I shove my hand under an insert to check the ice level, and remember what Sophocles said about love being a piece of ice we grip in our fist. Unintentionally—without *wanting* to get feeling again—I've laid myself open to rejection and abandonment.

Armouring myself, I push through the glass doors and approach the rooster, from the front to avoid startling him. "You hit that child."

"I didn't hit him. I cuffed him."

"You can't hit children."

"You hit me."

"I did not."

"Sure you did. Sauced, of course."

"I never hit you."

"Whatever you say, Mom."

270

"I would remember if I hit you."

"Like you remember all the jerks you fucked? Buzz off, I've got a job to do."

"When did I hit you?" I trail him. His tail drops feathers.

"When Peggy got mono you were supposed to cook dinner for me and Reggie."

"I did."

"Only when you needed to get into his liquor cabinet."

"What's this got to do with me hitting you?"

"After dinner you'd ask Reggie for ice cream money. He'd give you a ten and off we'd go to get ice cream only you'd buy me a Popsicle instead because it was 'healthier.' You'd keep the change."

My thoughts turn oily, slippery. I can't get a grip.

The rooster stops and faces me. "You *stole* from Reggie."

I look up at his beak. "Well, you stole from me. Maybe it's genetic."

"I stole from you once. Okay, twice. You were always stealing from Reggie and Peggy. You'd take loose change and small bills from Grandma's purse so she wouldn't notice. I bet you're still stealing from them."

"What's this got to do with me hitting you?"

"I threatened to tell on you. With fucking grape Popsicle dripping down my arm, I said I'd tell on you about the ice cream and the stealing, so you hit me."

A Mack Truck thunders towards us and I'm tempted to step in front of it. "I don't remember that."

"Of course you don't, you fucking waste of space."

"I'm not saying I didn't steal from them, but I don't remember hitting you."

"Then it didn't happen, right? If you, a boozehound who blacked out entire nights, can't remember it, it didn't happen."

"Is there a problem here?" An unshaven man in camouflage pants and jacket, wearing a ball cap and reflector wraparounds, grips my arm. I try to shake him off.

"It's okay," Pierce says. "She's my mother."

"She's interfering."

"I'm gone," I say, jerking my arm free.

"Good riddance," Greg Lem says. "Bitch."

The Popsicles I remember. Pierce took forever to pick one, leaning over the freezer bin, rummaging through the flavours until finally selecting grape, every single time. So annoying. We'd go to the park and I'd want him to climb the monkey bars or something, get out of my face. But he'd linger, licking the grape Popsicle, turning his tongue purple. "What are you waiting for?" I'd say, knowing he was waiting for his mother to show up. "Go play." I shoved him once, causing him to drop the Popsicle. He looked dolefully down at the frozen mess. Ants swarmed it and he asked if he could have another one and I said no. Because I wanted the money. Go play, I said. He looked frightened. My desperation for a few extra bucks meant I'd terrorize a little boy. That's what you do when you're a fucking waste of space.

Some people just shouldn't be parents.

TWENTY-SEVEN

"Trudy's sleeping," Liv says. "She needs sleep. So do you. You look beat, what happened?"

"Nothing."

"Have some tea."

"No thanks. We should get going." I'm not up for another interrogation session.

"What for? Let her sleep. Sit down. I'll get tea." Off she goes with her walker and I sit on the scratchy couch like a scolded child. I look beat because we ran out of fried chicken for the waffles. Corporate ordered enough waffle mix to feed an army but not enough plastic-wrapped fried chicken. We battered up a couple of boxes of chicken breasts with egg wash and spiced breadcrumbs, an expense that will alarm Corporate. When that ran out, we improvised a Tex-Mex sour cream and salsa topping that did not go over well with chicken-hungry customers. Siobhan and yours truly fielded complaints while Bob hid in his office.

As though the waffle chicken crisis were not enough, Daniel chose today to come out as a fat person. Lake, Daniel told us, is into fat boys and encouraged Daniel to accept his fatboyness. "Stop pretending you're only temporarily fat," Lake advised. Most fat people, according to Lake, think they could be thin if they only ate less and exercised more. They believe they are thin people waiting to climb out of fat people. According to Lake and Professor Bambo, this mode of thinking is the result of a self-love problem. They believe that fat people should accept and celebrate their size. Daniel celebrating his fatboyness gave Siobhan permission (according to Daniel) to further fat-shame him. They bickered in my office until I grabbed my throat and squeezed it, threatening to wring my neck if they didn't shut the fuck up. This worked but bruised my neck where Pierce bruised it the last time he tried to strangle me. Bruise upon bruise.

The rooster did not say another word to me after our did-I-or-didn't-I-hit-him discussion. For six hours he handed out flyers, taking only a fifteen-minute break. I packed a sandwich, a date square and a bottle of water in a bag and asked Helga to take it to him. They convened behind the dumpster, where she helped Pierce pull off his rooster head and told him about *Ghostbusters*. "He's really nice," she said. "A little shy maybe. Where'd he come from?" No one knew.

Liv shuffles towards me, somehow pushing the walker while holding a mug of tea. "Milk no sugar, right?"

"Right."

"Careful, it's hot." She pulls a photo album from a shelf and sits beside me. "I want to show you Ivy." She opens the album and carefully turns the pages revealing a blonde, blue-eyed, happy baby wiggling in a bassinet then progressing to a crawl then standing. Taking her first steps on wobbly legs, the toddler spreads her chubby arms for balance. Next she sits proudly on her pink trike, then straddles a red bicycle. As she grows, her white-blonde hair darkens to ash, she loses teeth, grows teeth, draws pictures of stick people, then houses, then butterflies, whales and horses. She prints three-letter words then short sentences. A bearded man carries her on his shoulders, his hands gently wrapped around her shins to prevent her from falling.

"Is that your husband?"

"He was always good with her. When she died, it broke him." Liv continues turning the pages and Ivy blossoms into a tween then a teen. In her powder-blue prom dress, she stands on tiptoes to kiss her father's cheek. In her graduation gown, she stares confidently into the camera, envisioning a long life ahead.

"Who Ivy was," Liv says, "had nothing to do with who her father became. It had to do with who he was before."

"Before what?"

"Before he failed at life. He was a mama's boy and never got over it. When his mama died it got worse. He was fired and never looked for another job, thought it was beneath him, refused to work at a job like mine.

With all that time on his hands, he turned angry and bitter and the only power he had was over me. Rapists don't get born rapists. Think about who your rapists might have been before they got so angry and bitter they had to exert power over you to feel like men. Only the before part of them lives in the child. You don't know the before parts of any of your rapists. They were all small once, like Trudy."

Liv keeps turning the album's pages and I see Ivy weakening, using a cane then two canes, then a walker, sitting in a wheelchair, lying on a hospital bed, wasting away. In the final shots she lies barely recognizable in a lair of tubes and wires. Liv closes the album and pats my knee. "The children have nothing to do with the act that made them."

"My son never looked like that."

"Like what?"

"Happy, sure of himself."

"Maybe he never looked like that to you. We get ideas about people we can't shake, illusions."

"I don't have any illusions about him."

"Sure you do. His father raped you. You think your son was born of evil. Clinging to that illusion inflicts suffering on you and the child. And whatever guilt you're harbouring, some of it justified, some of it pathological, it's wearing you down."

"That's not what's wearing me down. Listen, Liv, you've been incredibly kind but, honestly, I don't have the depth of feeling you're describing."

"Sure you do."

"No, I don't. I'm actually quite shallow."

"You said you don't believe in the love word or the trust word. So forget about the words. Some feelings can't be defined but you know them when they're there."

Trudy, holding her pink teddy, stands in the doorway. "Did my mom phone?"

"Not yet, but I was thinking we could go to Walmart and find you some shoes."

"Oh, wouldn't that be dandy," Liv says. "New shoes. Nothing like it."

"Can you come with us?" Trudy asks.

"No, sweetie, I'm a little tired. You two go have some fun. Are you hungry? Do you want to take some cookies with you?"

"Is Gyorgi coming over?" Trudy asks without looking at me.

"He has to work."

I avoided him, not wanting to interfere with whatever's brewing between him and Siobhan. Maybe, on the rebound from the Brazilian bombshell, she'll marry Gyorgi thereby enabling him to stay in Canada. This is the kind of help he needs, not communing in the dugout with a depressed, recently active alcoholic. Rejected and abandoned, I'm taking a piece of Bob's advice and accepting that the past belongs to the past. My preoccupation with the busboy is just another wound that will eventually scab over.

Normally I avoid Walmart due to its union-busting practices and my lacklustre career in Lingerie. But it has affordable kids' shoes and jackets. Initially shy about having a stranger buy her clothes, Trudy becomes emboldened as we look through the aisles, almost aggressive, searching racks and shelves within her reach for anything pink. Meanwhile I'm trying to gauge the right size.

"We're just here for shoes and a jacket," I remind her, carrying the sticks too big to fit in her backpack. "Find a pink jacket. Or pink shoes." She darts around, grabbing and fondling merchandise. As a former sales associate, I'm familiar with the aggravation caused by customers messing up stock. Hours must be spent refolding and rehanging discarded garments.

Finally I get her into a pink jacket. "Do you know how to do up zippers?"

"Yeah." She struggles with the zipper.

"Do you want me to do it?"

"No."

A harried mother and a sulking child step around us. Trudy watches them, apparently forgetting about the zipper. "I don't wannoo," the child whines as her mother pulls her along.

"Trudy? Do you need help with the zipper?"

The princess shakes her head and resumes, with intense concentration, fitting the zipper pieces together. A slouching sales associate tidies the turmoil left behind by Trudy, without looking our way. I know this trick: pretend you don't see the customer and maybe they'll disappear. Trudy manages the zipper but it sticks halfway. She keeps yanking at it, repeatedly saying fuckety fuck. I've never heard her use the f-bomb, and glance at the slouching sales associate, who continues to fold as though we don't exist.

"Let me do it," I say. "My zippers get stuck all the time." But before I can get my hands on it, Trudy pulls her arms free of the sleeves and wriggles out of the jacket.

"It doesn't work," she says, rifling through the rack.

I pick the jacket up off the floor and check the zipper. "It works fine. Look. You just have to be gentle with it."

"I don't want it."

"It's the only pink one in your size."

"I don't want it!"

I'd like to cuff her. This unfamiliar impulse suggests it is possible I hit Pierce. "How 'bout a fleece hoodie without a zipper?"

"Where?" She looks around.

I wave at the associate. "Hi. Excuse me. Do you have any fleece hoodies without zippers?" The associate has the pallor of someone who never leaves Walmart, who continuously folds and hangs garments mislaid by customers. "A *pink* hoodie?" I add. "It has to be pink. Or have some pink on it." The slouching associate shakes her head, continuing to fold.

"Fuck this," Trudy says, not sounding like Trudy, possibly like Sophie, or Yegor. Who knew a neglected child can behave as badly as the overindulged.

I take in a breath like Wolf did when he was exasperated with me. "Get with the program, Steve," he'd say. I never had the sagacity to ask, "What program?" Was it *his* program? Or was the program bigger than Wolf, spanning oceans and continents, eliminating thousands who failed to get with it.

"Trudy, get with the program."

"What program?"

Gulp. "Let's try shoes."

Once again the pink requirement must be met and I'm rummaging through pairs of runners tied together with nylon, guessing her size. It's not like the old days when a friendly salesman measured your foot and pulled the perfect fit out of a box. The princess tries to squeeze her foot into a pink sparkly shoe. "Trudy, that's too small."

"No it isn't."

"Try these ones. They have pink on them." Trudy tosses the small shoes and snatches the pair from me. "Please don't throw the shoes on the floor. Put them back where you found them."

"These look dumb."

"Why? They look fine. Are those pink flowers on the sides? Nice."

"They look like baby shoes."

"The shoes you were trying to squeeze your foot into look like baby shoes. These are for big girls."

"Where'd you put my sticks?"

I casually dispensed with them in the outerwear section, hoping she wouldn't notice. "I guess I put them down somewhere. I don't think it's fair I have to carry your sticks. If you collect them, *you* should carry them."

"Where'd you put them?"

"Where you were trying on jackets."

She starts to retrace our steps but another mother and child catch her attention. The orange-haired toddler, strapped into a shopping cart while his mother searches for shoes, chirps, "Hi."

"Hi," I reply.

"Hi," the toddler says again. I've never seen hair this orange. It's unearthly. Maybe he's an alien disguised to look human. "Hi," he repeats.

"Hi," I say.

"Hi," the alien says again.

"Trudy, can you say "hi" to the little boy?"

"Hi," she grumbles.

"Hi," the alien says.

"Stop saying hi," Trudy commands.

"Hi," he says.

"Stop saying hi."

"Hi," he says. Apparently "hi" is the only Earthling word he knows. "Hi."

"Stop saying hi." Trudy steps towards him as though she's about to slug him. I grab her hand, which I've never done before. It feels tiny, like I could crush it.

The orange-haired creature's mother, holding several pairs of toddler shoes, suddenly tunes in. "Is he saying hi? He loves saying hi, don't you, love bunny?"

"Hi," he says.

I pull Trudy down the aisle and let go of her hand. "Look, there are more shoes here."

"She called him love bunny."

"She did."

"That's dumb."

"Why?"

"Bunnies are white or brown or grey. There's no such thing as a love bunny."

"Why don't you try these? They've got pink laces and a pink stripe down each side."

Trudy grabs the shoes and, taking a moment to determine which to try on which foot, puts one on.

"You can't walk in them strung together, but just see if they fit." I tie the laces.

"Gyorgi's going to teach me how to do that."

"I can teach you."

"I want Gyorgi to teach me."

Without warning the resounding absence of the gypsy, in the dugout, in my life, bed—gay, bi, whatevs—becomes too much to bear and I sit on a bench with my head in my hands because I can't do any of this. Negotiate.

"Are you sick?" Trudy asks.

"No. Do you want those?"

"We got money for them?"

"We have a credit card."

"We can go in the change room and tear the tags off. My mom does it with her teeth."

"Really? Well, my teeth aren't that sharp." I take the shoes from her, knowing she will follow me because of them. Only one cash is open. We line up behind a disgruntled elderly woman in a Hawaiian shirt, pushing a cart full of *extra-scented scoopable clumping cat litter for multiple cats*.

"Don't you just love how they got just one cash going," the woman says.

"Just love it," I reply.

"People getting laid off left, right and centre, meanwhile we got to stand in line for half an hour. All that rigmarole to please the shareholders. Share this, I say. I'd like to see one of those chisellers lining up for half an hour."

"I don't think they shop at Walmart."

The line stalls due to a price check. If Trudy weren't with me I'd dip and seek solace in the woods. Instead, I arrange my face in what I hope is a benign expression while the woman in the Hawaiian shirt explains that global warming is caused by volcanoes and the heat from human bodies. Trudy keeps one hand on the pink shoes. She's not going to let them get away from her. "Do you want to hold them while we line up?" I ask. She nods and I give them to her. She cradles the shoes like a doll and begins one of her muted conversations. When she picks up sticks, she has muted conversations with, I presume, imaginary friends. Pierce talked to himself around me, probably because he couldn't talk to me. Trudy adds what looks like little dance movements to her muted conversations. She'll point a toe, flex a foot, toss a hand.

"Mommy," she squeals, dropping the shoes and running after a woman with a straw-coloured ponytail poking out the back of her ball cap. "Mommy, wait up!" The woman keeps walking. Trudy screams, "Mommy!" The woman, and many other Walmart customers, turn to stare at her.

"Who's your mommy?" A senior in a straw fedora places his hand on Trudy's shoulder, causing her to shriek more. "Have you lost your mommy?"

The woman in the ball cap walks on and Trudy wails, covering her eyes as though she can't bear to see. I grab the pink shoes, wrap an arm around Trudy's waist and carry her out of the store. She screams, flails and kicks but I hold on. People stare at Grandma and Baby Whale, but no one dares interfere. In a bus shelter stinking of piss, I sit with the distraught child on my lap in a straitjacket embrace. Pigeons peck at a muffin wrapper. The nylon tethering the shoes cuts into my fingers. I'd forgotten I was holding them. I shoplifted without tearing the tags off with my teeth. Slowly Trudy's cries fade to whimpers and she's almost still except for uneven breaths.

"That wasn't your mother, was it?" I ask.

She doesn't respond. We sit in lumpy silence. Gradually I release my hold and press the pink shoes into her hands.

Chester brings down Tiberius and lets Trudy feed the rat a Cheerio.

"It looks like he's holding a doughnut," Trudy says.

"That's right," Chester says. "Pure junk food. We can't give him too many."

While I stir-fry veggies, Chester informs us that, prior to being run over by a Caterpillar tractor, he'd planned to buy one hundred forested acres up north. "You need over eighty to get a permit to hunt on your property."

"Hunt what?" Trudy asks.

"Whatever you can eat. Moose, rabbits, geese. The plan was to buy a portable mill and clear enough wood to build a square house with a courtyard in the middle. And pull electricity from the air with Tesla's Free Energy Machine, making use of all those interacting particles. A wood-burning boiler would have kept me toasty all winter."

"I like that plan," Trudy says. "When I grow up I'm doing that."

"And I'll come visit," Chester says.

Sadness trickles under my skin. Not sure why. Trudy, Pierce, Gyorgi, my demented and undying parents. The meaninglessness of the love word.

I serve them at the rickety table.

"You're not eating?" Chester asks.

"I ate at the restaurant." This is untrue. Since witnessing the Siobhan/Gyorgi flirty interaction, I've lost my appetite.

"It's all happened before you know," Chester says.

"What?" Trudy tongues her wiggly tooth.

"Humans living on recycled dinosaurs. There's nuclear waste billions of years old, from ancient nuclear reactors, buried deep in the earth. But the new world order doesn't want the little people to know about it. The truth is we're making the same mistakes we made billions of years ago. The cycle keeps repeating itself."

Trudy insisted we check the mailbox and my messages. Her yearning for the mother who neglected and abandoned her never falters. Abused children cling, the counsellor with cherry red cat-eye specs and matching lipstick told me. I've inhabited a longing like Trudy's, hoping Peggy and Reggie would love me—before the rape shut everything down, before I recognized and repelled a similar longing in Pierce, before he went to Afghanistan and killed off a part of himself. The cycle keeps repeating itself.

My phone vibrates. I recognize Maya's number. "I'll take this in the bedroom. Eat up."

"Dick's girlfriend was in the car," she says. "*Her* car, a VW bug. I bet she's one of those people who put fake flowers in the dash."

"This was when he came to pick up his stuff?"

"She sat out there the whole time with her stereo blaring ABBA. What kind of person does that?"

"A person who likes ABBA."

"Now I can't get 'Dancing Queen' out of my head." She blows her nose. "I asked him, 'When did you stop loving me?' I wanted to know because I felt so stupid for not noticing. He said it wasn't that he stopped loving me but that his love for Felicity is different. So I said how is it different and he said, 'It's the kind of love men fight wars over.'"

"Dialogue from a bad movie."

"I know, right. He said it's time for me to get off the Dick train and go back to work."

"He actually said the Dick train?"

"He always talks about the Dick train and how lucky we are to be on it. I saw Felicity. She didn't look all that great, sort of average."

"It's not always about looks."

"You mean it's about pervy sex."

"He'd fight a war over it, apparently."

This makes Maya laugh and cry and I just listen, not knowing what else to do. I peek in on Trudy and Chester and find them coaxing Tiberius into a paper towel roll.

"You know those cheap glass ashtrays that used to be in restaurants?" Maya says. "We had those and my dad chain smoked. I was supposed to empty his shitty ashtrays, but I kept forgetting and the ashes and butts piled up. That's sort of how I feel. Like a shitty ashtray full of ashes and butts."

This brings to mind one of Siggy Moretti's word vomit poems that Helga showed us on her phone:

you smoked

me

so hard,

i burnt

your

fingers.

"Well," I say because Maya isn't speaking, "those ashtrays last forever. They're unbreakable. My father threw one at me once. It bounced off the wall."

"Oh heavens, I hear Katie. She has insomnia. Can you come over for brunch tomorrow? I really want the kids to be around someone who isn't caught up in all this."

"Can I bring a child?"

"A child?"

"I'm looking after a child. She's almost five."

"The more the merrier. Katie's four. They can play together."

Trudy playing with another child seems unlikely. She'll make Katie a prisoner and tie her up. "Can I bring a dog?"

"Absolutely, we love dogs. 163 Kingswood. Gotta go."

After Chester and Tiberius ascend to the penthouse, Trudy and I sit at opposite ends of the couch watching TV. The shows are inappropriate for a child, but I let her control the remote because she needs to control something. And forcing her to go to bed, only to have her wake up screaming, is not a cheering prospect. She surfs, criticizing the actions of TV characters, saying, "That's dumb" or "That's not very nice" or "She better watch it." She becomes engrossed in a crime drama that, as usual, begins with a dead and mutilated rape victim. "She shouldn't have done that," Trudy says of the rape victim partying in a flashback.

"Why not?"

"She looks slutty." This hints at conversations Trudy may have overheard in Sophie's apartment while trying not to "make noise."

"She's having fun," I say. "Don't you think she should be allowed to have fun?"

Trudy grips her loose tooth between her thumb and forefinger and wiggles it.

"Maybe there's something else on." I reach for the remote but she grabs it.

"I want to watch this."

"Okay, well, I don't. I'm getting ready for bed. You should too. You can sleep with Benedict in the blanket fort if you like." The mutt has morphed into a couch potato, staring blindly at the TV screen. "Do you need to do a dookie?" I ask him, but he ignores me. The Frisbee lies neglected in a corner. "Make sure you turn off the TV before you go to sleep."

African elephants are becoming smaller due to poachers killing large males for their large tusks, leaving only small males with small tusks. Small males produce smaller males. If African elephants survive poaching and loss of habitat, they will end up the size of horses. Or mice.

Trudy appears, offering her bloody tooth. "You said you'd give me a toonie."

"You're supposed to be sleeping."

She stands unmoving in her pink shoes.

"You want a toonie now?"

She nods. I feel around in my pockets.

"All I have is dimes and nickels. I'll give it to you tomorrow."

Her eyes hiss.

"I'm sorry. I promise I'll get change tomorrow."

"You said we'd go to Dollarama." The "you said" refrain is too familiar, too like her father. Suddenly the dugout feels hollow and shadowy.

"Can you check your messages again?"

I hold my phone to her ear. She maintains her strained bitch face despite what must be cavernous loneliness. I'd like to assure her that her mother left her to protect her. But I don't know this. Maybe Sophie was protecting herself by pushing her child away. Like I did.

"Go to bed, Trudy. It's very late."

"Don't you want the tooth?"

"Maybe you should keep it till I get a toonie." I turn back to my pencilled fragments because facing her burns. She returns to the couch, her pink shoes scuffing the linoleum.

"Can you turn the TV off?" I call after her. She doesn't. I hear gunfire and the gasping of actors pretending to suffer bullet wounds, then a soundtrack with soaring strings followed by mournful horns. Maybe this comforts Trudy. Maybe she's accustomed to falling asleep with the TV obscuring Sophie's activities.

If we could figure out why our parents did what they did, maybe we could unmake who we've become. Rewind. But that might mean we wouldn't recognize ourselves. Our traumas give us identity, help us to understand who we've become. If I'd been born to loving parents, and not been raped, I would not be me. And me is all I know, all I can manage. So what if I'm severely damaged, I can function. In my coffin.

Someone's knocking on the window, possibly Yegor after the pedo bait. I turn off the light and play possum. If it were Pierce wanting food or money, he'd let himself in. The knocking continues. Time to seal the exits. I slip off the bed to check on Trudy. She's asleep in the blanket fort, still wearing the pink shoes. I turn the TV off. Either the Bosnian or Chester plod down the stairs to open the front door.

"Well, if it isn't my communist friend. Did you try the buzzer?"

I crack open my door. Chester's wearing what looks like a satin boxer's robe and Crocs with socks.

"I'm not wanting to wake Trudy," Gyorgi says. He must have just finished his double shift. He sees me and holds up a plastic Barbie house. "For Trudy. Someone put to garbage. I clean like new."

"That's really nice of you," I say, feeling unjoined because I'm irrationally happy to see him.

"Well," Chester says. "I'll leave you to it." The heavyweight champion returns to the penthouse.

Gyorgi puts down the Barbie house. "I want to drop off before I go home. Surprise tomorrow, for her to put her plastic animals."

"Great idea."

"How are you, Stevie?"

"I'm fine, Gyorgi. How are you?"

"Fine also, but tired after double."

"No kidding."

"See you tomorrow." He winks and steps out the door. I catch it before it closes.

"I'm not working tomorrow," I say.

"Oh. Then day after."

"Has Siobhan got you doing another double tomorrow?" I watch his expression for clues he's lusting for Siobhan.

"Opening and lunch only. Short shift. Is okay."

"She was helping you today."

"Who?"

"Siobhan. I saw her helping you clear tables."

"She is nice girl."

Again I scan his face for glints of desire.

"Your son was good today. As rooster. I give him cigarette. We talk. He worry for you."

"Why?"

He shrugs. "Same I worry for my mother."

Pierce worrying about me, that's a stretch.

"Good night," Gyorgi says.

Before I can get my armour back on I say, "You can sleep here."

He looks at me, into me. "You sure is okay? Please to not feel pity for me."

"I don't feel pity for you." I slide my arms around his neck for another therapeutic hug, but his hands feel uncertain on my lower back. In a terrifying act of self exposure, I bury my face in his chest. He smells of Chappy's and active fruit ingredients. Then he's holding on to me as tightly as I'm holding on to him. Instinctively I wrap my legs around his hips. He lifts me up so we are face to face, eye to eye, mouth to mouth—unmoored—and I don't know the word for the feeling, can't define it. I just know it's there.

TWENTY-EIGHT

"When are we going to Dollarama?" Trudy's fist is clenched, probably around the toonie Gyorgi put outside the blanket fort before he left.

I spit toothpaste into the sink and rinse. "We can go now."

"You mean, like, right now?"

"Right now. On our way to have brunch with a friend of mine. She's got a girl your age."

"Can we bring the Barbie house?"

"If you carry it."

"Here." She opens her fist, revealing not the toonie but her tooth.

"Thank you." I take the tiny chunk of ivory. Trudy doesn't budge.

"Are you going to throw it in the garbage?" she asks.

"Of course not."

"What are you going to do with it?"

Not sure. It feels electric in my hand—Trudy's, Pierce's and my interacting particles. "I need a little box for it."

"You can get one at Dollarama."

"Good idea. I'll leave it here for now." I carefully place it on my bedside table.

"Yegor throws them in the garbage."

"Really? Well, I'm going to buy a special box for this one."

We hitch the mutt to a mailbox outside Dollarama. "We'll get you a doggy treat," I assure him.

Trudy searches the toy section for ponies that will fit in the Barbie house. We didn't bring the house because she couldn't carry it along with her backpack, purse and Samurai sword.

"There's no ponies," she says.

"What about the My Little Pony ones? They come in pink or blue."

"Those are dumb. Ponies aren't pink or blue."

"So you want a real-looking pony?"

She nods, scrutinizing a packet of plastic animals.

"Those look real," I say. "The label says they're ranch animals. There's one horse in there. And a pig and a cow and a goat."

"I've got a pig and a cow and a goat. And I don't want just one horse. I want a mommy and a baby." She fondles the horse through the plastic. "This is a nice horse."

"It is. I like the white on her forehead and hooves. Look, there's a zebra in the safari packet. That's kind of like a horse."

"Zebras aren't the same as horses."

"No, but maybe they could be friends. And the gorilla and the giraffe in the safari set are impressive. Check out the rhinoceros."

"I don't have a rhino."

"You're kidding? Oh, you've got to have a rhino. How 'bout *you* buy the ranch animals and *I* buy the safari animals? Then you'll have a horse and a zebra who might possibly be friends." I hand her the safari packet. She examines it carefully, turning it over to inspect both sides.

"I don't have a giraffe or a leopard."

"I think that's a cheetah, actually. Do you have a lioness?"

"I have a lion with a mane."

"Perfect, now he'll have a buddy."

She grips both the ranch and safari packets. "If *you* buy the safari one, can I play with it?"

"Of course. Now let's find a little box for your tooth."

In the gift wrap section we stare at an assortment of boxes. "Pick one," I say. She takes forever to decide, reminding me of Pierce dithering over Popsicles. Finally she settles on a pink box dotted with silver stars.

"Perfect," I say. "You hold it till we have to pay for it."

She grips the animals solemnly in one hand and the box in the other with her purse dangling from her wrist. We line up at the cash counter next to the greeting cards. There is only one cashier working, presumably to please the chiseller shareholders. Trudy studies the greeting cards as we shuffle along in the queue. Stalled in front of cards that say *To my darling granddaughter* or *To my sweet granddaughter*, I'm doused with guilt. The cards are decorated with flowers, princesses and fairies waving magic wands. Trudy pulls one out. "What's this say?" She holds up the card and points to the letters. "That's a *b*." She moves her finger to the next one. "That's an *l*, that's an *e* and those are *s*'s, right? Can you read it? I don't know how to read."

"It says 'bless you.'"

"What's bless mean?"

"In this case it kind of means thank you."

"For what?"

"For being a granddaughter."

"That's dumb. What's it say after that?"

"*My darling granddaughter, you light up my days.*
With your questions, giggles and fun-loving ways."

Trudy doesn't react, just stares at the card. "That rhymes."

"It does."

She carefully tucks the card back in the display.

"Do you want a candy bar?" I ask. "*I* feel like one. What about an Island Bar? Coconut covered in chocolate. Yum."

"Okay." She seems uncertain.

"Are you sure? Would you prefer a different kind?"

"My mom doesn't buy me candy bars."

"Well," I say, "*I'm* crazy about coconut." I grab two, and two packets of Trident. "We'll chew gum afterwards, to clean our teeth."

She shoots me a glance to check if I'm serious.

"Don't you chew gum?" I ask.

Trudy shrugs and looks back at the cards. She's as wary as her father was after two tours in Afghanistan. It took a war to severely damage Pierce. What severely damaged Trudy?

Maya's house is huge, renovated, glistening. It's like walking into Pottery Barn. Trudy, Benedict and I stand awkwardly on refinished hardwood, surrounded by refinished oak. On the nearest wall is an oil painting of an empty beach. The ocean and sky merge in the distance, obscuring the horizon.

"What a sweet dog," Maya says. "How old is he?"

"Old," I say.

"Katie, Liam," Maya calls, "come meet our guests and their doggy." She heads down the hall. "I'm making waffles."

"Waffles?" Just hearing the word triggers me.

"We're crazy about waffles."

"Isn't everybody?"

A ponytailed girl scurries down the stairs and after Maya. Clinging to her mother's leg, the girl sucks her thumb. Maya lifts her onto her hip. "Trudy's here to play with you, Katie. Do you want to show her your room?"

Katie shakes her head.

"Where's your brother?" Maya asks, but Katie only sucks her thumb. She looks frail, pale. Trudy seems bionic in comparison.

"Liam?" Maya calls. "He's probably got headphones on. If he's not gaming, he's watching Netflix. Never mind, it'll be just us girls." She kisses Katie and tries to put her down but the child won't let go.

"She's been really needy with all this stuff going on with her dad," Maya explains. "Sweetie, Mummy's going to make waffles. Why don't you show Trudy your bead collection? Do you like stringing beads, Trudy?" Trudy nods. "Go get your beads, sweetie." Katie climbs reluctantly back upstairs.

"Can I help with anything?" I ask.

"Oh, it's a no-brainer wafflemaker, with a timer and everything. Go relax in the living room." Maya looks strained from trying too hard around the people "not caught up in all this."

Trudy and I sit in the Pottery Barn living room on opposite ends of an overstuffed couch.

"Can I open my plastic animals?" Trudy asks.

"Of course."

She uses her teeth to tear open the packets, must have learned this trick from Mom. She tries to stand the animals on the pile carpet but they tip over.

"Try them on the wood floor," I say.

While arranging the animals, she keeps the prized horse in her left hand and has one of her muted conversations with it, holding the horse's head close to her lips. Benedict looks at me for some indication as to what happens next.

"I don't know, buddy." I give him another Dingo Nugget and look at happy family pics on the glass coffee table. Dick appears to be your average, middle-aged investment banker. The photos must predate cancer because Maya has breasts.

"You don't know what?" Trudy asks.

"Has the horse met the zebra yet?"

She ignores me and resumes her conversation with the horse. This doesn't feel like a house people live in. It's the kind of house you see in Diane Keaton movies about family get-togethers, where sisters and brothers, mothers and fathers feud then make up and live happily ever after.

"This house is big," Trudy says.

"It is. I know a guy whose house is so big his family texts each other in it." Wade moved out of the mansion to get away from his family, even though he never saw them in the mansion.

"That's dumb."

I text Conquer to check on Pierce. He texts back, "JC's son is on the prowl. Stay tuned."

I picture Jesus Christ's son, in her pink earmuffs and American flag scarf, stalking Pierce, and Greg Lem in his reflector wraparounds and camo, tackling her. This could work.

"What are you writing now?" Trudy asks.

"Haven't decided yet."

Being able to walk away from a blast doesn't mean you're not hurt. There are silent injuries. You can be symptom-free despite the pressure from the explosion entering your lungs and rupturing air sacs. Slowly you start to notice it's harder and harder to breathe. A pressure wave can rupture organs even if the skin isn't broken. Busted ear drums might indicate other internal injuries. Symptoms of blast-effect brain trauma aren't always immediately apparent.

I smell burning and speed to the kitchen where Maya's standing over the smoking wafflemaker.

"I can't even do this right," she says. "The batter keeps leaking out the sides."

"You're putting too much in." I turn off the wafflemaker.

"Dick used to do the Sunday waffles. It looked so easy when he did it."

The fire alarm beeps. I climb on a chair to remove the battery. "Maybe we should do something Dick didn't do."

"I so wanted things to be normal."

"They can't be normal. Make a new normal."

"He sneaked in early this morning to steal the iPod speakers, the turntable for his vinyl and this stupid wafflemaker. He said since *he* paid for them, *he's* taking them. I guess he'll be back for more as he's pretty much paid for everything."

"Mom," a long-haired, angular boy says. "What the fuck? You burning the house down?"

"It's under control, Liam. This is my friend, Stevie. She's having brunch with us."

"I ate already." He goes back upstairs.

"He's taking his dad leaving really hard," Maya explains. Katie reappears and clings to her mother's leg. "Hi sweetie, did you show the little girl your beads? What's her name again? Sorry, with chemo brain, my short-term memory's hopeless."

"Trudy," I say.

"Show Trudy your beads, sweetie."

"I don't want to."

"Why not?"

Katie reaches to be picked up again. Maya sits at the table and pulls her onto her lap.

"Why don't I scramble some eggs," I say, to get this show on the road so I can get off it. "Have you got eggs?"

"In the fridge. Thanks." Katie cups her hand around her mother's ear and whispers something.

"I know that, sweetie. Stevie, Katie won't have eggs. Pretty much all she eats these days are Bear Paws. I asked her doctor about it and he said not to worry."

"Okay, well, do *you* want eggs?" I shouldn't be here, should be at Chappy's running defence for Pierce, sharing smokes with Gyorgi.

"I love scrambled eggs," Maya says, still holding the thumb-sucker.

Trudy stands mightily in the doorway. "Where are your beads?"

"Show her your beads, sweetie."

Katie hides her face in her mother's neck.

This is nuts. "Maybe we should go."

"Oh, please don't." Maya extricates herself from the kid and sets her on her feet. "Come on, Katie, show Trudy your bead set." She gives Katie a little nudge and the kid heads for the stairs, dragging her feet. The princess promptly follows. One thing about Trudy, she gets shit done.

While Maya muses about her marriage and how she doesn't understand where it went wrong, I'm imagining JC's son head-butting the rooster.

"It's all because of the cancer," she concludes. Maya blames the cancer like I blame the rape.

I whisk eggs, pour them in a pan, stir them around. "Should we make toast?"

"Good idea. And coffee?"

"Please."

She pulls a couple of slices of bread from a package. "When you're young you have all these plans." She stands with a bread slice in each hand, apparently forgetting what to do with them. "Then they don't happen, or anyway not how you expected, and you're running out of time so it's sort of obvious they're never going to happen. It's depressing. I mean, didn't you have plans?"

I gently take the slices from her and slide them in the toaster. "I plan menus, not lives."

"You're funny."

We are not on a level playing field. The devoted mother with a potentially fatal illness, and the useless-piece-of-shit mother/grandmother with a potentially fatal attitude. It would be unfair to point out Maya's inner misogyny, explain that she doesn't need Dick to bring her down, she can do that herself.

"We're all on this giant hurtling space rock," I say, but she's adrift in chemo thoughts.

Katie, tearful, scrambles downstairs and resumes clinging to her mother. No sign of Trudy. A writhing inner discomfort starts up as I wait to hear what Trudy did to Katie.

"What happened, sweetie?"

"She made me sit in a corner and told me, 'Don't make noise.'"

"Why did she do that?"

"Trudy?" I call. "Come down please. It's time to go."

"You don't have to," Maya says.

"We do. I'm sorry, this isn't working out. I shouldn't have brought her." I hear the pink shoes on the stairs and grab Trudy's crushable hand. "Let's get your stuff and the dog."

"Are you coming back to the writing group?" Maya asks.

"Not sure." Since revealing my inner monster at Wolf's memorial, I haven't felt inclined to join Ashley Shutt's coterie. "We'll talk soon."

At Tim Hortons, seemingly unaware that she just terrorized Katie, Trudy orders a vanilla dip with pink sprinkles. She sits swinging her legs the way Pierce did.

"Did you make Katie sit in a corner and tell her, 'Don't make noise?'"

She swivels her head away from me. "No."

She's lying, but who am I to reprimand her, a lying, recently active alcoholic.

"I could understand why you'd want to," I say.

"What?"

"Get her to be quiet. She's pretty whiny. But you could've just asked her to be quiet. Making people sit in corners isn't the best idea. I mean, do *you* like being told to sit in a corner?"

"I do what I'm told."

"Yeah, but do you like doing what you're told?"

She opens wide to bite her doughnut. Sprinkles drop onto her lap. With impressive focus, she presses her index finger on one sprinkle at a time and pops them in her mouth. "She doesn't take care of her Barbies. Their hair's all messed. Some of them have no clothes on."

My phone vibrates. It's Conquer. "You better get over here. Some kid threw a rock at the rooster."

"What kid?"

"A kid on a bike. He's been zipping up and down the strip. Now he's circling him. Your son keeps spinning around in that chicken suit because he can't fucking see anything in it."

I call a cab that doesn't come. We wait for a bus on a bench beside a haggard Black woman with a bag of cleaning products on her lap. A spiky-haired middle-aged man in green leggings and a sweatshirt with a flamingo on it leans against the bus stop sign.

"How's it goin'?" he asks us.

"Fine," I say. The haggard woman stares past him. Trudy whispers to her horse. Benedict, at her side, listens intently.

"I've been in the pen for a few years," the man says. "Just got out. Feels good to be *alive*."

I give him a thumbs-up. Trudy shifts closer to me. The ex-con is frightening her.

"Your hair is way cool," he tells her, trying to touch it, but I grab his wrist.

"Hands off," I say. Benedict gets off his haunches to protect his princess.

"I'm just being friendly. You expect a white man to be racist, don't you?" he says to the haggard woman, who continues to stare past him. "Well, I'm not your regular white guy. I *jive*."

Trudy moves to my other side, distancing herself from the irregular white guy.

"I got the moves," he says, thrusting his hips. "Is she your grand-daughter?" he asks the woman. "I love her dress. Are you a princess, honey?

Or a fairy?" His assumption that the Black child belongs to the Black woman doesn't surprise me, but Trudy reaching for my hand does. I spot a cab and flag it.

Conquer calls again. "They've taken him to Scarborough General."

"Who's 'they'?"

"Emergency services. There were fire trucks, cops, the whole deal. The rooster tripped over the kid and fell, was rolling around on the ground. I didn't see the whole thing. We're in the middle of a rush here, some fucking Little League thing."

"What freaked Pierce out? The kid?"

"The kid took off. Anyway, they wrapped your son up like a burrito and whisked him away."

"Did you see a guy in camo and wraparounds?"

"Hard to say. There was a bit of a crowd, and World o' Chicken flyers blowing all over the place. Gotta go."

I redirect the cabby to Scarborough General.

"Where are we going?" Trudy asks.

"The hospital. Have you ever been to a hospital?"

"My mom went."

"Why?"

"I forget. They have a nice gift shop. Yegor bought me a lollipop."

Emergency is crammed with the usual Saturday-night-bleeding-into-Sunday-morning crowd. Pierce is nowhere in sight. We stand amid lacerated faces, drunken ramblings, a woman with two black eyes wearing a T-shirt that says *Blah Blah Blah*, a man in a worn blazer shouting about God's wrath being upon us. A frenzied drug addict demands that the nurse behind the triage window help him. "I'm in pain!" he shouts. "Why are you being so mean?" Within minutes two security guards escort him out. The snow princess stares at a boy whose eyes are swollen shut, probably from an allergic reaction. I take her hand. "Trudy, do you remember my son? You met him at my place. He had a backpack and was taking food out of the fridge. He's here somewhere. Let me know if you see him."

"The guy with frizzed hair?"

"That's right."

"Why's he here?"

"He got in a fight."

"Is he hurt?"

"I don't know." We navigate around patients on gurneys and chairs, inhaling the stench of bodies, Lysol, piss and vomit.

"The beds are too high," Trudy says. "I can't see." I hoist her onto my hip. She cranes her neck, looking around. A rotund man with bloodshot eyes and a split lip makes goofy faces at her and says, "Nice sword." She ignores him and points to a gurney down the corridor.

"That man's hair's frizzed."

I recognize the back of Pierce's head immediately because I've stared at it on my couch for months. The boy I barely knew has become a man disturbingly familiar. We stand over him. A sleeve of the chicken suit has been pushed up to allow for the IV needle. "Pierce?"

His eyeballs move without seeing, his face spasms, his legs and arms twitch as he pulls against the knit tubing tying him to the gurney.

"What's wrong with him?" Trudy asks.

"I'm not sure."

"Why's he in fuzzy yellow?"

"It's part of a chicken costume." I put her down and lean close to his ear. "Pierce? It's me. Mom." Calling myself Mom feels ridiculous. "Pierce, it's Stevie."

If he hears me, he's not letting on. He is trapped in the chaos behind his eyeballs. At war. There's nothing I can do for him. I can easily walk away.

TWENTY-NINE

"Do you know this patient?" a security guard asks.

"He's my son."

"Perfect, I'll let the nurse know you're here." The security guard has tiny ears and an unexpectedly kind face.

"Did they have to tie him up?"

The security guard pulls on one of his tiny ears. "He was pretty agitated, but he's quieted right down."

"Do you know where he is in the lineup?"

"The nurse took his vitals and got the story from the paramedics. The doctor had a quick look, gave him some meds and ordered blood work."

"What kind of meds?"

"They don't share that info with us, ma'am."

"How long does it take to get blood results?"

"Depends on how busy we are. As you can see, it's a full house." The security guard scratches his eyebrow with his thumb. "Do you happen to know why he'd think he was on fire? The medics said there was no fire at the scene."

This explains why Pierce was rolling around on the ground. To put out the fire. "He's a soldier. They get burned."

"Oh. Fair enough. Anyways, I'm supposed to keep an eye on him but, like I said, he's quieted right down."

"I'll watch him."

"You sure? I'll keep checking back."

"Do you go outside at all?"

"Outside?"

"The doors. I tied our dog to a post. A black lab. I'd be grateful if you could check on him when you're out there."

"No worries."

"And give him some of these." I pull the packet of Dingo Nuggets out of my backpack.

"His name's Benny," Trudy says.

"Benny, got it."

"Actually, sorry," I say, "would you mind keeping an eye on my son for a couple more minutes? I promised this child a lollipop."

"No worries." He directs us to the gift shop.

"You didn't promise me a lollipop." Trudy skips ahead.

"Must be your lucky day." I plod along, bodysnatched like Loretta, the hundred-year-old coal miner's daughter.

The princess bounces on the souls of her feet in the candy section.

"Pick two," I say. Around me are shelves of gifts that would make me want to die if I were close to death: stuffies, figurines, fake flowers, neck pillows, hemorrhoid cushions, foot and sitz baths, surgical stockings, happy-face mugs, best Mom and Dad mugs, wellness books.

"This is a nice shop," Trudy says.

"Aren't you a darling," says the senior behind the counter, wearing a *volunteer* tag. She looks like a real mother/grandmother, not a faker like yours truly. She beckons me to a corner and whispers, "You should do something about her hair. My daughter married a Trinidadian and I just about gave up on my granddaughter's hair, then I discovered these." She points to brushes with thick rubber bristles. "They're to stimulate the scalp but they work wonderfully on crinkly hair." She presses the bristles of one of the brushes into her palm. "See, they're soft. You start at the tips and move inwards so you don't hurt her."

I look at the brush then the woman. Lipstick bleeds into the wrinkles above her lip. Shaky liquid liner frames her eyes. This woman puts a face on before volunteering at the death-inducing gift shop. This woman is a life force. "Thanks," I whisper back, taking the brush, needing a drink.

Insurgents blocked a road with tires and set them on fire while little boys threw homemade bombs at the convoy. Pierce floored it to get off the road and onto the rough terrain. He couldn't see with all the smoke and dust, was driving blind, inhaling gas fumes from the explosives. All four tires blew. They were riding on the rims. "I'm on fire," Pierce screamed, "put me out! I'm on fucking fire!" His comrades had to assure him, repeatedly, that he wasn't on fire. Pierce told me this story as though it were a joke, and "I'm on fire" the punchline.

"That's not funny, Pierce."

"Sure it is, it's fucking hilarious."

"How long do we have to stay here?" Trudy asks. She's arranged her animals on the linoleum beside Pierce's gurney. The prized horse remains in her left hand.

"Until a doctor sees him."

"Where's the doctor?"

"With other patients."

She's still on her first lollipop, a ball with pink and turquoise swirls. She puts the ball in her mouth for a few seconds, closing her lips over it, then takes the lollipop out again. Which is why it's lasted over an hour. Most kids suck on lollipops, leaving the sticks dangling from their mouths like cigarettes. Trudy watches a lethargic girl, about her age, in the arms of her anxious mother, who tries to coax the child to sip from a juice box.

"What's wrong with that girl?" Trudy asks.

"Not sure. She might have flu and be dehydrated."

"What's dehydrated?"

"She might need water. They'll probably hook her up to a bag like my son's. See?" I point to Pierce's IV. "That tube drips water into his arm while he's sleeping."

"They did that to my mom."

"How long was your mom in hospital?"

She turns her face away. "I forget."

"Who looked after you?"

"Yegor."

The anxious mother holds the juice box straw to her daughter's lips again.

"Trudy, you didn't tell me if you got a chance to do some beading at Katie's."

She hands me her lollipop, rummages in her backpack and pulls out four small Ziploc bags of beads and some nylon thread.

"Katie gave you all that?"

Trudy nods but I suspect she's lying.

"How nice of her," I say. "Do you want me to tie a knot so you can string some beads?"

"We don't have scissors to cut the string."

I look in my backpack for nail scissors, always handy in my fingernail-destroying job. "Which bead do you want to start with?"

She opens one of the bags and pulls out a pink bead then carefully zips the bag closed. I hand back the lollipop and sit on the floor beside her, thread the nylon through the bead, tie a knot, snip the string and hand it to her. She passes me the lollipop before carefully opening another bag and selecting a second bead. It takes a couple of tries before she manages to fit the nylon through the bead's tiny hole. She carefully extracts beads from the bags one after another and struggles to push the nylon through the holes. I wait for her to become frustrated and ask for help. But she doesn't. This is a child unaccustomed to asking for help. A resilient and resourceful child who has had to adapt to changing circumstances for, possibly, her whole short life. Admirable, except that when we adapt, we give something up, let something go, and soon forget who we were before we adapted.

Months before Pierce's friend Jake committed suicide, he sat fidgeting at my rickety table waiting for Pierce who was late due to a subway breakdown. I made Jake coffee and a sandwich. He talked about Afghanistan. Women and children approached you in a crowd, he said, shielding the fighters about to kill you. He said men put women and children in the front seats of cars while they hid in the rear or trunks with guns. Using women and children as human shields was something Jake couldn't "get his head around." "I mean," he said, "you'd kind of assume that wouldn't be something any civilized society would do with their women and children."

You'd kind of assume that bombing women and children wouldn't be something any civilized society would do. Recently the Coalition mistook a funeral gathering for an ISIS meet-up. An air strike hit the house, killing eleven people, six children and three babies.

"They have toy guns over there," Jake said. "Kids point toy guns at us all the time, and we almost pull the trigger on them. I mean, what kind of person lets their kids play with toy guns in a war zone?"

Isn't that how kids adapt to unending war? They give something up, let something go, and play with guns.

Jake believed in the war at first, fighting counterinsurgency, supporting the Afghan people "and all that," but later he questioned what he called "the politics of it." "Providing security for a nation whose government falls because we ousted their leader is fucked up. Nobody likes being occupied. You just have to drive through a bombed village and see the people still trying to live in it to know it's fucked up."

Yet Jake wouldn't have traded his time in Afghanistan for anything. It made him "man up." Then he swallowed all the pills the VA prescribed and died in his mother's bathroom.

Conquer texts. "What's up?"

"We're waiting for the doc."

"Is he acting crazy?"

"They've drugged him."

"Call me when you've seen the doc."

"Will do." I won't, will not burden him with this.

Trudy puts the lollipop on her tongue for a few seconds. I pick up the rubber-bristled brush and start brushing her hair from the tips, moving inwards so I don't hurt her. She hands me back the lollipop and continues stringing beads as though having me brush her hair is perfectly normal.

A psychiatric nurse questions me about Pierce. She's not dressed like a nurse but in khakis and a navy pullover—possibly true navy—made of stretchy material. This makes me think of Greg Lem, and why he wasn't there to defend Pierce.

Trudy has fallen asleep against me. The psychiatric nurse squats beside us, jotting notes on Pierce's chart. She smiles too much.

I tell her what I know about Pierce's medical history and explain that he is a vet with undiagnosed PTSD, that the CF are not taking care of their psychically wounded, that this male-dominated organization continues to stigmatize PTSD, that many vets don't seek help for fear it will be seen as a sign of weakness, and the ones that do seek help can't get it, are stalled by voicemail and paperwork and put on waiting lists. The nurse smiles and asks about Pierce's sleeping habits, if he has outbursts of uncontrolled anger, irritability and/or difficulty concentrating. Is he hypervigilant, depressed, does he have problems with intimacy, suicidal thoughts, nightmares?

"All of the above," I say. "When do we get to see a doctor?"

"Your son's already been seen by the ER doctor. We're waiting for the psych resident, and he may want to consult with the psychiatrist on call." She looks at her watch. "Your son's in no shape to go anywhere just yet. You may as well sit tight."

I *am* sitting tight, so tight it's hard to breathe. "The spasms and writhing around he's doing, is that because of the medication?"

She nods. "Dystonic reactions are a common side effect of antipsychotics. Patients can get super crampy. It'll pass."

"Can we untie the tubing?"

"It's there for his protection. He was trying to pull out the IV earlier, got quite tangled up in it. Let's wait till the doctor sees him and take it from there."

Smiling, she asks more questions. Does Pierce experience panic attacks, anxiety? Does his behaviour ever become manic or violent? Is he excessively active? I realize how I answer her questions will determine whether or not he'll get out of here, and he will want to get out of here. So I don't tell her he tries to strangle me, or that he hit a kid, or that he's self-medicating with beer and I'm scared he's going to kill himself. I won't let them give Pierce a label he can't shake, a diagnosis that will make him unemployable. Finally I say, "Why don't you tell me something *you* know about him? What's written on that chart?"

"Not much. Just what the medics said on admission."

"Which was what?"

"That he fell on the ground and was extremely agitated, uncooperative and hallucinating." She straightens up from the squat with difficulty. Her stretchy navy pullover inches up her gut, revealing a roll of pasty flesh. She tugs the pullover down. "So, sit tight. I'll get this to the doctor asap."

"Is there any chance we can move my son out of the corridor?"

"I'll see what I can do," she says, which means she can't do anything. I make a pillow for Trudy out of my backpack and sweatshirt, and carefully shift her onto it. In a deep child-slumber, her mean face is replaced by the angelic one. The fingers of her left hand curl around the horse.

Standing beside the gurney, watching Pierce's drug-induced muscle contractions, I remember Gyorgi meeting my muscles' resistance with an equal amount of energy, enabling them to loosen slowly. I gently lay my hands on one of Pierce's thighs. Tied up, he can't throttle me. I add pressure—deep, firm, steady. When his muscles resist mine, I reduce the pressure slightly. As with Trudy when she freaks out, I don't let go or hesitate. When his tension ebbs, I apply more pressure. This barely perceptible energy exchange reduces his twitching, one muscle group at a time. My back starts to ache from leaning over him but I keep at it. He feels vulnerable under my hands, this boy who has seen more horror in his twenty-three years than I will see in my lifetime. This boy without a mother, who had to adapt, giving something up, letting something go. Who can't remember who he was before.

"Everything okay here?" the kindly security guard asks.

"Okay. The nurse came by. We're waiting for a shrink. Did you see the dog?"

"I did. He's really old, eh?"

"The dog," Pierce mutters groggily, pulling against the restraints. "Where's the dog?"

"Right outside, buddy," the guard says. "Take it easy now, you've been given something to calm you down. The tubing's on to keep you safe."

Heavy-lidded, Pierce tries to focus on the guard. "I killed a kid."

"You didn't kill anybody, buddy. You had a panic attack. You're going to be fine. I'll let the nurse know you're awake. Be back in two secs."

I can feel Pierce's tension rebounding. "Pierce, you've been given an antipsychotic drug. All the weird things you're feeling are side effects."

"Fuck this." He jerks against the tubing and yours truly, the human straitjacket, uses chicken-pounding arms to subdue him.

"If you fight them," I whisper in his ear, "they'll think you're really nuts and won't let you out of here. If you give them reason to think you might harm yourself or anyone else, they'll put you in the psych ward."

"I'm fucking dizzy."

"That's the drug. Close your eyes. Rest. Let's see what the doctor has to say."

"I don't need a fucking doctor."

"You need help, Pierce."

"Not pills. Don't let them give me pills. They turned Jake into a fucking zombie." He can't keep his eyes open. "Don't fucking leave me here."

"I won't. Try to relax." I keep my palm on his chest, applying steady pressure to his sternum. Other than when he's trying to strangle me, we've never been this physically close. For once I don't feel the rapists in him, possibly because he's tied up and in a fuzzy chicken suit. Or because handling Trudy has given me the ability to breach physical barriers. And handling and being handled by Gyorgi. I, avoider of human contact, have gone all touchy-feely.

"Don't let them dope me again."

"Don't act crazy, and they won't. They need the bed. They *want* to send you home. What happened to Greg?"

"He couldn't make it. Yesterday burned him out." He twists his head one way then the other.

Trudy, suddenly awake, stands, gripping her horse. "Can we go now?"

The security guard returns. "It's time to roll, folks," he says and starts pushing the gurney. "Shouldn't be long now, buddy. We're getting you in to see a psychiatrist. He'll sort you out."

In the ward, the guard draws the curtain around us. "You're in good hands now," he says, and I want to believe him. To our left, through the curtain, we hear a woman moaning softly. To our right, a man tries to get the attention of medical staff by insisting he's having a stroke.

I offer Trudy the only chair, but she shakes her head and arranges her animals on the floor. I hand her one of the Island Bars, which she quickly tucks into her backpack as though someone might snatch it from her.

"I killed a kid," Pierce mutters.

"You tripped over a kid. You didn't kill him."

"He got caught in the wheels."

"Wrong again. He took off on his bike."

"The dog was limping."

"The dog's fine. You didn't kill anything. You had a panic attack. Rest."

He drifts off again.

Feeling like an old ashtray, I remember I didn't replace the battery in Maya's fire alarm. The Pottery Barn house will go up in flames, the thumb-sucking child will cling to her mother while the gaming, angular teenager—deafened by headphones—won't hear his mother's desperate pleas to evacuate. I phone Maya, leave a message about the battery, and watch Trudy's muted conversation with her horse. Back on her feet, she does a little dance, flexing a foot, tossing a hand.

"It's fucking deaf or something," Pierce mumbles.

"What is?"

"The dog."

"The dog's blind not deaf. He's just outside, tied to a post."

The patient on the other side of the curtain who believes he's having a stroke warns hospital staff that technology is about to crash. "A satellite's going to fall from the sky. You watch. It'll start a world war. Over religion. A final world war."

"It's got bald patches," Pierce mutters.

I lean over him, my hands firmly on his chest, and look into his eyes, the same pond green as Trudy's. "You have to start making sense if you want to get out of here."

"Who the fuck called an ambulance?"

"A concerned citizen."

My phone vibrates. I don't recognize the number but answer it for something to do. It's Gyorgi.

"How can I help?" he asks. Hearing his voice reminds me there is another me who isn't an old ashtray full of ashes and butts—another me that's alive and feeling again. That me seems very far away.

"Where are you?" I ask.

"Warden station."

"Can you come and get Trudy? Hop on the McCowan bus? I'll give you money and you can take her to McDonald's or something."

"Sure. I am there in half hour."

"Thank you. Ask for Pierce Many. Tell them at reception we're expecting you."

"Okay."

I end the call before he does. On the rare occasions someone likes me, I worry they'll find out who I really am and not like me anymore. Better to cut them loose before this happens.

"Who's coming to get me?" Trudy, with her back to me, asks warily.

"Gyorgi."

She faces me. "Promise?"

"I promise."

"When?"

"In about half an hour. He has to take the bus."

She squeals, jumping up and down and clapping, startling Pierce. I lay a hand on his chest. "It's just Trudy."

"Who?" He lifts his head and squints at her. "What the fuck is she doing here?"

"I told you, I'm looking after her."

"For how fucking long?" He looks past me. "Is that a spider? Fuck. Where's my flashlight?"

In the dugout he checks for spiders with his flashlight. In Afghanistan there were spiders the size of his thumb. "It's not a spider, Pierce. You're in the hospital. I don't know what you're seeing, but there are no spiders here."

Trudy turns away from the crazy man in the chicken suit and retreats to her world of plastic animals and muted conversations. These two will never be anything but strangers. Their DNA can't compete with the trauma corroding their memories, causing them to doubt their experience—that it happened the way they remember it. Trauma convinces us that we are, partly, to blame. Ashamed, we try to block it with booze, bad sex, plastic animals. The products of my rape have adapted, given something up, let something go. They can't remember who they were before. Best to leave it that way.

THIRTY

The moaning woman has been wheeled away, and the patient predicting a satellite crash and a final world war sent home. In his place, a man with gastrointestinal problems belches and farts. Each time his gut makes a sound, he says, "Stop that." Trudy finds this uproarious and clamps her hand over her mouth to muffle her giggles. She leaps into Gyorgi's arms when she sees him, which is what I want to do. Instead, I hand him a twenty and some quarters. "Call me and I'll let you know what's happening."

"Sure."

"I really appreciate this."

"No problem. You okay?"

I avoid his eyes. "I'm okay. It's him I'm worried about. Did you see what happened?"

"Kid had Bic lighter. He flick it at rooster tail."

"Conquer said the kid was throwing stones."

"That also."

Pierce lifts his head and stares at us through fog. "It's the fucking busboy."

"Hello," Gyorgi says.

"Keep your fucking hands off my mother."

"Pierce, cool it." For hours now he's been drifting in and out of a discombobulated haze, babbling weird shit like "Get the fuck out of the

306

way," or "Quit faking it, you little fuck." I'm assuming the little fuck is the little savage.

He strains against the knitted tubing. "I can't believe you're fucking the busboy."

With Trudy on his hip, Gyorgi, unsmiling, says, "We will call." Off they go without me. Dejected, with gusts of guilt blowing from all directions, I sit on the chair.

"Get the fuck out of the way! What the fuck's the matter with him?"

"Pierce, you're in hospital. Please stop acting like a crazy person. You're scaring me."

"Scaring you?" He lifts his head to squint at me. "Scaring you? I can't fucking scare you. You scare me."

"How do I scare you?"

"Gee, let me think. By picking up pervs in bars and lying around in puke."

"I'm sorry about all that."

"Yeah yeah yeah." Buffered by drugs, his wrath lacks power. I am grateful for this. Now might be the time for some truth-telling.

"Why did you care?" I ask. "I couldn't figure out why you cared what I did when you had Peggy and Reggie."

"I sure as hell don't care anymore. Go ahead and kill yourself, be my guest. And fuck the busboy and whatever other losers want your sorry ass." He closes his eyes again, submerged in inner blackness.

Some clothing and personal equipment Pierce removed from dead soldiers was stored for reissue. A soldier replacing his combat pants might see the name of a dead comrade on the inside label of his new ones.

One convoy transporting food, water and ammunition also transported prisoners of war. The prisoners were bound, with bags over their heads, and given nothing to eat or drink. Two spoke some English and said they were forced to fight, told that if they refused, members of their family would be shot, one by one, until they joined the insurgents. With the bags covering their faces, Pierce couldn't tell if they were lying.

Once a boy collapsed on the road, convulsing. Pierce put his foot on the brake but his CO told him to keep driving. "It's the old fake-a-seizure trick," the CO said. Convoy drivers were ordered to think of all obstacles as "bumps in the road."

Anything in the way, including civilian vehicles, pedestrians, even children, was to be mowed down. Insurgents encouraged kids to play in the road because it stalled troops, making them easy targets.

Just as Pierce's vehicle bore down on the convulsing kid, the boy jumped up and scrambled out of the way. Pierce told me this as if it were a joke.

"That's not funny, Pierce."

"Sure it is. It's fucking hilarious."

"I can't believe you're still writing in that thing," he says. "Who the fuck's going to read that shit?"

"Nobody. It's not to be read."

"What's it for then?"

"Fun."

"Yeah, right. Untie me. I'm done with this shit."

"I already did."

He pulls his arms and legs free of the tubing. "Hallelujah."

"Don't pull out the IV."

"Let's get the fuck out of here." He manages to sit up. I place my hands on his shoulders and look into his eyes, still clouded by medication.

"Pierce, we're going to see what the doctor has to say so we can make sure this never happens again."

"Why are you touching me all of a sudden?"

The shrink-in-training pushes aside the curtain. He has a domed forehead and a cropped beard. For a second I can't take my eyes off his zigzag tie.

"I'm Dr. Himmelfarb," he says.

"Okay," I say.

He scratches his cropped beard while speed-reading Pierce's chart. "How are you feeling, Mr. Mony?"

"It's Many," I say. "Pierce Many."

"Many. Gotcha. How are you feeling, Mr. Many?"

"All right."

"Glad to hear it. Have you had panic attacks before?"

"If you read the chart," I say, "you'll learn that he was a soldier in Afghanistan."

"And you are?"

"His mother."

"Gotcha."

"It's all in the chart. The nurse asked me many questions about him. She made notes."

Dr. Himmelfarb pulls John Lennon specs from his lab coat pocket. He was speed-reading Pierce's chart without reading glasses. How reassuring.

"Are you taking medications for anxiety or depression regularly, Mr. Many?"

"No."

"For any particular reason?"

"They don't work."

Dr. Himmelfarb fondles his zigzag tie. "Well, you're on medication now and it's made you feel better, hasn't it?"

"I feel doped. Not better."

"Are you seeing a psychiatrist on a regular basis?"

"No."

"Would you like a referral for one?"

"No."

"Pierce," I say. "It wouldn't hurt to get a referral. You don't have to go."

"The truth is, Mr. Many, we can't do much for you on an emergency basis other than help you through a crisis. Given the limited clinical information available, all I can do is recommend psychiatric stabilization and agitation management, with a follow up in a couple of weeks."

"No way I'm coming back here."

"You don't necessarily have to come back here, Mr. Many, but you should be seeing a psychiatrist on an ongoing basis. At least until you're out of the woods."

"Woods?" Pierce says. "What am I, a bear?"

"Until you're *stable*, Mr. Many. I'm going to prescribe some medication just to get you over the hump. Benzodiazepines are addictive so we don't want you taking them long-term." He pulls a pad from his lab coat, scribbles a prescription, tears off the sheet and holds it out to Pierce, who doesn't take it.

"Thanks," I say, grabbing it. "Can someone take out his IV?"

"I'll get the nurse on that." Which means more waiting. Dr. Himmelfarb disappears behind the curtain. My phone vibrates. It's Conquer.

"What's up?"

"He's seen the doctor. We're waiting for a nurse to take out the IV."

"No we're not," Pierce says, pulling the IV needle out of his arm.

"Right. We're on our way."

"Wait by Emerg," Conquer says. "I'll pick you up." He ends the call before I can object.

"Was that your busboy?"

"It's my head cook. He's driving us home."

"Since when are you dinging the head cook?"

"I'm not dinging him."

"So why's he helping out?"

"Maybe because he likes me."

"Yeah, right. He wants to fuck you."

"Do you happen to recall what happened to the rooster's head?"

"I don't recall anything."

"Are you wearing the chicken suit home or do you want to take it off?"

Still sitting on the gurney, it takes him several minutes to disentangle his arms and legs from the suit then, out of nowhere, remorse tackles him. "I'm sorry I fucked up the gig. Like, I'm so sorry." He covers his eyes the way Trudy did at Walmart when she realized the ponytailed woman wasn't her mother.

I take the suit from him. "It's no biggie, Pierce. Seriously."

"I can't believe I fucked up in a fucking chicken suit." His shoulders start to quake. "Like, I can't even hand out fucking flyers."

"Everybody fucks up. It's no big deal." Although I suspect the disappearance of the rooster's head will cost me. The orange gloves, along with Pierce's wallet and keys, are in a plastic bag provided by the hospital.

"Can you hug me again?" His request is childlike, unfiltered, vulnerable. I shove the chicken suit in the bag and put my arms around him. We hold this awkward embrace while the hospital whirrs around us.

"Let's get out of here," I say, gently easing him off the gurney. "How do your legs feel?"

"Spastic."

"Can you walk?"

"Only one way to find out." He stands, steadying himself against the gurney.

"Lean on me." I grab the suit and my backpack, and slide his arm over my shoulders. We shuffle to the sliding doors. Nobody tells us we can't leave. Nobody notices, or cares.

He nods off between Conquer and me on the pickup's bench seat.

"Bit of a squeeze," Conquer says.

"It's good for him, physical contact. It's like with infants, you swaddle them to calm them."

"What do you know about infants?"

"Nothing. I've heard rumours."

The middle seat has no belt. I keep one arm around Pierce's shoulders and the other across his chest. Consistent pressure on his solar plexus seems to steady him. My neck, still sore from hauling Trudy's bag around, burns from the twisting required to keep my hands on him.

"We going to your place?" Conquer asks.

My place, where Trudy sleeps. There is no place else to go. "Yeah, but I'd like to get his prescription filled first."

We pull up in front of Shoppers. I carefully shift Pierce's head from my shoulder to Conquer's.

"What if he wakes up?" Conquer looks frightened, all traces of the Viking gone.

"Tell him I'll be right back. And restrain him. You can do that, you're stronger than he is, and honk if you need me."

The pharmacist is East Asian, her English difficult to understand. A deaf old lady, with a huge handbag, makes the pharmacist repeat everything. Next an old codger, his shirt pockets stuffed with lottery scratch cards, asks the pharmacist for something to fix his tummy trouble. The pharmacist leads him down an aisle in search of stomach remedies. I dash to the front of the store to check on the pickup. Conquer hasn't moved, sits staring straight ahead with Pierce's head on his shoulder.

The pharmacist sells the old codger some pills but he shows no sign of leaving.

"Excuse me, can you fill this?" I hand the pharmacist Pierce's prescription, not sure why I'm buying drugs he won't take.

Gyorgi calls. "You still at hospital?"

"No, we're heading home, just stopped to get his prescription filled. Where are you?"

"McCowan and Eglinton. We ate, now we have ice cream and take dog to park."

"Great. Can you call me in half an hour or so? I should know more by then."

"Sure."

This time I wait for him to hang up but he doesn't. "Gyorgi, we're not weird about last night, are we?"

"We are not weird about last night."

"It was really nice, but you can't sleep at my place with Pierce there."

"Of course not. I bring Trudy home then go."

"Great, although I may have another plan for her. So please call me."

"Sure."

Back in the pickup, Conquer growls, "What makes you think he'll take them?"

"I don't think he'll take them. They're for me."

"That's a joke, right?"

"Maybe."

"What are they?"

"Benzos."

"Mix them with some crack while you're at it."

"Do you think Liv would take Trudy for the night?"

"She'd take her but it might kill her. She was wasted after last time. Who's with the kid now?"

"Gyorgi."

"You left her with the busboy?" He makes his spitting sound without spitting.

Out the window, familiar strip malls and low-rises look threatening. I'm in Pierce country, where men in vans point guns at you and spiders the size of thumbs crawl under your cot.

"Why'd you leave her with the busboy?"

"Because there was no one else."

"Are you sleeping with him?"

"What's it matter?"

Before Conquer can explain why it matters, my jaw starts flapping. "All this attention devoted to who's sleeping with whom. Entire media empires are built on it. How fortunate for the magnates that we're so easily distracted from what's really going on."

"You *are* sleeping with the busboy." He swerves to avoid a squirrel. I hold tight to Pierce who mumbles incoherently.

"What's he saying?" Conquer asks.

"He talks in his sleep."

"You're going to have to tell him the kid is his."

"Why?"

"Because he should know. *I'd* want to know."

"Why? You never see your daughter who wants to become a divorce lawyer and skin the likes of you. How does your knowing she exists help you?"

"It's not about helping."

"What's it about then?"

"Accountability."

"How does making him accountable help?"

"It might sober him up."

"You've seen way too many feel-good movies, Conquer." My phone vibrates.

"You have other plan for Trudy?" Gyorgi asks.

"No. Just bring her home. I'll be there in twenty."

"Sure."

Conquer helps me ease Pierce out of the truck and into the dugout. We lay him on my bed. I slip one of the dissolving sedatives between his lips to help him sleep off the antipsychotic.

Conquer stands in the kitchen with his hands on hips. "How long have you been living in this fire trap?"

"Years. Thanks for all your help."

"You want me to go?"

"I want you to get some sleep so you can cover for me tomorrow morning. I may be late. If you tell Bob I've got female problems, he won't ask questions."

Conqer looks about to argue but says, "Whatever you say, boss. FYI the rooster head is in your office."

"Who put it there?"

"Your busboy. Call me if you need anything." He looks at me, his eyes are tongs with me in their grip. "I mean it. If your son tries to hurt you, you call me."

"I will." Watching him drive off, I'm the climber with the busted leg clinging to the frozen mountain while my partner heads to base camp for help. Neither of us believes I will make it back alive.

Gyorgi arrives with the princess asleep in his arms, her pudgy cheek resting on his shoulder, her mouth agape.

"Hang on to her for a minute." I find a Q-tip and gently slip it into Trudy's open mouth, holding it against her cheek for twenty seconds.

"DNA," Gyorgi says.

"Correct." I slip the Q-tip into a Ziploc bag and hide it in the back of the fridge. "Okay, let's lay her down on the couch." The pooch struggles to hop up beside her. I lift his rump. "She's starting to smell like the dog." I cover the mutt and child with a blanket and check on Pierce. He's right out.

"Is he okay?" Gyorgi asks.

"For now."

"It takes time."

"It does," I say, not knowing what "it" is exactly.

"You want cigarette?"

"Please."

We sit with our backs against the stucco.

"Did doctor help?"

"My son has no faith in doctors. A friend of his, also a soldier, saw many doctors and committed suicide."

The gypsy nods as though this is no surprise.

"Tell me about Chappy's," I say. "Something funny, like Bob stood on a chair and fell off."

"Bob mix up task binders. He give front of house binder to Chef and kitchen binder to Siobhan."

"Did they point out his error?"

"They hide both binders in dry storage room and find Bernardo with girlfriend."

"Of course."

He passes me the cigarette. "Also, Daniel is very excited about buy-three-get-three-free special for foaming body wash at Bath & Body Work. He tell us is best deal *ever* for foaming body wash."

"Amazing that someone so keen on bath products can smell unwashed."

"He is big man. He sweat."

"True."

"I had uncle was big man. So big he could not see his feet. He had children for to put on shoes."

"Seriously, he had children so they'd put his shoes on for him?"

Gyorgi nods, smiling, making me smile which I haven't done since the last time he smiled at me.

"When uncle died," he says, "no one put on his shoes. His wife say she want for him to walk barefoot in hell."

"Nice." I pass him back the cigarette. Wind rustles fallen leaves. A bus coughs along.

"Corporate spy was back," Gyorgi says. "She says washrooms are embarrassment. She show me how to clean them with microfibre. Spy want Bob to provide microfibre for to clean all of Chappy's. Should sparkle, spy says."

"What's she look like?"

"Blonde."

"As in bleached or natural?"

"What means bleached?"

"Dyed. Not her real hair colour."

"Oh. Bleached. And she wears clothes for to exercise."

"You mean like yoga pants? Tight and black?"

"Sure."

"How old is she?"

"Old enough for to have son work as manager at other Chappy's. She is fast. When she show me how to clean bathroom embarrassment, she move fast with microfibre."

"Yikes."

"People who move fast, they don't know for how to stop."

"You mean they miss things because they're always on the run."

"Sure. To stop is good. Like us now. Is good, no?"

"Yeah, it is good."

"Spy is not happy with Olaf's hair. She wants for him to get haircut."

"Olaf will never cut his hair."

"Do you know Olaf has good side? He take selfies only of good side. He tells me he has not found best angle for to hold his face. He try different angles and ask my opinion." Gyorgi imitates Olaf taking selfies from different angles. I start to giggle.

"I say to him, 'Olaf, all your angles are so good.'"

"Uh-oh."

"Is wrong?"

"You know he's bi, right?"

"Sure."

"So, he might interpret you saying all his angles are so good as in any sexual positions are so good. As in you'll try anything."

"You think so?"

"Just a thought. More a warning, actually."

"You think Olaf will ask me for to hook up?"

"Possibly."

"Whoopee." He winks at me.

"Daniel will get very jealous if you hook up with Olaf."

"Daniel was in break room taking selfies of all angles of Daniel."

"That could take some time."

"Days maybe." By now we're both chuckling. "Also, Edvar's new girlfriend take selfie naked, lying on stomach on bed, showing ass. Siobhan in state of super upsetness."

"Did the girlfriend have a nice ass?"

"Sure."

"That's gotta hurt. I bet Siobhan couldn't believe the new GF *literally* posted a naked selfie."

"Sure." He stubs out the cigarette and pitches it into the Bosnian's weed patch. He puts his arm around me and kisses my forehead. "You must sleep."

I fold into him and lift my leg over his, straddling him. In seconds we're sliding hands under each other's T-shirts, and within minutes we're having hanky-panky in the laundry room. I break it up to check on Pierce and Trudy, and to grab a condom. I'm like the teenager I never was, listening for the 'rents while unimaginable sensations ripple under my skin. As the gypsy and I try to meld, I understand why the French call orgasm petit mort. You die a little.

Then it's just us, a little closer to death, on the dirty linoleum with dust and lint in our hair, cradling each other's frailty.

THIRTY-ONE

I've never heard Pierce snore. His snorty inhalations suggest he really is asleep, for the first time in years. I crouch ninja-style beside the bed, watching for signs of consciousness. "Pierce," I whisper but he doesn't budge. "Pierce," I say a little louder. Nothing. Slowly, carefully I slide the Q-tip into his gaping mouth and hold it against his cheek for twenty seconds, bag it and hide it in the fridge.

Rapists aren't born rapists. Rapist number one, two, three and four once stood on wobbly legs, arms outstretched for balance, putting one toddler foot in front of the other. Then shit happened, robbing them of faith in themselves and the world. The products of rape have nothing to do with the act that made them. I repeat Liv's words to myself in the shower until the hot water runs out, brush my teeth and put on clean clothes in case anything untoward, as Chester would say, occurs. A quick check on Trudy then it's time to haul the zero-gravity lawn chair out of storage. Before the Bosnian dug hills in the yard, I sought sunlight out front, pushing the chair into the reclining position. I read Albert Camus—the outsider bonding with *The Outsider*—feeling sentenced to death in my zero-gravity chair. I haul it into the bedroom. It just fits between the wall and bed. Pushing it into full reclining mode, I try to doze off but of course can't. Suddenly, locating the pink box dotted with sliver stars becomes imperative. I scout around for my backpack, spotting it by the front door. Pink box in hand, I squeeze past the zero-gravity chair and reach for

Trudy's tooth on my bedside table. As I hold it between my index finger and thumb, an unfamiliar feeling of accomplishment tingles through me. This tooth would not exist if it weren't for me. Ha.

When she starts crying for Mama, to keep her from waking Pierce, I sprint to the couch, pick her up and swaddle her on my lap, rocking back and forth. Maybe I should sing a lullaby. Peggy sang them to Pierce but I can't remember any. The only tune currently going though my head is "Dancing Queen." Not knowing the lyrics, I hum the melody, periodically inserting the words dancing and queen. Gradually Trudy's muscles relax into mine and I lean against the pooch. Soon I too will smell of dog.

When her breathing becomes even, I ease the princess off me and onto Benedict and get back in the zero-gravity chair. If Pierce wakes, he'll have to climb over me.

"I killed a dog," he says.

"Why did you turn the light off?"

"It hurts my eyes." Streetlight seeping in the window reveals he's on his side, knees pulled in, hands curled into his chest. "Why the fuck are you sitting in a lawn chair?"

"You can see me in the dark?"

"I saw you when the light was on. You can sleep on the bed for fuck-sake, I won't bite."

"I'm fine here."

A couple of the Bosnian's cats fight outside the window. Her imperial highness clumps downstairs to break it up. The hissing and snarling subsides as she talks dirty Bosnian to them.

"I killed a kid."

"Pierce, you have to stop talking about killing. The kid took off on his bike."

"There was nobody on the road."

"What road?"

"In Kandahar. It was fucking freezing and the kid had no shoes."

"What kid?"

"The kid I killed."

I lean forward to try to see his face in the darkness.

"I thought maybe his village had been bombed."

318

A case of disconcerting disconnectedness jolts me. The Bosnian tromps back upstairs, presumably with a cat under each arm.

"There was nobody around," Pierce says. "He was waving a little American flag. I should've stopped."

"You weren't allowed to stop."

"I could've stopped."

"You were obeying orders."

"I thought he'd take off." He sounds injured, as though voicing the words hurts. "The kid got caught under the truck. I dragged him. I could feel it. He was screaming. He was *alive* under there. I started fucking blubbering, could hardly fucking see, and my CO was like, 'What the fuck's the matter with you? Keep driving, asshole. Do not slow down.'"

"You had no choice," I say, although I'm not sure this is true. If all the soldiers of the world said no to killing, there would be no wars.

"Then there's this weird thump and I see the kid in my rearview. He's still moving, and there's a truck coming up behind me about to roll right over him, and a bunch more after that, and I tell myself to keep driving, the kid's just roadkill. So I do, I keep driving. Don't look back, keep driving. Only I can't fucking see with all the tears, and snot's dripping out my nose mixed with dust and shit particulate and I'm like, 'I'm doing it. I don't know how, but I'm doing it.' It's like I'm not even in my body. I don't know where I am but I'm not fucking there."

The tranqs have enabled him to confess his crime.

"I know that feeling," I say.

"What feeling?"

"Being in the middle of something horrific and not knowing how you got there. Not being inside your body. Crying so hard you can't see, choking on snot, not knowing how you're going to get through it but somehow getting through it. Then hating yourself for getting through it, being ashamed, thinking you'd be better off dead. Wanting to be dead."

He leans on his elbow, trying to see my face like I'm trying to see his. We're both afraid to turn the light on and fully expose ourselves.

"When did you want to be dead?" he asks.

Leaning back in the zero-gravity chair, I stare into an abyss. "When I was raped."

He doesn't respond. Doesn't believe me. Like Reggie, he thinks I'm a slut.

"When?"

"Before you were born."

"By who?"

"It doesn't matter."

"Of course it does."

"I didn't know them."

"Them?"

"There were four."

"Christ."

A car pulls into a neighbouring driveway, its headlights briefly illuminating the crack in the ceiling. The Bosnian trods her well-worn path from the fridge to the TV. Life goes on.

"I heard an Afghan girl being raped," he says. "I didn't know anybody could scream like that. Then it got quiet. They must have gagged her. It was worse not hearing her. There was nothing I could do. We weren't supposed to interfere."

"All the things we weren't supposed to do. We spend the rest of our lives thinking what if we'd done them."

He's so quiet I think maybe he's fallen asleep again. "Pierce?"

"What?"

"I hit you. I know I did. You were right. I'm so sorry."

"Okay."

"That's why I started drinking. The rape, I mean. I didn't drink before that."

"Makes sense."

"I know you think I was a party girl. It was never like that. I was self-medicating, like you self-medicate with beer."

"Whatever."

"I'm so sorry, for everything."

"I get it."

I wait for something, I don't know what—a feel-good movie ending.

"I've got to piss," he says.

"I'll move the chair."

"I'm still spazzing."

"It'll pass."

He stays in the bathroom too long. Listening outside the door, I fret over potentially lethal items in the medicine cabinet: Advil, Tylenol, razors.

"Pierce?"

He opens the door. "I can't piss. I need to but I can't."

"That's another side effect."

"I'm still fucking woozy."

"You need to sleep it off."

Steadying himself against the wall, he makes his way back to the bedroom and crumples on the bed.

Combat used to be hand-to-hand, face-to-face. Over hundreds of years we have distanced ourselves from our enemies. Initially with muskets, cannons and rifles, then machine guns, grenades, tanks and poisonous gas. Killing enemies we couldn't see with binoculars became easy with rocket launchers, howitzers and mortars. Finally, the atomic bomb made it possible for one man to kill 200,000 unseen enemies, mostly civilians. Victory!

Now we have unmanned drones the size of planes carrying missiles, and hydrogen bombs capable of terminating mankind. All "the enemy" has is what arms dealers (probably American) sell them, plus homemade bombs and a seemingly endless supply of converts from all over the world willing to use their bodies or cars as weapons. Who's winning this war? Can it be won?

The soldier tries to get up.

"Pierce, what are you doing?"

"I forgot about Greg. I've got to make sure he's okay. Fuck, I've still got the spins."

"Put your head down. Sleep it off. Check on him tomorrow."

"What time is it?"

"Around four."

He puts his head between his knees. "She could hardly walk afterwards."

"Who?"

"The girl they raped."

This doesn't surprise me. Girls repeatedly raped can hardly walk afterwards.

"Was it like that for you?" he asks.

"I could walk."

"Nobody helped you."

"No."

"Did you go to the police?"

"No."

He lies back on his side, his expression unreadable in the darkness. "What did Grandma and Grandpa do?"

"I never told them."

"You were too ashamed."

"Right."

He rolls onto his other side and lies with his back to me. "Everything's so fucked."

"True."

"You reach a point you don't care anymore. You're sick with it, all that caring. It makes you sick. You can't do shit about it so who gives a fuck."

"I do."

"What?"

"I give a fuck. About you."

"Since when?"

"I'm not sure. Maybe always. Maybe I got sick with it because I couldn't do shit about it."

"What?"

I can't tell him he is the son of rapist number one, two, three or four. It doesn't matter.

"How did you keep going after that?" he asks.

"What?"

"Being raped."

"I didn't keep going. I pressed pause and drank myself numb."

"I get it."

"Try to sleep."

"My head's fucking throbbing."

"Another side effect. Sleep it off."

"Can you hold me again?"

I try to fit myself around him the way Gyorgi fit himself around me, easing tensions. That I, a used-up, low-on-battery creature, can offer comfort is miraculous. You don't know what you're capable of until there is no escape.

When his breathing turns to snores, fatigue sandbags me.

Trudy brings me All-Bran. I eat it to please her.

"Your son left," she says.

"So I see. Did you talk to him?"

"No. Where are we going today?"

"To Maisie's."

"I want to go to Liv's."

"Liv's tired. Maybe tomorrow."

"Why can't I stay here? I won't make noise."

"Trudy, we talked about this. I'm not comfortable leaving you alone."

"Are you scared the lady'll come over?"

"What lady?"

"The lady that looks in the fridge."

"Why does she look in the fridge?"

"Mom says the lady will take me away if there's no food and the place is dirty."

This sounds like a caseworker from Child Services. Sophie's got a file. Trudy is documented.

"Well, no lady's coming here. Anyway, if she did, she'd find food in the fridge and the place spotless because you and Gyorgi are such good cleaners. How often does she go to your place?"

She swivels her head away from me. "I forget."

"Since you were really little?"

"Since my burn."

"What burn?"

"At Christmas."

"What burned you?"

"A curling iron." She lifts her dress and points to two faint finger-length scars on her calf.

"How did that happen?"

"It was on the sink. I tripped on the cord."

"Of the curling iron?"

She nods, looking at the horse in her hand. "It fell on my leg and the doctor told the lady. That's when she started coming over. We never know when she's coming. Yegor gets mad. The lady says she'll get the police if we don't let her in."

"Okay, well, that lady and Yegor don't know where I live, so there's no way they can come here."

"Did you check your messages?"

I pull the phone out of my pocket, dial voicemail and hold the phone to her ear. She keeps listening even when there is nothing to listen to, invisibly grieving over the loss of a mother who neglects her, abandons her, maybe even burns her.

"How 'bout you take your beads to Maisie's?"

She scoots to the couch while I plot getting her into the bath. She's back in seconds, holding out a string of pink and purple beads. "This is for you," she says.

THIRTY-TWO

After dropping Trudy at Maisie's, I drag my sorry ass over to a DNA testing centre and use Visa to pay the $300 required to be ninety-nine percent certain the child belongs to Pierce. I am one hundred percent certain but need hard evidence for Child Services, or Pierce, who believes himself to be one hundred percent white.

The door to my office is closed. It's only closed when I'm in it. Conquer beckons me from behind the grill.

"Carol Sugg from Corporate is using your office for interviews."

"Who's Carol Sugg?"

Daniel flounces towards us, hands flapping. "Oh my god, oh my god, oh my god, the spy witch is, like, taking over, asking all these questions like we're criminals."

"Questions about what?"

"She wanted to know if I'd seen anything going on, like, with the servers. She wanted to know if I thought they were trustworthy, and that I should let her know if I *see* anything."

"She's saying that to all you cumdumpsters," Conquer says. "Seems there are discrepancies between what we're cooking and what you're selling."

"How can there be discrepancies?" Daniel asks. "It's not like the old days when customers paid cash."

"Tell that to Mizz Sugg," Conquer says. "She's batshit about monitoring portion control and minimizing wastage."

Daniel holds his hand to his moobs. "She talked to me like I was one of those bartenders who don't ring in all the drinks, charge the customer and keep the cash. I was mortally offended."

"Did you tell her where she could stick her bottles?" Conquer grumbles.

"I told her it's bad enough Desie's been *weighing* the bottles and insisting I measure out the wine. I told her I have years of experience in the service industry and have never been so insulted."

"What is the spy witch's title?" I ask.

"VP of Innovation," Daniel says.

Conquer tosses burgers on the grill. "Code name for hatchet/fix-it person."

"Like we need fixing." Daniel fiddles with his hair.

"Be warned," Conquer says, "the VP is all about quality assurance, fact-finding and functionality. Name a buzzword, the fixer uses it."

"Is she senior to Desmond?" I ask.

"She sure acts like it."

"Nobody's asked her? You're allowing her to interrogate you and you don't know her rank?"

"In my world," Conquer says, "VP means seniority. Anyway, don't piss her off. Maybe she'll get the fuck out of here if we act nice."

"I can't believe you two aren't taking this seriously," Daniel says. "We're talking about our jobs here." He glances over both shoulders. "I bet right this second we're on camera."

"Daniel," I say. "There are no cameras."

"Wrong." Conquer points to the exposed machinery above the walk-in fridges and freezers.

"You're kidding," I say.

"Nope. Cameras the size of ChapSticks hooked up to tiny transmitters. No need to run wires. High shelves, air ducts all make good hiding places."

"When did that happen?"

"When we weren't looking. She's got footage, boss. On all of us. In the interrogation room, formerly your office, she shows us our 'poor execution' on her laptop."

"She showed me me cutting Mocha Chocolate Cream Cake," Daniel says, "and squishing it by mistake, then eating it. I told her we're allowed to eat broken baked goods. She acted like I'd squashed it on purpose. Everybody knows how hard it is to make clean cuts on layer cakes with soft icing. Then she showed me me putting whipped on my coffee, like that's a crime."

Helga grabs an order. "She showed me me looking at my phone. I couldn't believe how fat my ass looked."

"The VP's got footage of everybody looking at their phones," Conquer says. "Smile, you're under surveillance."

"Does she have eyes in my office?"

"You'll find out soon enough."

"She kick-boxes," Helga says. "Is into blood and leather."

"How did that come up?" I ask.

"She's got good arms. I told her I've been trying to build muscle for, like, months, and my arms are still sticks. She told me she'd take me for a girls night out kick-boxing. Pretty trippy."

"She's only being nice to you so you'll spy for her," Daniel says.

"Who's in the interrogation room with her now?" I ask.

"Siobhan. And you can bet that bitch hussy is telling lies about me."

"Where's Bob?"

"Who knows. He's gotten so weird with all that qigonging."

Wade touchscreens an order, looking around furtively. "Where's the harridan?"

"Still in Stevie's office."

"Can we bolt the door from the outside?"

"Has she interviewed you yet, hot stuff?" I ask.

He nods. "It's all about the microfibre."

"She's making everybody clean," Daniel clarifies. "Like, if you're standing still for two seconds, she's waving microfibre rags at you."

Conquer flips the burgers. "It's all part of the Chappy's transformation."

"The what?"

"It's not called restructuring anymore, boss. It's called transforming."

"If she tells us one more time the place should sparkle," Wade says, "I may have to kill myself."

"Kill *her*," Daniel says, struggling to re-tie his apron around his girth.

Olaf swings by. "Dat she-devil be straight-up nasty, flexin' on my pants. I say dis be dope black denim, yo. Da witch go all la-di-da and say she want 'slacks with the correct waist size.' I say, 'Bitch, my pants is legit da correct size.'"

"No way did you say 'bitch,'" Daniel says.

"Your pants are not the correct size, Olaf," I say. "They hang off your ass. Try using a belt."

"Dat's da look, fam, da crew I chill wit', dat's how we do."

I call Desmond but he's not picking up. Siobhan slinks out of my office, tugging on her pleather mini. Carol Sugg, in what looks like four-way-stretch Lululemon, strides to the dining room. Short-haired and brawny, she could take down any one of us.

"We need to stick together," I say. "Don't talk smack about your co-workers."

"Too late," Daniel says.

"What did you tell her?"

"Just that Siobhan is flirty with everybody and all hoity-toity because she got a job interview at the Courtyard Marriott downtown. She says they were super impressed with her certificate from Algonquin College in hospitality and tourism."

"Siobhan doesn't look hoity-toity to me," I say. "She looks distraught."

"Oh that's because her closgay ex posted on Facebook, 'Does anybody have any ideas for a couples vacation?' Him and his new beard are going on a vacay together and the bitch hussy's like, 'How come he never took me anywhere?' Gee, I wonder why."

Wade, arms crossed and shivering even though it's hot, says, "It's a dumpster fire."

Holding what must be microfibre rags, Sugg returns from the dining room.

"FYI," Conquer mutters, "she didn't buy your women's problems excuse."

"Are you Stevie?" Sugg demands.

"Correct."

"I'm Carol Sugg, VP of Innovation. Do you have a minute?"

"Not right now, I'm afraid. I'm behind as it is and we've got orders coming in." I slip past her muscled frame and dump my backpack on the chair in my closet so she can't sit on it. In an instant she's at my door.

I grab my abdomen. "Damn these fibroids. I've bled through three pads already. So inconvenient. Would you mind using Bob's office for interviews? He doesn't appear to be around."

"I'm told he had to go to Emergency. Does that happen often?"

"Not at all. Bob is the picture of health."

"Desmond says he's easily distracted lately. There have been complaints from customers."

"What kind of complaints?"

"Enough to concern Corporate regarding Bob's mental state."

"Bob's mental state is excellent." I glance around for cameras the size of ChapSticks. They should be easy to spot. My closet is floor to ceiling drywall, with no crevices hospitable to spy gizmos. "If you don't mind, Carol, I've got to check the line. With the World o' Chicken menu, it's doubly important."

"You should know that Corporate was not happy with your battering chicken breasts for the waffle chicken."

"I was not happy with myself. But, as you know, the customer comes first. And customers wanted fried chicken with their waffles. If Corporate had supplied us with sufficient pre-prepped chicken, there would have been no need for such costly measures. The truth is, out here in the burbs, we get the short end of the stick." Clammy cold inside, I smile warmly at the spy witch and start checking stations. For a second it looks like Sugg's going to tail me, but she gets busy texting. I call Bob.

He picks up. "Is Bruce Lee still there?"

"Bob, you can't leave me alone with her."

"She had the nerve to ask if I'd noticed servers reversing out anything because of data-entry error, or a customer changing their mind. 'It's an old trick,' she said, 'the servers keep the difference,' like I don't know about thieving practices. 'You're insulting my servers,' I said. 'When you insult my servers, you insult me.' Next she questioned my leadership skills and waved data analysis and traceability gobbledygook at me. I told her my online course has taught me sensitivity is more important than strength, and that I must treat my staff emphatically."

"That's great, Bob, but we need to stand up to Sugg together. House and kitchen staff need to form a united front."

"Tell staff when feelings of peace and harmony are felt in the heart, and not just *understood* by the head, everything becomes clear."

"They need to hear that from you, Bob, which is why you should come back and use that emphatic sensitivity to make sure everything becomes clear. Where are you?"

"Emerg. I need to talk to Jordan about my pure feelings for Ashton. Self-knowledge comes through pure feelings, not words."

"Well, we're having pure feelings here, Bob. About Bruce Lee and her transformative mission. We need your guidance." With him here, it'll take the heat off me. "Please?" I add. "We got more Mocha Chocolate Cream

Cake in. I'm sure the VP wouldn't mind you having a slice if you pay fifty percent of the list price."

"I feel violated there."

"I think we're all feeling a little violated. Which is why we need your sensitivity."

"I completely understand where you're coming from, Stevie, but I have to put myself first for a change. You have no idea what it's like."

"Bob, you're the general manager. You should be here. Sugg can't be ignored."

"There you go using 'can't' again. I bet if you counted the number of times a day you say 'can't' you'd be up to a hundred or something." He ends the call. I finish prep check and discover Bernardo in the break room with his tongue down the throat of one of his women.

"Clear out," I say. "And Bernardo, do up your shoelaces."

"So sorry, Miss Stevie." He makes no move to tie his laces.

"There are regulations about footwear, Bernie."

His girlfriend applies lipstick and flips her hair.

"How you feeling, Miss Stevie?" Bernardo asks without tying his laces.

"About what? The fact that you should be prepping and not swapping spit in the break room?"

"To tell the truth you been looking a little tense lately. I can sell you neck massager. You try it and tell me how you feel about it. No obligation."

"Potatoes need peeling, Bernie. Get on it."

The spy witch catches up with me in my closet and explains that, as VP of Innovation, it is her job to improve process modelling, define, measure, analyze and control. "My focus is change management and strategic thinking," she adds, "taking into account deliverables, timelines, soft skills, baselines, human capital and, of course, resources."

Sleep-deprived, I feel like I got on the wrong bus.

"Desmond tells me there is no one better in the kitchen than you, Stevie. Corporate appreciates all the good work you do. The same cannot be said regarding other members of the team."

"Really? I think we perform like a well-oiled machine." Gyorgi, bussing tray in hand, passed me outside the break room, smiled and winked, and I smiled and winked back. Is this on camera?

"Your loyalty to your staff is commendable, Stevie, which is why Corporate has sent me to do the heavy lifting. I'm not here to be liked."

I grab my abdomen. "Oh my god, sorry, it's the fibroids again. Excuse me, I've got to use the toilet."

This works until Helga raps persistently on the door. I let her in and make room for her around the sink. She reapplies her cat-eye liner. "It's illegal to have cameras in bathrooms, isn't it?"

"Let's hope."

She appraises her reflection, tipping her head from side to side. "Siggy told me I look like Justin Bieber. He said he's been thinking I look like Justin Bieber ever since we met but didn't tell me because he didn't want to offend me."

"Are you offended?"

"I can't figure out if it's one of those backwards compliments, like 'you're kind of pretty even though your mouth is small.'"

"Well, if it's any consolation, I don't think you look like Justin Bieber."

"Daniel says it's because Siggy's gay."

"Daniel thinks everyone's gay."

"But what if he's right? I mean, Siggy's been such a gentleman, and he writes all that experimental lit, it makes sense he'd be gay."

"Just because he's a gentleman, and writes experimental lit, doesn't mean he's gay."

Sighing pensively, she sits on the toilet lid. "I just don't get how we're supposed to meet decent guys. I met this comp sci dingus at a party who wasn't too obnoxious, but I got the vibe he'd overstay his welcome, like, not figure out once I sober up you need to leave 8 a.m. latest, none of that 10 a.m. shit, like, don't go expecting eggs from me. He says to me, 'Wow, your glasses make you look hot,' and I'm like, 'Really? Because their intended purpose is to prevent me from walking into things.'"

"I've never seen you wear glasses."

"I use contacts at work."

I peek out the door to check for Sugg.

"Men are garbage," Helga concludes.

"Oh come on, don't give up on Siggy just yet. Millions of people, male and female, think Justin Bieber is seriously hot. Which means Siggy thinks you're seriously hot." My phone vibrates. I don't recognize the number. Must be Pierce.

"Greg's gone," he says.

"Maybe he's with Tara."

"I called her. She has no idea where he is."

"Well, he'll probably be back."

"He took all his gear—all the shit he backpacks with up north. He used to go there before he got injured. Like, on leave, to get his head straight. He'd hunt and forage, eat berries and shit, dig up roots. Tara used to call him her wild man. Anyway, since the blast, with all the surgeries and injections and shit, he hasn't been able to go and it's been driving him nuts. He says the only place he feels normal is up north. It's not like here, where he's a freak."

"So, maybe he needs some time up north alone."

"His meds are here. Like, all of them."

"Maybe he didn't take them because they turn him into a zombie."

"He can't fucking function without the narcotics."

"Maybe he's going cold turkey to find that out. Maybe he won't need drugs in the woods where he doesn't feel like a freak."

"Don't you get it? He's going there to fucking die."

"You don't know that."

"I know where he goes. He's got it all mapped out, has shown me his coordinates. It's fucking brutal. He says it makes you feel alive because it can kill you."

"You don't know for sure he's gone up north, Pierce. Wait awhile and see if he comes back."

"He can't *function* without his injections. The pain cripples him. There's no way he'll be able to make it on his own. I need money to go get him. Can you lend me three hundred bucks?"

"How do I know you won't spend it on beer?"

"I'm not going to spend it on beer. My best friend's gone to *die* up there, like, I know he's going to die. I don't want it to be like with Jake, me doing nothing then all of a sudden he's dead. *Please* lend me the money."

The little boy appears in my mind, staring down at ants crawling over his shattered Popsicle. The little boy who asked for another Popsicle and didn't get it. Who didn't cry when his mother hit him.

"Okay," I say, "but I have to go to the bank, and I can't leave work till after the lunch rush."

"Just say when and where."

"The TD at Warden and St. Clair at three."

"I'll be there."

"I may be late."

"I'll wait." He ends the call.

Sugg tracks me down sorting veg, tossing the mouldy stuff, my mind jammed with images of Pierce being mauled by bears.

"You're not throwing that out, are you?" the VP asks.

"It's old produce."

"As kitchen manager, you should know that subpar veg goes to the prep cook for soup."

"These are rotting, Carol."

"I'm fine with you throwing out perishables like salad stock, but it's essential we minimize wastage. Whatever's left at the end of the night should be wrapped and reused. The processed items, even when thawed, are designed to last days in the fridge."

I rotate stock on auto. A headache's growing over my right eye again. Maybe Bob's tumour is contagious.

"Most of the food shrinkage takes place during the night shift," Sugg says. "I'll be speaking with the night manager shortly. He may be unaware that food is going out the back door."

"Perry is unaware of anything going out the back door because we have a lively bar scene at this location, meaning the night manager is fully occupied with front of house. If Corporate insists on cutting costs by hiring low-paid part-timers, there's bound to be shrinkage as they usually have mouths to feed."

"Having mouths to feed does not excuse leaving with a backpack containing a box of chicken fingers."

"Doesn't it? Anyway, if most of the food shrinkage is during the night shift, what's it got to do with me?"

"Apparently a busboy on the day shift was caught stealing crackers and condiments."

"I spoke with him. He won't do it again."

"When staff are caught stealing, they should be dismissed. Immediately. We have cause."

"Of course, but this boy is an exceptional worker. He performs tasks no one else will do, like clean a homeless man's shit off a banquette."

This blindsides her. "What was a homeless man doing in Chappy's?"

"Seeking shelter and coffee."

"Homeless people should not be in Chappy's."

"That's not my department, as you know."

"I'll speak with the house manager. The long and short of it is we need to simplify prep and production. Streamline." This is Corporatespeak for fewer staff doing more work. Fewer staff requiring minimal training as simplifying prep and production means more plastic wrapped pre-prepped items. It also means fewer managers needed to provide the minimal training. Heck, maybe even cheap labour will be streamlined. If bots can drop bombs, they can shove food into a microwave.

Jamshed, the slowest man alive, stands before us. "Chef says you're needed on the line." Conquer doesn't need me on the line. He's rescuing me again, from Sugg.

Pierce isn't at the bank at 2:50. I withdraw $300 and sit outside on the steps with wind whipping my legs and futility surging through me. What's the point of saving Greg Lem, who may have gone up north to die? But then what's the point of anything? Siggy sent Helga more word vomit in response to her dismay about looking like Justin Bieber:

> you look like
> the star
> every
> body
> wants a piece of
> every
> body
> wants to be
> but you're you
> yourself
> and you
> is all I want.

"What's he mean by 'want'?" Helga asked us. No one knew. "Like what's his point?" She yanked up her Cat Woman boots. I told her I banged a stoner once who told me I looked like someone from Minnesota. I was experiencing my usual weed-induced paranoia and demanded, "What's your point?"

"No point," the stoner said.

"There has to be a point."

"To what?"

"To it."

The stoner winced, holding smoke in his lungs. "Let it happen."

So I told Helga, "Let it happen." Which is what I should be doing re Greg Lem.

"It" is too enormous, too abstract, like the prospect of extinction by over-population and the planet's climate warming a few degrees. Who isn't deadened to the images of devastation and atrocity crowding our screens? Better to open Twitter and scan what's trending, keep up with who's shagging whom.

"Have you got the money?" Pierce asks. With his hoodie pulled low over his forehead, he looks ready to commit a crime. I hand him the envelope of cash, plus a ham and Swiss sandwich VP Sugg will catch me making on one of her ChapSticks.

"Thanks."

"When are you leaving?"

"There's a night bus."

I expect him to take off but he sits on the steps to eat the sandwich. Cars zip past in another dimension where wounded soldiers don't escape to the woods to die.

"How old were you when you were raped?" His hoodie hides his face.

"Oh. Umm. Young."

"You had me when you were sixteen."

"Correct."

"You said you were raped before that. So what were you, fourteen?"

"Something like that." I pull my jacket tighter around me.

"How'd you get booze?"

"I didn't."

"You said you drank yourself numb."

"Oh, right. Well, it didn't take much in those days."

"Where'd you get it?"

"Where anybody gets it."

"You were underage. Did you steal it?"

"Of course not."

"So where'd you get it?"

"Men buy underage girls drinks, Pierce."

"Did my dad?"

"What?"

"Buy you drinks."

"I guess so. Can't remember."

"Because you were drunk."

"Right."

"Where'd you do it?"

"What?"

"Fuck my dad. In a car, a bar, his place, what?"

"I forget." This is what Trudy says when she lies.

"Because you blacked out."

"Right. We've been through this."

His face remains masked by the hoodie. "How did you know you didn't like my father if you blacked out and don't remember anything?"

When Pierce was old enough to ask about his father, I told him we never saw him because I didn't like him. Keeping the lie alive heats my face and I'm glad he isn't looking at me. "Well, gee, sonnyboy, do *you* remember every one-night stand in detail?"

"Pretty much. I'm not proud of them."

"Me neither. Did you ever force a woman?"

"What?"

"Did you ever force a woman who was incapacitated by alcohol?"

He faces me. "You mean, like, did I rape anybody? How sick are you? Fuck off."

"Some men can't stop themselves."

"What are they supposed to do if you're too sauced to tell them to back off?"

"If a woman is too sauced to tell you to back off, you shouldn't be fucking her. That's called rape."

"Oh grow up, Mother."

A small girl, gripping her mother's hand, takes the steps one at a time. "What's it like to walk on the moon?" she asks. Her mother, eyeing Pierce warily, doesn't answer. "I bet it's like bugga bugga boom," the little girl says, "and bugga bugga bing."

Pierce watches them climb into an SUV. "So you're saying you drank while you were pregnant."

"I was too nauseated to drink while I was pregnant."

"So you quit drinking then started again after I was born?"

"Correct."

He nods, considering. "I thought maybe I was an FAS kid, like, that that might be why I'm fucked up."

"You weren't an FAS kid. And you're not fucked up."

"There's a bus. I gotta get supplies." He sprints to the bus, the soldier who days ago would not leave the dugout, who hours ago could hardly walk. The son I lied to, again, for fear the truth would destroy him.

"Call me collect," I shout into the wind.

I wrote on the note tucked in with the cash: *I know I don't know shit about what happened to you in Afghanistan. I get that I can never understand what it was like for you, how horrifying, terrifying, exhilarating, soul-destroying. And how it became normal to you. And how what the rest of us do—we who haven't seen what you have seen and felt what you have felt—seems abnormal to you. That I can never understand doesn't mean I don't care.*

The bus roars up Warden and dips beyond the smudged horizon. An empty plastic bag spins in the wind—suburban tumbleweed. I pull Trudy's string of pink and purple beads from my backpack and finger them like worry beads.

THIRTY-THREE

Maisie says she needs to talk to me about Trudy, who sits balled up in her usual corner, having a muted conversation with her horse. I wait in the kitchen while Maisie helps parents get their preschoolers into jackets and out the door.

Sugg accosted me to tell me she's noticed recipes have "drifted" in prep and on the line. Towering over me the VP added, "It's not unusual. People form habits, and sometimes even management stops noticing or remembering the original recipe."

All afternoon I felt the ChapSticks on me. It was like I was wrapped in plastic—a piece of waffle chicken, stiff and dry.

"Most of these slip-ups," Carol explained, "stem from attitudes like 'This is how we've always done it so why change it.' The cooks decide making the meals according to the specs is too labour-intensive."

She showed me a vid of Tareq plating a kebab dinner with rice. "What's missing here?" she asked me.

"His ear."

"I mean on the plate."

"Potatoes. And parsley garnish."

"You see how easily items can be missed? It's not acceptable. Corporate wants meals prepared the same way in each location, each and every time. It's time to tighten up by giving the cooks a binder with all the spec sheets." She handed me a binder.

"They can't read English," I said.

"Then you'll have to show them how it's done. From now on we'll be expecting you, and your staff, to work from these sheets. I will regularly check up on the line and prep kitchen to make sure that specs are being followed."

Looking up at the bleached blonde into blood and leather, I marvelled at how you can coast along miserably managing the idiots in your life, thinking, "Well, at least I can handle these idiots." Then you're thrown a new model of idiot and suddenly your psychic space is crammed with the new model's idiocy. The plastic tightens around your stiff and dry self as you pine for the previous idiots. How happily you would have managed them if only you'd known about the blood and leather coming to town.

The horoscope in the paper on the table tells me that the Sun and Jupiter sit in my house of career, reputation and responsibilities. It's important to let my trustworthy side be known.

Conquer texts, "Liv wants you here for dinner. 7 sharp. Resistance is futile."

"It's a date," I text back, still hoping Pierce will call and tell me Greg's returned and it's all good. Why do the soldiers suffer debilitating shame and self-loathing, but not the politicians who send them to unwinnable wars?

Huffing and puffing from picking up toys, Maisie joins me. "Trudy gave a bead to each kid."

"How nice."

"They could've choked on them. Don't let her bring beads here."

"Right. Sorry."

"Anyways, she didn't mean any harm by it."

I'm not so sure. Choking simpering toddlers with beads sounds like a Trudy scheme.

"She likes cats," Maisie says. "She was all over my neighbour's."

"Really? Well, we've got plenty of cats around."

To waylay Maisie from banning Trudy from the premises, I point to the paper. "Did you see this? There's a multi-billion-dollar robot that can consume one million books' worth of knowledge per second. With each new bit of info, the computer gets smarter. They say it's just a matter of time before it's read so many books it'll be smarter than the smartest human."

Maybe we won't need soldiers, just smart combat bots. No more will humans have to get off the couch to kill humans.

It's too early to go to Liv's. The princess and I hang out at McDonald's.

"Why did you give beads to the toddlers?" I ask.

"I forget." She scampers to the PlayPlace and disappears up a tunnel.

Jake, before he killed himself, told me he was getting "overly mad about stupid shit." He'd "lost it" with a salesgirl at Fido. "It freaked me out how scared she got, like, I don't get why I get like that. I mean, I'm not that kind of guy. And it's messing with how my friends and mom see me. When I get like that they say it's like I'm a totally different person." Which made Jake feel like a freak. Like Greg Lem. Like Pierce. The world changed for them, became crueller, deadlier, not to be trusted. The world was a disappointment. And they were a disappointment to themselves. They grieve, silently, for the person they were before, and the person they might have been.

Pierce was ordered to run over the child. He betrayed himself in that split-second decision to obey his commanding officer. Betrayed himself for a military that then betrayed him.

When I told him counter-insurgency-based warfare blurs the lines between right and wrong, he said, "You don't know shit about right and wrong." True, but then who does? And yet you hear it all the time: "I did what was right." How many madmen have said that, how many murderers? The people using their bodies and cars as weapons think they're doing what's right. The soldier remotely dropping a bomb on the Syrian wedding party thinks he's doing what's right. We all do. And we could all be wrong.

Liv makes the most delicious tuna casserole I've ever eaten. The secret, she tells me, is a sprinkle of sugar. Conquer and I do the dishes while the girls play tiddlywinks.

"What are we going to do about Sugg?" he asks.

"Nothing. Hide."

"She'll hunt us down."

"What vids does she have on you?"

"Sudoku, solitaire, scratching my balls."

"The usual."

"You?"

"She couldn't locate the chit on her ChapSticks for the tuna sandwich and date square I fed the rooster. She accused me of making unpaid-for food."

"What'd you tell her?"

"That feeding the rooster was a promotional expense."

"Did she back off?"

"For a nanosecond."

"She's collecting chits off the spike."

"That's a mindfuck. She doesn't need them. She's got the data, down to the individual order, available on her ever-present laptop. What I want to know is, where's Desmond? He's not answering my calls."

"She fired him."

"What?"

"Drug use."

"She had proof?"

"Who needs proof." He leans against the counter. "You look lousy. Did you get any sleep?"

"Some."

"How'd it go with your son?"

"He's heading up north to search for his psychotic soldier buddy."

To escape Conquer's strobe-light stare, I put plates in the cabinets.

"You're freaked out," he says.

"A little."

"I guess that means you care about him."

"Maybe."

"Funny how that sneaks up on you."

We hear a blast of guitars and tambourines from the living room.

"That's Liv playing the Gypsy Kings," Conquer says. "She's wild about the sleazebags."

"Billy?'" the wolfwoman calls. "Come dance with Trudy."

"Just finishing up here."

Liv drags her walker into the kitchen. "Wait till you see Billy dance."

"The music's a little loud, Olivia," Conquer says.

"Bah. Come dance. Billy used to be a rock star."

"Not a rock star, Olivia."

"He made the girls cry."

"I bet he did more than make them cry," I say.

"His band was called Bent Penny."

"What did you play?" I ask.

"Bass."

"Of course. Now I know why the nineties were so memorable for you. Why'd you quit?"

"The band took up a collection to *make* me quit."

"They changed the name. What'd they change it to, Billy?"

"Twisted Nickle."

"Come on, child." Liv grabs his hand. "Show Trudy your horse dance. She *loves* horses."

I sit on the scratchy couch and wait for the show to begin. Liv, with one hand on her walker, swings her free arm and leg out flamenco-style then changes sides. She even wiggles her hips to the gypsy beat. Trudy flexes a foot, tosses a hand and performs wobbly pirouettes. Conquer, head and knees bobbing, gets into the groove.

"Do your horse dance," Trudy commands. The Viking kicks up a foot and canters forward then spins around and canters back. The princess collapses into giggles.

"Come on now," Conquer says, still prancing, "*you* do it. I bet you can do a wicked pony." Trudy jumps up and canters.

"You can add reins," Conquer advises, holding up his hands as though gripping reins. Trudy tries it, laughing her tinkly laugh.

Liv pats my knee. "Up you get, girly, it'll do you good."

I get off the couch and start jumping around to the gypsy rhythms and wails, swinging my arms and legs, rolling my neck and shoulders.

"Do the horse dance," Trudy says, breathless and galloping.

"Gotta lift those knees, boss," Conquer instructs, "to get the back leg action."

The three of us horse around while Liv does her walker shimmy, croaking volare along with the Gypsies.

Later, with Liv and Trudy focused on an alphabet puzzle, Conquer and I drink cantaloupe water in his boat.

"What's in the photo album?" I ask. He hands it to me and I flip through it. "All I see is old barns."

"I like old barns."

"Why?"

"They remind me we used to be able to do shit, like build barns. Old barns make me misty." He looks mournful suddenly, deconstructed, unsure what to do with his face.

"Did you sing in the Twisted Nickle formerly Bent Penny?"

"Fuck no."

"Did you have a Rod Stewart do?"

"You betcha. So sexy."

"Did you have groupies?"

"How do you think I met my wife?"

"Is that why it didn't last?"

"The marriage or the band?"

"The marriage."

"She balled the drummer."

"Ouch."

"Exactly." He lies back and stares out a porthole at stormy seas. "What are we going to do about Sugg?"

"You already asked me that."

"You didn't answer."

"Don't have an answer."

"We have to do something or she'll downsize the lot of us."

"She'll do that anyway."

"I expected you to put up a fight. Must be the busboy is making you mellow."

"It's just business as usual, Conquer. Corporate expansion—careless, self-absorbed, greed-driven destruction."

"So I better look around."

"I'll do what I can to stall her. I'm still not clear on the endgame, if HQ sent her to whip us into shape or if transformation means a whole new, low head-count, pre-prepped Chappy's."

"Makes me miss Stan."

"I always miss Stan." I flip through more old barn photos. "Whatever you do, don't quit. Let Sugg make the cut so you get EI."

"Copy that."

A skeleton of a barn, its rusted roof buckled, its remaining timbers leaning and weathered, gets me pondering the barn builders from when-ever ago and if they were, in fact, any smarter than we are.

"Did you know," I say, "part of wagon-train morality was leaving the weakest behind to freeze in the mountain passes? Survival—not looking after each other—was what the settlers were all about. That and stealing land from Indigenous peoples. Careless self-interest was what made America great."

The Italian neighbour's rooster crows. Conquer takes a swig of canta-loupe water and resumes his gloomy rumination out the porthole. "It sucks to suck," he says.

Back in the living room, Trudy's passed out on the couch. Liv points to a teapot on the coffee table and a cup. "Camomile. Help yourself."

"I should get her home."

"Let her sleep a little. She's had a big day." She pours the tea and hands it to me. "Who's this Gyorgi fella?"

"The busboy. Why?"

"She can't stop talking about him."

"Well, he's pretty special."

"Are you two an item?"

"Not an item, exactly."

"Exactly what then?"

"Not sure, exactly."

"But you like him."

"I do."

"You more than like him."

"He's teaching me about sex. All those years of slobbery tongues, aggressive gropings and blundering penetrations deadened my nerves. He's rewiring me."

"Aren't you lucky."

"The thing is there's so much going on right now with my son, and Trudy, and my demented parents, and new management at work, it's not a good time."

"Bah."

"Seriously, I can't handle looking after anybody else."

"Who says Gyorgi needs looking after? Sounds like he's looking after *you*."

"I don't want that either. I can look after myself."

"Looking after yourself and nobody else gets tiresome. It also causes trouble, everybody looking out for number one."

Billy appears. "Break it up, girls. I'm driving you home, no argument. Olivia, it's bedtime."

We stop by Chappy's to check in with Perry Meeker re what Sugg's done about the chicken finger thief. As usual, Perry doesn't seem to hear me but jaws about Oliver urinating in the condo. "I decided to ignore it and walk the pup so he wouldn't get all emo and suffer Catholic-type guilt for his piddle. Something must have scared the poor baby to make him lose control like that. Most likely the construction noise from the condo going up next door. And both pups are obvi stressed over the new sofa because they can't get up on it, which means I have to crawl into the giant doggy bed to give my babies extra snuggles. So adorbs. The hitch is now they expect me to always get in the doggy bed with them. Like, they get all whiny if I sit on the new sofa. So we have to watch *Game of Thrones* from the doggy bed, lol."

"Perry," I say, louder, "did Carol Sugg talk to you about a staff member stealing chicken fingers?"

"Who?"

"Carol Sugg, VP of Innovation."

"Oh my, she has two huskies she got for 500 bucks, what a sweet deal. The only problem is they're both male and from the same litter so they fight all the time, like, lock teeth and everything. Carol and her hubby have to pull them apart. I told her huskies are pack animals, programmed to compete for dominance. I said you better give one of those babies away before they rip each other's throats out."

"Good plan. Do you happen to know if she fired anybody?"

"Who?"

"Carol Sugg, VP of Innovation. The woman with the huskies."

"Why would she fire anybody?" He sips from his *Slay All Day* mug. "Oh, now, wait a sec, she told me to cut Abeo's hours, like, not put him on the schedule, so I guess that's like firing, lol."

Already the hatchet is swinging.

I get a call in the pickup and hope it's Pierce. "What's up?"

"Hello?"

"Who is this?"

"Is that Stephanie?"

"It is."

"Oh, thank the lord. I wasn't sure I had the right number. It's Carmella Schmurlich, your parents' neighbour from down the street?"

"Hi, Carmella. Is everything all right?"

"Well, I'm here with your father. Your mom won't let him back in the house. He was taking the garbage out and Peggy locked the door on him."

"Why?"

"She seems to think your dad has designs on me." Carmella titters uncomfortably. "Reggie and I were just having a little chat out front. I was telling him about this new lawn fertilizer that works a treat and should be applied before the first frost, you know, before a big rain. It's on special this week at Canadian Tire, I told him, and your mother poked her head out the door and started calling me all manner of names and whatnot. It was quite embarrassing, actually. Anyway, he was out there in his PJs so I thought I better bring him home before he caught his death. I'm sorry to say he must have soiled himself because he smells something awful. I was hoping you could come and get him and let him back in the house."

"Of course. Does he understand what's happened?"

"He understands he's locked out, but for a while there he seemed to think Peggy was his mother. Apparently his mother locked him out when he came home late."

"I'll be right over."

"It's number fifty-nine."

"Thanks. See you in a bit."

Conquer stays in the truck, guarding sleeping Trudy. Carmella's house reeks of Febreeze. She must have sprayed an entire can to eliminate Reggie's stench. He droops on a stool, rubbing his hands as if removing engine oil.

"He's quite changed, isn't he?" Carmella's fuchsia lipstick matches the fuchsia flowers in her coordinated capris and blouse combo. "That poor Chinese girl who looks after them has the patience of a saint."

"She's Filipino."

"Is she? Well, what a darling. Peggy mistreats her something awful."

"You've seen them outside?"

"Oh yes. Peggy puts up a terrible fuss every time that poor girl shows up. The girl has to talk to her for maybe ten, fifteen minutes before Peggy lets her in the house."

"Does Peggy hit her?"

Carmella purses her fuchsia lips. "I wouldn't say she hits her. It's more like a little shove, you know, in the shoulder. Nothing harmful."

"Carmella, if you see the situation escalate, please call me. I really appreciate you keeping an eye on things. I've been meaning to ask you, have you seen Hilda Wurm's daughter around?"

"That slatternly soul. Good heavens no." Carmella shakes a Chiclet from a box and chews thoughtfully. "There was a police raid at the drug house two streets over. I don't know if she ever stayed there. A girl overdosed in the basement last week, poor thing—such a sad story. They say she'd wanted to get clean, even went to her doctor to get a referral for rehab, but the waiting list is months long."

"Do you know the girl's name?"

She shakes her head. "It's like Grand Central over there. We're hoping the police will shut it down finally. This used to be such a nice neighbourhood."

"Well, thanks for all your help."

I take my father's hand like a child's, lead him slowly back to the bungalow and open the front door.

"I don't want him here!" Peggy shrieks. "He's a no-good two-timer!" She tries to swat him. I stand between them like a referee.

"You think I don't know what's going on around here," she says. "You're no good, is what you are. I want a divorce!"

"Mom, he was taking the garbage out." Reggie slumps on the hall chair but Peggy keeps swinging. I wrap my arms around her in a strait-jacket hold and whisper calmly into her ear. "He doesn't have it in him to flirt with Carmella, Mom. And he shat himself. He's *your* Daddy. He needs you to look after him." Peggy's pillowy body against mine feels intrusive, as though she's been shoved against me in a crowded subway car. Her chocolate marshmallow breath inflames my headache. After a few minutes, overcome with sleepiness, she releases into me. I guide her to her room and onto the bed and pull the comforter over her.

For years I've wanted to hurt my father as he hurt me. But this sack of scrambled brain, flesh, bone and shit is not my father. There is no pleasure in wielding power over a mentally absent tyrant. Leading him to the tub, stripping and hosing him down is no payback, only pay-more. This could go on for years after he loses the ability to shove food into his mouth. Will bots feed and bathe our mentally eroded and withered bodies when we no longer know who we are? Maybe spoon-feeding and diapering the demented and decrepit are bot-proof skills—the coveted jobs of the future.

Conquer and I sit at my table drinking Sleepytime, keeping an eye on Trudy asleep on the couch.

"Where are *your* parents?" I ask.

"Around."

"Do you ever see them?"

"I cut 'em loose."

"Why?"

"They did squat for Liv when Ivy was sick, then went and blamed her for her deadbeat husband's death. Said she could've saved him, didn't phone 911 fast enough."

"*Did* she phone 911 fast enough?"

"Who knows. Who cares."

"Do you have siblings?"

"A sister. We don't talk."

"Because?"

"We can't stand each other."

"So the only person you really care about, other than the daughter who wants to skin you alive, is Olivia?"

He nods then fixes me with a Viking gaze. "Who do *you* really care about?"

"Not sure. Probably nobody."

Chester or the Bosnian clomp downstairs to do laundry. The washer and dryer thump and rumble through the wall.

"FYI I am sleeping with the busboy."

"I figured."

"Are you mad?"

"Nope."

"Are you jealous?"

"Nope."

"Do you think it's bad, him being younger and illegal and all that?"

"I think you should be careful."

"About what?"

"Being used."

"Don't we all use each other? Isn't that what relationships are all about?"

"Maybe in your world."

"What about in *your* world? The waitresses you plough, aren't you using them?"

"It takes two to tango."

"Precisely. It's when we're of no use to anyone that we despair."

"Sounds like you've been listening to Liv."

"I'm a little crazy about her to be honest. Even more now that I know she took too long to call 911."

He rinses his cup in the sink. "I should head back, make sure the old gal went to bed." He offers me his fist. We bump knuckles.

"Your horse dance is amazing by the way," I say. "The best horse dance I've ever seen, no lie."

"I'll horse dance for you anytime, baby."

I walk him out and on the return trip encounter Chester in his satin boxer robe, carrying a basketful of laundry.

"Everything under control here?" he asks.

"Moderately."

"How was your day?"

"The Sun and Jupiter sat in my house of career."

"How'd that work out?"

"So-so. How were things at base camp?"

"The cat lady had the constabulary over again. No idea why."

"She needs someone to talk to besides her cats."

"A waste of taxpayers' money, I say."

"Come by for dinner tomorrow, Chester. Bring the Roman general."

"With pleasure. Tiberius always enjoys a night out. Any chance my communist friend will be there?"

"I'll ask him."

Letting the mutt out for his dookie, I worry that maybe Gyorgi was forced to sleep on the floor because a bed wasn't vacated by a Slovakian. Now hold it right there, girly. He doesn't need you looking after him. He's managed a difficult life just fine without you. Maybe the gypsy in him frees him from forming attachments to people and beds. With his searchlight intelligence, he can always move on, floor surfing. The only constant in his life is his love for his mother. I envy this and try to decide if worrying about Pierce being mauled by bears equals really caring. The fact that I'm trying to decide suggests otherwise.

The dog hears Trudy calling for Mama and stumbles blindly back to the dugout. "This way, pooch." I guide him with my flashlight through the front door then hurry to the couch and wrap Trudy in my straitjacket embrace.

THIRTY-FOUR

Bob and Sugg duke it out in his/her office while I dutifully demonstrate prep as per the spec sheet instructions. The South Asians raise their eyebrows, evidently thinking I've gone soft in the head. With cameras on me I can't gesture to indicate that none of this is my doing, that we must obey Corporate's commands or get transformed. How do you tell new immigrants that social and economic stability, even in Canada, is an illusion that only lasts as long as the going is good for business? Befuddled, they follow my instructions, exchanging looks and muttering in various tongues. When I show the binder to Conquer, he spits without spitting.

"You're on camera," I murmur. "At least *look* compliant."

"Fuck that noise."

Bob's door swings open and out the she-devil strides. I hold the open binder in front of Conquer. "Just nod," I say. "Please." He barely perceptibly nods. Sugg inspects the plated orders and heads for the dining room.

"She always looks like she smells something bad," Daniel observes.

"That's just her face," Wade says.

Daniel checks his hair on his phone. "Turns out she's an alky. Her and Perry were talking about their fur babies when she suddenly said, 'Shit, I'm late for AA.'"

Olaf's eyes pop. "No way dat straight-up bitch said 'shit.'"

Already I'm working out the alky bonding angles. There is no sister/brotherhood like AA. No need to mention I've never been to a meeting.

"According to Perry," Daniel says, "the spy witch caught the writing bug and is working on a kid's book about two beagles."

"Really?" A fellow auteur—another bonding opportunity.

"She says beagles have three types of howls or barks, each serving a different purpose, like for hunting rabbits or whatever. So this one little beagle is the best howler ever, like he can be heard for miles. The other beagle is bigger but sucks at howling."

"Does the big beagle tear the little beagle's throat out?" I ask.

"Not at all, that's what's so cute about the book. The big beagle protects the little beagle from a coyote. And the little one howls on behalf of the big one to win the heart of a lady beagle."

"Cyrano de Beagle," Wade says.

"Did anybody talk to Bob when he came in?" I ask.

"He told me to open myself to my inner goodness," Daniel says, "which is kind of what Lake tells me. He says the power of my inner strength can neutralize the body-shamers."

"Did Bob seem all right to you?"

Olaf tugs up his still beltless dope jeans. "Does you mean all right like da old bro or da new bro?"

"Either."

"He didn't do any qigonging." Daniel applies lip balm. "Apparently he's discovering all kinds of inner pathways to success now he's found pure love with Ashton. Crazy, eh? Both of us clubbers finding pure love at the same time but not in clubs?"

"Crazy."

"So, what's the scoop with your busboy?" Daniel asks. "Who beat him up?"

"What?"

"He's all beat up."

Olaf jabs gangsta gestures. "Dat dude is cut up real bad, fam."

My plastic heart pumps so fast it hurts. I find the gypsy emptying a bussing tray. "What happened to your face?"

He doesn't look at me. "I fall."

"You should put ice on those bruises."

"Not to worry, Stevie."

If not for the ChapSticks, I'd pull him into my office and ice him myself. "The swelling won't go down unless you ice." Already his swollen right cheek is starting to close his eye. "You won't be much use if you can only see with one eye. Come with me."

He reaches for the hose and rinses the tray. "Please, not to worry."

"Come with me. Now." He follows me to the break room. "Sit down. I'll be right back." Scooping and bagging ice, I scan for the spy witch. Praveen, spec binder in hand, points to an instruction he doesn't understand. "It means set the slicer to the lowest possible setting," I tell him. "Thinner than you've ever sliced before. Okay?" He nods, looking frazzled. I grab the first-aid kit and return to the break room, where there's bound to be a ChapStick hidden in the shelves. "Pretend we're strangers for the camera," I say.

"Sure."

"I'm going to put disinfectant on the cuts."

"Is okay, Stevie. I already wash with soap and water."

"Better safe than sorry. Hold still. Where did you fall?"

"On street."

"Did you sleep on a bed last night?"

"Sure." He's lying. Some beefy Slovakian slugged him.

"Did they find out you're Roma?"

"Please, not to worry."

I tear open two square bandages. "I'm going to put these where the skin is broken, otherwise the wounds might get infected."

"Sure."

I want to hold him, tell him everything will be okay. Instead I hand him the bag of ice. "You're sleeping at my place tonight. Chester's coming for dinner. He asked if you'd be there."

"Where is your son?"

"He went up north to find his soldier friend."

"He is okay for to do that?"

"No, but I couldn't stop him. So come to my place tonight. If you want to."

"I want to."

We lock eyeballs, electric currents pulsing between us. "Keep the ice on it for ten minutes. I'll cover for you."

My phone vibrates. I grab it and head for the dishpit. It's Maisie. "Did you take Trudy's beads out of her backpack?"

"I did."

"She thinks somebody stole them."

"Let me talk to her."

Maisie calls Trudy and hands her the phone. A weighty silence.

"Trudy?" I ask.

"What?"

"*I* took the beads. I forgot to tell you. I'm sorry. Maisie doesn't want the little kids playing with beads because they could choke on them."

"You shouldn't touch my stuff."

"I understand that, but we were in such a hurry, and you were in the hall showing your safari animals to the cats, so I just took the beads out. I'm sorry. Trudy?"

"What?"

"Your beads are safe at home. You can string some later." I hear the TV blaring and toddlers squealing.

"There's too much noise here," Trudy says. "It's driving me crazy. Does my mom know how to get here?"

"She has my number. If she calls, I'll give her directions." That's if Sophie isn't the girl who overdosed in the "drug house." If Sophie was that girl, did she seek a rehab referral from the same doctor who'd informed Child Services about Trudy's burn? Was Sophie hoping the doctor would report her request and thereby prove her intentions to be a better mother?

"All I want is peace and quiet," Trudy says, sounding much older than her years, possibly like Sophie.

"Guess who's coming for dinner tonight?"

She doesn't guess.

"Gyorgi," I say.

"Promise?"

"I promise. And Chester's coming too, with his rat."

"Yay!"

"I'll pick you up after work and we'll decide what to cook. Okay?"

"Okay." She hands the phone back to Maisie who says, "Now don't go playing prisoner. Go sit on the back porch. It's a nice day and the kitty's out there. Off you go, sweetie. Stevie, you still there?"

"Yep."

"Between you and me, I have a hunch her mom's a self-harmer. One of the little ones scraped his knee and Trudy wanted to put a Band-Aid on it. She said she puts them on her mom all the time. I said, 'Why's your mom need Band-Aids?' She said, 'When she cuts herself.' So I said, 'When's that happen?' And Trudy said, 'I forget.'"

"Cutting herself doesn't necessarily mean self-harming. She might have just accidentally cut herself."

"Maybe, anyway I just thought you should know. One thing's for sure, Trudy knows how to put on a Band-Aid. She's got great hand–eye coordination for her age."

"Do you think her mom might have burned her?"

"Burned her?"

I grab a rinsed bussing tray to take to the dining room. "She's got a couple of burn scars on her leg. She said the curling iron was on the sink and she tripped over the cord and the curling iron fell on her leg."

"That sounds like something somebody told her to say."

"That's what worries me."

"What a strug. Seriously, Stevie, the kid's pretty wrecked. You need professional help with this."

The VP spots me.

"Gotta go." I pocket the phone.

"What are you doing with a bussing tray?" Sugg demands.

"Taking it to the dining room."

"You have a busboy for that."

"He's on break."

She checks her phone. "Do you think surfer necklaces are appropriate?"

"Excuse me?"

"Several of your cooks are wearing surfer necklaces."

They buy these baubles off Bernardo.

"Really? I hadn't noticed."

"It's not hygienic. They should not be wearing jewellery, except, obviously, wedding rings."

"I'll talk to them."

"And make that Mexican do up his shoelaces."

"He's Colombian."

"There is no question your soft skills need improvement, Stevie. Data shows food costs at this location have exceeded thirty percent. It's pure carelessness on the part of your staff. I saw a cook plate rice and potato with fried chicken."

"Maybe a customer ordered it with rice and potato instead of fries."

"The spec sheets specify no substitutions."

"Some of the regulars are seniors and can't eat fries due to heart conditions."

"Absolutely no substitutions. Make that clear to your staff." She looks back at her phone. "Corporate wants consistency. Customers should get the same meal regardless of the store." She starts texting. I take the tray to the dining room and grab a full one.

Olaf holds up a club sandwich plate. "Yo, wassup wit da fries, cuz? Dis dawg say da plate look legit empty, you know what I'm saying?"

"Explain to the dawg that portion sizes are being measured to Corporate standards."

"I tell him dat and da shizz will slam."

"Let it slam."

All this measuring and weighing is slowing the line. Chits pile up.

"Where are my Westerns?" Wade whines. He's been glum all morning due to developers building a ski resort on grizzly bear habitat.

Helga returns an omelet. "This customer asked for Swiss, not cheddar."

"Tell him we no longer make substitutions," I say.

"You're kidding, right? This guy always orders Swiss instead of cheddar in his omelet."

"Tell him Corporate is enforcing a no-substitutions policy. Any dissatisfied customers should contact head office." I grab chits and play catch-up on the line. Sugg eagle-eyes every plate going out the hutch, making sure specs are followed. Not once does she lend a manicured hand.

When the she-devil leaves for a meeting at HQ, I knock on Bob's door. No answer, and it's locked but I can hear his heavy breathing. "Bob? I know you're in there. It's only me. Bruce Lee left. Can I talk to you for a minute please?"

He opens the door but appears to be in one of his qigong/online course trances.

"So this is how you're dealing with Sugg?" I ask. "Locking her out? What went on between you two?"

He closes his eyes and places his hands on his chest. "A loving attitude towards myself protects my inner tranquillity when faced with pressures."

"Bob, we really need to stick together here. Customers are complaining about portion sizes and Siobhan's tired of making excuses for Corporate. She may have a job at the Courtyard Marriott, and Conquer's looking around. We're going to lose good people if we let Sugg have her way."

"I explained to her it's when staff are at their lowest ebb that we must restore their self-belief."

"And she said?"

"She's full of unwanted thoughts and feelings."

"Sugg said she's full of unwanted thoughts and feelings?"

"Those feelings can only end when she truly accepts her inner truths. I told her cooperation comes when there is love for the task and trust in the special part each staff member plays. You don't love your tasks, Stevie. This has always been just a job to you. Now your faith is being tested."

When did he turn into a wise old Chinese man? In a second he'll call me grasshopper. The headache over my right eye jabs.

"Faith can move mountains, Stevie, but it needs three ingredients to work—belief in yourself, belief in others and belief in your ability to draw on your *inner* strength. I've always believed you have inner strength, but you need to be liberating yourself from the chains of useless and negative thinking. Think of yourself as a traveller through life." Bob spreads his arms, palms facing upward. "Free yourself of the past and future and fully embrace the present."

"The present involves Sugg."

The wise old Chinese man clasps his hands and nods sagely. "An enlightened person welcomes the ideas of others."

"They're not *her* ideas, Bob. They're Corporate's. And anyway, weren't you two arguing? She was in here for almost an hour."

He holds up the hairy digit. "Never say 'I alone am right.'"

"I didn't say I alone am right." It's like I'm talking under water.

The wise old Chinese man taps his temple. "Honesty creates a clear and clean conscience."

Siobhan bangs the door open. "Desmond's church lady mother is here and she's mad as hell. She wants to know why Desmond got fired."

"Not my department," I say, slipping past her, heavy with unwanted thoughts and feelings. I grab another full tray, take it to the dishpit and start loading the washer, my chains of useless and negative thinking clanging. Gyorgi, holding the icepack against his face, helps with his free hand. When we're done he looks at me with the eye not swollen shut.

"Want cancer stick?"

"Definitely."

We smoke out of camera range on the other side of the dumpster. "How's your face feeling?"

"Good."

"We'll ice it more later."

"Sure."

I rest my head against his shoulder. He rests his chin on my head.

"I can't stop worrying about my son."

"I know."

Sirens wail, traffic stops, fire trucks speed past, traffic crawls.

"You can't let the Slovakians beat you up again," I say. "You can stay with me till my son gets back. We don't have to sleep together. You can sleep on the couch and Trudy can sleep in the blanket fort."

"You sure is okay?"

"I'm sure."

We don't move, just lean on each other.

Trudy orders a vanilla dip with sprinkles and carefully arranges her animals on the table. Her lips move as they silently converse.

Wade showed me the bufflehead courtship dance on his phone, the male and female bobbing their heads, raising their breasts out of the water and flapping their wings.

"Doesn't it make you a little sad," I asked, "that your lovebird never danced a courtship dance?"

"She's blind and raised in captivity. That's all she knows."

"So all we know is all we need to know?"

"If we're raised in captivity, yeah. She'd perish in the wild."

Aren't we all raised in captivity, within the confines of our houses/coffins, living our lives as expected? We'd perish in the wild.

My son didn't smell like rapist number one, two, three or four. He smelled like hospital and his old teddy bear. Peggy put the bear on the bed in his room—formerly my room—when he went to war.

For years he has dreamed up a father with a good job, a nice wife and legitimate spawn. A white, fleshy-faced, pant-straining, average dad who didn't get the chance to love his son born of the useless-piece-of-shit mother because he didn't know he existed.

"What are you writing?" Trudy asks. "Is that a *d*?"

"It is."

"And that's a *t*?"

"It is. How 'bout we pick you up a notebook so you can practise letters? Would you like that?"

"You sure we got money for that?"

"Of course."

She looks at her horse.

"Have you finished your hot chocolate?"

She nods.

"Great. Pack up your animals and we'll go to Walmart."

In Men's Sleepwear, two old duffers arguing about a tennis player block our access to the pyjama shelves. "His legs are too thick," the one with a fleshy growth over his eye says.

"It's his serve," the wizened one in a Raptors jacket replies.

"It's got nothing to do with his serve. It's his legs. They're too thick. It takes him too damn long to get going and too damn long to slow down."

"Excuse me," I say, wedging between them to find a pair of PJs to replace Reggie's shit-stained ones.

"He'll never make the top ten with those legs," the man with the growth says.

"He'll do all right in the top twenty."

"Yeah, they still make a million bucks in the top twenty."

"*I* used to play tennis, had to stop because of my knee."

"Excuse me," I repeat, trying to reach around the Raptors fan for a size medium. The tennis aficionados smell unwashed.

"He won't stay in the top twenty with those legs," the man with the growth says.

I grab a medium and retreat, looking for Trudy. "Trudy?"

No answer. I check the aisle. "Trudy?" I call, startling the old men who finally acknowledge my presence. "There was a little girl here. Did you see her?"

"What little girl?" the man with the growth says.

"I didn't see no little girl," the Raptors fan says.

Trudy, expert at making herself invisible, has vanished. "Trudy!" I call louder. Shoppers stare. Already I'm imagining Yegor luring the child into the back of a van by promising to take her swimming with the dolphins. "Did anybody see a little girl?" I half scream, chasing after a stooped white-haired sales associate. "Excuse me, can you help me? I've lost a child. I mean, a child's missing. She's tiny, five years old, Black."

"You'll have to go to Customer Service," she says. "They can page her." She points to the front of the store and I bolt to the service desk, my knees burning, my plastic heart twisting. Disgruntled customers stand in line, clutching items to be returned. "Can you please page Trudy?" I shout over them. "Please, a little girl is lost! Please page Trudy."

A security guard with acne scars grabs my arm. "Calm down, ma'am."

"You need to page her right now. Trudy."

"What's her last name?"

"Oh. Umm. Wurm."

"What's your relationship to the child, ma'am?"

"I'm her grandmother."

The security guard steps behind the service counter to confer with several blue smocks, who send me sidelong glances. This is all taking too long. I charge back to Men's Sleepwear and run up and down the aisles, calling for her. The PA system crackles and a flat voice says, "Can Trudy Wurm report to the service desk at the front of the store. Your grandmother's waiting for you. Trudy, please report to the service desk at the front of the store."

No one will miss her. Pierce will never know.

What must be sorrow pummels me, forcing me to grab hold of a shelf. The stooped white-haired associate sees me. "Did you check inside the square racks? Sometimes kids hide in there behind the clothes." She pushes aside bathrobes hung on a square rack and peers inside. "Not here, but you might want to check some of the others."

"Good idea." I spin around, checking rack after rack. Despair floods me, pools in my eyes, drips from my nostrils. "Trudy!" I full scream now because this can't be happening. I can't lose them both. She is so small, so mighty, so weary, so wise. She has remained her singular self due to sheer force of will, despite neglect, abandonment, burns. She can't hold on much longer among strangers who see her as a product to sell, a product devalued with use. "Trudy!"

The stooped associate catches up with me and taps my shoulder. "Follow me." We walk past Men's Wear into Ladies'. The associate stops beside a square rack and pulls aside coats. "Looks like she wet herself."

I crawl under the rack. The coats fall into place behind me like a curtain. Trudy sits curled up in her puddle of piss, her face buried in her arms. "Trudy, I'm so sorry." I don't know what for. Everything. Unexpected feelings saturate me I can't define. She doesn't move. We're in darkness except for the fluorescent light leaking between the coats.

"Why didn't you answer when I called?" I don't expect an answer, don't know what to expect. "Were you playing hide and seek? My son used to play hide-and-seek. I'm pretty good at it but I need to know we're playing, you know, so I can close my eyes and count to sixty." Some mindless pop tune drones from the sound system, the bass beat battering the dense hush between us.

She keeps her face buried in her arms. "I was scared you'd be mad at me."

"I'm never mad at you."

"You sounded crazy."

"I was a little crazy. I was scared I'd lost you."

She rocks slightly back and forth. "You're not my grandmother. My grandmother's dead."

The stooped associate pulls the coats aside. "Are you two coming out so we can clean in there?"

"Yes. Sorry. We'll be right out." I want to comfort Trudy but don't know how. It's like with Pierce. I don't know anything about her war. "Maybe we can play hide and seek tonight with Gyorgi." Appalling how I use him as bait. "What do you want to cook? Or should we order pizza?"

"I know how to order pizza."

"Is that what you'd like?"

"I'm sick of pizza."

"Fine, then we'll cook something. How about spaghetti? Do you like pasta?"

"I only know how to cook Alpha-Getti."

"*You* don't have to cook. We'll make it together with fresh vegetables. Do you like zucchini?"

"What's that?" She faces me for the first time and my heart untwists a little.

"It's green on the outside and white-ish on the inside. We'll slice it and fry it lightly with onions and peppers."

"What's peppers?"

"I'll show you. But first let's get you some dry clothes."

"I can't go out there. People will see."

"Not if I carry you. I'll bunch the wet part of the dress under my arms so no one can see it."

The stooped associate pushes the coats aside again. "You have to get out of there, ma'am. The cleaner's here."

I take Trudy's hand. "Come on."

When I lift her onto my hip, she hides her face in the space between my neck and shoulder. Feeling her piss seeping into my jeans, I know I can never let her go.

THIRTY-FIVE

Gyorgi puts a guitar case on the floor. "Cool jeans," he says, seeing Trudy who leaps into his arms.

"Why do you have Band-Aids on?"

"I fell."

"Why are they square?"

"For me to look like pirate." He winks at her.

"We're making spaghetti."

"Smells good." He holds an arm out for her to swing on. He seems practised at allowing children to use him like a jungle gym. The swelling on his face has gone down a bit. "How are you, Stevie?"

"I'm fine, Gyorgi, how are you?"

"Fine also."

"I guess you play guitar."

"You guess right."

Trudy tugs at his backpack. "What's in here?"

"Clothes and toothbrush."

"Does that mean you're sleeping over?"

"Sure."

"Yay!"

"Go play," I tell them, taking the pack off his back. "We'll let the sauce simmer for a bit."

"What's simmer?" Trudy asks.

"Cooking on low heat."

Walking home she stepped on ants, very deliberately, as though they had done her wrong.

Chester arrives. The humans and the albino rat commune in the living room. I make a salad and phone Ducky to update her about the lockout and Reggie's new PJs hidden in his closet, beyond Peggy's reach. Ducky will have to stand on a chair to find them.

"Mrs. Many told me she is marrying an Olympic skier," Ducky says. "She wants me to take a love letter to him. She doesn't want Mr. Many to know."

"Is this crazier than usual?"

"It's all because of Mrs. Schmurlich. Oh my goodnuss, Mrs. Many is so jealous of her."

"At least she doesn't think *you're* trying to steal her Daddy."

"She couldn't find the napkins. When I told her they're where she always puts them, she looked in the oven."

"Well, that's pretty standard, isn't it? The oven's her go-to place for lost items."

"I left an invoice for my extra hours, did you see it?"

"Yes, sorry. I meant to leave a cheque for you. I'll drop it off next time I'm by." I'm delaying till payday.

"If you don't pay me for extra hours, I can't do them next week."

"No worries, I'll drop a cheque off by the end of the week." I hear Peggy raving in the background. "I'll let you go, Ducky. Let me know if you need anything."

"I need my pay."

"Of course," I say, as though job security at Chappy's is alive and well. "We'll talk soon."

When VP Sugg returned from HQ, she showed me the vid of yours truly making the ham and Swiss sandwich for Pierce.

I handed her the receipt. "I paid for it when I got back."

She scrutinized it, wrinkling her nose as though something smelled bad.

"I'd have paid right away," I said, "but my dog was sick and I had to take him to the vet."

"You have a dog?"

"Of course."

She looked directly at me for the first time, her eyes hawkish. "I wouldn't have taken you for a dog person."

"Are you kidding? I'm canine kooky."

"Me too," Sugg said, seeing me in a whole new dog-person way. "What's wrong with him?"

"Who?"

"Your dog."

"Oh. He's blind."

"That's terrible."

"He gets around okay. He's old. By the way, Perry told me you have two beautiful huskies. That's awesome." And on it went, canine yakety-yak. The she-devil showed me pics of her huskies wearing deer antlers, gnawing on rawhide, sleeping, and pretty much doing everything but shitting. "Aren't they divine?" she asked and I nodded warmly, not letting on I knew the pack animals wanted to rip each other's throats out. So busy were we doggy bonding, Sugg failed to notice Rinkesh plating very generous Butter Chicken Burritos with piles of rice for his Bengali buds in the dining room. He waved through the hutch at his compadres, all cab drivers, who'd linked tables and were loudly chitting the chat while ogling waitresses. This could be why Rinkesh was fired from his previous place of employment.

Gyorgi leans his shoulder against my door frame. "You okay?"

"Okay."

"Your son did not call."

"He did not."

"He is far from phone."

"Possibly."

"He will call."

Chester holds forth over dinner about what he calls the IMF criminals in Basel, Switzerland. "Economics is a device cooked up by the criminals. It's got nothing to do with the people. Anytime some smartass starts talking economics at you, ask him where the people are."

"Can we dance now?" Trudy asks.

"What a fine idea," I say. "What kind of music should we play?"

"Disco," Chester suggests. "Or ballroom. Or how about some salsa? You name it, I've got it. Be right back." He goose-steps up the stairs.

"We have DJ," Gyorgi says.

"Do you think he can dance ballroom, disco *and* salsa?"

"Maybe before Caterpillar tractor." Gyorgi lies on the floor and instructs Trudy to balance her belly on his raised feet while he holds her hands. He straightens his legs, raising her up. "You fly." Trudy squeals with delight, and I flop on the couch trying to free myself of the past and future and fully embrace the present.

Chester plays Donna Summer belting "Last Dance," "She Works Hard for the Money" and "I Feel Love." We shake our booties and bump cabooses. Then, of course, he plays *Saturday Night Fever* hits.

"Do the horse dance," Trudy commands.

"You show them how," I tell her and she does, adding reins. Soon we're all cantering around the dugout. Chester maintains his marching-band-leader posture while lifting his knees. Next he plays ballroom, demonstrating the foxtrot for us. We do our best, stumbling into one another. "Chins up," Chester coaches because we keep staring at our problematic feet. Then he turns on the salsa.

"Time out," I say, collapsing on the easy chair. In Crocs with socks, Chester dances the best salsa I've ever seen. Even Trudy is mesmerized by his twitching pelvis and fancy footwork. Gyorgi picks her up and dances with her, copying Chester's lusty moves with ease. The dugout is ablaze with Latino trumpets.

Knocking on the door makes me leap up, hoping/fearing it's Pierce, although he'd use his key. It is the Bosnian's henchmen. Not the same cops as last time. They must take turns servicing her.

"We've had a complaint about the noise," the one bulging out of his bulletproof vest says.

I step back so they can listen to my stereo. "Does Marc Anthony seem overly loud to you?"

"Just take it down a notch, ma'am."

"The complainant plays her radio loud 24/7 and I don't call the cops."

"She says she hears domestic violence down here," the one leaking snot says. He dabs his nostrils with a Kleenex.

"When does her calling you to complain about me, and you knocking on my door stressing me out, qualify as harassment?"

"To be honest with you, ma'am," the bulging one says, "we have her down as an EDP."

"What's an EDP?"

"An emotionally disturbed person."

"In that case why do you come here every time she calls?"

"We have to answer every complaint, ma'am."

The marching band leader turns off the music and joins us. "We do so enjoy your visits, officers, but all the good lady has to do is ask us herself to turn the music down and we shall do so post-haste. No need to draw you away from more important matters."

"Anyway, it's off now," I say. "Have a good night."

"Let us know if we can be of any further assistance," Chester says as I close the door in their faces.

Back in the living room the gypsy and the princess have disappeared. "Where did they go?" I ask.

"They were here a minute ago."

"Oh, well," I say, "I guess we'll have to eat *all* the ice cream ourselves."

"We're here!" Trudy trumpets, popping up behind the couch. Gyorgi, looking hunted, gets up off his knees.

"The cops are gone," I say. "They won't be back."

His chronic fear of police is embedded in his nervous system. He will never be free of it. Just as I will never be free of my fear of men loitering in parking lots, and Pierce will never be free of the war at his back.

"I've been looking for wall art," Chester says. "Something from the sixties. Maybe Pollock. Nothing too busy. Have you had any experience with wall peels?"

"No," I say, watching the rat scurry between Trudy and Gyorgi. The gypsy seems far away, cowering in his echo chamber.

"It's like wallpaper," Chester says, "but coated with adhesive. You peel off the backing and the paper sticks to the wall. My ex put it in her granddaughter's bedroom."

"Not *your* granddaughter's bedroom?"

"Eugenie's child-bearing years were over by the time we met." He scrapes the last of his ice cream from his bowl and sets it on the table. "It was clouds, the wall peel. When you walked into the room you were in the sky."

"Trippy." Helga's word. She was in a state of super upsetness this afternoon because a New Zealander at Zumba asked her to hang out in a "friend way" and not a "date way." Because the New Zealander was hot, Helga only wanted to hang out in a date way. She wasted my time asking whether or not she should go. "Just go," I said gruffly. With Sugg on my case, I've become wearily belligerent with staff.

"It took me three years to decide what colour to paint my old place," Chester says. "I'd like to move a tad faster on this one."

"Well, I think a wall peel of clouds sounds great."

"Or planets. The solar system is also available."

"That might be too busy with Pollock."

He nods, fondling the keys on his lanyard. "Eugenie suffered from anxiety, had panic attacks, migraines and so on. The medication didn't help. I thought she should get off the pills but she insisted they were the only way she could cope. Her daughter told me she died leaning on the bed like she was praying. I'd never known Eugenie to pray."

Not sure what to say here, I start to clean up. Gyorgi, on the floor, absently watches Trudy put her plastic animals to bed under squares of toilet paper in the Barbie house. I hand him a pack of frozen peas to put on his face.

"Decor decisions have never been my forte," Chester says. "I suppose I could move the couch. Or get rid of it. Eugenie wasn't a fan of that couch. Vintage seventies, she called it."

"Do you ever see her daughter?" I ask.

"No, no, she never took to me. Understandably."

"Why understandably?"

"I stole her mother."

I try to imagine having a mother worth stealing.

Trudy stands. "Chester, we forgot about your orange Jell-O with marshmallows."

"Oh, now that's a delicacy not to be missed."

We all spoon Jell-O.

"I miss her," Chester says. "The wife. Don't get me wrong, it wasn't all rainbows and unicorns. Eugenie was in the habit of saying, 'The worst is yet to come.' Certainly true in her case."

"In most cases," I say, wishing Gyorgi would share a glance with me, repair me with his smile.

I help Trudy print *cat* in her notebook. Next she draws what might be a cat, although it's bigger than the stick figure next to it. "Is that a cat?" I ask her. She nods. I point at the stick figure. "Is that you?" She nods, which means in her world cats are bigger than she is. She has spent her life making herself invisible and inaudible.

Chester pats his mouth with a napkin. "She always had difficulty sleeping, Eugenie, and, of course, required more and more pills. On several occasions I was unable to wake her in the morning."

"Sometimes my mom doesn't wake up," Trudy says.

"Is that right?" Chester says. "Well, sometimes a little extra sleep is deserved. Particularly on Sundays. By the by, did you happen to notice the deceased woodpecker last Sunday?"

I shrug. "Dead birds are pretty common around here due to the cat infestation."

"Ah, but this chap wasn't mauled. He was at the foot of the tree out front. It was as though he'd decided to call it a day and leaned against a tree trunk. Reminded me of Eugenie leaning on the bed to pray. I buried him."

"Did the Bosnian catch you digging in her hills?"

"She did and was unduly disturbed. I'd say that hydrant is about to blow."

There's a ceaseless whirring in my head. When Chester starts reminiscing about his days as a Boy Scout leader, I say, "I forgot to take the dog out." The pooch hears the tinkling of his leash and hobbles towards me. "We'll be back shortly."

No dogs or humans frolic in the park. And Benedict doesn't fetch the glow-in-the-dark Frisbee. Tree branches, competing for space, rub against each other in the wind, mournfully squeaking. November gusts swat my face. The temperature must be lower up north. What supplies did Pierce buy with $300: thermal blankets and socks, long johns? Are they sleeping in hollowed-out tree trunks like Johnny Appleseed?

A man shuffles pigeon-toed around the park, his bony frame clenched and twisted, punching invisible people, possibly children as he throws the punches at waist height. What's going on in *his* coffin?

The spinning cat crowds my brain box. I hit it on Lakeshore Boulevard years ago, didn't see it, only felt it, knew I'd struck something but couldn't stop the car without causing a pileup. The feline spun in the rear-view mirror, presumably because my wheel hit its head. Multiply the horror of the spinning cat a billion times and you have a sense of the endless reel playing behind Pierce's eyes: the boy mangled but still moving, the oncoming trucks about to crush him. The little American flag, no longer in his grasp, taking flight in the wind.

Gyorgi sits with his back to the stucco. I join him, relieved he puts his arm around my shoulders. We huddle against the chill. Traffic rumbles.

"No cancer stick?" I ask.

"I quit."

"Why?"

"I smoke because I have deal with Slovakian. Now no Slovakian."

"How many cigarettes was he giving you?"

"Three."

"A day?"

He nods.

"It was nice of you to share them with me."

"Is better not to smoke."

"It is." Sharp breezes scatter shrivelled leaves.

"Chester and Trudy are playing cards," he says.

"I hope he teaches her to cheat."

Gyorgi smiles, making me smile. "Chester was born with upside-down kidney. Backward also. He had operation when he was six for to put it right side up, but is still backward."

"The man's a medical miracle."

"He has plan for to be rich."

"Which is?"

"He design biodegradable cigarette filter." The pooch flops down beside Gyorgi.

"Sounds marketable. Why isn't he rich yet?"

"It cost thousands to patent design. Cowboy does not have money. He worries someone to steal his idea."

"What's the biodegradable butt made of?"

"He says it can be made from anything. Is all in his design of filter. Is top secret." Gyorgi rubs Benedict's tummy. Garbage trucks lurch past, grind to a stop, pick up garbage, lurch on, grind to a stop, pick up garbage. A dog walker allows his hound to whiz on the weed patch.

"When I was child," Gyorgi says, "my mother let me have dog. He was small. I thought he would live long time and we would be for years together. He got tumour and died. This felt wrong to me. I was older than dog. I should die first."

"Didn't your mom tell you dogs don't live as long as humans?"

"I not believe her. She always was warning me about bad things to happen. I don't listen."

"Yeah, we're deaf to warnings after a while."

I rest my head on his shoulder. He rests his chin on my head. A couple of the Bosnian's cats hiss and spar.

"Are you sure is okay I sleep here?"

"It's more than okay. I want you to sleep here. If you want to sleep here."

"I want to sleep here."

He presses his face into my hair and I turn into him, slide my hands inside his jacket and straddle him, carefully kissing the skin around the bandages. His hands are up and under my sweatshirt and in seconds we're escaping into each other, temporarily freeing ourselves of disconcerting disconnectedness. I break it up to guide the dog into the dugout and grab some laundry plus a condom. "We're just doing some laundry," I tell the card players, who don't bother to look up.

THIRTY-SIX

"Bob quit," Daniel tells me.

"Please tell me you're joking."

"No joke. He came in with a couple of empty Dollarama bags, filled them with his owls and stuff and left. He's not answering his phone."

Without Bob's lunacy, there is no buffer between me and the she-devil.

"How dey hangin'?" Olaf swings by with a plate. "Dis dawg say da steak be straight-up hard to chew, yo."

"Didn't Sugg tell you to tie your hair back or get a haircut?"

"Fam, you gotta put a leash on dat she-wolf's tongue. She be high-key vicious."

The Viking glowers at the hard-to-chew steak. "The fucker ordered it well." To Conquer, well-done is sacrilege.

I grab the plate, nudge Conquer aside and toss another steak on the chargrill, where it sends up a hiss of smoke. This I can do. My hands move speedily while my brain stalls. Daniel and Helga, oblivious of the peril around us, yabber about a cosmic bar that serves glow-in-the-dark drinks: green grasshoppers and blue lagoons. "Pretty trippy," Helga says.

"Had a ball-breaking session with the VP this morning," Conquer grumbles. "Seems like it's her way or the highway."

"Who's supposed to replace Bob?"

"Sugg's moved into his office, wiped it down with disinfectant wipes. Where were you?"

"Dentist."

Not true. I was at the DNA testing centre. The probability of Pierce's paternity is 99.9996 percent. Now I have to tell him. Everything. Or nothing.

"Boss, you got to run interference if any of us are going to survive here."

"I'll talk to her. Bernardo?"

"Miss Stevie, how you feeling? You don look so good."

"Do up your laces, Bernie. Now." I flip the steak. "Ahorita!"

"Right away, Miss Stevie." He bends down but hesitates, as if he's forgotten how to tie shoelaces.

Wade, looking wounded, picks up two orders of fish and chips.

"How's the VP of Innovation treating you out there?" I ask him.

"It's all about the dust motes."

"Dat she-wolf wants us dustin' da ledges and crevasses. Dat ain't right, cuz, you feel me?"

"I refuse to dust," Wade says.

"She say polish da brass railing and clean da cabinets. I says, 'Yo, we is waiters, not cleaners.' I tells her dis gig be hella finite—no extra gwop, no side hustle."

I plate the steak and hand it to Olaf. The she-wolf speeds past. "Stevie? A word in my office."

"Sure, I'll just finish up here."

"There is nothing here your staff can't handle. If they can not adequately perform their duties, there will be new hires."

I follow her into Bob's office and am astonished by its transformation. Freed of clutter, it feels almost spacious. On the desk is a copy of *Secrets of the Millionaire Mind*. I glance around for ChapSticks.

"Have a seat." She pushes up the sleeves of her yoga top, readying for a fight.

"Where did you find an extra chair?"

"The break room. Which will no longer be a break room. Staff have abused it long enough and we need the floor space to optimize efficiency."

I never know who she's referring to when she says "we." Are there bots at Corporate with whom she's planning our destruction? "What are you intending to use the break room for?"

She clicks at her laptop. "We're breaking down the wall and installing another walk-in fridge and a bank of microwaves."

"We don't need another fridge or microwaves."

She narrows her eyes at her screen, scanning data. I feel like the kid who has no idea why she's been called into the principal's office.

Sugg folds her hands on Bob's desk and looks at me sternly. "Our goal is to improve performance by systematically removing waste and reducing variation. As we'll be shifting to more prepared inventory, we'll need more fridge space."

"Are you talking about prepared foods we have to unwrap and zap in microwaves as opposed to foods we cook fresh?"

"I'm talking about efficiency. You saw we just wasted another steak due to poor execution. Our goal is to guarantee a level of quality. We will microwave chicken, pork and beef dishes with presets, then heat up the finished plate in another microwave with presets. Same with cooked veg. Meals will be prepared to exacting standards every single time. No waste."

"Low-grade meat and vegetables topped with sauces made in a lab sounds like TV dinners."

Ignoring me, she checks her phone. "The complete new menu won't be available until the new year. In the meantime we'll make small additions. Our first innovation will be to replace Build-a-Pasta Night with pasta bowls. We've tried them at other locations and they're very popular."

"You mean the pre-made bowls marketed to be healthy that are, in fact, loaded with salt, sugar, artificial flavours and fat?"

"The Asian bowls are particularly in demand, followed by the Mexican and Mediterranean."

"They're as fattening as Big Macs."

She crosses her arms tightly, possibly to restrain herself from punching me. "If we're to move forward together, Stevie, it's important you understand that *my* expertise is in business process management." She pushes a strand of bleached hair out of her eyes. "My mandate is to eliminate unnecessary steps in the process of food production from the moment it comes in the back door to the moment the dirty plates are returned to the kitchen. Quality assurance is critical which means that, ultimately, to streamline production, the flattop, stovetop and chargrill will be removed."

I gasp inwardly. The chargrill is the reef to which I cling. Where Stan trained me and told me I did whiz-bang jobs. Without it I will be pulled out to sea.

Desolation clobbers me and all I can do is mutter feebly, "Chappy's is known for its steaks."

"This location, according to the office report which this Chappy's failed, isn't known for anything. Chappy's should be a brand. The customer should know exactly what he's getting. No deviations."

"You can't microwave steaks."

"Steaks are not on the new menu. Burgers and grilled chicken will be shipped in frozen. The line cooks will simply unwrap the food, put it in microwaves at fixed settings, add pre-measured sauces and toppings, buns, sides, etc. Quality will be assured with minimal skills."

Removing the chargrill is removing this old elephant's teeth. My trunk feels around for them. "Then you don't need me."

"Not in the same capacity. I'm taking charge of all hiring and scheduling during the transition process. But I can't be here long-term, and as we will no longer require a kitchen manager, ultimately we would like you to be general manager." Looking like something smells bad, she resumes clicking at her laptop. "Head office is offering you an opportunity, Stevie, despite my concern that you are change-resistant and too lenient. Corporate believes in you."

"No, Corporate likes me because I'm cheap and can work every station."

"Certainly your experience is valued. And you have good rapport with both kitchen and front of house staff. As I've said, your soft skills need improvement where efficiency and discipline are concerned. But, from what I've seen, you are reliable."

Corporate intends to crown me the puppet president, to pull my strings, fooling staff into believing my actions are my own. My "good rapport" will disguise the inevitable obsolescence of their jobs. And when the culling is done and the branding complete, Corporate will cut me loose.

"Just to be sure I understand you correctly," I say, "Corporate is transforming Chappy's into a fast food joint."

"We're repositioning Chappy's to fit a changing marketplace. Sit-down chains are seeing a decline while fast food and delivery is picking up. Unlike a fast food chain, Chappy's will maintain a pub theme, serving alcohol and offering ambiance. Excellent customer service will be a must."

"Excellent customer service means offering substitutions and freshly grilled meat."

"Not for the Millennial demographic. They want comfort food fast and a variety of beverage choices. The bar tab at this location in particular indicates that pub food sells."

"The bar does well here because Perry is an excellent bartender."

"So excellent he doesn't notice employees stealing supplies."

"You're telling me 'transitioning' means offering the kind of food that kills people."

"Good business modelling requires making changes to meet demand." She pushes up her sleeves again. "As labour and food remain Chappy's two biggest operating costs, our first initiative will be to cap hours to avoid paying benefits. Starting today no one on an hourly rate will get more than thirty hours a week, consequently full-timers will eventually leave of their own accord. Throughout the changeover, I'll be weeding out poor performers. To blue-sky it, we'll have part-timers only, and wait staff that present well."

"Did you just use blue-sky as a verb?"

"Ultimately, we want only attractive servers on the floor. We all know they draw male customers who spend more."

"How do we all know that?"

"Don't think your negativity goes unnoticed, Stevie. If we're to work together, you're going to have to dial that down. My job is not an easy one, but I get it done." She resumes clicking. "Wait staff are minimum wage, it's the kitchen staff at different pay rates that add cost. We'll cut the higher-paid cooks' hours. I'm still crunching numbers to determine the timeline required to transition completely to minimum-wage part-timers."

"I'm not firing anybody," I say.

"*I* will cut hours as staffing needs change. Once the expensive cooks' shifts are cut, they will leave of their own accord, giving me the opportunity to hire less skilled workers and part-timers. Staff costs *will* go down."

I must look strange because she looks at me strangely, like she's a husky and I'm a creature it's never seen before. The husky can't decide whether or not to rip my throat out.

"It's a lot to unpack," she says.

"It certainly is." Bob's photos of Elvis and the Dalai Lama are gone. And his poster for *Eat Pray Love*. Only traces of sticky tape remain.

Sugg no longer looks ready to chomp but stares past my head like a bored lifeguard.

"As GM," I say, "would I get a raise?"

"Certainly as your job description changes, you will be entitled to ask for appropriate compensation."

Which means no raise.

She leans towards me, smelling of disinfectant wipes. "None of what we've discussed is to leave this room, understood?"

I nod, knowing I will tell Conquer everything asap.

"You look a little pale," she says. "Is it the fibroids again? Do you want some Tylenol?"

"No thanks but I have to admit, while unpacking all this, a shot of JD wouldn't hurt. Just kidding, I can't touch a drop." I look at my watch. "Better make my AA meeting tonight, maybe even phone my sponsor."

"You're in AA?"

"Of course. I'm an alcoholic."

She glances around as though someone might be listening and whispers, "So am I."

"You're kidding?"

"It's not something I kid about. Alcohol ruined my life. I've been building it back, brick by brick, but it hasn't been easy."

"You can say that again."

"I'm actually writing a memoir about my renewal."

"Really? That's impressive."

"I'm calling it *Transcendence*."

"Nice."

"How long have you been sober?"

"Four years, eight months and nineteen days. You?"

"Three, six and two. You're doing better than me."

"For now." Best not to mention the Moscow mules.

"Oh Stevie, you can't let innovation upset you. Have you tried meditation? Meditation changed my life. But you have to stick with it."

"I square breathe a lot."

"Good for you. Try identifying to reduce stress. It really helps."

I don't know what "identifying" means but nod anyway. Sugg attempts an encouraging smile but the muscles of her face resist—possibly because of the Bobo—and she looks back at her screen. "I have stats from previous changeovers that give us an idea of how many high-cost staff we need to lose per week."

"How many?"

"1.2."

"So that's one whole cook plus .2 of another cook. What's .2, an entire hand or just a couple of fingers?"

Siobhan charges in, panicked. "A table literally dined and dashed. Olaf thought they were going for a smoke, but they're getting on their bikes."

"Where?" Sugg demands.

"They locked them to the fence on the other side of parking lot."

The VP takes off like a superhero. I scurry to my closet and spot Bob's note on my desk: *Daer Stevie, A difficult sitaution is a test of our abilties to rise above the jugement of others. If we recognize our inner resuorces and use them accordingly poeple will trust us. Be humble and recognize that there is always something to be laerned. Clamness and centredness act like an air conditioner in a hot room. Wishing you all good things. Yours paecefully, Bob.*

Bob has moved on to discover his inner pathways to success while I dodge Sugg's blows because I can't afford to quit. We become who we are out of necessity, not choice.

Trudy tore leaves off shrubs on our way to Maisie's. Pierce did this at her age. I thought he was trying to get my attention so I ignored him. Now I understand he was trying to have an effect on the world. He wanted to be noticed. Like Bob. Like all of us.

"Why are you tearing leaves?" I asked Trudy. She stopped because I'd noticed.

We three genetically linked malcontents, motherless, attention-deprived, are shadowed by a presentiment of loss.

I asked Gyorgi if he played guitar in the Slovakians' apartment, thinking this may have tipped them off about his being Roma.

"No. In subway."

"For money?"

"Sure."

This seemed punishingly sad, the gypsy boy, far from home, missing his mother, busking for change. Then he played for Trudy, soft melodies unfamiliar to me, Romani tunes probably centuries old. I lay on my bed listening, wanting to be consoled by the gentle thrums and fingerpicking. But a presentiment of loss loomed over me. "The worst is yet to come," Chester's anxious wife said, swallowing pills until she knelt down and died.

My phone vibrates. It's a collect call.

"I found him," Pierce says. "We're all right."

My plastic heart stops for a second then jerks into overdrive and my eyes balloon tears.

"Are you crying?" he asks. "I can't believe you're crying. Stop worrying. We're good up here. You wouldn't fucking believe it. It's so quiet. It's like all you hear is birds and shit, and then night comes and you hear different sounds but it's not like noise. It's this blanket over you. Greg says he doesn't have night visions up here. He's so tired at night, he just listens to the quiet and passes out."

"Aren't you cold? I mean, it's getting colder."

"This is nothing. We're fine. You wouldn't believe the colours, like everywhere you look is a painting. We see deer and rabbits. We ate a rabbit. And the sound of the water, it washes over you, just goes on and on and you kind of forget everything."

This is not the Pierce I know, inert, drained of hope. Energy crackles through the phone.

"Greg met this guy Mike, who lent him a canoe. We get going in that thing and it's like, it's like we're *alive*."

"That's really wonderful," I say. "I'm so proud of you. Did you call Tara?"

"Yeah, she even talked to Greg. She's back in the apartment. Anyway, the thing is we need more supplies and meds. He's cutting back but still needs some shit. The VA covers his drugs but we need other stuff."

"So you have to come back."

"Just for a day. The problem is I need more money. This is the last time I'll ask, I promise. Next week we start working for Mike. He clears driveways and supplies firewood for locals and cottagers. He's going to pay us cash. Greg knows how to run a plough and I can stack and chop wood and shit. Whatever's going. Mike does property maintenance. So, can you spot me another couple of hundred?"

"Of course." I just received the two-hundred-plus bill for his ambulance ride.

"Can you meet me at the bank again?"

"When?"

"Tomorrow night? I'll get the morning bus down. Can we meet around seven?"

"Okay."

"You're the best. Thanks for this. I'll pay it back. I will."

"Don't worry about it."

"See you soon." He ends the call and I feel carbonated because he's safe, for now anyway. I pull the DNA test report from my backpack and stare at the columns of numbers. The "child" and "the alleged father" have some of the same numbers circled but not all. I reread: *Based on the samples received from tested parties whose identities cannot be independently verified, I, the undersigned Laboratory Director, Veselko Popovic, declare that the genetic data is correct as reported on 11/09/2014.*

I don't have to tell Pierce, don't have to destroy his newfound wonder at Mother Earth.

Daniel and Wade pile into my closet.

"Oh my god, oh my god, oh my god, you have to stop the she-devil."

Wade leans his forehead against the wall. "She's making us clean the server stations."

"Did she catch the dine-and-dashers?"

"She's holding them prisoner until the cops get here," Daniel says. "Which is why we can stop cleaning for two seconds while she plays sheriff."

"I hate to be the bearer of bad news, boys, but changes are afoot. Carol Sugg is here to stay."

"Time to die," Wade says.

Daniel squirts hand lotion from his turtle key chain, making the office reek of lavender. "What kind of changes?"

"I can't share deets," I say, "but be advised it wouldn't hurt to look for work elsewhere."

"That bitch hussy got the Courtyard Marriott job. She's acting like it's a major career move."

"Did she give Sugg notice?"

"It doesn't start till next month. She figures if she tells the she-devil, she'll cut her shifts."

"She'll cut her shifts anyway. Sugg's taking over all scheduling."

"Classic VP of Innovation behaviour," Wade groans.

Daniel tucks the turtle back in his pocket. "She's a fat-shamer. She made me bend down to clean the baseboards behind the bar and kept making comments about my size, like pretending she was concerned it was too hard for me to bend over. I said, 'Excuse me for being a big person.' Next she gets me on my knees to clean the fridges and keeps asking if I can reach all the way back. I'm squeezed in there, and I'm like, do it yourself, bitch."

Wade, still with his forehead against the wall, says with great melancholy, "She told me I'm her best server."

"Even though you refuse to dust?" I ask.

"It's because he's pretty," Daniel says.

"And wears a belt," I add. "She likes pants to stay on."

Conquer sticks his head in. "What'd the terminator say?"

"We'll talk later."

"You mean off the premises?"

"Oh my god, oh my god, oh my god, are you two dating finally?"

"We're getting married," Conquer says. "And you don't get to be a bridesmaid." He closes the door.

"Why's he always so alpha with me? I bet he's a closgay."

"Boys," I say. "Don't burn yourselves out working for the VP. Follow the tips around town. Christmas season is fast approaching, restos will be hiring."

Siobhan barges in. "Get back on the floor, hot stuff. And we need three pitchers, lardy ass."

"Don't fat-shame me, bitch."

I steer them all out and close the door, feeling bereft because Chappy's is about to be process-managed to pieces.

Conquer and I pick up Trudy and the mutt and sit in the park. As usual, Trudy keeps her distance from the other kids.

"Not a joiner, is she?" Conquer asks.

"Only if she can take prisoners."

"Like you."

"Nah, I don't wanna be no warden."

"Says you."

"Sugg's cutting shifts. She doesn't want full-timers, thirty hours a week tops."

"Who's supposed to cook?"

"Cheap labour and microwaves. Seriously, Conquer, you need to look around."

"I already did."

"And?"

"A chick I went to George Brown with works at the CN Tower. She's going on mat leave and getting me in there."

"That's great," I say, hollow inside because without Conquer, one kick from Sugg will topple me. "When?"

"Three weeks. What about you?"

"What about me?"

"She keeping you on?"

"If I comply."

"I can't see you doing that."

"I can't see me doing anything else."

"Boss, you just got to get your CV out there."

"Not till everybody is safely off the ship."

"Make sure you save a spot on a lifeboat for yourself."

A monarch butterfly lands on my armrest. "Aren't you supposed to be on your way to Mexico?" I ask it.

"She's talking to somebody." Conquer points to Trudy getting coaching tips from an older girl on cartwheel technique. Trudy tries one but topples sideways.

"You're getting a second chance with that kid," Conquer says. "Don't blow it."

"My son called. He's loving it up north. Feels alive. Eating rabbit."

"Did you tell him about Trudy?"

"Of course not. Why ruin it?"

"Because he has to know."

"Why now? Why ever?"

"So he has a chance."

"He won't want it."

"You don't know that."

"What if he raped her?"

"He didn't rape her."

"How do you know?"

"Because she gave her back to him. If he'd raped her, she would've given the kid to anybody but him."

Benedict forces a dookie, which I bag and drop in the trash can. Back on the bench, Conquer looks like he's on his boat, staring out a porthole, getting misty about old barns.

"A girl OD'd in our old neighbourhood," I say. "It's not beyond the realm of possibility that she was Trudy's mom."

"All the more reason to tell him. If he's all that little girl's got."

"She's got me."

"Kids want parents."

Unless I make my son's paternity official, I will have no legal right to Trudy. She attempts something like her twentieth cartwheel.

"She don't give up easy," Conquer observes. "Definitely your acorn."

A small hairy dog sniffs Benedict's ass and crotch and every inch around our bench. The dog's owner has a shock of white hair and is wrapped in a fluffy coat that looks suspiciously like a bathrobe. She yanks on the dog's leash. "Step on it," she tells the mutt, who doesn't budge. "My god, it's like walking an old Italian man on a rope." She picks up the dog and stomps off with him.

Conquer continues to stare out the porthole in his mind.

"I don't know how I'm going to manage without you," I say.

"Me neither."

We sit with the indefinable bulk of our intimacy between us.

"Child-rearing is weird shit," he says. "They start out attaching themselves to you because you're there and feeding them and seem to know what you're doing. Then they start figuring out you're not perfect, maybe even as scared and confused as they are. But you act tough and keep cheering them on, making them strong so they don't need you, even though without them you think you'll die. They get bigger and smarter then split and you never know when you'll see them again. It's like having the better part of yourself walking around unattached to you. You're always feeling your better part missing."

"I never felt that."

"You do now. Stone cold sober, you're feeling it."

A bouncy ball rolls towards us. Conquer grabs it and gently tosses it back to a small freckled boy, who startles himself by catching it.

"I'll try to get you in at the Tower, boss. Wouldn't that be something? Us badasses on top of the world?"

"That would be something."

"Nobody grills like you, baby."

Some starlings swarm a tree, chirping wildly. The freckled little boy hugging the ball stares up at them, bewildered. A homeless man with matted hair meanders around the swings, arguing furiously with an imagined foe. The little boy watches him until his mother scoops him up and straps him into a stroller.

"You know what I miss most about drinking?" I ask.

"Feeling super sexy?"

"Besides that. Booze shut down the outside world. I didn't even look out windows. There was a stillness to it."

Trudy lands a perfect cartwheel and stands triumphantly. I jump up and applaud shouting, "Way to go, Trudy!" She launches a smile my way and nails another cartwheel. I keep cheering her on—the better part of myself—making her strong so she won't need me, even though without her I think I will die.

THIRTY-SEVEN

I've been trying to find myself for years and, all the while, I was at Chappy's. Now, in touchless Gitmo-style torture, I'll lose .2 of my self-respect daily until, once again, I'll be lost.

Sugg told me the transformed menu will offer chicken wings. Wing Day every day. Dismembered chicken tossed and sauced in artificial flavours: orange-glazed, teriyaki, jerk, chipotle and, the most poisonous and popular of them all, Southern fried wings that will arrive pre-breaded and ready to be hot-dropped into the fryer.

When will we, the angry and disenfranchised, unite like pack animals and rip out the throats of the oligarchs?

Gyorgi leans against my door frame. "She is asleep."

"She's so in love with you it's scary."

"Why scary?"

"Because when you're not around she misses you."

"Is bad?"

"To be that invested in someone, yeah."

"Better to not invest?"

"Better to invest wisely."

"I am not wise investment?"

"You're not a safe investment."

"Why?"

"Because you're illegally in this country and could be sent home at any time."

He nods and stares at one of the Bosnian's cats mauling a bird just outside the window.

"Another sparrow down," I say.

"And not you?"

"What?"

"Scary in love with me."

"I don't know how to do that."

"Me also." He raps his knuckles against the window, shooing the cat.

"While we're on the subject, do you happen to have any idea what's going on between you and me? Just asking."

"No idea."

"Me neither," I say. "Wade told me zebra finches grow new brain cells when mating season begins and they have to sing to attract mates. Maybe you and I are growing new brain cells while having survival sex. Because that's part of it, isn't it? We're fucking for our lives."

"Maybe we should sing like zebra finches."

"While we mate or just anytime?"

He starts to sing softly in Romani and I pull him onto the bed.

"You sing," he says.

I sing "Dancing Queen" like I did for Trudy, humming the melody then singing the words dancing and queen. My fingers feel for his belt buckle and his hands slide inside my jeans and we're back to breathing sensation into one another, growing new brain cells.

Afterwards we lie intertwined, me mystified by the intense coherence and unity I feel curled around him.

Later he reheats the chicken, green pepper and potato stew he made for dinner. The fridge puckers open and whooshes shut—a comforting sound. For once there is no Bosnian background noise. I think of Pierce under the blanket of quiet in the woods, sleeping peacefully.

We sit on the bed slurping stew.

"The spice is paprika, right?" I ask.

"Right."

The dog clacks towards us and rests his snout on the bed. I feed him some boneless chicken.

"Do the Roma believe in an afterlife?" I ask. "Heaven or something?"

He shrugs. "Some."

384

"Not you?"

He places our empty bowls on the bedside table and lies back with his hands folded on his abdomen, a scientist pondering a formula. "Everything what I am," he says, "what I think, feel, conscious or unconscious, is electrochemical activity of billions of brain cells. They are joined together with almost infinite number of synapses. When my brain dies, I die."

"So humans are dancing a transient electrochemical dance."

"What means transient?"

"Temporary."

"Sure."

"Considering how temporary we are, it's weird how we tribalize. You'd think we'd just want to get along with each other for the duration."

"What means tribalize?"

"Divide up, form camps, so it's us against them."

"Who is in your camp?"

"You. And Trudy and Pierce. And Conquer and his auntie."

"Who are we against?"

"Them."

He smiles and I place my hands gently over his face, feeling every contour, wanting to remember it with all my transient molecules.

Siobhan has a meltdown in my closet because Edvar went to the Riviera Maya with his new squeeze and posted a pic of the two of them in sarongs, Tequila Sunrises in hand, with the caption "We're going to make beautiful babies together!!!!!"

"Classic," Wade says.

Siobhan does the jazz handsy thing. "He literally told me he didn't want kids."

"Consider yourself lucky to be done with the deadbeat," I say. "By the way, congrats on the Courtyard Marriott gig. That's a major career move."

"Daniel, you were supposed to keep that under your hat."

"The she-devil won't let me wear a hat."

"How are things going out front with the VP?" I ask.

"She literally wants us to wear form-fitting clothes," Siobhan says.

"Not like Hooters skin-tight," Daniel clarifies. "More like a sports bar look. She's benching Olaf until he gets pants that fit."

"Leaving you short a server because Olaf will never wear pants that fit."

"She wants fewer servers on the day shift anyway," Siobhan says. "If anyone stops moving for literally a second, she thinks we're overstaffed."

Daniel works gel into his hair. "If she says, 'If there's time for preening, there's time for cleaning,' one more time I may just slap her."

"Promise?" Wade says.

"Helga deep-Facebooked her," Daniel adds. "Turns out the spy witch has a Down syndrome son. Like, not little and cute but weird looking in his twenties."

"I thought her son managed a Chappy's," I say.

Daniel checks his do on his phone. "That's the younger one. There's pics of her with the Down's son all over her Facebook page. She's always fund-raising for Down's. Helga's been following her on Twitter and says Sugg constantly tweets about her struggles with anger and control issues."

The VP has been angering and controlling staff all morning. They move around uncomfortably, like animals forced to walk on hind legs. We've been cleaning places we didn't know required cleaning, like under equipment. She insists we use no-name brand cleaning products. She points to directions on labels the South Asians can't read. "Use a little less than the recommended amount per litre of water," she advises—another innovative cost-cutting measure. Tareq and company ignore the strumpet and more than double the formula to make the cheap cleaner effective. Sugg scolds and reprimands while making them scrub the crap out of the back walls, fridges, freezers, hoods, dry stock room, etc. Conquer and I can't manage the orders piling up.

"Carol," I say, "we need cooks on the line. Maybe save some scrub duty for after the lunch rush."

She wrinkles her nose and squints at the board. When her phone demands attention, I signal the crew to return to their stations. For a sweaty two hours the VP eagle-eyes portion sizes and execution.

With lunch over, I hide in my closet. In minutes servers crowd around my desk. Helga's in another state of super upsetness due to Bryan the OkCupid dud tweeting that she is a cocktease. After blocking her on Facebook, Bry had the nerve to text her, inviting her for all-you-can-eat sushi. When Helga, for no good reason other than low self-esteem, agreed to sushi, he texted, "do u want to fuck before or after lunch." Helga texted back that he was garbage.

"I am so not a cocktease," she says.

"You are so not, bae," Daniel agrees.

"What happened to Siggy?" I ask. "Why are you bothering with Bryan when you have Siggy?"

"Siggy's come out as non-binary. He doesn't want to be identified as male or female. From now on he's a 'they.'"

"Iconic," Wade says.

Daniel applies lip balm. "'Theys' confuse me. I always think they're talking about more than one person."

"Well," I say to Helga, "when you're with Siggy you don't have to use any pronoun but 'you.' Never let a pronoun stand in the way of romance."

Daniel snaps the cap back on his balm. "How'd coffee with the Kiwi go?"

"Pretty lame," Helga says. "I definitely got not-going-anywhere-with-my-life-because-my-dad's-rich-and-I'm-a-fuck-up-type vibes. Anyway, I think he's sleeping with a Zumba instructor. They're, like, all over each other at the gym."

"Just because he's sleeping with a Zumba instructor," Daniel says, "doesn't mean you shouldn't date him."

"Helga," I say, "why do you feel you have to date *anybody*? You can be a 'she' unattached to a 'he.'"

"And end up like you. Awesome."

"Sick burn," Daniel says.

"Anyway, kids," I say, "have you started job-hunting?"

Helga yanks up her Cat Woman boots. "Sugg needs us now she's cut Olaf."

"She won't need you once she hires staff that look good in skin-tight clothes. Seriously, get out there and hustle."

They all sag, the air sucked out of them.

"Applying for jobs," Wade whines, "is an exercise in futility."

"So random," Daniel agrees.

"I can't even," Helga says. "It's a lot."

Like yours truly, they will let the VP cut them .2 pieces at a time. If we quit, we get nothing. If she lays us off, we get EI.

Sugg opens the door into Daniel's girth. "I've just about had it with these little gripe sessions," she says. "House staff should be on the floor."

The three amigos slink out with the she-wolf nipping at their heels. I close the door behind her.

When Gyorgi was little, his mother had a relationship with an African who had long dreadlocks and taught Gyorgi card tricks. Gyorgi didn't under-stand what was going on between his mother and the African, whose name was Henri, but having a man around made him feel safe. Henri told Gyorgi he'd escaped a merciless dictator whose soldiers dragged people from their homes, slashed them with machetes and crowded them into prisons. "You are lucky here," he said. Gyorgi didn't feel lucky because his mother cleaned people's houses and was never home when he returned from school. He had to make himself supper. "No, no, no, mon petit prince," Henri said. "You must understand you are living a life that is an exception, not the rule. Where I come from it is normal be misérable, to work non-stop for little money, to suffer at the hands of tyrants, to fear weather that can drown you or starve you or crack open the earth. You are lucky here." Henri looked around their dismal apartment and smiled, revealing big uneven teeth.

When the police came for Henri, Gyorgi's mother stood in front of him, locking her arms through his. When she refused to step aside the police hit her with truncheons. Henri did not resist arrest and pleaded with Gyorgi's mother to let him go. "Lâche-moi, ma chérie," he said. The police beat her until Henri was the only thing keeping her upright, then they beat him until he gently released her to the floor. After they took Henri away, Gyorgi lay beside his mother, holding her where she said it didn't hurt. She lay still for a long time. Gyorgi knew she was alive because her ribs moved against his. They never spoke of Henri again.

"Henri was not wise investment," Gyorgi said.

Sugg pushes open my door again and I try to be emphatically empathic like Bob, reminding myself that the VP too has suffered, has a Down Syndrome son and fundraises for Down's. "What are you writing in the logbook?" she demands.

"Oh, just an idea I have for a kids' book I'm working on. I don't normally write at work but sometimes I jot down ideas so I won't forget them."

She holds a hand to her breast. "That's incredible, because I'm also working on a kids' book."

"Really? As well as the transcendent memoir? That's impressive."

"Writing is my secret passion."

"Mine too. What's your kids' book about?"

She describes the beagle book and I try to look impressed because I hope to last a few more weeks at this job, maybe even score some severance.

"Tell me about yours," she says.

"My what?"

"Your children's book."

"Oh." My brain freezes for a second. "It's about a butterfly."

"Why a butterfly?"

"When I was a kid, we sang a song in school about the world being like a butterfly with frail blue wings. My book's called *Blue Wing*, which is the name of the butterfly who outsmarts a tyrannical beetle despite having frail blue wings. It's a story about moral courage."

"Sounds fascinating. We should share our manuscripts sometime. Brainstorm."

"That would be awesome. How's the cleaning going?"

She waves her hands as though shooing bugs. "I can't get them to stop wasting cleaner."

"Well, if it gets the job done on kitchen-grade grease and dirt, why complain?"

"You see, that's exactly what I'm talking about with you, Stevie. You let things slide." She says this woefully, as though I've hurt her feelings. The doggy/alky/auteur bonding is paying off. The VP wants me to like her. "Please get the dishwashers to clean the garbage areas thoroughly, and under all the mats."

She said *please*!

"I'm on it," I say.

"Did you call your sponsor?"

"Oh. Yes."

"Was it helpful?"

"Very."

"The other thing that works really well for me," she says, "is walking without touching anything."

"Except the ground."

"What?"

"If you're walking, your feet touch the ground."

"Of course. I mean not touching anything with my hands. Not my body or my face or my clothes or walls. No leaning or sitting, just moving through space without connecting with anything. You'd be surprised how challenging that is. You really need to focus. I'm a bit of a germaphobe anyway, always washing my hands after touching doorknobs, elevator buttons, that sort of thing."

I slide my logbook into my backpack and zip it closed, picturing Sugg caring for her Down Syndrome son while moving through space without touching anything. "Okay, well, I better get out there and snap the whip about the garbage areas."

"That's the spirit."

How does the son manage such a mother? But then, how does my son manage me? There are no pictures of us together on Facebook.

Buses come and go in a cold, greasy mist. Pierce should be here by now. Bleary and empty-eyed bank customers step around me. I try to keep my mind off my son by imagining where the customers live, how they manage, what gets them up in the morning. Wade told me the defining characteristic of an organism is to strive. None of us appear to be striving, only plodding familiar paths well worn by yesterday and tomorrow.

A full moon skulks behind the mist. Stan used to say the moon left him cold; it was the stars he admired, dying brightly all those bazillions of miles away. He kept a bottle of whiskey and a couple of stubby tumblers in his locker, and after what he considered to be a rat-arsed day, we'd sit out back stargazing while imbibing JD and water in what he called highfalutin style. We talked about work, politics, weather, the tragedy of his neighbour's bipolar son turning tricks for crystal meth. "Addiction's a terrible thing," Stan said, letting me know he understood how fierce and present it was, barely contained. When I stopped drinking for real and passed on the amber liquid in the tumbler, he said, "Brave girl."

I don't feel brave, shivering, trying to figure out what's right and what's wrong, knowing that everyone's right is someone else's wrong.

"Hey," Pierce says behind me. "Sorry I'm late." He looks bigger, livelier. I hand him the envelope.

"Thanks, Mom, seriously, you're the best."

This is the second time he's called me the best. If only I'd earned such praise for something other than handing over cash.

"Can I buy you dinner?" I ask. "There's a Tims just up the street."

"Okay."

He eats as though he hasn't for days, which calls into question Greg's ability to hunt and forage. So intent is Pierce on his soup and turkey-bacon club, he doesn't hear me when I say there's something I need to tell him. Around us teenagers talk rapidly. An ancient couple, maybe Greek, nibble at muffins. She's in a black pageboy wig and has a tremor. Her hand shakes when she sips from her paper cup. Her balding husband, his glasses perched on the end of his nose, carefully places small plastic bags of purchases into larger plastic bags. The couple say little but seem to be all right with each other. A diamond sparkles on her wedding finger as she adjusts her wig.

A diamond from whenever ago when she had hair, and life was up ahead, not far behind.

"Pierce," I say, a little louder. He looks up as though he'd forgotten me and smiles. Trudy flickers across his face.

"Are we all right with each other?" I ask.

"What do you mean 'all right'?"

"This mess between us. Our relationship. It's complicated, I know. But it's ours."

"We have a relationship?" The smile dissolves and he resumes eating and I, toothless old elephant that I am, retreat behind my coarse hide because I'm not strong enough for all this, am just quietly waiting to starve to death.

"What's your point?" he asks.

"No point really. I was just hoping there might be a relative all-rightness between us. After all these years."

"You want forgiveness."

"Absolutely not."

He wipes his fingers on a napkin. "What was it you needed to tell me?"

My tongue clutters my mouth. There is too much to explain.

"Is it about the rape?" he asks.

"Which rape?"

"Yours."

"Yes."

"So. Say it."

"It's difficult."

"Say it."

The ancient Greek couple decamp slowly, both using canes, clutching their plastic bags.

"Fucking say it," Pierce says.

"That's how I got pregnant. With you."

He nods without looking at me, and bunches up his napkin. "I figured."

"How did you figure?"

"Because you're a shit liar. And because nobody's a fucking drunk at fourteen." He crumples his sandwich wrappings. "What else? Is that it? I gotta get my bus."

"Two of them were Black. The rapists."

This stops him. The bones slide from his face and his eyes lose their sheen.

"Half of you is Black," I say as though this needs explaining.

"For fucksake." He shakes his head repeatedly in, I guess, disbelief. After a moment, anger shoves his bones back in place and he starts to quake, rocking in his chair the way Trudy rocked in her puddle of piss at Walmart. What looks like a car salesman moves to another table, presumably to distance himself from Pierce's combustibility. The soldier resumes shaking his head and the car salesman pulls out a phone and intently scrolls. The rapidly talking teenagers plug their ears with earbuds and bounce to rhythms we can't hear. With everyone riveted to tiny screens, an otherworldly quiet engulfs us.

Pierce stops rocking and turns his empty paper cup around and around on the table. "So I'm not who I thought I was. And you're not who I thought you were."

"We're still us. It doesn't change anything between us."

"Are you fucking nuts? You've been lying to me my entire life."

"To protect you."

"To protect yourself."

"I didn't think you needed to know. The child has nothing to do with the rape." The words sound tinny on my lips, lacking Olivia's gravitas. He turns the cup around, his military-trained face unyielding.

"It doesn't mean I don't care about you," I say.

"Oh fuck off, seriously."

"I am serious."

He mashes the cup. "Now what? Am I supposed to feel sorry for you?"

"Not at all. *I* don't feel sorry for me. Women get raped all the time. While we're sitting here women are being raped."

He stares off at something unseeable. "Does this mean I'm Black or white?"

"Does it matter? You're you."

"Thanks, Mom," he says with the old, familiar loathing. As Chester's praying, pill-popping wife said, the worst is yet to come.

"Now I get why you've always hated me," he says.

"I've never hated you."

His hands jerk as though he's about to grab my throat. Instead he says quietly, "Why the fuck are you telling me this now?"

"Because the child is yours. That little girl I'm looking after, Trudy, she's yours." I pull out the DNA report and spread it on the table. "I took a swab from your mouth after the hospital."

"While I was unconscious. I can't fucking believe you." He doesn't touch the report, only stares at it. I point to his name.

"Sophie's her mother. She left this note for you when she abandoned Trudy at Reggie's." I lay the note on the table. We are suspended in a completely altered reality, an unrecognizable, menacing place.

He touches the note like it's delicate parchment and pulls it towards him. "Where's Sophie now?"

"I don't know. She got in a car with a man and drove off. Ducky gave her my number but she hasn't called. The child is amazing, Pierce. She's smart and strong and brave. She learns incredibly fast. You can show her something once and she'll remember it. I've never seen anyone work things out the way Trudy does. She's had to look after herself so much her self-reliance is astounding. She hasn't even started school yet. I'm teaching her to write three-letter words."

A choking silence. His pond green eyes chisel at me but I can't look away.

"You love her," he says. It is an accusation laced with resentment.

"I don't know. Maybe."

"Like you never loved me. Go fuck yourself, seriously, I'm done with your shit." He takes off at soldier speed and I scramble to collect the papers, my hands shaking like the ancient Greek woman's. When I look up he's vanished into the murky night.

I wrote on the note tucked in with the cash: *If I'd been able to see who you were and not where you came from, if I'd been able to understand that you were my anchor and that if I'd held onto you I would have been safe, you might not hate me so much. The bottle enabled me to let you go. To forget. You know this. With enough alcohol in your veins, your mind becomes a tranquil lagoon. For a while. Then the gators and snakes are back taking chunks out of you. You know this. I am so proud of you for staying sober.*

Peggy and Reggie cared for you as they never cared for me. That's all you needed, I thought. You were lucky you had them, I told myself. I didn't understand that Reggie and Peggy weren't capable of caring deeply for anyone but themselves, so absorbed were they in their narcissism. You and I were props in the badly acted stage play that was their marriage. You were the son they always wanted. It would be different for you, I told myself as I abandoned you. A more harrowing abandonment than Trudy's because I kept showing up for cash, booze and shelter, and you thought I was coming back for you.

I abandoned you like Sophie abandoned Trudy, on the steps of the bungalow. It was the biggest mistake of my life, and I've made many. The regret and sorrow lives in me, a virus that flares and recedes. Incurable. I don't want this for you. I want you to know your daughter, to feel the indefinable bond between you. A bond so strong it frees you. Whatever shit is going down in your life, the tug of that anchor steadies you. Trudy taught me this, made me realize that if you, my son, were trapped in a burning building I would run through walls of fire to find you.

I never told you how proud I was that you went to Afghanistan because I wasn't. You know I don't believe in war. I am proud of you for surviving Afghanistan, for enduring an unendurable situation. You'll never shed the self-hatred you suffer for following your CO's command. You will always feel the thump of the boy's body under your wheels. Sometimes the terrible acts we commit teach us to see, to care, to live. I can't give you the sixteen-year-old loving mother you deserved. The only mother I can offer is an alcoholic, pushing forty and working at a dead-end job. But I see you. And I care.

Trudy doesn't know who you are. She doesn't know you exist. She doesn't know who I am. She tells me her grandmother is dead. I am a stranger, in a long line of strangers, with whom she stays until her mother returns for her. This is what Trudy believes, that Sophie will be back. She watches the door, yearning for her mother as you yearned for yours.

I don't know where it goes from here. I'm in the dark, feeling my way around this child's life. Maybe my actions on her behalf are futile, I have no way of knowing. As I had no way of knowing the effect my actions would have on you. The future, in my world, has always been obscure. I have come to appreciate its darkness. To see far ahead—to know exactly what is to happen—robs us of unexpected sparks.

Please call me. Sometime. No pressure.

He won't bother to read this, will crumple the note like his sandwich wrappings and toss it in the trash. Or he'll read it, then crumple and toss it. Too little too late.

Walking without touching anything, not feeling my feet connect with the pavement, I head south to Warden Woods instead of north to McDonald's, where Trudy and Gyorgi are waiting for me. The cold moon slips in and out of clouds. The woods smell of skunk and rotting leaves. Branches creak and moan forlornly. I sit in the damp undergrowth, grateful that the creeping cold grips my ass because it's tangible, not like the shifting winds of indefinable feelings that keep batting me about. "In the end nobody can save you but yourself," Stan said before he died alone in the hospital with cold feet. He warned me not to get my hopes up about people, about anything. "Hopes are traps you set for yourself," he said.

"We have a relationship?" Pierce asked. I set this trap for myself.

My phone vibrates and I know it's not him.

"You okay?" Gyorgi asks.

"Okay."

"Your son is gone?"

"He is." A huge raccoon scrabbles down a tree trunk, stops and stares, wondering what a human is doing on his turf at this hour. I stare back.

"Trudy made friend," Gyorgi says.

"You're kidding. Where?"

"In PlayPlace. Trudy showed little girl plastic animals."

"That's incredible."

"Is more incredible. Are you ready for to be shocked?"

"I'm ready."

"She let Fatima hold her horse."

"Oh my god." I start trembling again, with what? Relief. Pride.

"Trudy wants to talk to you."

"Put her on."

"Stevie?"

It is the first time she's said my name. "Yes?"

"Do you know how to cook cake?"

"Of course."

"Can we cook cake later?"

"Of course."

"Yay!" She hands the phone back to Gyorgi. The huge raccoon stares, unmoved.

"She is different, no?" Gyorgi asks.

"She is."

"Is because of you."

"Maybe. Listen, I'll meet you guys back at the apartment. I kind of just want to walk for a bit."

"Sure."

"We'll make a cake."

"Sure."

I wait for him to hang up while "MacArthur Park" plays in my head: someone left the cake out in the rain.

"Stevie," Gyorgi says.

"Yes." I gaze up at the slippery moon.

"Your son will be back."

"I hope so," I say, setting another trap for myself. I end the call and have a blinking contest with the raccoon, an animal Gyorgi admires because it has no fear. So much fear all my life, never-ending, crippling, for what?

The raccoon, done with waiting for me to get off my damp ass, resumes clambering down the trunk and waddles into the undergrowth.

CORDELIA STRUBE is an accomplished playwright and author of 10 critically acclaimed novels including *Alex & Zee*, *Teaching Pigs to Sing* and *Lemon*. Winner of the CBC literary competition and a Toronto Arts Foundation Award, she has been nominated for the Governor General's Award, the Trillium Book Award, the W.H. Smith/Books in Canada First Novel Award, the Prix Italia and long-listed for the Scotiabank Giller Prize. A two-time finalist for ACTRA's Nellie Award celebrating excellence in Canadian broadcasting, Strube is also a three-time nominee for the ReLit Award. Her 2016 novel, *On the Shores of Darkness, There Is Light*, won the City of Toronto Book Award.